ON

ACKNOWLEDGEMENTS

My thanks to those who have encouraged me to write, in particular Hilary Mellon; to my readers, Jean, Joan and Mary; and to my husband, who gave me the idea for this novel's plot, helped me with so much of the factual detail and has always supported everything I have ever set out to do. Huge thanks also go to Dr. Steve Carver, for his critical support, encouragement and championing of this novel.

ON THAT DAY

E.A.PARKER

All characters in this publication are fictitious
and any resemblance to real persons, living or dead,
is purely coincidental.

ISBN: 978-1-5272-8888-1

To Patricia,
for guiding me along the path.

"A time to dance and a time to weep…"

(Ecclesiastes 3;4)

13th February 1993, 7.30 a.m.

Before School

Chapter One

The day began as all days begin, even those days that end in a disaster. It was February 13th, 1993, a date that is etched on the national consciousness as well as on the village memorial in Easton St. Matthew.

'Do you remember where you were?' people always say of national calamities.

I do. I was there.

I'll start with the wait for the school bus. It was 7.30 on a cold morning and the potato clamp where I always left my bike gave no shelter from the wind. Ronnie used to say, 'Fen winds blow straight from the North Pole, there's nothing between but tater fields.' But let's leave Ronnie for the time being; he will, of course, take centre stage later in the story. I felt sick as well as freezing as I waited, and the sick feeling was all about what I thought I knew would happen later that day and how I could avoid the repercussions. In the event, of course, what happened on that day was far worse than I could ever have imagined.

In front of me was the River Nene, dead straight and dead deep, as it was almost high tide. The water was dark and threatening, whipped up by the east wind, and swirling round the channel posts. A solitary gull was battling its way downstream. Far to my right, I could see the two lighthouses which marked the entry of the river into the Wash estuary. Far to the left was the swing bridge over the main road, which opened whenever a ship made its way downstream from Wisbech port to the North Sea. Behind me stretched Wrong Drove, a typical fen road, stuck up above the eroded landscape at right angles to a line of pylons and leading, like a ruler, to the mud of the Wash saltmarsh that we called simply 'the Marsh'. And three quarters of a mile down Wrong Drove were two semi-detached cottages, clinging together in the middle of the vast flat fields of brown soil. I lived with my mum in the left-hand cottage.

I stamped my frozen feet and shivered. The sweat I had worked up cycling down the drove had cooled and my neck, under its school tie, was itchy. I looked at my watch and willed the bus to arrive, peering along the road to Franklin's Cottages where I knew it would emerge. And in this way, at least, the day was no different to a hundred others since I had started secondary school. A small yellow square turned the corner from King John Bank and gradually expanded as it approached. The school bus was on its way.

I was glad to climb up into my usual front seat next to the wheezy heater. I was the first pick-up on the run. By the time the bus arrived at Sir William Smith High School (or 'Sir Willyum's' as everyone called it), having made its steady way for nearly an hour through straggling villages and past isolated farmhouses and bungalows there would be a warm fug and my feet would have thawed. I also liked my seat at the front because it gave me some protection. I knew that my fellow-pupils would not try to torment me if I was sitting next to the driver.

Now, as an adult, I can look back at my suffering and wonder what it was that marked me out, from my first day at

Sir Willyum's, as a victim. Was it my appearance? I was in those days small and skinny. I had inherited my father's red hair and my mother's short sight, which meant I wore thick-lensed glasses. Or was it my name? I still cringe remembering the moment on my first morning when our form tutor asked me to confirm my full name. She did not hear my mumble, so asked me to speak up. I squeaked, 'Stephen Sydney Stringer, Miss,' which was met with titters around the classroom and the collapse across his desk in hoots of laughter of Dwayne Tubbs. This was the same Dwayne Tubbs who, throughout my time at Sir Willyum's, always sat next to me because Tubbs came just after Stringer in the register; who was always behind me in corridors to trip me, always in the dark corners of cloakrooms to thump me and whose memory still sits on my shoulder.

Mrs Pritchard had tried to rescue the situation. 'Sydney? That's an unusual name for a boy nowadays. Is it a family name?'

'Yes, Miss,' I managed.

I wasn't going to tell anyone at school about our family tradition, that I was, like my father and his father before him, named after an original Sydney Stringer, who had been mayor of Kings Lynn in 1816. But the damage was done; what I had been proud of became a nightmare. From my first day I was known at Sir Willyum's as 'Sydney', and I can even now hear the taunting chant: 'Sydney! Sydney! Kick him in the kidney!' the terrifying preface to a vicious attack under the stairs or in the toilets.

But let's return to the school bus. Let me shut my eyes and remember that journey, repeated every morning until that day. Writing this story now, I wonder if I can really remember the details of that day or if what I think I remember is actually an amalgam of all my memories of days at that school; welded into one six-hour long movie, played in my head over and over again with a terrifying sense of premonition. Through the wide front window of the school bus I can see again King John Bank stretching into the distance, with its line of dark poplars bent into strange shapes by the wind. A kestrel is hovering high over the grass verge, a few ducks are making use of a flooded corner of a field of winter wheat, a man is walking his dog along the old sea bank.

The bus negotiates a double bend and draws to a halt at an isolated bus stop. The automatic door swishes open. A girl climbs aboard, tripping over the top step as she is pushed from behind by two boys, and in the sudden rush of cold air I hear what I think is the call of the geese. As the bus pulls away I look up and see them, a faint curved line in the sky, then another behind the first, then more and more. As the bus draws closer to their flight path the skeins become clearer as they fly in regimental formation across the grey clouds. The pink-footed geese are on their way from their roosting grounds far out on the mud of the Wash to feed in the harvested sugar beet fields. There are thousands of them, at least seven thousand I reckon (Ronnie has taught me how to estimate their numbers), and the sky will be filled with their cries, although I cannot hear them, trapped as I am in the teenage cacophony.

'Can you sleepover tomorrow? My mum says it's OK and…'

'Didya see that goal for Man U? Fucking fantastic! Wham! Straight in the back of the net!'

'What yer looking at me like that for, dickhead?'

'…and like in the queue was Samantha Stevenson with her mum and I said like "Hiya" and she just blanked me, stuck-up cow!'

I would just sit and listen because no-one ever talked to me except Dick Gosling the bus driver, and on that morning he was probably too busy concentrating on the slippery road surface. There wasn't much room for error on the humpback bridge over the Relief Channel. I knew that the Relief Channel was dug as part of the 1960s flood prevention system. I knew this because Ronnie told me when we went fishing there. Most of what I know about the world about me, even now, I know because Ronnie told me.

I can picture him now, sitting outside his shed watching Gyp, his old yellow Labrador, nosing along the hedge or leaning on the gate of the wildfowl pen, watching his birds. A fag is hanging out of the side of his mouth and his cap is pushed to the back of his head, as he takes a break from something or other – turning the compost heap, cleaning out the chickens, taking a rotavator to bits – with me perched on an upturned bucket at his feet, like a disciple.

'You need a proper education, boy, not just that stuff the teachers learn you. You need to use your eyes and ears, get your nose out of them books you're so keen on! Look at that wagtail over there. It's got young somewhere round here. How do I know that, eh?'

'I dunno, Ronnie. Tell me.'

And he would. Ronnie knew everything there was to know about nature, and shooting, and country life, and fen history (and most other things that were at all important, it seemed to me). I would spend hours with him, listening to him, asking him questions, soaking up the lore. My education was practical too. It was Ronnie who taught me how to use an axe properly, how to skin a rabbit, how to handle a ferret, how to clean a shotgun. He gave me a catapult for my eighth birthday and an airgun for my tenth. At eleven I shot my first wood pigeon with a twenty-bore shotgun he had adapted for me. When I was twelve and he judged I was just about tall enough he taught me how to drive his van on the concrete farm roads, with two cushions at my back so I could reach the pedals.

Ronnie was our next-door neighbour and I grew up spending as much time in his house as in our own. When I was tiny I was looked after by Ronnie's wife, Beryl, so Mum could work, and toddling around after Ronnie was a habit I never lost. I suppose he was like a dad to me, for my own dad had died in a motorbike accident soon after I was born.

'I don't know how I'd manage without you, Ronnie,' my mum would tell him when he fixed the bathroom tap or cleared the snow from the front path. 'And you're so good to Stephen. I keep telling him not to pester you, but he just adores the ground you walk on. It's always Ronnie this and Ronnie that. I tell him it should be *Uncle* Ronnie but…'

'Don't you worry your head about that, girl. I'm right fond of the little old boy. And I know it makes things easier for my Beryl, having your Stephen around,' and Ronnie would suddenly change the subject, before Mum could look sympathetic and murmur something like, 'I know, it must be terrible for you.'

Ronnie and Beryl's only son, Duncan, had been killed cycling on the newly-built arterial road when he was just ten. My mother had told me the story a thousand times, vowing never to let me have a bike, except that Ronnie and Beryl bought me one for my eleventh birthday and she didn't want to hurt their feelings. Even so, the day after my birthday she walked me and my bike to the main road and showed me where I was to get off and walk across. She made me promise never to cycle on that road, in the same way that she had made me promise never to get on a motorbike while she was alive.

'I can't be doing with losing both of you!' she said.

Come to think of it, I never disobeyed her about cycling on the main road (even if I do now own a Triumph Bonneville, just like my dad's). I even got off and walked across the road on that last terrible bike ride on that day.

For the last part of our journey to school we joined a long cavalcade of buses crawling along the main street of Easton St. Matthew, because nearly every pupil at Sir Willyum's was bussed in. Easton St. Matthew, like most fen villages, was a stretched-out sort of place with all the houses lined up along the main road for nearly a mile, with their back gardens abutting the flat fields behind. There was only one crossroads, where Church Lane met Main Street, and on one corner was St. Matthew's Church and opposite was the *Dog and Duck*, which had a large car park where the school buses could turn. That was where we got off.

When the door hissed open I took up a safe position behind Dick as he attempted to supervise the general barging and shoving that constituted the 'disembarkation', as it said in the 'County Guidelines for Carrying School Pupils' (which I knew by heart because it was posted up above my front seat). I waited until everyone else was off the bus and well on their way before I got off.

'See you later,' I said, although, of course, after what happened on that day I didn't ever see him again.

'Bye, lad. Take it easy now!' he answered, as he always did.

It took only a minute to walk along Church Lane to Sir Willyum's, and I would make straight for the left-hand door of the pupil entrance, passing under an ornate Victorian sign which read 'BOYS 1885' and was right next to another which read 'IRLS 1885', the 'G' having been chipped off when Rodney Thompson (father of Rebecca in Year 10) kicked a football at it in 1974, so Ronnie told me. I was the register monitor, a role which no other pupil volunteered for, but which I valued because it meant I was allowed into school before the bell. Inside a school without pupils was a much safer place for me than a playground. It meant I could use the toilet if I needed to, as I didn't dare visit the toilets if there were other boys about. If I sauntered along the corridors and hung around reading notices on walls, I could fill in the fifteen minutes until the bell and be outside the staff room to offer Mrs Pritchard the register and a red pen, check she'd got her reading glasses and walk under her protection to the form room.

It was during those fifteen minutes every morning in the empty school buildings that I got to know about parts of school life that no other pupil even thought about. At the school office while waiting for Mrs Duckworth, the school secretary, to put out the registers, I watched her straight back and listened to her answering the telephone in that bright smiling voice she had.

'Sir William Smith High School, good morning, can I help you? Oh, good morning, Mrs Evans … dear, dear, and has he been sick too? Well, you'd better keep him in bed then … Well I find soaking the sheets first is best, it gets rid of the stain … What form is he in? 8B? Of course, Mrs Evans, hopefully we'll see him tomorrow.

'Sir William Smith High. Oh, hallo David … Oh dear, your car won't start, you say … have you called the AA? ... Oh, I see, your brother-in-law … Yes, I'll tell Mr Godley to cover you up to morning break.'

All the time she was taking these constant calls she was slitting open envelopes, reading the contents and sorting them into piles while simultaneously feeding the photocopier. I don't know how

Mrs Duckworth managed to do so many things at the same time. Then Mr Godley bustled in, with a huge pile of exercise books, which he dumped on top of the photocopier. Mr Godley was the deputy head and he was always rushing everywhere because, according to Ronnie, he actually ran the school, even though we had a headmaster.

'Morning Maureen! What's happening this morning? Who's broken their leg? Whose washing machine's flooded? Whose kid's got measles? Just tell me the good news, the bad news can wait until tomorrow!' and he would chuckle and jerk his head sideways, a nervous habit he had.

'Good morning, Stan. Not too bad today, but David Jewson's car won't start. His wife will run him in when she's dropped off the kids at primary school. He should be in by Period 2.'

'Again! He needs to get rid of that pile of scrap metal and get himself a bike! I bet he's got 9C first period, he hates that class. I'd better cover it myself or there'll be an insurrection in the staff room.'

'You do too much for them already, Mr Godley, and all they do is moan. Anyway, you can't cover Period 1. You're due to do a health and safety check in the kitchen instead of Ronnie.'

For Ronnie was not only my next-door neighbour, my guru and my substitute dad, he was also the caretaker at my school. That is, he had been until that day.

Ronnie had told me a great deal about what was going on at Sir Willyum's. Caretakers know everything in a school because they are ever-present but never noticeable. They can read documents left out on desks, they can find things they shouldn't in desk drawers, they have keys to filing cabinets, they can listen to conversations through open windows, they can watch when no-one realises they are watching. I therefore knew things about the teachers that no pupil really ought to know. I knew that if you turned around the dart board that hung on the staff room wall you would see a photo of Mr Crumb the headmaster with his nose as the bulls-eye; I knew that Mrs Pritchard, the RE teacher and my form tutor, drank Bailey's in her store cupboard (because Ronnie once found the empty bottles in the box with the spare Bibles); I knew that Mr Crumb, the headmaster, kept copies of *Penthouse* magazine in the bottom left hand drawer of his desk. Ronnie detested Mr Crumb and was contemptuous of all the teachers except Mr Godley.

'That Stan Godley's a real gentleman, Stevie, and the only proper teacher in the place. I don't know how the school would keep going if it wasn't for him, runs it all, he does. Good job too, old Crumpet couldn't run a whelk stall.'

Ronnie knew everything about Mr Crumb's appointment as headmaster.

'Got the job because that old bird Mrs Westley-Lewis fancied him, I reckon.' Mrs Westley-Lewis was the wife of an important local farmer and the Chair of the school's governing body. 'I heard her going on about him when they did the interviews. I was in the stationery office and you can hear everything from there. 'He'll be a safe pair of hands,' she said. Too true, I say, 'cos he keeps his hands safe in his bloody pockets! Never does any headmaster work, never even moves a bit of paper from the in-box to the out-box, and when have you ever seen him bother to take his hand out of his pocket to shake hands with a parent, eh?'

The pupils detested Mr Crumb too, but Mr Godley was loved and respected by all of us because he had been loved and respected by our parents. Stan Godley had been at Sir Willyum's as long as anyone could remember. This gave him a position of omnipotence in the community because he knew every family. We called him 'God', and not just because it was a derivative of his surname.

On that morning he ruffled my hair as he rushed out of the school office.

'Morning, Stephen. How's your mum? Still working at the Shell garage?'

'Yes, sir. Don't forget your books!' and, as usual, I rescued his pile of exercise books and ran after him with them.

Meanwhile Mrs Duckworth was dealing with another phone call while sorting the registers and talking to Robbie Brown from 7B.

'What is it, Robbie? Sir William Smith High School, good morning.'

'It's my hamster, Harry, Miss. Can you look after him until Period 3, Miss? He's for my talk in English, Miss. Please Miss.'

Robbie pushed a scrabbling cardboard box up against the reception window. Mrs Duckworth got up from her desk, slid the glass window across and picked up the box, still talking into the telephone jammed against her shoulder.

'Yes, Robbie, but don't forget to fetch him after school, will you. He won't be happy in that box overnight. Yes, Mrs Dickens, Deirdre has the flu, you say? What form is she in?'

Robbie's mention of English talks reminded me of what I was carrying that morning, and which had weighed so heavily on my mind as well as my handlebars as I had pedalled against the wind to meet the bus. I had been wondering how I was going to hide it until lunchtime.

'Oh Mrs Duckworth,' I asked, as she turned back to close the reception window, 'could you look after this for me please until lunchtime? I need it for an English talk too.'

She stared at the cricket bag which I lifted towards the window. It was an old bag and the zip didn't work which was why the handles fell apart, revealing what was inside. She peered inside the bag.

'Oh my God, it's a gun! Stephen, what are you doing with a gun?'

'It's all right, Miss, honestly it is. It… er it doesn't work. It's an old airgun of Ronnie's. I'm just going to er… explain to the class how it fits together,' which was all lies.

'Well, if you're sure it's not dangerous,' she said, still sounding hesitant. 'Have you got permission to bring it into school? I'm surprised your mum let you, and what about Miss Ferguson? Does she know you're bringing a firearm into class?'

I thrust the bag further through the open window where she took hold of it gingerly and laid it on her desk as if it were a bomb.

'It's all OK really, Miss. I er… asked permission last lesson and Mum said it was OK and have you got the registers?

'But Stephen, are you sure?'

Fortunately, the phone began to ring at that moment and I rushed off with the registers before she could ask any more questions.

*

Every morning I first went to the music room, because Mr Took, the music teacher, never went to the staff room. Mr Took didn't fit into the staff room very well because he was a 'bit of an oddball', to quote Ronnie. Although as a lad I did not really think much about such things, I realise now that what Ronnie meant was that Jeremy Took was gay. He was a small quicksilver man who walked 'as if two hairs on his arse were tied together', to use Ronnie's fruity expression. In the past, when I had taken him his register Mr Took would be scurrying about the music room straightening desks or licking his thumb to count out photocopied worksheets or writing the date very neatly on the blackboard, all the time humming classical music.

'Stephen!' he would cry, 'You've brought my register, you angel! How very kind of you. And how are you, dear heart, this fine morning?' and he would advance on me.

'Fine, thank you sir,' I used to answer, placing the register on the desk, and backing away to get out of the room, because although he was great fun in lessons, I felt uncomfortable when he was too close to me as he smelt of a strange mixture of aftershave and liquorice.

But now, of course, because of what had happened earlier in the year, he had been muted. On that morning he was sitting at his desk with his eyes shut when I placed the register on his desk. He did not move.

'Your register, sir,' I said.

'Thank you, Stephen,' he said, quietly, without opening his eyes. 'Shut the door behind you, would you please?'

On the way to the staffroom, I would often come across Mr Crumb on what Ronnie called his 'smoking patrol'. On that morning he was on the top floor of the main block, training his binoculars on the bushes at the back of the playground, a favourite site for those pupils who were regulars at his lunchtime smokers' detentions.

He made me jump as I passed. 'Got him! That's Harrison again!' he shouted out in glee. 'Twice this week!' He got out a tiny notebook from his inside jacket pocket and added to his list of culprits using a silver propelling pencil.

Mr Crumb spent most of his time trying to catch smokers. He was very good at lurking in dark corners and suddenly pouncing on an unsuspecting unfortunate just as he was taking his first drag at break time. And unfortunate they were, those who found themselves at Mr Crumb's lunchtime smoking detentions, for Mr Crumb's other obsession was country dancing.

I had sometimes watched Mr Crumb demonstrating a step.

'I want to see it done like that Morgan pay attention or you'll be here after school now line up.' Mr Crumb always talked in a continuous monotone.

The dancers would shuffle into position, two lines facing each other, agony on their faces.

'Are you ready first couple form the arch come on Dickinson thank you Mr Took.' Mr Took had to miss his lunchtime to play the piano.

A tall boy would flap his arms in the vague direction of a girl's outstretched hands and, as Mr Took played the next bit with breezy enthusiasm, the rest of the dancers would shuffle through the wonky arch and return to their places, the girl wiping her palm on her skirt to remove traces of the boy's sweaty grasp. But Mr Crumb would not be satisfied.

'No that's not good enough we want to see some energy we want to see you dancing with joy on a midsummer morning don't we Mr Took now let's do it again,' and the torture would be repeated, as Mr

Took pounded it out once more, and another two victims formed an arch and stared away from each other in embarrassment.

Mr Crumb was so keen on country dancing that we all had lessons in it once a week. On the timetable it was called 'Cultural Activity' but Ronnie called it 'prancing around like a prat' and most pupils would have agreed with him, except that it beat ordinary lessons when they had to write things. Of course, country dancing lessons at Sir Willyum's became notorious after that day. There was something particularly poignant, according to the tabloid press, about the fact that it happened while children were dancing.

That day was a Monday and on Mondays I had to take the weekly dinner list to the school kitchen on my way to the staffroom. I dreaded this task. Although Mrs Tubbs, the school cook, was a cheerful friendly woman, she was, unfortunately, Dwayne Tubbs's mum, and he was often with her in the kitchen, cadging food. It was even more unfortunate that Mrs Tubbs had no idea about the true relationship between Dwayne and me, and thought we were still the close buddies we had apparently been at mother-and-toddler group, although I can't remember that. It meant that I had been invited to Dwayne's birthday parties all through primary school (and made to attend by my mum), and it also meant that Mrs Tubbs continued to work on cementing our 'friendship' when she could.

'Oh look, Dwayne,' she cried, as she wiped her hands on her apron, 'it's Stephen. Now, when are you going to come round after school and have your tea with Dwayne? You two always played so nicely together.'

'I'm not sure, Mrs Tubbs. Mum likes me to get straight home after school.'

Dwayne leered at me from behind his mum. His mouth was full of yesterday's left-over jam tart and he was sniffing loudly.

'Stop that sniffing, Dwayne, for Chrissakes, and blow your nose boy!' said Mrs Tubbs, and she pulled a large handkerchief out of her apron pocket and thrust it at him.

'What's for dinner today, Mum?'

'Sausage and mash or cottage pie. Upside down cake and pink custard.'

'No chips?' groaned Dwayne.

'Friday's chip day, Monday's mash. County hinstructions. Now get off that counter before you get snot all over it and bugger off. I've got a busy day and Muriel's off sick and there's an 'ealth and safety check with Mr Godley this morning so as we can get a new sustificate.'

'But it's cold outside Mum!'

'Fresh air'll do you good. And look at them crumbs you've gone and dropped on my nice clean floor. Geroff with you! And don't get into any trouble today, d'you hear, especially not with that Jimmy Buckland.'

'But he's left school, Mum.'

'I don't care if he has. How many times have I got to tell you. He's a pikey, and you're not to go around with pikeys, the thieving buggers.'

'But Mum…'

'Never mind "but Mum", just do as I say! You need to spend more time with Stephen, he's nicely brought-up, he'll be a good influence on you.' She had spied me leaving the list on the counter and trying to sidle out without being noticed.

Dwayne turned his curranty eyes on me and grinned.

'Oh hallo, Sydney. I didn't notice you there,' and I am certain he licked his lips. 'Do you want a game of footie before registration?'

He flung his arm around my shoulders and began to shepherd me through the door. I tried to resist, but he was bigger and stronger than me, and before I knew it I was out in the corridor and Mrs Tubbs had shut the door on us with, 'Off you go boys!'

My mouth felt dry and suddenly I wanted to go to the toilet.

'Leave me alone!' I ventured in a cracked whisper.

'What? Don't you want to be friends, Sydney?' and he knocked the pile of registers out of my arms and they scattered across the corridor floor. 'Whoops! Oh dear, look what you've done now, Sydney? What will old Crumpet say when he sees you've gone and spoilt his registers!' and he stamped on one or two that had fallen open, leaving muddy marks.

I knelt on the floor, trying desperately to gather them together.

'That's right, pick them all up and toddle off to the teachers, tell them what that nasty Dwayne has done,' and his voice suddenly lowered to a hiss, 'and see what you get!'

The next thing I knew my back was up against the wall, and his hot jammy breath was in my face.

'I hope you haven't forgotten what you were supposed to bring today, Sydney! We wouldn't like it if you had copped out like the snivelling chicken you are.'

'Get off me, I've got it, don't worry!'

'Well, let's hope it all goes according to plan, eh? Or else!' and he slammed my head back onto the wall and made off.

On the way to the staffroom I sometimes visited Ronnie. He would be in what he called his 'office' at the back of the boiler room, which was actually a store cupboard and was crammed so full of stuff that there was never room for me to take more than one step inside. He would usually be having his first tea break of the day, for he started work at six o'clock every morning, and the room would be warm and smoky. He used to sit in an old teacher's chair squeezed into the corner, with his kettle and the 'makings' neatly set out on a school desk next to him and an old maroon transistor radio tuned to Radio 2 playing quietly on the shelf above his head.

'Morning Stevie,' he would greet me. 'What's on today?'

I would tell him what lessons I had that day. He always listened, and I could tell that he was proud when I told him about my test results, which were always good (I was what Dwayne called a 'boff' and was quietly proud of it), but I knew that Ronnie thought formal schooling was an irrelevance and did not understand my love of books.

'All you need, boy, is to be able to read, write and reckon up. That, and a good dose of common sense, will get you everything you need in this life. Look at me – what more do I want? I've got a roof over my head, a good wife, bless her heart, and a job that gives me plenty of time to go after the geese. Get your priorities right, boy! All this book-learning is a load of squit! Look at these bloody teachers! Like a load of spoilt kids they are, never had to grow up, straight from school to college and back to school, no experience of real life. You don't want to end up like them!'

It was true that school hadn't done much for Ronnie. He never knew his father, being the product of a chance encounter with a lorry driver when his mother worked at a transport café. She was still working there eight years later when she met another lorry driver and ran away, leaving Ronnie to be brought up by his grandfather,

Reg Rawlinson, a famous wildfowler, who lived in the last houseboat left on the Marsh. Knowing the Marsh, the birds and the right kind of shot to use was the old man's idea of education and Ronnie was taught to 'work hard, shoot straight and not take no shit from no-one'. He attended school as infrequently as possible and left as soon as he could, working as a farm labourer until he landed a 'nice cushy job sitting on a great big ol' drag line' at the land drainage company. Privatisation and cost-cutting led to his redundancy and the caretaker's job at Sir Willyum's, which suited him well, as it meant he had the afternoons to go shooting or fishing.

But on that morning, of course, Ronnie was not in his room. I had put my head round the door out of habit and experienced a shock when he wasn't there. And then I remembered: Ronnie was no longer the caretaker at Sir Willyum's. Everything seemed as usual, as if at any moment he might bustle in, swearing about the teachers. Everything was in its place – the brooms and buckets, the polisher, his toolbox, the sink plunger, the boxes of toilet roll, the pile of paint tins – except for Ronnie. I remembered how Ronnie's van had still been parked outside when I had left for school that morning and realised that I had hardly thought about him because I was so full of my own anxiety about the day ahead. But I was worried about him. There was something the matter, and it wasn't just that he had lost his job. Nowadays, when we were talking, he would sometimes slip out of being Ronnie.

'What's that?' he would suddenly say, if I asked him something, and he would look at me as if he didn't know me.

I found that unsettling. He had been one of the certainties of my life. But then, on that day all my certainties collapsed.

Chapter Two

Opposite the staffroom was a big window that looked out onto the carpark and the road beyond. While waiting for Mrs Pritchard I used to look out of that window. I could see the carpark filling up, teachers closing their car boots with their elbows and struggling into school with their briefcases and piles of exercise books.

I looked at the stream of cars drawing up at the front gate and disgorging pupils. A white BMW had double-parked and was blocking the way for one of the school buses. The bus driver was leaning on his horn and everyone was beginning to turn around and look when the passenger door opened and out swung Josie Davenport. She stood for a moment, adjusting her skirt so it was really short and then, swinging a large pink bag over her shoulder, she turned and gave a big V sign to the bus driver before swaggering off on the kind of high heels that girls weren't supposed to wear to school and which made her hips sway in a way that made me grow hot.

Josie always made me feel hot. We had been at school together ever since reception class at Easton St. John's C of E Primary, when we used to play together in the Wendy house and she announced that she was going to marry me. Nowadays she hardly noticed me, and when she did it was to be as insulting as everyone else in the class. But that didn't stop me fancying her something rotten, which had nothing to do with her personality but everything to do with the length of her legs and the shape of her bum and the way she pushed her lips out as if she was kissing someone when she was concentrating. I spent a lot of time day-dreaming about her, and when I remembered how, as six-year-olds, we once showed each other our private parts under the table in Class 1, the fantasies became quite difficult to control.

The V sign was typical of Josie. Ronnie, who had had a number of run-ins with her over graffiti in the girls' toilets, called her a 'nasty piece of work'. He was probably right, but I can't help but feel sad when I remember what happened to Josie on that day.

The other thing I remember about standing at the window on that particular morning was that the tramp wasn't there. Beyond the school gates you could see the bus shelter and in the bus shelter sat the tramp. The tramp was always sitting in the bus shelter, because it was his home. Except on that day.

According to Ronnie the tramp had lived in the bus shelter for years. He had walked into the village one day carrying a huge bundle and sat down in the shelter, as if to wait for a bus. But the bus service into Wisbech had been discontinued years before and when no bus came, he stayed, stowing his bundle of belongings under the bench and covering himself with a green plaid sleeping bag. Early in his 'tenancy', Ronnie told me, the parish council had tried to move him on and demolish the bus shelter but, having been coaxed into the vicar's car and driven to a hostel for the homeless in Kings Lynn, he had merely walked back again the next day. After that no-one had the heart to demolish his home, and although the parish council was always discussing the 'eyesore of the bus shelter' they never did anything about it except to organise the donation of extra blankets to keep him warm in winter. The tramp had just become part of the scenery in Easton St. Matthew.

He was a tall gaunt man with a tangled beard and he wore a long black overcoat and a red knitted hat. Sometimes Mrs Tubbs used to take him leftovers and, on the day of the school Christmas dinner, a turkey dinner and a mince pie, but apart from that everyone ignored him. Except Ronnie. Ronnie said he knew 'Old Badger' from when he had lived with his grandad in the houseboat.

'Used to see him on his way back from flight sometimes. Never said much, even in those days. Wouldn't ever stop for a natter, even with Grandad.'

'Is that his real name?' I once asked.

Ronnie pushed back his cap and scratched his head. 'Far as I know.'

Badger was always in the bus shelter during school days, sitting and watching the school. At other times he could be seen walking the long fen roads with a slow forward-leaning stride, and sometimes, at weekends, when I was bird-watching, I would come across him standing motionless on the edge of a field or on top of a bank. Once I tried saying hello, but I got no spoken response, although he did point across the field, and when I trained my binoculars on the spot I saw a stand of golden plover, a rare sight at the time. When I turned back to him he was gone, stalking away like a black heron.

Ronnie said he was a great expert on the birds and that 'in the old days' he had been the best wildfowler on the coast.

'What Old Badger doesn't know about the sport of wildfowling isn't worth knowing. Used to be a marsh guide, you know, made money taking all them toffs from London out after the geese. And even today, if you want to know where to go on the Marsh to get a nice pair of ducks, or where the geese are heading, he's the person to ask. Not that he'd tell you in so many words,' he added. 'Never been much for talking, has Badger, and seems to have forgotten how to do it at all nowadays, poor sod. Haven't heard him say a word for years!' Badger was what I now know is called an elective mute.

Sometimes Ronnie would go and sit in the bus shelter with Badger, sharing a fag and having a one-sided chat.

'It doesn't hurt to pass the time of day and I get more sense out of Old Badger than out of them teachers.'

'But he doesn't talk.'

'Exactly!'

Once, when we were collecting driftwood on the other side of the river at low tide, we came across the remains of a wildfowling punt rotting in the mud.

'That's Old Badger's punt,' Ronnie said. 'He was the best punt-gunner on the Wash in the old days. Used to bag birds regular and sell them to make a living. They say there's pictures of him in his punt in books about wildfowling.'

'What happened? Why doesn't he do it now?' I asked.

'That's something I don't rightly know, boy. There were stories at the time – some said there was an accident with a gun, others said he got 'turned' from shooting, like that Peter Scott. Others say he drunk all his money and ended up down-and-out, like we see him now.'

I found it strangely disturbing that, on that day, Badger was not at his post.

Most of the teachers had by now arrived in the staff room. The door was open and I could see inside and hear bits of conversation.

Mr Spencer, the history teacher, was reading a newspaper and talking loudly, as he usually did. He was always the first teacher to arrive in school. According to Ronnie that was because he wanted to commandeer the best armchair and the staff room copy of the *Times Educational Supplement.*

'Thinks he's king of the staff room, that tosser does!' was Ronnie's opinion of him.

'Nice job for you here, Ken,' said Mr Spencer to Mr Foster, who was on his knees stapling worksheets, 'bursar at a girls' school in Dubai. Just up your street, eh? Lots of lovelies for your harem and nothing to do all day but count the money!'

There was a smell of coffee coming from the staff room.

'Do you want a coffee, Peggy?'

That was the voice of Mrs Dipfield, the cookery teacher, and 'Peggy' was Mrs Pritchard. I could see her because she always sat in the corner opposite the door, with her little fat legs spread and her glasses on her nose, and she was always knitting. Perhaps it helped her to relax in the staff room, because she certainly did not have a very relaxing time anywhere else in Sir Willyum's. She taught religious education and her lessons were always a riot; no-one ever listened to her although she would shout at the class to be quiet. The only way she could teach us anything was to write things on the board, which she did by standing on a stool because she was so short. Then, because she had her back turned, all sorts of things would happen. Fights would break out, someone would pinch the board rubber from her desk or hide her handbag, girls would start doing their nails and boys would ping bits of chewing gum at each other or even at her. She was always having to send me for Mr Godley to sort out the discipline in the class, but as soon as God put his head round the door and said, 'Now, what's all this about?' the class became instantly quiet.

'We're doing work on Muslim festivals, sir,' some wit would reply, who happened to be clambering over a desk when the door opened but who had read the title on the blackboard and therefore salaamed to the blackboard ostentatiously, 'and we're pretending to pray to Allah!'

Mr Godley always arrived for staff briefing a few minutes before the first bell when the door was firmly shut for about five minutes. Then, when the bell went, he would usher the teachers out, saying the same thing every morning: 'Your classes await you, ladies and gentlemen!' and I would hand out the registers and then walk with Mrs Pritchard to the form room.

On that particular morning, it was as we were crossing the walkway to the science block that I saw both Ronnie and Badger by the minibus garage. Ronnie had his back to me and was fiddling with the lock of the garage door and Badger was tugging at his arm. My first feeling was relief. Ronnie was all right, he was here at school where he belonged. But then I remembered that he shouldn't be in school today and worry surged again. Why was he here and what was he doing?

I slowed, making to turn towards him, but Mrs Pritchard said, 'Come on Stephen, don't dawdle, it's an assembly morning,' and so I had to trot to catch her up. When I looked back over my shoulder I saw Badger pulling at Ronnie's arm as the garage door swung open, and then Ronnie shrugging him off and pushing him away, and, from the look of it, swearing at him. That wasn't like Ronnie. But then it wasn't like Badger to be on the school site. What was going on? I saw nothing more, as I had to follow Mrs Pritchard, who had turned the corner.

But there was more to worry about that morning than Ronnie. Registration meant sitting next to Dwayne Tubbs, because Tubbs still came after Stringer in the register, and although I had asked Mrs Pritchard if I could move, she said yes but never did anything about it. I did not tell her the reason for wanting to move seats. The school had an anti-bullying policy, which was stuck up on every classroom wall. It told you to tell a teacher if someone was nasty to you, but no-one ever did because everyone knew that if you did you suffered even more afterwards, because not only were you a victim but you were a 'grass' too. In our world, the world that the teachers knew nothing about, a 'grass' was just about the worst thing you could be, far worse than being a 'boff' or a 'queer' or a 'girl'.

I was right to be apprehensive about Dwayne on that day. Sometimes he forgot about me for days on end and I lived in a state of agonising tension knowing that something terrible was going to happen but not knowing exactly when. But on that morning I had already seen the glint in those little black eyes.

When we arrived at the form room Josie Davenport was leaning out of the door on one leg so that her skirt had ridden up and I could almost see her knickers. She was screaming 'Whore!' at some girl down the corridor. When she saw us coming she dodged inside with a cheery 'Morning Miss!' She ignored me.

The form room was, as usual, hot and noisy. Pupils were spread across desks and chairs, their bags filling the aisles between the rows. One or two of the girls were completing homework, but most were in huddles gossiping with Walkmans plugged into their ears. The boys were shouting about football, or laughing at jokes, or playfighting. Mrs Pritchard nearly tripped over Jessica White's guitar case as she struggled to her desk and there was a burst of laughter.

'Quieten down everyone and sit in your places. We need to do the register.'

Nobody took any notice. I tried to slide into my seat invisibly, glad that Dwayne was turned in his seat talking to Peter Slingsby, who sat behind us. But as Mrs Pritchard opened the register and looked down at it, pen at the ready, my head was suddenly and violently pushed onto my desk, squashing my nose and scraping my glasses. It was so unexpected that I bit my tongue painfully.

Mrs Pritchard must have noticed the movement out of the corner of her eye and looked up.

'Dwayne! What are you doing?'

'Nothing, Miss!' and with a final vicious push, he released my head.

'Are you all right, Stephen?' said Mrs Pritchard.

'Yes, Miss.'

She looked unsure. 'I hope you weren't bullying Stephen again, Dwayne. Remember the little talk we had about that?'

The 'little talk' had been in Year 7, when she had come around the corner of the corridor to find me up against the wall trying to shield my stomach from a thumping by Dwayne. That 'little talk' from well-meaning Mrs Pritchard had resulted in a split lip and chipped tooth which were so obvious that I had to explain them to my mother as an accidental trip on some concrete steps.

'Just having a laugh, Miss, me and Stringer. Weren't we?' and he turned towards me with a leer and nudged me sharply in the ribs.

'Yeah,' I said, 'It's all right, Miss,' and, relieved, I saw her return to her register.

But the chant had started. 'Sydney! Sydney! Kick him in the kidney!'

Up and down the desks it spread, like the swishing of distant waves, the words hissed so quietly that to anyone who didn't know, and that included Mrs Pritchard, they were unintelligible. She rapped her pen on her desk.

'Hush now, 9P! Let's get on with the register.'

No-one took any notice but Dwayne, who saw himself as the class leader, turned round and bawled: 'Shut up! Register!'

It was suddenly quiet, and Mrs Pritchard took advantage.

'Richard?'

'Yes, Miss!'

'Gillian?'

'Yes, Miss!'

Morning registration proceeded, while I sat, like a tensed spring, waiting for the next assault. This was why I did not notice that my school bag was being passed round the class. I didn't realise what was happening until it had reached Jamie Cunliffe, who sat by the classroom door. He was emptying it into the waste paper basket, item by item. He had just unwrapped my sandwiches, inspected them, and taken a big bite, when the bell rang. There was a great scraping of chairs and a crowding towards the door in spite of Mrs Pritchard's 'in one line please, 9P, don't push!' and in the turmoil what remained of my sandwiches were trampled into the floor. I waited until the room was empty, put my stuff back in my bag, put the squashed bread and cheese in the bin and hurried after the class to assembly. Not having anything to eat was the least of my problems on that day.

I soon caught up with my form group. By the time I reached the main corridor, where all the classes from different parts of the school amalgamated in a huge river of bodies, the river was sluggish. Bodies were slowing, then stopping, and bodies behind them, not looking where they were going, were bumping into those in front and being thumped, and then doing some thumping themselves. There was a blockage ahead.

'Ducks!'

The message rolled back along the river and as it did everyone got more and more excited, until it became a rhythmic chant…

'Ducks! Ducks!'

The whisper grew in volume until it was being shouted like a war-cry and then it got faster and faster.

'Ducks! Ducks!'

Ducks were a common sight in Easton St. Matthew. They could be seen all along the Seventeen Foot Drain that ran parallel with the school playing field. Attracted by food litter, they had over the years become so tame that they frequented the school grounds, flying up with a squawk if a football was kicked in their direction and waddling around the playground at break time hoping to be fed, often with a brood of ducklings behind them, to be cooed over by girls. They were always being driven away by Ronnie, especially when they tried to follow us indoors, and he was always bemoaning 'fucking duck droppings being trodden into the fucking floors!' It wasn't that he didn't like the ducks. He kept an eye on them and would give me updates on their family situation.

'That little ol'ol' mallard duck with the missing tail feather, she's hatched eight, bless her, saw 'em in the dyke this morning.'

But he didn't want them in the school buildings, and woe betide any girl who picked up a duckling.

'They're not pets. They're wild creatures and they belong in their own habitat, on the river or flying up in that there sky, where I can get a decent shot at 'em!'

That might sound contradictory to someone not born in the fens but to Ronnie it made sense; he was a hunter, and they were his legitimate prey. He loved them in life and respected them in death, once giving me a painful clipped ear when, as a young kid, I had thrown a dead pheasant at the shed wall just for the fun of it, as young kids do.

'Don't you ever let me see you treat a wild creature like that again, boy! It's not a toy!'

But Ronnie wasn't being a caretaker on that day and, as the queue pushed sideways, with cries of 'Mind yer feet! Look out! Ducks!' I saw through the bodies a mallard duck leading a procession of nine ducklings along the main corridor from Reception.

From where I was standing there were internal windows into the assembly hall, and I could see Mr Crumb in position on the stage with his assembly book open and his glasses on his nose.

'What is that noise Mr Godley?'

'Er… I think it's ducks, Mr Crumb. I'll see what I can do,' and Mr Godley's head did a huge sideways jerk and he scurried out into the corridor, with a loud command: 'Quiet!'

It was suddenly very quiet, except for the duck's gentle quacks and her progeny's squeaking.

Mr Crumb's monotone continued, now clearly audible to everyone in the corridor.

'Whoever it is Mr Godley take the names for lunchtime detention…'

Mr Godley hurried towards the ducks, his head jerking like a piston and the ranks of pupils fell back and over themselves before his advance. But then he stopped, halted by Mr Crumb's continuing monotone:

'…and why are there no chairs in the assembly hall Mr Godley? Why hasn't Rawlinson put out the chairs?'

There were, of course, no chairs set out because Ronnie was no longer the caretaker. Every morning one of Ronnie's jobs was to put out two hundred chairs in rows for assembly and then to stack them up again afterwards, ready for Mr Crumb's lunchtime country dancing detention. He hated this job.

'Waste of bloody time! As soon as I've got them all out in straight rows it's time to put them back again, and you should see the chewing gum the little sods leave sticking on the underneath of the seats. And it destroys my polished floor, all that scraping when you lot are up and down for the bloody hymns.'

Mr Godley paused in his pursuit of the ducks and hesitated.

The voice didn't stop: '…and if anyone else makes a sound they can join in too that applies to you Benton see me at the end of assembly…' and we filed into assembly, shepherded by Mr Godley, who had decided which was the greater evil: duck shit on the floors or the whole school out of control.

'No chairs today. Just stand in your lines. No, don't sit on the floor! No, leave those chairs alone, Dominic, we'll manage without.'

Assembly was a mess. To ask two hundred adolescents to stand still for fifteen minutes is asking a lot. It was impossible to sit and daydream, which was what most people did in assembly, and there was a lot of whispering, sniggering, nudging and general messing about. Even Mr Godley found it difficult to control, although Mr Crumb just went through his assembly routine as usual.

'Good morning school what is that commotion that boy see me after assembly quiet now blessed are the merciful for they I shall not continue until there is total silence Mr Godley please take names they shall receive mercy I can give out punishments if this continues thank you school now this is the fifth beatitude found in the fifth chapter of St. Matthew's gospel it tells us that we all need to be merciful and that is what I expect to see in your behaviour…' and so on, up to 'Let us pray!' when he recited the Lord's Prayer, accompanied by a general susurration of mutters and grunts. Then there was a hymn, the words of which were projected onto a big white screen at the back of the stage and which Mr Crumb sang loudly, accompanied by Mrs Pritchard and a few girls who were in the choir. If I remember rightly, the only hymn that anyone else ever joined in was 'All things Bright and Beautiful' because of the possibilities for 'All tits large and beautiful, all fannies tight and small'. The hymn was followed by notices. Mr Crumb read out the list of pupils in smoking detention, Mr Godley performed a very big head-jerk and told the boys not to throw wet paper towels at the ceiling in the boys' toilets and a girl mumbled what I think was a report about a netball match. Then assembly was over and it was time for lessons.

The school day stretched ahead of me, four hours of anxious waiting.

9 a.m. Lesson One

Chapter Three

My first lesson on that day was Art with Ms McCarthy. I enjoyed art lessons, but I found being with Ms McCarthy uncomfortable. This was because we had history.

I first saw Ms McCarthy upside-down as two black leather legs striding towards me on top of a large purple bosom, which was on top of a lot of bushy red hair out of which two very large round earrings pointed upwards (but really dangled, of course). This strange vision was the result of being hung by my legs outside the window of Room 3, just above the school entrance. Dwayne Tubbs had hold of my right leg and Jimmy Buckland my left. Mrs Pritchard was in the store cupboard looking for Bibles. I was used to this treatment, although I was always terrified, hanging there with the blood throbbing behind my eyes, trying to stop my glasses from falling off. I knew that as soon as someone hissed the warning: 'Miss!' they would haul me up and drop me on the floor ready for Mrs Pritchard's 'What's all this noise about?' as she emerged from the cupboard.

But Ms McCarthy didn't know this. It was the day of her interview and I was the first sight she got of Sir Willyum's.

'Jesus!' she screamed.

She stood stock still for a moment looking up at me with her mouth open and then she rushed underneath me into the school entrance. Dwayne and Jimmy dragged me up smartly and sat me in my chair, Dwayne next to me with an innocent smile on his face and a hand on my shoulder as a reminder of what would happen if I told.

Then the fire alarm went off.

I overheard afterwards, from an excited Josie Davenport, who had been sitting in reception with a sick bowl on her lap, that a strange woman with lots of red hair had rushed into reception and pounded on the glass of the reception window shouting 'Quick! There's a boy hanging from a window! Get someone before they drop him! Quick!'

According to Josie, Mrs Duckworth slid open the reception window, just as if this was a normal occurrence.

'Good morning! Can I help you? We would be grateful if you wouldn't knock on the glass as it easily shatters. There is a buzzer just to your left.'

'For Christ's sake help!' shouted Ms McCarthy! 'He'll land on his head if they drop him!'

'Now what is it, dear?' I can just imagine the way Mrs Duckworth said it, calmly, with that well-rehearsed smile.

But Ms McCarthy could do *talking to stupid people* too. She answered very slowly and loudly, 'Like you do when someone's deaf,' said Josie.

'Outside that door,' (pointing), 'a boy is hanging upside-down from one of your upstairs windows. They are swinging him by the legs like this,' (demonstrating), 'and if they drop him there will be a fatality. That means he will die. D, I, E. Do you understand?'

Mrs Duckworth must have realised by now that something was seriously amiss. Either one of the pupils was about to be dropped on his head from a height or there was a mad woman loose on the premises. In either case, she knew what to do. She removed one of her shoes and rapped the heel on the glass of the fire alarm situated next to the reception window. A deafening blare erupted across the school. Josie said it was so sudden it made her barf into the bowl.

'Well, Mrs Duckworth goes, "Get the registers, Gillian!" at Miss Sweeney, who was like in the office, and then Old Crumpet came out of his office with a newspaper and goes, "What is that infernal noise, Mrs Duckworth?" and Mrs Duckworth said, "There appears to be an emergency, Headmaster," and he said (and Josie held her nose in order to imitate Mr Crumb's peculiar nasal tone), "Not another false alarm Mrs Duckworth tell Mr Godley I want the culprit in my office by breaktime and tell Rawlinson to turn that appalling noise off," and then he like goes back in his office and slams the door, and Mrs Duckworth got that megathingy out of a cupboard and told me to follow so I left the bowl in reception.'

Back in Room 3, the rest of the class had rushed out before Mrs Pritchard came out of the cupboard.

'Oh dear, what's happening?'

'It's all right, Miss, it's just a fire alarm,' I said, and I held the door open for her.

We walked together along the corridor and down the stairs. Like lemmings, pupils were pouring out of classrooms and rushing towards the fire exits and then into the playground. Occasional bleats of 'Single file!' and 'Don't run!' could be heard but made no difference.

It was always bedlam when we had a fire alarm, which was at least once a month and sometimes more often if people got really bored and needed a break from lessons. One well-remembered day, there were three on the trot, each starting just as everyone settled back into their classrooms. It was great fun for kids, but not for the caretaker.

'Fucking kids!' Ronnie would complain. 'Every time they do it I have to get to my room to see where the fucking red light is flashing and then I have to get to wherever it is and change the fucking glass, and who is it that has to phone the fucking fire brigade and explain that it's just the fucking kids larking about again? Woe betide everyone if there ever was a real emergency in this fucking school!'

He was right, of course, but with Mrs Pritchard puffing along beside me, I just enjoyed the excitement around me: boys whooping and jumping on each other, revelling in the sudden freedom; girls trotting in groups, giggling and waving and calling to each other, 'Hi Trace! Come and stand with me in our line!'

Staff were irritable, it was obvious, as they fetched their registers. I could hear some of the comments.

'That's the third false alarm this term.'

'I'd just got them quiet and settled.'

'Why does it always have to be in my free period?'

A group of boys in football kit clattered past in football boots, a Year 7 class in cookery aprons were shepherded past by Mrs Dipfield.

'We'd just got the Victoria sponges in the oven. I wish you'd let me know when this is going to happen,' she complained to Mr Godley, who was by then in position on the steps of the back entrance, megaphone in hand.

We were supposed to line up with our form and I had taken up position right at the front of our line, where it was safest. While Mrs Pritchard tried to get the line straight and quiet, I gazed up at the sky, which was white-blue and clear. I remember spotting a kestrel hovering above a hedgerow in the distance and wondering what it had sighted. It swooped just as Mr Godley's dalek voice began to address us.

'Listen school!' There was a lot of shushing. 'The evacuation took…' he consulted his wrist watch '…exactly eight minutes and thirty-three seconds.' Cheer. 'That is not good enough.' Groan. 'That means we will have to practise at break time.' Louder groan. 'Now there is obviously no fire, so I need to know who it is who set the alarm off, and no-one is leaving until I know.' Another groan. 'If we have to stand here…' he continued, when suddenly the fire alarm stopped ringing.

There was total silence broken only by a few stifled giggles. Ronnie had inserted a new glass in the fire alarm. As if out of nowhere, there was the sound of a cuckoo calling, the first I had heard that year.

'…until home time,' Mr Godley carried on, 'we will stand here until I know who…' But nothing more could be heard but a high-pitched whistle from the megaphone. Mr Godley could be seen mouthing into it, his head jerking, but all we could hear was the static. There was another cheer. He tried fiddling with the volume control and as he did so Mrs Duckworth whispered something in his ear. Suddenly the megaphone found itself again.

'What did you say, Mrs Duckworth?' came the amplified squawk, 'A mad woman in reception?'

There was an even greater cheer. Mr Godley went into a huddle with Mrs Ducksworth. The lines began to sway and bulge, as if at any moment they would break up completely and dissolve into chaos.

Mr Spencer made his usual contribution. 'If we keep them here much longer, Mr G., there'll be a mutiny. Get your finger out!'

Then suddenly there was the sound of the fire engine siren from the village and that brought the loudest cheer of all.

The fire drill disintegrated and there was a charge for the door. I waited, watching the mayhem. I didn't want to get involved in any pushing and shoving as it was likely to end up in kicking and trampling underfoot. Some of the teachers tried to impose order, but it was hopeless to maintain any sort of authority in that crush. They soon gave up and did their fair share of pushing and shoving to get to their classrooms.

When most people had gone I began to return to Mrs Pritchard's classroom, but on the way past reception I was waylaid by Mrs Duckworth.

'Ah, Stephen, just the person we need. This lady has come for an interview today. Could you take her for a tour of the school, please?'

And so I came face to face with Ms McCarthy for the second time that morning, but this time the right way up.

'Well, hi!' she said, smiling. 'We meet again. Are you OK?'

'Hallo!' I said, 'I'm fine, thanks,' and I could feel myself blushing.

'Don't be too long, Stephen; change of lesson is in ten minutes time, and Miss McCarthy has her interview at ten o'clock.'

'Ms,' said Ms McCarthy.

'I beg your pardon?' said Mrs Duckworth.

'It's "Ms" not "Miss". I'm not a dried-up old spinster.'

Mrs Duckworth prickled. 'Well, that's as maybe, *Miss* McCarthy. I think you will find that pupils will call you "Miss". It's easier to say for them.'

'We'll see, shall we? And it's "Ms" not "Miss" please, er…' and she bent forward and stared closely at Mrs Duckworth's name badge which was pinned to her left breast, '*Mrs* Duckworth.'

Mrs Duckworth looked like thunder. Ms McCarthy smiled at her. I decided that I liked Ms McCarthy's smile. It was not a false dutiful smile like Mrs Duckworth's or a warm but weary smile like Mr Godley's, but a full-blooded and wide grin.

'Lead on, MacDuff!' said Ms McCarthy. I didn't understand the reference, but I led on, at a reasonably fast trot, to complete the tour before the stampede which was change of lesson. I was one of Mrs Duckworth's 'go-to' tour guides and I set out on my regular route along the main corridor, where we caught glimpses of lessons taking place: a teacher pointing to a blackboard; a sea of hands up; heads bent over books; the flickering of a video in a dark room; a boy jumping over a desk; a girl yawning.

'This is English, with Miss Ferguson,' I said, as I opened the door on bent heads and concentration.

'This is Science, they're doing an experiment,' I told her, as I revealed considerable chaos in the science lab and quickly shut the door again.

'What's your name?' she asked, with another of her smiles, as we went up the stairs.

'Stephen Stringer, Mi…' I stopped myself just in time from saying 'Miss'.

She smiled at that. 'Well, Stephen, you're a very good guide, and a very tactful one too. You can call me 'Sidney', if you like. All my friends do.'

That stopped me suddenly. I could not help looking up at her and I know that I blushed again. It was so strange to hear my dreaded nickname being used so casually, as if it was a perfectly acceptable name, used among friends. It wasn't the way teachers usually talked to pupils either; the very idea that a teacher had a Christian name was somehow embarrassing, and as for using it…

'You look as if you recognise that name, Stephen. Do you know someone called Sidney? It's quite an unusual name for a girl, but my dad called me after his best friend. I think he wanted a son.'

'It's my second name,' I blurted out. 'After my dad, and grandad. But…' I stopped talking. I could not go on to tell her anything else about the way the name tormented me, even though she seemed so warm and friendly that I almost thought I could.

'Well, fancy that,' she said. 'It looks like we Sidneys had better stick together eh?' and she raised her right hand for a high-five.

I didn't know how to respond at first, so I just stood there, but she didn't move and just grinned at me in that special way she had, so that eventually I raised my hand to meet hers. It was a moment I will never forget.

We continued along the first-floor corridor until we passed a boy standing outside a classroom. He was picking his nose and eating the snot.

'You'll catch something nasty!' was Ms McCarthy's comment to him.

I couldn't help laughing as he gazed at her with his mouth open. For a teacher, I rather liked her.

Later, as I looked out of the window on the way to the library at lunchtime and saw her gliding out of the carpark astride a huge gleaming Harley-Davidson, I decided that she wasn't like any other teacher I had ever met and that I certainly liked Ms McCarthy.

Later that evening, when we were cleaning out the chicken house, I talked to Ronnie about Ms McCarthy.

'Did you see that new teacher with the red hair? I showed her round. She's all right.'

'Yes, I saw her,' said Ronnie. 'Replacement for that twat Rodney Rushbridge, what's run off to the south of France with someone else's missus, so I heard.'

'She's called Ms McCarthy, and we mustn't call her Miss.'

He grunted. 'Load of trendy nonsense!'

'And she's called Sidney, she told me, same as me, and…'

'Bloody stupid name for a woman!'

'…she's got a great sense of humour,' I continued, not aware of Ronnie's growing irritability. 'She said to this boy who was eating his snot, "You'll catch something." You should have seen his face. I couldn't help laughing.'

'Are you going to empty that bucket of shit or am I going to stand here all day waiting? I've got a dog to feed this evening, never mind bloody art teachers and snotty boys.'

'But I was only telling you how much I like her.'

'Teachers aren't there to be liked,' he growled.

When I had emptied the bucket onto the compost heap I returned to the subject.

'And, Ronnie, she rides a motorbike. It's black and chrome…'

'Yes, I know. I bet it left a bloody great pool of oil in the car park! Now shut your noise and bring that sack of layers pellets from the back of my van.'

Looking back, I think that conversation, and my enthusiasm in particular, might have sparked the jealousy and dislike for Ms McCarthy that grew in Ronnie over the next few months.

*

Ms McCarthy's lessons were fun. It wasn't so much that she taught different things, but she did it differently and she treated us as if we were equals and had important contributions to make to the lesson. She taught us drama as well as art, and I even found myself enjoying those lessons although in the past drama had been a kind of purgatory because no-one would work with me.

She had been at the school only a couple of weeks and we were stacking the chairs round the edge of the drama room after a lesson when Ms McCarthy called out over the hubbub.

'Stephen, would you mind if had a word before you go please.'

Everyone looked at me and I could feel my ears go red. There were some giggles and Josie sniggered.

'Oh Sydney, you've made a conquest!'

'Teacher's pet!' hissed Dwayne and placed the foot of his chair onto my foot and pushed it down hard.

'Ow!' I couldn't help shouting, for the pain was excruciating.

'Oh dear, Sydney!' He smirked at me. 'Have you hurt yourself?'

When the class had gone I limped over to Ms McCarthy.

'You wanted to see me, Ms McCarthy?' I was always very careful not to call her 'Miss', although everyone else did.

'Why Stephen, you're limping, have you hurt yourself?'

'It's nothing, Ms McCarthy, honestly.'

She perched herself against her desk. 'I wanted to talk to you privately, Stephen,' she said.

That embarrassed me. It wasn't what teachers said to pupils.

'It was great seeing you the other day, Stephen, with your binoculars.'

She was referring to an encounter the previous Saturday morning when I had met her on the Marsh.

I had been with Ronnie and we had gone with the intention of walking out at low tide to the Trial Bank (a sort of hump about half a mile out on the saltmarsh), to see if we could see any seals and to give Gyp a good run and splash in the salty creeks. When we had arrived at the Marsh parking area, we could see a motorbike parked on top of the wall which had left deep ruts on the grass slope.

Ronnie was livid. 'Look at that! Someone else without legs! Can't they read the bloody sign?'

He was referring to the weathered noticeboard planted next to the parking area, which warned members of the public that 'riding horses and driving any motorised vehicle on the sea wall' was prohibited.

He parked the van and marched up the slope ready to give somebody a piece of his mind. I followed him, with some trepidation, for I thought I had recognised the helmet parked on the motorbike saddle.

About twenty yards along the wall on the marsh side stood a figure in leathers with a camera on a tripod which was trained on the horizon, where, above a line of grey, the sudden swoops and swirls of thousands of waders could be seen. Above the black leathers was a riot of red hair.

'Ronnie, it's Ms McCarthy,' I hissed.

But Ronnie was too worked-up to listen properly. 'I don't care who the fuck it is! That motorbike's not allowed!' and he yelled, 'Here you! Get that bike off the marsh! Can't you read, you dozy twat?'

I hurried after him, anxious.

Ms McCarthy turned her head towards us. Ronnie stopped.

'Fuck me, it's a woman!'

Ms McCarthy had recognised me and walked towards us.

'Why, it's Stephen Stringer isn't it? Fancy seeing you here. What are you doing out here in this lonely place? With binoculars I see. Bird-watching?' She turned to Ronnie. 'And don't I recognise your companion here?'

'It's Mr Rawlinson,' I ventured.

She looked unsure.

'The caretaker,' I explained, miserably embarrassed.

'Ah, of course! Mr Rawlinson. And are you bird-watching too? It's so beautiful out here, isn't it? Wild and empty. I thought I'd get some sky shots for my collage,' and she smiled at us in that disarming way she had.

Ronnie cleared his throat.

'Well that's as maybe, ma'am…'

I looked at him; I had never heard him call anyone that before.

'…but this area is protected. It's a Triple SI, that's a Site of Special Scientific Interest for those that are hignorant, and that means motorbikes are not allowed. So could I ask you to remove it as soon as possible from the sea wall.'

'Why of course I will. Special Scientific Interest, eh? Because of the wild-life?'

'Yes,' I couldn't help myself from answering. 'The Wash is the most important wetland site in the country. Did you know that it supports over half the total world population of knots, probably about 180,000, and as for pink-footed geese…'

'OK, Stevie. You don't need to show off,' said Ronnie. 'I'm sure your teacher's got the message.'

'Yes, I certainly have. It's obviously a very special place and I can understand why you're so enthusiastic, Stephen. I'd love to learn more. Perhaps you can teach me, eh? I could be your pupil for a change,' and she grinned at me. I blushed. She had a special brand of charm, that woman, and I was a sucker for it. 'But first, I must obey the rules and move my bike. Let me just pack up my stuff, I've got enough shots for one day anyway.'

Later, when she had packed her photographic equipment into her haversack and wheeled her motorbike down the slope, we watched her riding away along the long concrete farm road.

'So that's the new teacher, eh?' said Ronnie.

'Yeah! She's great!'

He looked at me thoughtfully. I could see something was on his mind.

'What?' I asked.

'I don't quite know what to make of her, that's what.'

He never did quite work her out. And to Ms McCarthy, Ronnie must have seemed like a throwback to a former age. It was a clash of cultures.

But I was telling you about the end of the drama lesson.

I stood there, wondering what this was all about and wishing I could escape to examine my foot, which was really hurting.

'Have you ever used a camera, Stephen?'

'Not really, Ms McCarthy.'

'Because I was wondering if you would like to go with me on a little photography expedition I'm planning for next Sunday. You'd have an opportunity to take some photos of those birds you love so much. I've got a Canon SLR, an A1 with all the lenses and it takes wonderful wide shots. If your mother doesn't mind, that is. What do you say?'

I had no idea how to say no to a teacher and the idea did appeal to me. So I said yes.

It wasn't until afterwards that I remembered that I was due to go fishing with Ronnie on the coming Sunday. Ronnie went fishing throughout the fishing season on Sundays because that was when Beryl went to church, and I usually went with him.

When I was a little boy I had begged him to take me with him. I took to playing out front, so that I could meet him on his return, pretending with a bit of cane and string that I was catching fish in Mum's round rose bed in the front garden.

'Did you catch anything, Ronnie?' I would shout, before he could even get out of the van. I would be jumping around with excitement.

'Give me a minute to catch my breath, boy. Let's see now,' and he would open the back of the van, take out his rod and line and stool and all the fishing paraphernalia that I found so fascinating, and he would give me his catch bag to carry. We would repair to his shed, and there he would show me what he had caught. The usual catch in those wide slow-moving fen rivers was perch or roach with the occasional pike and I can to this day remember the smell of fen fish, cool and earthy. But most times there wouldn't be anything, and I would just climb on the bench and hang the bag on the designated hook.

'Just nippers today!' Ronnie would comment.

'Nippers, Ronnie?'

'Yeah, little'uns, just like you, still got a lot of growing to do.'

'But I am growing Ronnie, look!' and I would stand up against the shed wall, where he would, on every birthday, measure me with his long ruler and chalk a mark on the wall with the year and my age. 'Look, Ronnie, I am growing. Am I old enough to go fishing with you yet?' Ronnie had insisted for what seemed like years that I was as yet too young to go fishing with him.

'Little'uns can't go fishing until they sit still, and you've still got too many ants in your pants,' he would say.

Then, at last, when I was eight, Ronnie and Beryl bought me a fishing rod. I was by turns ecstatic and frustrated, because my birthday fell within the close season for river fishing, and I had to make do with sleeping with the rod laid carefully on the bed beside me and practising by casting over the bannisters when Mum wasn't looking.

Ronnie had timed my initiation well. Once I started I never had any problem with sitting on a bank for hours, with Ronnie just up-stream, watching the brown water or ripples round my line, and soaking in the life of the river around me: the moorhens and ducks, an occasional heron, the caw of a rook or clatter of a pheasant on the field behind me. I enjoyed my fishing trips with Ronnie.

But photography was something new. The only camera I had ever seen was Mum's old box Brownie which she got out if we ever went on holiday, and I wasn't allowed to use it. The idea of using a camera like I used my binoculars, to see a bird and zoom in on it or pan out to see it in its setting, and to be able to record that sighting by clicking a button, seized my imagination.

But I can see how it must have looked to Ronnie. When I got home from school that day I went to find him, as usual. He was digging in his vegetable garden, Gyp sitting upright next to him, watching every turn of the spade for traces of any old bones.

'Ronnie! Guess what? Ms McCarthy has asked me to go on one

of her photography trips, and she said she'll teach me to use her camera, you know with the tripod and wide angle and all that.'

He stopped digging and looked at me.

'Mm. Miss who?'

'Ms McCarthy, that new art teacher, the one with the motorbike that we saw on the Marsh last week, you know, the one that we mustn't call Miss.'

'Ah, her.'

I was so excited that I did not notice that he was being unusually reticent.

'Yeah, I think that she's great, not like normal teachers. She said if Mum says yes she'll pick me up on Sunday at ten o'clock at the top of the Drove.'

'Sunday?'

I stopped, suddenly aware of the implications of the timing of the trip.

'Oh, yeah, that means I won't be able to go fishing this week. Sorry. But we haven't been getting much recently, have we…' I trailed off.

He was still digging.

'Ronnie?'

'Yes, Stevie?'

'Is that OK? I mean, you don't mind, do you?'

He continued to dig.

'Mind? Why should I mind? I go fishing on Sundays. It's you that was always so keen on joining me.'

'Yeah, well. I'll want to go again next week.'

'Yep, I expect you will.'

I was at a loss, aware that something was not quite right, but not sure exactly what it was and what to do about it.

'I must go and ask Mum. I'll see you later, Ronnie.'

He didn't stop digging.

Later, having promised my mum to ask for a 'proper letter, with details and all that' from Ms McCarthy, and to find out how much it would cost and what time I would be back, I happened to look out of the back window because it had started raining. Ronnie was still digging, but Gyp had got fed up and left him alone.

*

That first photography trip with Ms McCarthy was the most exciting day of my life so far, and a big part of that excitement was the motorbike ride. I hadn't told my mother about the Harley-Davidson, of course, and that was why I had arranged to meet Ms McCarthy at the top of the drove. When I arrived, there was no sight of her and I wondered if she had forgotten or I had got the time wrong. I checked my watch and gazed intently along the road to the double bend by Franklin's Cottages. Fen roads on Sunday afternoons were often empty of traffic and it was very quiet. All I could hear was a persistent thrush. It was a very warm day; I could smell the ripening sloes on the blackthorn hedge on the opposite side of the road and a freshly-hatched swarm of midges was busy above me. It was low tide, and it was so still I could hear the air bubbles plopping in the mud.

I was just beginning to feel disappointed and to consider whether I should wait any longer, when I heard a faint chug and saw a headlight emerge from the bend and then gradually, as if being blown up on a balloon, the motorbike got larger and larger. She slowed down when she saw me, lifted one hand from the handlebars to wave, and then came to a halt right beside me, engine still running, black-leathered legs astride the bike.

'Hi Steve,' she said as she took off her helmet. 'That's some straight, that bit before the bend – must be nearly a mile dead straight, got her up to ninety easily. That's the beauty of these fen roads. I never had a chance to do those kind of speeds in Liverpool. Are you ready? Hop on then.' She reached back to retrieve another helmet from its position strapped to the back of the seat. Just like that! As if I rode pillion on a motorbike that did ninety miles per hour every day! I was so excited I felt sick as I put on the helmet and climbed onto the seat.

'Are you OK? Hold on tight then. Off we go!'

I gripped her round the waist and I certainly held on tight!

What followed was totally exhilarating. We overtook every other vehicle on the road, accelerating to what felt like a dangerously high speed on the empty stretches. At the big roundabout outside Kings Lynn we met the Sunday-afternoon-out traffic on the coast road, and how exciting it was to weave in and out of the cars and then feel the powerful engine between my legs as we surged away from them.

Halfway to Hunstanton we turned left for Snettisham Beach and then bumped along a rutted track lined with ramshackle beach huts between a lake and the sand dunes, stopping at a gate where a sign read 'RSPB Reserve. No shooting. Please do not disturb the birds'. We left our helmets with the bike, climbed over the gate and carried the camera equipment through the dunes.

The tide was right out and before us stretched miles of flat sand and mud, shimmering where the sun shone on patches that were still wet. It was a clear day and opposite, across the expanse of the Wash, I could see the dark line of the Lincolnshire coast.

'But that's the Lighthouses!' I pointed in amazement to the two lighthouses that guarded the mouth of the Nene, tiny verticals on the dark line.

Ms McCarthy was setting up the tripod.

'The light is perfect,' she said. 'You should be able to get some magical shots.'

I soon got the hang of the wide angle and the zoom, and spent a happy two hours, under her direction, composing my shots: waders strutting around on the sand or circling far out over the shallows a few feet above the waves; a boat at its moorings; a close-up of a black-headed gull swooping; a ship far out in the channel bound for Kings Lynn port; and even a few shots of the way the sun lit up shapes on the sand ripples. It was a perfect afternoon.

'I'll get these developed this evening, Steve, and bring them into school to show you tomorrow,' she said as we packed up the gear. 'I'm planning to set up the art store cupboard as a dark room, so soon you'll be able to develop your photos yourself.'

They were beautiful photographs. I still have them; no longer hanging in their frames where Mum had proudly placed them over the fireplace in the front room – as they were until the day we moved out of the cottage – but stacked in my studio along with all my other photos, because that afternoon was the start of a hobby which I still enjoy. Looking at them now I suspect that they were not my unaided work. There is an artistry about the composition and the use of light which I am sure I did not have when I was thirteen and using a decent camera for the first time. And if they are indeed hers then I am glad, for it means that I still have something to remind me of her.

So began a happy few weeks. That half term Ms McCarthy took me on three further expeditions to the North Norfolk coast. She told me she was putting together a collection of photographs called 'Shifting Coasts'. On these trips I learnt more about how to use a good camera, how to compose shots, and use light effectively, lessons which have formed the foundation of my own photographic work ever since.

Much as I enjoyed the photography, however, it was the motorbike rides that I looked forward to most of all, and if she had arranged a trip for the following Sunday I spent all week in a buzz of anticipation. Speeding along the A17 straight or the Kings Lynn bypass, clutching her leather jacket as we overtook all the other traffic with a satisfying roar, the wind tugging at my trouser legs and stinging my cheeks, on the edge between excitement and fear, was one of the great experiences of my childhood. And although as an adult motorcyclist I have often ridden at speeds well beyond the limit, I have never been able to re-live the excitement of those rides as a thirteen-year-old on that old Harley with my idol.

For during those first few weeks I idolised Ms McCarthy. She consumed my waking hours and I measured everything and everyone against her. She could do no wrong. At home it was 'Ms McCarthy says…' and 'Ms McCarthy's got one like that,' and so on until my mum lost patience.

'Anyone would think you were in love with that teacher, Stephen. You'll be telling me the colour of her front room curtains next. Give it a rest!'

I could have told her that Ms McCarthy had blinds not curtains in her flat, but I bit my tongue in time as I wasn't sure my mum would have approved of me knowing. Ms McCarthy would usually take me home for tea after a trip, and I thought her flat at the top of a warehouse overlooking the Town Bridge in Wisbech was the ultimate in cool residences. It was utterly different from my own home and from any other home I had visited.

The living room stretched the length of the flat, with wide windows at each end letting in striped sunbeams across an off-white fitted carpet, of the kind that my mother would have deemed 'impossible to keep clean'. The furniture was sparse; there was a long low black leather sofa and two black glass coffee tables, and the only other places to sit were two large bean bags, one orange and one yellow with black stripes. I had never seen such things before and I found them an interesting, if unpredictable, sitting experience, especially when the sudden sideways shift made my doughnut slide from my plate. One wall was covered with paintings, abstracts in blocks of colour which I assumed were her own work. But what impressed me most was that the other wall was covered from floor to ceiling with shelves and on those shelves were not the kind of knick-knacks and souvenirs which I was used to seeing on shelves at home, but hundreds of books. These books fascinated me, not just because of the wide range of interests they represented, but simply because there were so many of them.

'How many books have you got?' I asked her once, as I wandered my fingers along the titles of a shelf at my height.

She looked surprised at the question. 'Do you know, Steve, I don't really know. I've never counted them. I suppose I've got so many because I can't bear to part with a book once I've read it. To me it would be a bit like parting from a friend, someone who's given me something precious. I hate to think of a book being thrown away. Mind you,' she laughed, 'some of them are Kath's.'

Kath was Ms McCarthy's flatmate. She was small and bouncy with bubbly blonde curls and she didn't look much older than some of the girls in Year 11 although she was actually a history teacher at the grammar school.

The other unusual thing about Ms McCarthy's flat was that there was no television. I was used to my mum watching telly every evening after tea and in Ronnie's house Beryl had it on all day even when she wasn't watching it. 'I wonder what they do in the evenings,' I thought, but then there were all those books to read, and photographs to develop, and there were piles of exercise books on the coffee tables, which Kath used to complain about.

'I've got to mark two sets by tomorrow morning. I sometimes wonder why I wasn't an art teacher, with no marking to do!'

'But then you wouldn't have your Sunday evening tipple!' replied Ms McCarthy, and she told me how Kath would intersperse marking each little pile of ten books with a slug of Jim Beam. 'And at exam time, when there are loads of exam scripts to mark, she's as pissed as a newt by bedtime!' she said and they laughed.

The sophistication of all this impressed me mightily; I had never heard of Jim Beam bourbon.

9.40 a.m. Lesson 2

Chapter Four

My second lesson on that day was science, which was my favourite subject. I wasn't enjoying it very much though, because we were doing a practical assessment and my partner was Ashley Darbyshire. It's not that there was anything wrong with Ashley as a person. I had known him since I was five years old, when we used to get on quite well. No, there was nothing wrong with Ashley himself. The trouble with Ashley was Ashley's mum.

I remembered Mrs Darbyshire from my primary school days. Long after we were old enough not to be collected by our parents, Ashley was met at the school gate by his mum, who would take hold of his hand to cross the road to the car, even when he was eleven. She still stood outside the gate at Sir Willyum's, but Ashley now refused to hold her hand. At primary school Ashley had always been away ill; Ashley was allergic to certain foods, Ashley had asthma, Ashley couldn't do PE because… I can't remember why. In summary, Ashley's mum was over-protective and Ashley was what my mum called 'spoilt'. Being invited to Ashley's birthday parties was great because there was always a bouncy castle in the garden and presents in little bags to take home, and for his tenth we went to the local roller-skating rink. I can remember thinking that I wouldn't mind putting up with a fussy mum like Mrs Darbyshire because of the benefits of being 'spoilt'.

At secondary school Mrs Darbyshire was still fussing about Ashley, although he didn't seem to have asthma anymore. He wasn't as quiet as he used to be, and he was sometimes horribly rude to teachers, particularly women teachers. I don't know if he ever said to his mum the things he said to them, but I wouldn't have dared speak to my mum like that. I used to wince sometimes at how cruel he was to Mrs Pritchard, who never dared to correct him.

I can remember one occasion when Ashley had got into trouble with Miss Ferguson.

I happened to be in reception, with a bent pair of glasses in my lap and a pad of tissues to my nose trying to stop a nose bleed occasioned by the attentions of Dwayne & Co, when Mrs Darbyshire arrived. Mrs Darbyshire was very over-the-top; she was overweight, over-dressed and over-loud, so when she arrived in reception everyone noticed. She pushed past Sadie Johnston, who was standing at the reception window waiting for some photocopies for Mr Dawson, and rapped sharply on the glass.

Mrs Duckworth was at the photocopier, and when she saw who it was, she stayed there.

'Shop!' shouted Mrs Darbyshire, rapping again.

'Just a moment, Mrs Darbyshire, I'll be with you shortly,' Mrs Duckworth called.

Mrs Darbyshire continued to rap on the glass. Mrs Duckworth continued to photocopy. She took her time tidying the sheets and then took them to the reception window and opened it.

'Excuse me, Mrs Darbyshire,' she said, thrusting the papers out through the opening. 'Sadie, tell Mr Dawson to give me more notice next time, and it's going on his departmental budget.'

An arm poked round the side of Mrs Darbyshire and grabbed the photocopies.

'Ta Miss!' said Sadie and ran off.

'Now, Mrs Darbyshire, how can we help you?' Mrs Duckworth smiled a tired smile.

'I am not happy with this school,' started Mrs Darbyshire, waving a letter.

'Let me just see if Mr Godley is available,' said Mrs Duckworth. 'He's very busy but if you just take a seat I'll see if he has a moment.' She slid the window shut and went to the telephone on her desk.

Mrs Darbyshire rapped again.

'I don't know why I never get to see the headmaster!' she shouted.

'Do you want me to tell you,' muttered Mrs Duckworth, probably forgetting I was there. 'Ah, Stan, sorry to disturb you but Mrs Darbyshire is in reception again. I didn't get the details but it's some kind of complaint…

'I know but there's no-one else…

'But she'll just stand at the window and rap on the glass. It's the third time she's been in this week…

'No, I can't get rid of her – she takes no notice of me. You'll just have to work your charm on her again.'

There was a pause while she listened. Mrs Darbyshire continued to rap.

Mrs Duckworth's voice lost its telephone manner. 'Stan, for Christ's sake, get her out of reception, she's doing my bloody head in!' She took a deep breath. 'OK, I'll tell her. Thanks Stan.'

She went to the window and opened it.

'Mr Godley is on his way, Mrs Darbyshire. Do take a seat.'

'I don't know why I always have to see Mr bloody Godley. He's just a waste of space. Last time I complained to the school I had to see him, and did he sack the bloody teacher what was rude to my Ashley? Did he fuck? And what I want to know is where is that headmaster what never shows his face? What has he got to hide, eh? And as for you, Mrs Whatever-you're-called, you're nothing but a…' but Mrs Duckworth had slid the window shut with a bang, so I didn't hear Mrs Darbyshire's description.

Then Mr Godley arrived.

'Ah, Mrs Darbyshire, how nice to see you again. Do come this way.' He tried to usher her towards the corridor, his head jerking.

But Mrs Darbyshire would not be moved.

'No, Mr Godley, if I'm going to say it, I'll say it here, if you don't mind. I haven't got all day to sit around and pass the time of day. It's about my Ashley. I'm not going to have him bullied by your teachers. It's not fair when teachers pick on him the way they do. I've told you before. He comes home yesterday with this letter,' and she waved it,' crying his eyes out he was, poor lamb, because his English teacher put him in detention. I've already told you, Mr Godley, I don't believe in detentions. The school day is long enough already, especially with Ashley's eyes weak the way they are. I'm not going to allow him to be kept behind and made a spectacle of. He's a very sensitive child.'

'But we do have a clear detention policy, Mrs Darbyshire,' said Mr Godley. 'As I have explained to you before, we do expect our pupils to behave well, and we need to apply sanctions if they don't.'

'Oh, I know, Mr Godley. Don't think I don't support your discipline. I believe in strict discipline, especially for these yobs you've got at this school. Bring back the cane, I say. There are a lot that deserve it at this school. But Ashley didn't do anything, Mr Godley. He was picked on, like what your teachers are always doing.'

'What did he get the detention for?' asked Mr Godley, jerking like mad.

'It says here "insub… er… ordinariation",' said Mrs Darbyshire, pointing to something in the letter, 'whatever that means. When I asked Ashley, he said his teacher accused him of being rude. Now I can't accept that, Mr Godley. I've brought Ashley up to be polite and he's the sweetest, gentlest child, and always does what I tell him. So this is all a load of squit. She's just picking on him, and I won't have it!'

I remembered the incident. Miss Ferguson had told Ashley to pick up a crisp wrapper that he had thrown at the waste bin and missed. He had refused, saying, 'That's what cleaners are for,' and when Miss Ferguson had said she wasn't allowing the class to leave until it had been picked up, and everyone had groaned, he had said 'Pick it up yourself, then,' and walked out.

'Can you leave it with me, Mrs Darbyshire?' said Mr Godley. 'I can understand how you feel if there has been a miscarriage of justice. Let me look into it and see exactly what happened. I'll give you a phone call tomorrow. Would that help?'

'But I'm not having him in detention tonight! Tuesday's his bath night and I need to see to his toenails.'

'No, of course not. We'll look into things first shall we? Now if you'll excuse me, I have a class waiting.'

Mrs Darbyshire was always in reception complaining about something. Ronnie told me that once she had tried to ambush Mr Crumb as he backed out of his parking space.

'"Ah, the headmaster at last! I need a word with you," she says, standing there in front of the car with her hands on her hips. Christ that was some sight, she ain't 'alf got an arse on her, that woman! Well, old Crumpet, he just ignored her and went on driving. So she did her usual trick, that rapping on the window, and he just winds the window down and says, you know how he talks, all posh like, "I don't know who you are madam and I don't want to know but I am warning you that if you don't remove your filthy hands from my motor car and remove yourself from this car park in that order and within ten seconds I will be obliged to call the police to have you removed which is my right under the…" some regulation or other that he quoted. And then he just drove away. I tell you, it was a right laugh!'

But Mrs Darbyshire wasn't really funny. That woman was pure poison, as Ronnie was to find out. Her first victim, though, was Mr Took.

*

It's quite difficult to explain nowadays how people felt about things like homosexuality and paedophilia in the early nineties, as the zeitgeist has shifted. In those days it was still quite common in our part of the world to call a homosexual a 'queer' or a 'poof' rather than 'gay' or 'LGBT', and to call anyone who was a bit different in any way a 'pervert'.

Unfortunately for him, Mr Took was quite eccentric. He had a camp style of talking and walking and was rather feminine in little ways. For example, he would use an embroidered handkerchief which poked out of the top pocket of his jacket to blow his nose, with little high-pitched snorts and a lot of wiggling of his nose and wiping afterwards. But there was no obvious evidence that he was a homosexual.

He lived with his elderly mother. I knew that because he was the church organist and choirmaster at St John's, and Beryl had told us how he would bring his mother in from the car, 'Like a little old-fashioned gentleman he is, arm in arm with his old mum,' and seat her in the front pew before starting to play the organ before the service. 'She can't stand up to sing, you know, bent double she is with that arthritis, but she never misses church and her Jeremy playing the organ, bless her,' added Beryl.

He was a good music teacher. As well as his classroom lessons, he gave instrumental lessons after school and he was the conductor of the Boys' Band. The *Sir William Smith Boys' Band* was an institution in our area. It had been started in the fifties when someone had donated some trumpets and it had been going strong ever since. As a small child I remember watching the Boys' Band, which by then had girls in it as well as boys, marching with the floats at the annual Wisbech Rose Fair, and it was still in demand for village fetes. 'Being in the band' was an ambition for many of Sir Willyum's' pupils when they first started school, and I was no exception. My mum had paid for trumpet lessons for about six months until it became obvious, even to me, that I had no musical talent. But Ashley Darbyshire was different; he was musical and was soon playing trumpet in the Boys' Band and being taught the French horn by Mr Took after school.

Of course, Mrs Darbyshire embraced Ashley's membership of the Boys' Band with enthusiasm, which meant she attended all the after-school rehearsals. And it was at one of these rehearsals that Ashley's musical career came to an abrupt halt. I had long departed from the band, and I heard about the incident from Ronnie.

'I was just finishing polishing the hall floor when in comes this girl, stamping her feet right across my floor she was, and shouting blue murder.

'"Mr Rawlinson, Mr Rawlinson, come quickly we need you the door won't open and Ashley's stuck with Mr Took and he's screaming!"

'"Hold you hard," I says, "get your breath and tell me slowly. What door?"

'And she told me how Ashley had gone into the music store cupboard for something, and he'd pulled down a load of stuff from the top shelf and there had been a big crash and Ashley had screamed and Jeremy Took had gone in there to sort things out and then when he tried to come out the door had stuck and wouldn't open, and Ashley was screaming even louder.

'By the time I got to the music room he was still screaming and so was that mother of his.

'"What are you doing to my Ashley? Come out of there, you pervert!" and that sort of thing.

'A right palaver it was. Well, I soon sorted out the door; it had got some papers stuck under it and when I got there Jeremy was on his hand and knees trying to tear them away. He looked petrified! I had to laugh to myself. But it was soon sorted.'

But, unfortunately for Mr Took, it wasn't 'sorted'. Ashley's days in the band were over but, what was worse, from that day Mrs Darbyshire insisted that Mr Took was a paedophile and had been trying to touch up her Ashley in the cupboard. The rumour spread fast, and suddenly all the members of the band except Kirsty Philpott were withdrawn by their parents, and you can't really have a band with one trombone player, can you?

What was worse for Mr Took was the way the pupils treated him. Chinese whispers thrive in schools. What started out as members of the band telling their friends that, 'Ashley had dropped something in the store cupboard and when Mr Took had gone in to help the door had stuck,' ended up within a few days as Mr Took locking himself and Ashley in the cupboard, pulling Ashley's trousers down and molesting him.

Ashley didn't help the situation.

'Hey Darbyshire, is it true? Did Tick Tock try it on with you in the music room cupboard?' asked Connor Soames.

'Yeah, Ashley,' added Josie Davenport. 'Did he really make you take your trousers down?' Her eyes sparkled. 'That's disgusting!'

Ashley had just come out of a science lesson and I was behind him, so I heard it all.

'Perhaps he enjoyed it!' said Michael Thompson, and everyone laughed. He began nudging Ashley in the ribs. 'Did you, Ashley? Did you like being touched up, eh?'

'Ooh, Ashley!' said Josie. 'You're not a queer, are you?'

There was more laughter. Ashley had blushed bright red and looked from side to side for escape, but there was quite a crowd round him by now.

'Come on Ashley, tell us your secret. You're in love with Mr Took!'

There were loud guffaws.

'No!' spluttered Ashley. 'No, of course not. It was horrible. I couldn't get out!'

'So he attacked you did he?' said Connor and added in a posh voice, 'Filthy swine!'

There was more laughter.

'Yes,' protested Ashley. 'He was all over me. My mum's made a complaint!'

'Really?' said Josie. 'What? To Old Crumpet?'

'Perhaps he'll lose his job,' said someone else.

'Good thing too. He's a creep!'

'Never mind, Ashley, Mummy'll look after you!' said Josie.

'What's all this?' said Mr Brighton, the science teacher, who had come to the door. 'Ashley, get a move on, old chap, you're blocking the door, and you lot will all be late for your next lesson. Now disappear!'

In spite of his eccentricities, Mr Took's lessons were fun and no-one messed about too much, but now things began to change. I noticed that in our next music lesson no-one took any notice of him when he asked people to listen. He looked quite surprised.

'I said, 'Quiet everyone', I want you to listen to this…' but most people just went on talking. He rapped on his desk with the baton he used to beat out rhythms.

'I said quiet!'

He waited and gradually the noise subsided.

'That's better. I don't know what's the matter with you all this afternoon, my lovelies. It must be the way the wind's blowing. Now listen to this and I want you to tell me what instrument it is.'

We were doing instruments of the orchestra. He beamed at the class, just like he usually did, and paused his right finger over the button on the tape recorder in a dramatic way, just like he usually did. But instead of a sea of expectant faces and the 'one, two, three' we usually chanted, there was silence and we just stared blankly at him. I felt very uncomfortable, although I didn't know why. Mr Took looked shocked.

'Now, what is it, my dears? Have I got a bogey hanging from my nose, or are my flies undone?'

There was a horrible silence. Normally someone would have shouted, 'Bogey, sir!' and we would have collapsed in roars of laughter, Mr Took included, but instead people sat completely still, staring at their desk, or looked sideways at each other.

Somehow, he got through that lesson, but from that day there seemed to be no more fun in our music lessons. Mr Took still taught us conscientiously but he no longer made his little jokes and often struggled to keep order. People had always made fun of him, pinging paper pellets at his backside when he bent over to help someone with a keyboard or making farting noises when he said, 'Listen to the silence,' but he had always taken it all in good part. But now things began to happen which were quite nasty. For example, someone wrote 'Took is a poof' on the whiteboard and one day Dwayne pinched his baton. This had often happened before, and it would have been passed round the class and waved around, with Mr Took joining in and thoroughly enjoying the prank. But this time the baton was hidden and then put back on the teacher's desk, bent out of shape.

'How did this happen?' asked Mr Took, picking up the wonky baton and looking sadly at us.

No-one said anything.

Chapter Five

Mrs Darbyshire decided that Mr Took must go, and she not only complained to the school, she also organised a petition. This was in the days before social media made it possible to get thousands of signatures, so she stuck copies of the petition under the windscreen wipers on cars parked near the school. Some of them blew away and were cleared up by Ronnie.

'Look at this poisonous rubbish!' he said, dragging a crumpled muddy piece of paper out of his pocket and laying it on the table. He had just come back from locking up the school. 'All over the carpark they were, blowing everywhere.'

It was my day for having tea with Ronnie and Beryl as Mum was working late. I was sitting at the kitchen table idly looking at the *Daily Mirror* while Beryl cooked my favourite tea of eggs and home-cooked chips. The kitchen was engulfed in a fog of cooking oil and Gyp was sitting next to the cooker looking very interested. Ronnie took his coat off and went to hang it up behind the door. Beryl peered at the paper, spatula in hand.

'What is it then?'

'Some petition that stupid cow Mrs Darbyshire's gone and got up. Wants Jeremy Took sacked because he got stuck in the cupboard that time.'

'What? Jeremy Took the organist at the church. But he's a lovely man!' She shook the chip basket vigorously. The oil spluttered.

'Well, that's as maybe, but he's certainly not a pervert, which is what she says in this 'ere petition. I was there. I saw his face. I think he was more frightened than the boy!'

He sat down and began to take off his boots.

'It's not right, spreading this poison about someone. He might be a bit of a weirdo, but he doesn't deserve this!'

I reached across for the petition, but he snatched it away.

'Best you don't see this, Stevie. It's not the sort of thing that a kid needs to know about.'

'But those petitions are everywhere, Ronnie,' I protested. 'There was one being passed round in History this afternoon.'

'What is the world coming to?' said Beryl, as she cracked an egg into the frying pan.

'It's not right, that's what I think,' said Ronnie.

He returned to the topic while we were eating.

'I just hope Stan Godley sorts this out, 'cos I wouldn't want to see a chap suffer for something he hasn't done.'

'But Ashley Darbyshire says he did do it,' I said.

'Then he's a liar, I tell you,' and he pointed his eggy fork at me. 'That's the same toe-rag that made Peggy Pritchard cry the other day. He's a nasty piece of work I tell you – takes after his mum. I don't want to see you being mates with him, boy!'

'He's not my mate,' I said. 'It's just that we're both in Set 1 for things.'

'What was that about Peggy crying, Ronnie? Peggy Pritchard what's husband's church warden?' asked Beryl.

'Yeah. Came across her in her classroom the other day. Sobbing her heart out she was, head down on her desk and all.

'"Now, buck up, Peggy," I said. "What's the matter love?"

'"It's the children, Ronnie, they seem to be so nasty nowadays, and I don't seem to be able to do anything with them. I had to send someone for Stan Godley twice today, and as for that Ashley Darbyshire!"

'Well I got her to blow her nose and that, and she told me what that nasty little piece of dirt had called her. I won't repeat it here, love, because of the boy and out of respect to you, but I tell you, if any son of mine had used that sort of language to a lady he'd have got a hefty clip to the side of his ear!'

'Dear, dear,' said Beryl. 'What is the world coming to?'

'But they do give her the run-around, the kids. Too soft with them, that's the trouble. No wonder she resorts to the Baileys! I can't blame her.'

Ronnie wasn't the only member of staff to be up in arms about the petition. I heard the teachers talking about it one morning when I was waiting outside the staffroom for Mrs Pritchard. Ms McCarthy had come striding past me as usual but looked very worked-up. She didn't say 'Hi, Steve!' like she usually did.

'Look what I picked up in the carpark?' she announced to the staffroom, and she waved one of the petitions. 'It's a disgrace!'

'What is?' said Mr Spencer, 'dropping litter or touching up the pupils?' and he looked round the room grinning.

'It is not funny, Jim,' said Ms McCarthy. 'It's character assassination, and it's happening to one of our colleagues.'

'What is, Sid?' said someone.

'Who's being assassinated?' said someone else.

'Archduke Ferdinand,' said Mr Spencer, but no-one laughed.

'Listen to this!' said Ms McCarthy, and she began to read: 'Sack the Pervert! If you want your child to be safe from the clutches of Jeremy Took, music teacher at Sir William Smith High School, who is a proven paedophile (which is spelt with an 'f' instead of the 'ph'!) then sign below and return to Dulcie Darbyshire, 15, Singleton Estate, Sandford St. James.'

'But that's terrible,' said Mrs Pritchard, 'saying those things about Jeremy.'

'Where did she get the idea from?' asked someone.

'I expect it's from when he got stuck in the cupboard with Ashley Darbyshire,' said Mrs Dipfield. 'My Julia was at that band rehearsal, but she's dropped out of the band now and I can't get her to change her mind because all her friends have left. It's such a shame. Jeremy wouldn't harm a fly.'

'Serves him right,' said Mr Spencer. 'Flouncing about like a pansy. I don't mind people who bat for the other side, as it were, live and let live I say.'

'But Jeremy doesn't play cricket, Jim,' said Mrs Pritchard.

'He means being homosexual, Peggy,' said someone.

'Oh!' said Mrs Pritchard, 'I'm sure he isn't one of those.'

'Don't you think you are all being prejudiced,' said Ms McCarthy. 'I don't know about Jeremy's sexual preferences and I don't want to know as it's none of my business, but I do know that he is a colleague and I do not believe for a minute that he would do anything like this. This is a case of persecution by a stupid woman and I, for one, won't stand for it. I'm going to Mr Crumb about this at breaktime.' With this, she disappeared into the Ladies'.

'I'd take off your leathers first, young lady, or he might not concentrate,' commented Mr Spencer.

'But it's not funny, Jim,' said Mrs Dipfield. 'She's right. It's awful for Jeremy.'

'So what exactly can Old Crumpet do about it? The damage is done,' said Mr Spencer, 'and you watch, it'll be all over the papers.'

'Mm, he won't like that.'

'And do you seriously think Old Crumpet'll take any sort of action that involves getting off his backside?' said Mr Spencer.

But Mr Crumb did take action. We were in a Maths lesson when a Year 7 girl came into the classroom, gave a bit of paper to Mr Warrington, and shot out again.

'Ashley? Mr Crumb wants to see you.'

Everyone looked up from percentages. I could see Ashley's shoulders stiffen and his neck go red. But he didn't move.

'Come on Ashley, lad,' said Mr Warrington, 'when the call comes… Don't let's keep the headmaster waiting, eh?'

Slowly, as if in great pain, Ashley stood up and walked unsteadily to the classroom door, every eye following him.

'Get a grip boy,' said Mr Warrington. 'You look as if you're on the way to the gallows. It can't be that serious.' But we knew it probably was. Going to see the headmaster was very rare at Sir Willyum's.

Twenty minutes later Ashley returned. His face was crumpled and his eyes red.

'I've got to get my bag, sir,' he said, and made for his desk, where he crammed his books and pencil case into his bag any-old-how and hurtled out of the room.

Everyone looked at each other with expressions of excited

smugness. It had been serious.

We soon found out what had happened, because Josie Davenport brought the news to the queue outside the Geography room for next lesson.

'You'll never guess what!' she began. 'I've just seen Ashley Darbyshire crying!' She grinned. 'Bawling his eyes out, he was. It looked right weird.'

People gathered round for the gossip.

'Really!' said Jaynie Carter. 'What? A boy crying?'

'Yeah. It was cool. I heard it all, there was him and his mum and Old Crumpet said, "Deal with this woman please Mr Godley I can't stand hysterics in a woman," and slammed his door 'cos Ashley's mum was screaming blue murder. It was in reception and I'd just gone to the loo…'

'Oh yeah?' said one of the boys. 'Since when was the girls' loo in reception, Jose?'

'Well, I'd slipped out for a quick one, hadn't I?'

'But why was Ashley crying?' asked someone. We all cried sometimes, of course, but the idea of someone crying in public at school was somehow interesting.

'I think it was to do with that thing he said about Tick Tock touching him up in the cupboard. 'Cos God said, "I hope this has taught you to always tell the truth, Ashley," and that made Ashley's mum livid and she started shouting something like, "Don't you call my son a liar!" and grabbed Ashley's arm and started dragging him to the door and he was sobbing real loud and he'd got like hiccups, like this…' She demonstrated a sort of gasping hiccupping kind of weeping. 'And then God went into Old Crumpet's office and I heard them 'cos he didn't shut the door and he said something like it being a false ally… allygumption, or something like that, and old Crumpet said, "That woman gives me a headache," and God said, "I'll go and see Mr Took after school, headmaster," and Old Crumpet said, "Yes, I leave it to you, Mr Godley," and God turned round and saw me and said, "Josie, what are you doing out of class?" and I said, "On a message sir," and scarpered.'

In assembly the following day Mr Godley made a short speech.

'Now, I want you all to listen very carefully as this is a serious matter. We have just had to deal with a case where a pupil has made a false allegation about a member of staff. It has now been dealt with, but I want to make it clear to all of you that such allegations are completely unacceptable and will be dealt with very seriously. The student involved has been excluded for a week. I expect the member of staff in question to be treated with the utmost respect in future.'

Ashley was away for a week. It was a bit awkward in music lessons for a while, but over time the atmosphere relaxed and things got back to normal, although Mr Took had lost his flamboyance. Mrs Darbyshire had vowed to take Ashley to another school, but he came back after his exclusion. At first, he was treated as a celebrity. He basked in the notoriety but that didn't last either, and everyone forgot about it.

Chapter Six

It was Mrs Darbyshire who couldn't forget.

She focused on Ronnie next. It all started when Ashley got his trousers wet.

It happened at Angling Club, which was an after-school activity that Ronnie ran. That makes it sound much more official than it was. Actually, it was me and six other boys who went fishing with Ronnie after school on Tuesdays in the summer term when the evenings were light and when Mr Godley volunteered to do the locking up. Ronnie used the school minibus to take us to good spots where the bream and tench were particularly easy to catch.

Ashley joined the Angling Club to keep his mum quiet.

'You know that fishing thing you do on Tuesdays, Stringer?'

We were supposed to be doing a biology worksheet, but the class was being taken by a supply teacher so there was a lot of chatter and not much work. I had finished the work sheet and was reading a book.

'Yeah,' I said. 'Why?'

'Can anyone join?'

'I suppose so,' I said, and turned back to my book, not really interested in having a conversation with Ashley.

'So I could come next Tuesday, could I?'

I looked up from my book.

'What did you say?'

'I said could I join the fishing club on Tuesdays, the one that Mr Rawlinson does?'

I was surprised. I couldn't imagine Ashley sitting on a river bank with a fishing rod, especially if it was raining. He wasn't the outdoor type.

'I've got to do *something*,' he said, reading my thoughts. 'Now I'm not in the band anymore Mum wants me to be in the school play and I hate drama. I thought if I did another after-school thing she'd stop going on at me.'

'Can't you do chess?' I suggested.

'Nah, it's too boring.'

'Well, fishing can be pretty boring too. You have to sit and do nothing for hours.'

'Yeah, I know, but you do catch fish, don't you?'

'Sometimes,' I said.

'Well, that's what I want to do, so you can't stop me!'

'I'm not trying to stop you, Ash. It's up to you if you want to come. We meet at the minibus garage at half-past three and you need wellies.'

So there he was the following Tuesday afternoon, with his wellies and his mum.

'Where exactly are you taking them, Mr Rawlinson?' she asked.

Ronnie was loading the gear into the back of the minibus.

'Well, I don't rightly know yet exactly where we'll end up. Somewhere on the Middle Level probably. Depends how I feel when we get going.'

'But what if I need to come and find you? How will I know

where to come?'

'Mum!' pleaded Ashley.

'Now why would you need to do that?' said Ronnie.

'Well, my Ashley's not used to fishing. He might not like it and want me to come and get him.'

'Mum!' pleaded Ashley again.

Ronnie stopped what he was doing and looked at her.

'Look here, missus, if he doesn't want to come he doesn't have to. No-one's forcing him.'

'But I do want to come,' said Ashley.

'Well, what time will he be back? I don't want Ashley home too late. It's his bath night.'

'Mum!' Ashley sounded desperate.

'Get in the bus, lad,' said Ronnie, and he shut the boot. 'We'll be heading back sometime between seven and eight and I'll drop the lads off at their homes safe and sound as I usually do, so don't you worry, missus. I haven't lost one yet.'

Everyone got in the bus.

'Don't sit at the back, Ashley, in case there's an accident,' shouted Mrs Darbyshire.

'Don't sit at the wrong end of the bath, Ashley,' shouted Kevin Drubbs, who was a bit of a wit. 'You might fall through the plughole!' Everyone laughed.

When we arrived, Ronnie helped Ashley set up. He showed him how to put the worm on the hook, set his float, cast out and then how to reel in, doing his first cast for him.

'Now you watch that float, lad,' said Ronnie, 'as if your life depended on it and if it wobbles you shout. Right?'

'OK,' said Ashley.

'If you've got any questions, call to Stephen just up the bank there. He knows what's what.'

For the first ten minutes Ashley just sat and stared at his float.

'You don't have to stare like that, Ash,' I said. 'You'll feel it move.'

A further ten minutes passed.

'What do I do if a fish bites, Stringer?' he called.

'Jerk your rod upwards and pull the line 'til it's taut. And shout for us to help you.'

Twenty minutes passed.

'How much longer have I got to wait, Stringer?'

'A long time. We've only been here half an hour. You probably won't catch anything the first time anyway?'

'Why?'

'I dunno. People don't.'

Ten minutes later Ashley called out, 'What if I want to go to the loo?'

'You put your rod down and go and piss in the nearest bushes.''But what if I want to do number twos?'

'For goodness sake, Ash, go and do it in a bush. No-one's looking.'

'But I haven't got any toilet paper!'

At that moment his float did a nose dive. It was so obvious that I noticed it from twenty yards away.

'Ash! You've got a bite! Quick! Jerk your rod!' I shouted. 'Ronnie!'

Ashley stood up suddenly and threw his rod upwards and over

his head so dramatically that he overbalanced and fell backwards, landing on his backside and then sliding down the steep bank and into the river, ending up sat up to his waist in the reeds. As he went he howled.

Ronnie came running.

'What the hell's happened?' he panted.

'Ashley got a bite and jerked too hard.' I said. 'He's fallen in.'

'So I see,' said Ronnie. 'Stevie, come and see to his rod will you, while we get him out. Just stop hollering, boy, will you,' he said to Ashley. 'You're not drowned, but I tell you, you will be if you don't put a plug in it, you're doing my head in.'

By now the other boys had arrived. I tried to sort out his tackle, which had got in a muddle when he fell and let go of it. The fish had long gone.

'Now. Let me see,' said Ronnie, and he pushed his cap back on his head, which he always did when he was thinking.

'We'll pull him out, Mr Rawlinson,' said Kevin, and he started down the bank.

'Hold you hard, boy!' shouted Ronnie. 'That there bank's damn steep and damn slippery. I don't want you *all* swimming. There's a life belt on the bridge up yonder, under the sign, a couple of you boys run and fetch it for me.'

Damien Dawson and Dean Fipps rushed off.

'Now sit still boy,' warned Ronnie,' if you don't want to go swimming. That flow's fast out there in the middle and it's some years since I passed my life-saving.'

By now Ashley had stopped howling and was whimpering instead.

'But it's cold,' he gasped. 'And I'm getting wet.'

'Well, Ash, it is bath night, it'll save Mummy having to scrub your back later,' said Kevin. I couldn't help laughing.

The boys with the lifebelt were soon back and Ronnie carefully slithered his way on his backside down the bank until he could throw it towards Ashley's head. It hit him on the right ear and he yelped.

'Get it over your head and shoulders, boy, and hold on to it tight when we pull,' instructed Ronnie. 'Now lads, spread yourself along this here rope and when I give you the word we all haul. Right?'

It was great fun. We all got hold of the rope and Ronnie shouted, 'Are you ready? One, two, three, heave!' We heaved. 'And again!' shouted Ronnie.

'Yo-heave-ho!' sang Kevin, and we laughed and joined in.

It took three heaves and Ashley came slithering up the way he had slithered down, flat on his back. He was shaking.

'I… want… to… to… go home.'

'Well, you can't go home, lad. We've only been here half an hour.'

'But… I'm… wet.'

'A bit of water won't hurt you, you're not a sugar lump, you won't dissolve, and it's a warm evening. Now empty out those wellies and get yourself set up again. You've gone and lost your fish in all this palaver.' Ronnie began to wind up the rope.

'But… I'm… cold.'

'Shut up, Ash!' I said and got a very dirty look back.

For the rest of the time Ashley just sat on the bank looking miserable. He didn't bother with his rod and I couldn't be bothered to help him, especially as the tench were biting and I caught two. Ronnie came along to see how we were getting on.

'What's the matter, lad?' he said to Ashley. 'Are you still cold?'

Ashley nodded and shivered. I am sure it was just for effect.

'I'll tell you what,' said Ronnie. 'I've got a pair of over-trousers in my gear, keep them there for foul weather. What if you changed your trousers and we hung them up to dry – the sun's still warm. Would you like that?'

Ashley looked up at him and nodded again. Ronnie fetched his over-trousers and offered them to Ashley, who just stood there holding them.

'Go behind the minibus, lad, and get them wet breeks off. Off you go!'

A few minutes passed. Ronnie and I admired my catch.

'Mr Rawlinson,' called Ashley from behind the minibus.

'What is it, lad?'

'I can't get my trousers off! They're stuck to my legs.'

'Oh, for Chrissake, Ashley,' I muttered.

'Watch your language, Stevie,' said Ronnie, and he went off to help Ashley.

I don't know exactly what happened behind the minibus, but I do know that a few minutes later Ashley emerged in a pair of over-trousers tied round his waist with baler twine and Ronnie emerged carrying a wet pair of trousers, which he hung on a bush.

I thought nothing more of this incident with the over-trousers. If I thought about that fishing expedition at all in the days that followed it was to remember how Ashley had fallen in and to think what a wimp he was.

*

The next day Ashley informed me that he wasn't coming to angling club any more. I wasn't surprised.

'Oh yeah?' I said, not really that interested and certainly not bothered. As far as I was concerned his whingeing had been a real pain, although seeing him fall in the river and having to rescue him had been fun.

'My mum was livid,' he said.

'You only got wet, Ash. You weren't in any real danger.'

'But she said I could like catch pneumonia from sitting around in wet trousers and I've started a cold already.' He coughed a bit, to prove the point. 'Anyway, she's going to complain to the school.'

'That'll make a change, I said.' I don't think he noticed my sarcasm. 'Anyway, you didn't sit long in wet trousers. Ronnie lent you his over-trousers to go home in.'

'Yeah, that's what she's really mad about.'

'Why?'

'Because Mr Rawlinson took my trousers down behind the minibus.' He looked quite proud as he said this.

'But that's because you asked him to, you dipstick, because you couldn't get them down yourself, you said they were stuck to you or something. I heard you say it.'

'My mum says that's like taking advantage of a minor child, or something like that. Anyway, she's complaining to the school and I'm not allowed to go fishing again.'

'That's crazy, Ash. Ronnie's not like that!'

'Well you would know wouldn't you, Stringer, seeing as you're so matey with him. How do we know what you two get up to when you're on your fishing trips.'

'Fuck off, Darbyshire!' I said.

As the day wore on I brooded on what Ashley had said and couldn't wait to get home to warn Ronnie. I watched out for the van arriving back after locking up the school and was fidgety and preoccupied all through tea.

'I said, "Do you want a doughnut for afters?"' said mum.

'What? Oh, no thanks,' I said.

'Are you sickening for something? I got them specially when I saw them reduced in the Co-op 'cos usually you're mad about them. They won't keep, they go stale.'

'Oh, OK Mum. Thanks. I will have one.'

I didn't enjoy the doughnut. I was listening for the sound of next-door's back door slam shut, which was the sign that Ronnie had finished his tea and was off to his shed. When I heard it, I was up and on my way out, cramming the last of the doughnut into my mouth.

'Not so fast, young man. Sit down and finish your tea properly, or you'll get indigestion. What are you in such a hurry for anyway?'

'Nothing,' I said.

I sat down, chewed as fast as I could and swallowed.

'Can I get down, Mum, please.'

She looked at me carefully. 'You know, son, sometimes I don't know what to make of you. I wish I knew what goes on in that head of yours.'

I didn't reply, but just fidgeted on my chair.

'Oh, off you go,' she said, but as I hurtled through the kitchen, she gave a parting shot.

'What about homework?'

'Haven't got any?' I shouted as the kitchen door slammed shut, which was a lie.

Ronnie was in his shed and was planing wood. He was making a new broody coop out of some driftwood he'd picked up on the tideline. He didn't look up when I went in.

'Put the wood in the hole, boy. The ferrets are out.'

There was a lot of scrabbling in the corner where the two ferrets were investigating the inside of Ronnie's wellington boots, which had fallen over in the fun. I stood and watched his hands as they worked the plane. He was deft and skilful, and the wood was being transformed before my eyes. Now that I had the opportunity I didn't know what to say, how to start, how to explain how worried and angry I had been all day, and how frightened I was for him.

'What's eating you, then?' he said as he turned the wood over and began to plane the other side.

That's how well he knew me! I shifted from one foot to another, thinking how to start.

'Come on, boy. Spit it out!'

'It's Ashley's mum, Mrs Darbyshire, she's going to complain about you taking his trousers down and it was his fault because he's such a wimp and… and…'

'And what, son?'

Ronnie had stopped planing and was looking at me.

'…and I don't want people to say you're a pervert like they do about Mr Took!' I felt the tears burn and blinked hard, trying desperately to stop them flowing.

'Let's you and me have some cocoa, shall we?' said Ronnie, and he put the little kettle on the camping stove and lit the gas. 'Park your backside, boy, and then you can tell me all about it.'

So I sat on an upturned crate and told Ronnie about my conversation with Ashley, while he picked up a couple of mugs, inspected them for spiders and added three or four spoonfuls of cocoa and sugar into each one. He smelt the contents of a quarter of a bottle of milk and when the kettle began to whistle, poured water into each mug.

'There you are, lad,' he said, as he settled himself into his old ladder-back chair and took a sip of his cocoa.

'But she's going to complain to the school, Ronnie!'

'She already has, boy.'

'What? When? Oh Ronnie, what are we going to do?'

'Now, just calm down, Stevie, and I'll tell you how it happened. I was on my way across reception with a load of chairs on my trolley when I runs into that Mrs Darbyshire on her high horse. She was laying into Maureen Duckworth good and proper, she was.

"'I demand to see the headmaster," she says, "and I'm not moving from this spot until I see him in person. No, don't fetch that Mr Godley, he's as much use as a feather duster in a coal hole. I am not having my Ashley molested by the staff at this school. It's full of paediatricians and perverts and I've made one complaint and no-one did anything about it and I am not laying down this time," and so on. She really had her dander up. And then she sees me.

"'There he is," she shouts, with all her spittle flying everywhere. "There's the pervert that undressed my son," and she advances on me. It was a good thing I had the trolley between me and her, I tell you, because she's a large lady and she looked like she meant business.

"'What have you to say for yourself, you pervert?" she shouts. "Getting my Ashley to take his trousers down and, what's more, taking him behind the minibus. I'll have you in court, you pervert.

They should castricate people like you!" and lots more stuff like that.'

'But what did you say?' I asked.

'I didn't have a chance to say nothing, boy. She was well under way, like a fire engine she was. Well, the noise brought Old Crumpet out of his room.

"'What is going on?" he says, and then he sees Mrs D. and he turns round and goes straight back again.

"'You might think you can run away from me, Mr Crumb!" shouts Mrs D. "But if you won't see me I'm going to the police!" and then she turns to me and she says, "You won't hear the last of this, you pervert," and off she waddles, like an angry hippopotamus.'

I didn't laugh, even though the idea of Mrs Darbyshire being like a hippopotamus was funny.

'But what if she does go to the police, Ronnie?'

'Don't you worry, Stevie, she won't. She's all wind and piss, stupid cow. And if she does,' he took another sip of his cocoa, 'and if she does, I've got nothing to be ashamed of. I've done nothing wrong, we both know that, don't we, and so does that lad of hers, poor kid.'

'But Ashley doesn't always tell the truth, Ronnie.'

'And who are they going to believe, eh? A grown-up man with a clean record in a steady job, who's held a shotgun certificate for donkey's years and a clean driving licence with not even a speeding ticket? Or a silly young lad with an ignorant woman for a mother?'

He sounded so confident and I believed him. But, of course, he was wrong.

Chapter Seven

It was a policewoman in plain clothes who interviewed Ronnie. It happened at school about a week later and she also interviewed Ashley and everyone in the Angling Club, including me.

'There's a cop car in the car park!' was the whispered rumour that swept the school during Period 3, closely followed by, 'It's plain clothes!'

'Perhaps someone's murdered Old Crumpet,' said Kevin Drubbs at change of lesson.

But I wondered if their visit was about Mrs Darbyshire's complaint, and my heart started to beat fast. Then, in Maths, a message came that Ashley Darbyshire was to go to Mr Godley's room.

'I told you, Stringer,' he hissed as he got up. 'My mum's gone to the police about your precious Ronnie Rawlplug!'

I felt sick all through maths and when Ashley came back he looked as if he'd been sick too. But I didn't get a chance to hear what had happened because he said to Mr Warrington, 'Mr Godley wants to see Stephen Stringer,' and it was my turn.

'This is PC Walker, Stephen, she's from the Child Protection Team of Fenland Police, and this is Mrs Stibbings from Social Services,' said Mr Godley when I got to his office. His head jerked towards the policewoman. 'Stephen was taking part in the fishing activity.'

The policewoman was short and fat and the social worker was short and thin; otherwise they looked identical, both with short grey hair and glasses and both wearing saggy cardigans. I sat on the edge of a chair facing them and Mr Godley sat at his desk.

'Now Stephen, we would like you to tell us exactly what happened when your friend Ashley fell in the river and how he came to be wearing Mr Rawlinson's trousers,' said the fat one.

'Take your time, but make sure you tell us the truth,' said the thin one.

I did as they asked.

'So Ashley called for help to get his trousers off?' asked the fat one.

'Yes, he was wet through and he said he couldn't get them off because they were sticking to his legs.'

'Were you surprised about that?'

'Not particularly. He's a right wimp.'

'Why didn't you go to help him?'

'Why should I? He's old enough to change his own trousers, isn't he?'

'Were you surprised when Mr Rawlinson went to help him?' asked the thin one.

'No. Ronnie's a grown-up, he was in charge, like a teacher sort of thing and he probably felt responsible 'cos Ashley had fallen in and got wet.'

'Ronnie? Do the pupils call the caretaker by his first name, Mr Godley?'

'Stephen lives next door to Mr Rawlinson, they're close family friends,' said Mr Godley, and his head jerked again.

'Ah,' said the thin one. She looked at the fat one. 'Now, Stephen, I want you to think very carefully before you answer this question and when you do to answer completely truthfully. Do you understand?'

I nodded.

'Has Mr Rawlinson ever helped you to dress or undress?'

I stared at them. It seemed such a weird question. Why did they want to know that? Mr Godley, who had been leaning back in his chair, suddenly leaned forward, his head jerking like mad.

'Is that question really necessary?' he asked.

'We have to explore all possibilities, I'm afraid, Mr Godley. It's about protecting children,' said the fat one. 'Well, Stephen?'

'I suppose he might have done when I was a littl'un and him and Beryl were looking after me for Mum, putting on my pyjamas and stuff. And he did help me with my waders the first time I wore them.'

Mr Godley got up. He looked worried and I could see that he was building to a very big jerk.

'I think Stephen has given us enough help,' he said. 'You can go back to your class, Stephen.'

I felt terribly guilty as I walked back to my Maths lesson. Although I couldn't put my finger on exactly why, I felt that I had betrayed Ronnie. At the time I had no idea what those two women were on about. Now, as an adult, I do.

*

I didn't have the courage to ask Ronnie about his interview, but he asked me about mine. We were on the way to the supermarket in Wisbech the following Saturday morning. We were supposed to be fishing but I had asked Ronnie to take me shopping so I could buy a birthday present for my mum. I knew she loved Quality Street chocolates and Beryl had said that Tesco had the big tins on offer.

'We'll go on Saturday morning, when your mum thinks you're out fishing; then it'll be a surprise,' said Ronnie.

'You can get a card at the same time,' said Beryl. 'And Ronnie can get her a card from us while you're about it.'

'Have you got enough money, boy?' asked Ronnie.

'I've still got £4.50 of my Christmas money left. Is that enough?'

'Yes, love, should be,' said Beryl, 'but here's an extra fiver in case you need a bit more. Keep the change; you're a good lad and give Ronnie a hand regular I know.'

'Thanks Beryl.'

So there we were on the way to Tesco.

'I hear them two women from the police had a word with you,' he began, 'about that daft lad what fell in the river.'

'Yeah.' I didn't say anything else because I didn't know how to express how I felt about that interview.

He looked sideways at me.

'And was it OK?'

'Yeah.'

There was a pause as he negotiated the big roundabout on the edge of town.

'They had a word with me, too.'

'Yeah, I know.'

'I just told them what happened, didn't mince my words, told it as it was.'

'Yeah, me too.'

'Warned me to be more careful in future, they did. Something about always having another adult around if I needs to touch pupils, something like that. Not that I'm likely to be touching any of 'em, am I?'

'No.'

'Not that they don't deserve a good clip round the ear, some of 'em.'

I laughed briefly.

'But I'll have to resist the temptation like, won't I?'

'Yeah,' I said and I laughed again.

After this conversation I felt more comfortable. But that was before we met Mrs Darbyshire.

We had found the chocolates and chosen the cards, and Ronnie had put a packet of his favourite biscuits in the basket and we were on the way to the checkout. It was busy and there was a queue. We were just standing waiting and I was looking at the checkout sweet display, wondering whether to use some of Beryl's money to treat myself, when we heard her.

'There he is, Barry! There's that pervert from the school!'

We both looked round. Bearing down on us was Mrs Darbyshire, with Ashley behind her. Next to her, pushing a trolley piled high with groceries, was a little man with receding hair. This, I assumed must be Mr Darbyshire, although I hadn't realised that Ashley had a dad.

'Don't go to that checkout, Barry,' continued Mrs Darbyshire in her screeching voice. 'I don't want Ashley to be anywhere near scum like that.'

Obediently, Mr Darbyshire manoeuvred his trolley towards the neighbouring checkout, but the assistant chose that moment to put her barrier across and say to him, 'Sorry, love, this checkout's closing. You'll have to join the queue.'

Mr Darbyshire steered his trolley back to where he had started from and settled behind us. He looked tired.

'I think it's disgusting!' bellowed Mrs Darbyshire. 'Allowing perverts to roam freely where there are children. Ashley! Keep behind me.'

I looked at Ashley and attempted a smile of greeting. He ignored me. He looked tired too. Ronnie said nothing, but he turned and looked at Mrs Darbyshire.

'You ought to be locked up, you filthy bugger!'

People in the queue began to look curious.

'Excuse me missus, but what did you call me?' Ronnie's voice was very quiet.

Mrs Darbyshire's voice was not quiet. 'I called you a filthy bugger and I'll say it again. I'll shout it from the rooftops if needs be. People like you should be locked up.'

'And what exactly do you reckon I've done that I've got to be locked up?'

'Molesting young boys, that's what. You're a pervert!'

The people in the queue looked even more interested.

'And where did you get those fanciful ideas from, if I may ask, missus?'

'My Ashley told me what you did to him behind that bus. As if it wasn't enough to half-drown him you had to take his trousers down and touch him up.'

By now some of the other shoppers had paused at our queue for the entertainment. I felt acutely embarrassed. I tugged on Ronnie's arm.

'Let's go, Ronnie,' I whispered.

He ignored me. He was staring at Mrs Darbyshire.

'And you won't get away with it! I've told the police. I hope they put you down for a long time.'

'I'll tell you something, missus,' said Ronnie. 'I think you need to watch that mouth of yours, 'cos it runs away from you. And what's more you need to get your facts right before you go making false accusations.'

He turned away from her.

'Did you hear that, Barry?' shouted Mrs Darbyshire. 'He's just called me a liar. What are you going to do about it?'

'Give it a rest, Dulcie,' said Mr Darbyshire. 'Let's just get the shopping done and get home for the match, eh?'

'Typical!' bawled Mrs Darbyshire. 'A fine husband you are. Your wife is insulted by a paediatrician and all you can do is moan on about your bloody football.'

At this point the queue moved forward. I was glued to the spot.

'Come on Stevie, it's nearly our turn,' said Ronnie, and he put his hand on my shoulder and ushered me forward with my basket.

'There you go!' screamed Mrs Darbyshire. 'What did I say? He just stands there and puts his arm round that boy. You need to keep your hands to yourself, you dirty pervert!' She suddenly grabbed me by the arm and yanked me away from Ronnie.

'Hey!' I shouted.

Ronnie took a step towards her.

'Leave go that boy, missus, or I won't be responsible for my actions,' he said, quietly.

'Did you hear that, Barry? He's just threatened me.'

Fortunately, at that moment the store manager arrived.

'Now then,' he said to Mrs Darbyshire. 'Would you like to go to checkout 3, madam. It's just opened.' He firmly took hold of Mr

Darbyshire and his trolley and led the family away. The people in the queue looked disappointed.

When we were back in the van with our purchases, Ronnie took a deep breath. 'I tell you, Stevie, that woman needs to stop her yammering, 'cos if she doesn't, I'll swing for her.'

I could tell that Ronnie was angry because of the way he drove back. It was not like him to drive fast; normally he pottered along at 35 m.p.h. whatever the speed limit was. But today his hands were clenched on the steering wheel.

'Don't you know what indicators are for, you stupid cow?' he shouted as a Peugeot suddenly changed lane in front of us and he had to brake suddenly. 'Are you fucking blind?' and he leant on the hooter. 'Bloody women drivers!'

I kept quiet.

By the time we had arrived at Middle Level, he had calmed down and we had a good afternoon. Between us we got four bream and Ronnie nearly landed a pike, but his line got caught up on something and he had to break it. By the time we got home he was the old Ronnie again, even whistling as he unloaded the van.

'How are you going to get that into the house without your mum seeing?' he asked, as I picked up the tin of Quality Street. 'You can keep it in the shed for now, if you like. Give it here.' He looked at his watch. 'Hey, we're a bit later than usual. You'd better get straight in for your tea or your mum will have my guts for garters. Off you go boy.'

Ronnie continued to unload the gear and I went home. When I entered the kitchen there was a note on the table.

'Next door with Auntie Beryl. Tea later. Bread and jam if hungry. Mum.'

As I didn't fancy bread and jam when there might be one of Beryl's chocolate cakes next door, I decided to join them. There, huddled at the kitchen table with Mum's arm round her was Beryl, in floods of tears.

'I've never been so humiliated in my life, Myra,' she managed to gasp between sobs.

'I know, dear,' said Mum, and she pushed a box of tissues towards Beryl and gave me a disapproving look, gesturing with her head towards the door through which I had just arrived. I chose not to understand her. Beryl took a tissue and crammed it into her eyes and screwed it up in her hand.

'Didn't you see my note, Stephen?' said Mum.

'Yeah, but I thought I'd come and see… er… see where you were. Are you all right Beryl?'

Beryl started crying again.

'It's Auntie Beryl and no, she's not. She's had a bit of an upset this afternoon. Why don't you go and do your homework, I won't be long.'

'Mum, it's Saturday afternoon. I've done my homework.'

At this point the back door opened and Ronnie came in.

'Beryl? Love? What's up?' He threw his cap on to a chair and rushed to her side, crouching down at her lap and taking her hands in his. He looked up into her face, which was red and puffy.

'What is it, Princess?'

I was surprised. I had never heard him call her that before and I don't think I had ever seen him touch her. He wasn't physically demonstrative. I think Mum must have been surprised too. She gently removed her arm from Beryl's shoulders and edged her chair away.

Beryl stopped crying and took great shuddering gasps of air.

'Oh Ronnie!' she cried. 'It was awful!'

'What was, love? What was awful? Tell me! Come on, I'm here now, love. Tell me all about it.'

'It was at Ladies' Circle, Ronnie, you know at the church, and it was that Rosemary Chichester, her what does the flower rota with me. I can't ever do the flowers again, I know I can't, not if people are saying things like that,' and she broke down again in tears.

'Saying things like what, darling?'

Beryl made a big effort to stop crying and blew her nose.

'Well, we were just having a cup of tea after the meeting and she comes up to me and she says, all smarmy like, "Oh Beryl dear, I felt I must just come and say how sorry I am and how awful it must be for you," not that she looked sorry, mind you. So I says, "What do you mean, Rosemary, what's awful for me?" and she said… and she said… Oh Ronnie, love…' Beryl couldn't go on and started sobbing again.

Ronnie looked at my mum in desperation.

'Apparently there's a rumour going round the villages,' she whispered, 'about some allegation.'

'Allegation?' said Ronnie, and I saw his face change from concern to anger.

'Everyone's saying you're a pervert, Ronnie!' blurted out Beryl. 'And I can't bear it. I'll never be able to show my face again!'

Ronnie took a deep breath. I think he did that to take control of himself because he looked thunderous.

'Now look here, Beryl,' he said. 'Look at me, look at my face, darling. Please!'

Slowly Beryl looked up at him.

'This is me, sweetheart, this is your husband, the man who married you twenty-two years ago…'

'Twenty-three, Ronnie,' sobbed Beryl, but she kept gazing into his face.

'Is this the face of a pervert? Don't you know me, darling?' And he, too, almost sobbed.

I felt uncomfortable and rather emotional at the same time. Even Mum sniffed, and she got up, steering me towards the door.

'Oh I know it's not true, Ronnie love, of course I do. But everyone's saying it, and they don't know you like I do and I just can't bear to imagine them saying it about you.'

'Come here, love,' said Ronnie, standing up and pulling her into his arms.

At that point Mum pushed me through the door and we went home.

Later, when it was almost dark, I went outside to the dustbin and I saw Ronnie standing at the bottom of the garden, with his back to the wildfowl pen, gazing out over the fields. He looked lonely and I somehow wanted to comfort him, so I joined him. Gyp was sitting so close beside him that he was almost sitting on his feet. Ronnie finished his cigarette and stubbed it out on the sole of his boot.

'Ronnie?' I said.

There was no answer. He lit another cigarette. He didn't usually chain smoke. I waited for a bit. Gyp was gazing up at Ronnie's face.

'Is Beryl all right, Ronnie?'

There was still no answer. I waited a bit longer. Then, just as I was about to leave him and go inside, I heard his voice, a voice I didn't recognise, cracked and rasping.

'That's my woman, Stevie, and I may not always show it but I loves her, I worships the very soles on her feet and she knows that, she does. And when I married her I promised her I'd always protect her, come what may.' He took a drag of his cigarette. By now it was completely dark, and all I could see of his face was the glowing cigarette end. 'And now she's been hurt, she's been hurt bad and I wasn't there to sort it out for her.' I saw the sudden glow again. 'And it's all the fault of that woman, that bloody stupid woman with her big mouth and her wild imagination. And I tell you, Stevie,' he threw down his cigarette and ground it into the grass with his boot, 'I'll swing for her, that I will.'

Gyp whined quietly.

*

The rumours spread. A few days later I came home to find Beryl in our kitchen, in tears again. Mum had her arm round her, again.

'There now, love, don't take on so. It's just your imagination.'

'But everyone looks at me funny, Myra, as if they know. It's horrible. I went into the newsagents to get my magazine this morning and that man that runs it he asked if I was feeling all right because I looked a bit down. And I know he was saying that to be kind but I just knew that he knew.' She started a fresh bout of sobbing.

'I'm sure he didn't know anything, Beryl dear. He was just being kind. He is a friendly sort of man, he talks to everyone.'

'But that's just it, Myra. That's why he knows, because he talks to everyone and they talk to him and they've all being saying those things about Ronnie and I just can't bear it. I can't go anywhere anymore.'

Mum gave me a significant look that said, 'leave us alone', but I was hungry.

'I'll just get myself a jam sandwich, Mum.' I opened the bread bin.

'Oh, what shall I do, Myra?' wailed Beryl. 'I daren't tell Ronnie because he's already so angry. I don't want to start him off, but I just can't go anywhere anymore.'

She didn't either. Beryl had been a happy soul with lots of friends in the area. As well as the Ladies Circle at St John's she went to the WI once a month and played bingo every Tuesday evening in Wisbech. Now, suddenly, she stopped going out.

The next Tuesday evening I heard the following exchange when I was putting my bike away.

'I'm ready, love!' called Ronnie. He had the van parked by the back yard and the passenger door open ready to take Beryl to Bingo.

She didn't emerge. He looked at his watch.

'Hurry up or you'll miss the first session!' he shouted. Seeing me, he added more quietly, 'Bloody women! Never on time, always having to titivate themselves.' And he laughed.

But Beryl did not come out.

'Where the hell is she?' he muttered and went to investigate.

A few minutes later he was out again. He slammed the door and backed the van back into its parking place.

'Isn't Beryl going to Bingo tonight?' I asked.

'Says she doesn't feel very well.' He shook his head. 'It's not like her, she loves her Bingo, never misses if she can help it.'

Then, a week later, it was Ronnie in our kitchen.

'I don't know what to do, Myra, I really don't,' he was saying. 'She keeps saying she doesn't feel well and she spends all her time moping around. It's not like her at all.'

'Oh dear,' said Mum.

'Do you think it's anything to do with… well you know, what's happened to me, the police and that?'

He looked worried.

'I don't think she's found it very easy, Ronnie. Between you and me, I think she can't get it out of her head, the injustice of it, and she thinks everyone is talking about it, when actually I haven't heard a murmur for over a week now.'

'But what can I do, Myra?'

Mum took a deep breath. 'Perhaps she needs a break, you know, to get away from round here for a bit.'

'You may be right. But our holiday's already booked for August and I won't be able to get any other time off.'

'I don't know how you're going to take this, Ronnie love, but have you thought that she could go and stay with her sister for a few days, the one in Swaffham, what's her name?'

'Sandra? Yeah, I suppose she could. But would she go, do you think, without me?'

'Why don't you ask her?'

He must have done as my mum suggested, and Beryl must have said yes, because the next day she came in to say goodbye.

'I'm just off for a few days to Sandra's. Ronnie thought it might do me good. You will keep an eye on him won't you, make sure he eats regular and that.'

And there was Ronnie packing a suitcase into the back of the van. They drove off waving.

For a few weeks I saw even more of Ronnie as Mum insisted that he have his tea with us.

'I'm not going to let you eat rubbish from the chip shop,' she said to him. 'I always cook a proper meal for Stephen and me and you are very welcome to join us, it's no trouble.'

Beryl phoned him every evening, he told us.

'She seems much better, been gadding about with that Sandra. But I'll be glad when I get her home again,' he would say cheerfully, when Mum asked how she was.

But I noticed how lonely he was, in spite of his meal with us. He spent much less time pottering with things in his shed and much more time than usual standing at the bottom of the garden staring out across the fields in the dark, as a pile of cigarette ends grew at his feet.

*

'Hey, Sydney!' Connor Soames confronted me one day in the corridor. 'I hear you're the caretaker's pooftah!'

Everyone turned and looked at me, curiosity lighting up their faces. Connor and his cronies from Year 10 stopped and looked at me, where I was standing in the queue with my nose in *The Observer's Book of Birds* waiting for Mrs Pritchard to arrive. I pretended I hadn't heard.

'Hey! Cloth-ears! Are you deaf? I'm talking to you!'

I kept my eyes firmly fixed on the book, praying for a teacher to happen along. The whole corridor round me had gone still.

'Did you hear me? Are you the caretaker's pooftah? Answer me, you fucker!' He jerked the book upwards out of my hands. 'Listen when a Year 10 asks you a question, you dirty little prick-sucker!'

Josie Davenport giggled. I bent down to pick up the book, but Connor kicked it away.

'Do you know what we do to pooftahs, Sydney? Eh?' he said, thrusting his face close to mine.

Fortunately, at that moment Mrs Pritchard opened the classroom door and the queue began to surge forwards. It was always a rush going into R.E. because everyone tried to get the seats at the back of the room and Mrs Pritchard couldn't control us. On this occasion I joined in the rush, to get away, leaving my book on the floor outside.

Later in the lesson it was returned to me by a grinning Josie, on her way to the classroom rubbish bin, ostensibly to sharpen a pencil.

'Here, you dropped your book, Sydney,' and she slapped it down on my desk.

Some of the beautiful illustrations had been scribbled on in ballpoint pen, some pages had been torn and inside the front cover, where my mum had written 'To Stephen on his seventh birthday from Mummy with love,' the 'Mummy' had been crossed out and 'Rawlplug' inserted. There was a crude drawing of a penis directed at a large bottom with 'Poof' written underneath in big capitals.

When I saw what they had done, tears smarted my eyes, but they were not the tears of fear, they were the tears of fury. It was the first time I had felt angry rather than frightened about being bullied. By the end of that lesson I certainly knew what Ronnie meant by that phrase 'I'll swing for her!' Something I treasured had been violated and I had hatred in my heart.

For some time after that I had to endure a new kind of persistent name-calling. Dwayne seized on the idea with vicious enthusiasm and 'Pooftah!' took over from 'Sydney!' as my label. But what was somehow nastier was the way all my class, even the 'nice' girls who had just ignored me before, pretended I was untouchable and made a big show of shrinking away from me physically as if I had something catching. Then, as was the way in school, it became boring and I went out of fashion and was able to slide back into relative anonymity. But I didn't forget, and I began to fantasise about revenge and to imagine horrible things happening to my tormentors.

But, of course, I never dreamed of anything as horrible as what actually happened.

10.20 a.m. Morning Break

Chapter Eight

At the end of the science lesson I stayed behind.

I was pleased when break time came immediately after a science lesson because it meant I could stay in the science lab and make myself useful rather than venturing into the dangerous playground. On that day Mr Brighton asked me to water the pelargoniums that sat in pots on the window sills, so I had an excellent view of the playground and beyond.

The bus shelter was still empty. Where was Badger? What had been going on between him and Ronnie at the minibus garage earlier that morning? It must have been serious for Badger to come onto the school site; I had never known him do that before. Why was Ronnie on the site if he had been sacked? Perhaps he had just come into school to get some of his things, I thought, but I couldn't think of anything that he kept in the minibus garage. Where was Ronnie now? His van wasn't in the carpark, so he must have left the school site. What was going on? While I worried, I filled the plastic watering can and began the watering.

The playground looked cold. There was a bit of football going on, but I reckoned that most boys were in the canteen queueing for the soggy biscuits that Mrs Tubbs sold at break time. There were some groups of shivering girls sheltering next to walls, and I could just see, through the glass of the door, the duty teacher, Mr Spencer, leaning against the radiator reading a newspaper.

Then I saw Dwayne and his latest sidekick, Keydon Bartley, come across the playground. Dwayne was stuffing the remains of a biscuit into his mouth and Keydon was dribbling a football. In the middle of the yard they waylaid Robbie Brown and encircled him to prevent him from escaping. I could see him arguing but eventually he opened his school bag and handed over a Tupperware container. Dwayne opened the lunchbox, inspected the sandwiches, threw them on the floor and took the crisps, handing a yogurt pot to Keydon, who looked at it with disgust. Dwayne laughed then grabbed the pot and emptied it over Robbie's head so his hair was covered in pink yogurt. He ran away towards the door, where he was stopped by Mr Spencer, who listened to him and then just nodded and went back to his newspaper.

Dwayne and Keydon began to kick a football around and took to kicking it at Margaret Jackson who was huddled up against the wall near the corner drainpipes. She put up with this for some time before Dwayne kicked it very hard at her face. I winced. I hated seeing her being badly treated and hated even more the helplessness and guilt I felt as I watched it. Eventually she moved to stand near one of the groups of girls, which closed ranks, excluding her. The two boys continued to kick the ball towards her, but after what looked like a foul-mouthed request from one of the girls to go away, they sauntered off laughing.

Margaret made me feel guilty because she had been my friend, probably my only friend, during my first two years at Sir Willyum's. But friendship with her had become complicated and guilt-ridden.

Everyone else in the school thought Margaret Jackson was a freak and so did I when I started at Sir Willyum's. Her appearance didn't help her. In Year 7 she was tall and fat with the beginnings of huge breasts. She dressed very differently from other girls, with their short skirts or tight trousers. Her skirt was long and pleated, her shoes were clumpy black lace-ups and she wore a transparent waterproof mac as a coat. She had mousy brown hair which she wore in a long plait down her back.

Like me, Margaret was a victim at Sir Willyum's but she wasn't taunted or assaulted, she was just ignored, and in a very obvious way. People always left a space around her, as if they didn't want to be associated with her. If asked to explain they would have said, 'She smells!' but I know that actually she didn't smell, except of lavender soap. She was certainly cleaner than Susan Sedgely who had awful BO and always looked grubby.

Margaret lived in an isolated row of cottages not far from us where the council housed the 'bad debts' and which locals called 'the reservation'. She lived there with her older sister Doreen, who looked just like her except that she was fatter and had a huge hairy mole on her cheek.

Like the other pupils, at first I didn't take any notice of Margaret, even though I was often left to pair up with her in lessons and, like me, she spent her lunchtimes in the school library.

For both of us the library was a haven of peace and quiet. Mrs Daventry, the lady who ran the library, was a stickler for behaviour and was always 'shushing' anyone who even whispered. Not that many other pupils used the library at lunchtime, unless it was raining, when girls tended to come and look at the magazines so they didn't have to stand around in the wet playground. I always sat at the table next to the shelf labelled '300. Religion', because no-one ever looked at the books on religion, so I could read in peace.

The books I liked were those on Natural History. I remember there was a huge reference book called *Fauna Britannica* which kept me engrossed for many a lunchtime.

Margaret didn't sit and read, like me. She couldn't read very well and therefore she was always in lower sets, which must have been hell for her because that was where all the disruptive boys were. But she did love books. She once told me that she loved the feel and smell of them, and sometimes she would just sit and turn the pages of an encyclopaedia and look at the pictures. Mrs Daventry had given her a 'librarian' badge and she liked helping with things like stamping books and dusting and arranging the shelves. Margaret liked doing things with her hands.

Life went on like this for the first few months at Sir Willyum's. But then one day Margaret became a real person for me, and even a person *like* me.

It started in a cookery lesson. Margaret enjoyed cookery.

'It's a good job I do,' she told me later. 'It's me that has to cook tea 'cos Rene works in the greenhouses until six o'clock.'

Doreen worked in Beacon's Nurseries, which was at the back of the council houses.

'What about Sundays?' I asked, thinking of Mum's roast dinners.

'Oh, I do that too.'

'What? With roast taters and Yorkshire?'

'Yeah. It's easy.'

She certainly was good at cookery, and in lessons I was grateful that we shared the same work station, because I benefited from her help.

I can't remember exactly what we were cooking in that particular lesson, but I do remember the onions, because that is what started it all. Being so good at cooking, Margaret was well ahead of the rest of us and she had started chopping her onion while I was still struggling to peel it. I didn't see it happening, but I suppose that as she chopped her eyes began to water and she probably wiped her eyes on her sleeve, which would have made them smart and water even more.

It was unfortunate that Mrs Dipfield noticed this and decided to use it as a teaching point.

'Stop what you are doing for a moment, 7P. We need to talk about the best way to chop onions. I want you all to look at Margaret.'

Everyone in the class stared at Margaret, with her red streaming eyes. There were a few giggles, quickly stifled.

'Now it looks as if she's crying, doesn't it? Why do you think this is?'

There was a long pause. Everyone looked either puzzled or bored. Then Josie Davenport put up her hand.

'Yes, Josie, do you know?' Mrs Dipfield sounded surprised.

''Cos she's so ugly?'

The class disintegrated into laughter.

'Josie! What a rude nasty thing to say! Go and stand outside the room! I will speak to you later.'

Josie flounced out with a triumphant air. Mrs Dipfield tried to restore order and to divert attention from Margaret.

'Now listen everybody!' She rapped on her desk.

The laughter stopped.

'When we chop onions, chemicals containing sulphur are released and that has an irritating effect on our eyes. If this affects you badly, you need to put your onions in very hot water. Now get on with your task or we won't get the dish finished in time.'

I stole a look at Margaret, who was standing completely still with an onion in one hand and a peeling knife in the other. She was bright red and the tears were streaming down her face. I didn't know if that was because of the onions or because of her humiliation, but I felt a sudden stab of pity for her. I took her onion and began to chop it for her. It was a particularly strong onion, and my eyes were soon watering too. I looked up at her and smiled tentatively. She looked desolate.

After that I began to notice Margaret and to feel sorry for her but there wasn't anything I could do about it. I needed all my emotional resilience to cope with my own troubles. However, a few weeks later I came across Margaret out of school, and that is how our friendship started.

It was on one of those long warm evenings in early May, and after the bus dropped me I didn't go straight home because I wanted to check out a heron nest that Ronnie had said was in a dyke near Beacon's Nurseries. I turned off the road and began to cycle along a narrow track beside the dyke, making for the greenhouses in the distance. It was tough going because the lane was covered in tractor ruts and puddles and I was looking into the dyke, not where I was going, so I had several dangerous moments when I nearly caught my wheel and came off. Eventually I reached the expanse of concrete next to the first line of greenhouses, and that was when my luck ran out. My front wheel caught in a broken edge of concrete and I fell off heavily, landing sideways with one leg caught under the collapsed bike.

'Fuck!' I shouted. I liked to swear whenever I could, out of earshot of my mum or Ronnie, whose language was often very fruity but who wouldn't allow me even to say 'Damn!'

'Wash out your mouth, boy!' he would say, if he heard me trying out a satisfying curse. 'Until you're old enough to know what "fuck" means I don't want to hear you cussing, d'you hear?'

On this occasion, well away from anyone, as I thought, I let rip.

'Fucking sodding bike!'

I disentangled myself and kicked the bike, stung to anger by the pain, as I had fallen with my weight on my right knee which had scraped on the rough concrete. I looked down at the knee of my trousers which was torn and bloody.

'Bloody hell!' I shouted, thinking of what Mum would say, and I kicked the bike again.

It was then that I saw her. Margaret Jackson was running across the concrete towards me.

'Are you all right, Stephen?'

It was the first time that I had heard her voice properly. Normally, at school, when we worked in a pair, she just mumbled 'Yeah,' and left me to do all the work. It was a surprisingly light and musical voice for someone so physically large.

Embarrassed at the idea of anyone witnessing what had just happened, I was gruff in return.

'Yeah, I'm fine thanks. I think there's something wrong with this bike.' I pretended to examine the front wheel.

'But your knee's bleeding.'

'It's nothing, just a graze.' I didn't want to lose face any further.

'Come and see if we can stop the bleeding,' she said, and she took the bike from me and began to walk towards her house.

I didn't immediately follow, feeling somehow at a disadvantage. She turned back towards me.

'Aren't you coming? I'm good at first aid, and there's some coke left.' She smiled. I realised that I had never seen her smile before. It was a surprisingly lovely smile, and I followed her.

Half an hour later, with the grit washed out of my knee and an Elastoplast in place to stop the bleeding, I was sitting at the kitchen table in a pair of Margaret's baggy pyjama bottoms drinking coke and eating my way through a packet of chocolate biscuits while Margaret effected a minor miracle of darning on my trousers.

'There!' she said, offering them for inspection. 'I don't think your mum will notice, 'cos I've used matching thread, so if we just sponge away the blood like this...'

The expression 'She'll make someone a good wife' was a perfect description of Margaret Jackson. She was not only extremely organised and very practical, but she was one of the warmest and most caring people I have ever known. No doubt she would have eventually grown from an ugly duckling into a swan and made some bloke a happy man.

That was how our friendship started and how I learnt not to judge people by their appearance. After that we spent quite a bit of time together. I would cycle to see her sometimes in the evening to help her with her homework. We would sit together at the kitchen table and I would explain how equations worked or make up a story which she would write laboriously in her English book to my dictation. Or, when the summer holidays came, she would borrow Doreen's old sit-up-and-beg-bike and I would take her bird-watching. I showed her my fossil collection. She showed me her dolls. She had a collection of porcelain dolls, which stood on a long shelf in her bedroom. She found them in the car boot sales which Doreen was addicted to and made all the outfits for them with remnants of worn-out clothes or curtains, using an old sewing machine that Mrs Beacon at the nursery had lent her. I was very impressed when she first showed me, but found the dolls themselves rather disconcerting as they sat in a row and stared at me, glassy-eyed and motionless.

Another unsettling feature of Margaret's home was a huge picture of Jesus which was on the wall above the mantelpiece in the living room. This picture dominated everything because Jesus's eyes seemed to follow you everywhere. Doreen was very religious and asked me, when I first met her, if I had 'given my heart to the Lord' yet. I was very embarrassed, and I didn't know what to answer. I think I um'd and ah'd a bit and Margaret saved me by saying, 'We're just off out, Rene,' and dragged me outside.

'Don't worry, she asks everyone that,' she told me. 'I'd just say "yes" if I were you or she'll start quoting from St Luke and trying to convert you. She's born again, you see. I'm not, yet. But I expect I will be eventually. Come on!' She led the way towards one of the empty greenhouses at the nursery, which had become our den.

There we would sit leaning against the polythene wall and eat jam doughnuts or Mars Bars and talk. We would talk about our interests, our favourite TV programmes. I told her about Ronnie and she told me she had twenty-three cousins but she never saw them because Doreen had 'denounced her family' when she joined the Baptists. We told each other about our ambitions; she wanted to be a fashion designer, I wanted to be a game-keeper. But we never talked about school. Sir Willyum's was taboo when we weren't there. Moreover, we did not take our friendship into school with us. We both knew, without needing to voice it out loud, how it would be misunderstood and scorned, and we suffered enough already. We continued to work together sometimes in lessons, of course, and sometimes chatted in the library at lunchtimes, but apart from that, we ignored each other at school.

But now we were in Year 9 and things had changed. For a start, I had stopped spending time with her out of school, having become rather bored with her company. Ms McCarthy's photography expeditions by motorbike were much more exciting. We were both growing up too. I was becoming more aware of the secrets that Josie Davenport might offer, and, by contrast, Margaret was decidedly unattractive, although as I watched her on that day from the science lab window I had to admit that she was changing. She was still tall, but what had been a lumpy body was now what might be called 'buxom'. She no longer wore out-of-date clothes but black trousers and trainers like most of the other girls, and her long hair was no longer plaited but fell round her face to her shoulders. And was that eye make-up? I couldn't quite see from where I was, but I wondered how she had managed that without attracting Doreen's criticism, as I remember her telling me how her sister believed make-up made a woman into a 'whore', a word I hadn't properly understood at the time.

My thoughts were interrupted by Mr Brighton.

'Oh Stephen, you're still here!' he said cheerfully. 'Good lad! Can you pop to reception for me and pick up the worksheets for Year 11 Period 3. Tell Mrs Duckworth they're the ones on the periodic table.'

I took one more shameful look at Margaret, and with a certain amount of relief left to run Mr Brighton's errand. The main reason I felt guilty was not for drifting apart, but because of the fear of being known as her friend, and what that fear had led me to do.

*

It was in reception that breaktime that, for the first and last time, I heard Badger speak.

When I arrived, there was the usual queue at the reception window. I joined it as Mrs Duckworth opened the reception window.

'Now what can I do for you, Jessica?' (who was first in the queue).

Everyone answered at the same time.

'Please Miss, can I look in lost property for my coat, it's got my name in it.'

'Please Miss, I've got my money for the geography trip.'

'Please Miss, Mr Budworth says please can the caretaker clean up the sick outside Room 17.'

I joined in: 'Can Mr Brighton have the worksheets on the periodic table please Miss.'

A small group of Year 7 girls came running into reception. One was red-faced and screaming. The others pushed to the front.

'Please Miss, Daisy's got knocked over.'

'It was Richard Barber, Miss.'

'She's cut her knee bad, Miss.'

'Bring her into reception and I'll sort it out,' said Mrs Duckworth. 'Do stop that noise, Daisy, it's only a graze. Don't be such a baby!' This made Daisy scream even louder.

Mrs Duckworth was just embarking on her usual feat of multi-tasking, opening the lost property cupboard, pushing the photocopier button and writing a receipt for the trip money, when the phone rang. She stuck the receiver under her shoulder while stacking the copies as they emerged from the photocopier.

'Good morning. Sir William Smith High School. Can I help you?'

At that moment Badger lurched through the front door and into reception. His breath was rasping and he glared from side to side, making high-pitched muttering noises.

'Mm! Mm!'

There was a universal gasp and then a sudden silence. All the other pupils in reception edged away from the counter and took refuge in a huddle behind the visitor seats. I froze, feeling I ought to do something, but not sure what it was.

Mrs Duckworth looked up from the photocopies and saw him. She frowned, then approached the reception window.

'Yes? Can I help you?'

'Mm! Mm!' Badger shuffled towards the window.

'Can I help you?' Mrs Duckworth repeated, wrinkling her nose as the full force of Badger's unwashed person wafted across the reception counter.

Badger continued to shuffle on the spot. He looked round desperately and noticed me.

'Mm! Mm!' he said to me, obviously recognising me as someone who had once tried to communicate with him. 'Mm! Mm!' He was very excited about something.

'What is it, Badger?' I said.

He opened and shut his mouth a few times, then finally managed to blurt out again, 'Gun! Mm! Mm!' He caught hold of my arm in his anxiety to make me understand.

At this Mrs Duckworth felt she had to intervene.

'Excuse me, sir, can I help you? Stephen, do you know this gentleman?'

'It's Old Badger, Miss. The tramp from the bus shelter.'

One of the girls giggled.

'Well, Mr Badger, or whatever you're called, I haven't got all day. How can we help you?'

Badger turned his attention to her and leant through the reception window.

'Gun! Mm! Mm!'

'I can't understand what you are saying, sir. Could you repeat it.'

With a huge effort Badger made his important communication.

'He's got a gun! Mm! Mm!'

In a flash I thought I understood. He must have seen me arrive at school with the airgun. I remembered what Ronnie had said about the mystery surrounding why he had given up wildfowling. In his mind (simple? deranged?) he had jumped to the conclusion that I was going to shoot a gun in school. If it hadn't been such a strange situation I might have smiled at the irony of it, as I knew what the airgun waiting under Mrs Duckworth's desk was intended for. But, of course, when I think about what actually happened that day I could weep, not smile, at the irony.

'It's all right, Badger. It doesn't work, it's just for a lesson. You don't have to worry.' I turned to Mrs Duckworth. 'It's all right, Miss. He just saw my airgun this morning, the one you're looking after for me. He sort of thought… er… he sort of misunderstood. And he doesn't… er… talk much.'

Badger was clutching on to me desperately as he continued to try to communicate.

'Mm! Mm! No! Ronnie! Gun! Mm! Mm!' He shook his head violently, spittle flying everywhere.

'No, Badger, it's me with the gun, not Ronnie. Ronnie's not… er… he's not in school today,' I said to him. 'He knows Mr Rawlinson, Miss,' I explained.

'I see,' said Mrs Duckworth, looking weary. 'Well, if you know this gentleman, Stephen, would you mind seeing him off the premises and taking him back to his… er… home.'

'Yes, Miss. Come on Badger,' and I guided him out of the front door.

All the way across the carpark he was repeating his message: 'Mm! Mm! Ronnie! Gun!'

I settled him on the bench in the bus shelter and disentangled myself from his clutching hand. He clawed at me, still muttering, but I backed away.

'It's all right, Badger, you're back now. I'll tell Ronnie to come and see you!'

How can I make him shut up? I thought.

'It's all right. I understand. You've seen the gun. Thank you for telling us. We understand.' I made my escape.

But, of course, we really *didn't* understand what he was trying to tell us. It wasn't until I began to write this story that I realised that he couldn't have seen my airgun as it was concealed in the cricket bag.

I never saw him after that day. I wonder what happened to him?

10.50 a.m. Lesson 3

Chapter Nine

Checking the time, I hurried back from reception with Mr Brighton's worksheets because my next lesson on that day was PE and I always tried to arrive in the changing rooms before the other boys. This was to avoid the hoots of derision that had once greeted the removal of my trousers on a never-to-be-forgotten occasion early in Year 7, when I was still naïve and thought everyone wore the kind of underpants my mum bought for me. If I could be already dressed in PE kit before the horde arrived I could hide in the toilet cubicle next to the showers until I heard Mr Parkin, the PE teacher, arrive with his whistle and his, 'Now then, Year 9, let's be having you! Twice round the football pitch,' and the horde of football boots would clatter past and I could sneak out and follow them on to the playing field.

On the other hand, I had found to my cost that it was wise not to arrive in the changing rooms too early. Once, I had arrived in the middle of morning break into a particularly steamy atmosphere of hot damp boy left behind by the last class. I ventured across the soaking wet floor, littered with odd socks and wet towels, and peered through my misted-up glasses. I could see some blazers and school bags hanging on the pegs, as many boys left them in the changing rooms at the beginning of break time if they had PE immediately afterwards, and in the far corner…

I realised I was not alone. He had his back to me but even in the steamy fog I saw who it was. Jimmy Buckland was rifling through a bag and I saw him take out a pencil case, unzip it and take out two coins which he pocketed. I froze. He moved on to another peg, put his hand into the inside pocket of a blazer and withdrew a five-pound note. I decided I needed to get out fast before he saw me, but as I turned my foot caught a football boot lying on the floor.

Jimmy's head spun around and there was one of those moments when the hunter and the hunted stare at each other. It was like the time when I hadn't been able to shoot a hare even though it sat up in front of me not twenty yards away. We just gazed at each other for an instant before it bounded away across the field.

'Witchcraft,' Ronnie had called it. 'They have the power, them there hares. You're not the first, Stevie boy, to come under their spell.'

But on this occasion, the hunted turned into the hunter. The expression on Jimmy's face underwent a series of startling shifts, from shock to fear to desperation to cunning before finally settling on innocent charm.

'Where did you spring from, Sydney?' he grinned at me. 'D'you know which is Tubbs's blazer? He's asked me to get him his money for tuck.' He was always a fast thinker, was Jimmy.

I stared at him and I saw that he knew that I knew.

I turned and headed for the door, but he was too fast for me and planted himself in front of it. He was still smiling but I saw menace in his eyes. My mouth felt dry.

'Not so fast, Sidney. You haven't answered my question. "Where did you spring from?" I said. It's very rude to ignore someone who's talking to you, isn't it, Sydney? It doesn't show respect.'

I looked away from him and gazed at the floor, seeing nothing.

'Why are you ignoring me, Sydney? I'm sure your mummy has brought you up to be a polite little boy, hasn't she?' He put his hand under my chin and forced my face up towards him. He was still smiling.

'Talking of your mummy, Sydney, my Uncle Jake rather fancies her, you know, reckons she's got real big tits, that's what he told me. Now, if you're a bad boy and open that snivelling mouth of yours about this little meeting, my Uncle Jake will have to pay her a little visit about her snitch of a son.'

Jimmy's Uncle Jake was the patriarch of the Buckland family, who lived on the traveller site on the edge of Wisbech industrial estate. He was notorious in our area for his fighting, which included semi-professional prize-fighting as well as the run-of-the-mill Saturday night drunken brawls. He was the principal reason that most of the pubs in our area had signs outside saying 'No troublesome van-dwellers'. He was the stuff of myth to me and I certainly did not want him anywhere near me or my mum.

'Well, Sydney? Do you understand? You know how we all hate people who tell tales, don't you?'

I nodded. He let go of my chin.

'Well, don't you ever forget, eh?'

I hadn't forgotten. For weeks after that incident I lived in fear of Jimmy and his Uncle Jake. Every time I came across Jimmy he would wink at me and then pretend to be really chummy, laughing if the other boys questioned why he was talking to me, as he was very much his own person and didn't care what he said or did. This false friendliness made me very uneasy.

Every morning I would see Jake Buckland's pick-up truck,

usually loaded with scrap iron, pull up outside the school and Jimmy would climb out; but all I saw of his uncle was a shadowy figure at the steering wheel and a muscular arm resting on the open driver's window, sometimes raised in farewell to his nephew.

However, one morning I actually came face to face with Jimmy's Uncle Jake.

I was in reception with a message from Mrs Pritchard, when in through the school door came a giant of a man with thick curly black hair and long sideburns. He wore an open-neck shirt with the sleeves rolled up, even though it was a chilly day. He was carrying a badly-wrapped loaf of cut bread.

'Now then, sonny,' he said. 'Where do I go to find my nephew, eh?'

I pointed towards the reception window. He approached it and pressed the buzzer firmly. He was so tall that he had to bend down to speak to Mrs Duckworth when she slid the window open.

'Now then, petal!' he said and Mrs Duckworth, for once, was speechless; I don't expect anyone had ever called her that before. 'Our Jim left his sarnies in the truck this morning. I found 'em under the seat when I was looking for my baccy. Good job the dog didn't find 'em first, eh? I've sort of re-wrapped 'em but tell him some of 'em might be a bit mucky, the floor under that seat didn't look too clean to me.' He pushed the loaf of sandwiches through the reception window. At one end they were coming out of the waxed wrapping paper and grated cheese and pickle spilled onto the reception counter.

Mrs Duckworth collected herself and regarded the sandwiches with distaste.

'And your Jim is in which form, Mr… er?'

'Buckland's the name, missus. Jimmy Buckland. Named after his old grandad, James Ebenezer Buckland.'

Mrs Duckworth examined the sandwiches, looking unsure. Then she noticed me.

'Ah, Stephen, you're in Jimmy Buckland's class, aren't you? Can you take his packed lunch to him please and say his… er… father…'

'No, love, the poor lad ain't got no dad no more; got stabbed in a ding-dong in Peterborough a few years back. I'm his uncle.'

Mrs Duckworth took one of her big breaths.

'…and say his uncle has brought it in and he needs to be less forgetful in future.'

She pushed the disintegrating pile of food back through the reception window.

'Off you go now!'

'But I've got a message from Mrs Pritchard, Miss.'

'Oh, tell her I'll send Mr Godley when he's got a minute, if I can find him.'

I turned and began to walk away, cradling Jimmy's sandwiches in my arms.

'So you're a mate of our Jim, are you, son?' said Jake Buckland.

I looked up at him. He had the same colour eyes as Jimmy and they were cool and calculating like Jimmy's; he even grinned just like his nephew.

'Er… well, not exactly,' I said.

'Wait a bit! I know you! You're the lad that lives in the cottages up Wrong Drove, aren't you? Along of Ronnie Rawlinson. You're Myra Coatley's boy!'

I felt my throat go dry. Coatley was my mother's maiden name.

'What's your name, son?'

'Stephen Stringer, sir,' I said.

'Yes, of course, I remember now, she married that John Stringer that went to grammar school. Why, I remember Myra. We went to school together, you know – that is until I left school. Me old dad, he didn't hold with schooling. "That's for them Gorgios," he would say. "We don't need none of that."

'Mm, I remember your mum; she was a right swinger, she was! Fancied her rotten I did when I was fifteen! Them tits, eh?' He put out his huge hairy hands and squeezed two imaginary breasts.

I felt my face burn. Jake burst out laughing. It was a booming laugh. In fact, he was a booming sort of man, and I found it hard to escape from his overwhelming presence. I stammered something like, 'Excuse me, sir, I have to…' before scuttling away up the corridor.

On the way back to the classroom I stopped under the stairwell and opened the sandwiches. I looked round to ensure I was alone and then I deliberately and carefully spat on them, gathering the saliva in my mouth and letting it dribble all over them. Wrapping them again, I carried them back to the classroom. It was only a small act of defiance and invisible to all but me, but as I watched Jimmy eat his sandwiches at break time it was with great satisfaction, heightened even more when he offered one to Dwayne and I saw him stuff it complete into that big mouth.

*

It wasn't long before the end of Year 8 when Jimmy Buckland followed the example of his Uncle Jake and left school. He boasted about it in form time one morning.

'I'm leaving school when I'm fourteen.'

'Oh yeah?' said someone.

'Yeah! I'm leaving on my birthday, that's next Friday.'

'But you can't,' someone else said. 'It's not allowed.'

'Who says?' retorted Jimmy.

'It's the law. You can't leave 'til you're sixteen.'

'Well, sod the law! I'm fucking leaving school! My Uncle Jake says I can so I can!'

There were some dubious looks, but no-one argued with what Uncle Jake said.

'The welfare'll come and find you, you wait and see,' said one of the more envious.

'Yeah, and then your uncle'll have to pay a fine.'

'Oh yeah?' said Jimmy. 'I'd like to see them try to make him.'

We thought about Uncle Jake and understood what he meant.

True to his word, Jimmy stopped attending school that Friday.

'Does anyone know why Jimmy's away?' asked Mrs Pritchard the following Monday, when she was calling the register.

'He's left, Miss,' said Dwayne.

'What do you mean Dwayne? Of course he hasn't left,' said Mrs Pritchard. 'You can't leave in Year 8.'

'But he has, Miss,' said Josie. 'He said his Uncle told him he could leave when he was fourteen and his birthday was last week.'

'Well, we'll see about that,' said Mrs Pritchard. 'I'll get Mrs Duckworth to give his mum a ring.'

'He hasn't got a mum, Miss,' said Josie.

'And they're not on the phone, Miss,' said Dwayne. 'They live on the traveller site.'

'In that case,' said Mrs Pritchard, trying to sound in charge, 'we will ask the welfare officer to call.'

'Best of bloody luck!' muttered Dwayne.

'What did you say, Dwayne?' asked Mrs Pritchard.

'I said, 'He'd better be careful, Miss. The Bucklands have got dogs.'

I forgot about Jimmy Buckland for a few weeks. Then one day Jake Buckland arrived at school, and he was not in a good mood. I heard about it from Ronnie.

'We had a right kerfuffle this morning,' he reported to Beryl, as he took his boots off after arriving home from his afternoon shift. I was hanging around their kitchen because Beryl had been baking.

'Really love? What happened?'

'Well, I was just picking up a delivery from reception when that Jake Buckland, you know the big pikey, the one what fights, he comes storming in through the door.

'"Where's that fucking headmaster?"' he shouts. '"I'll show him! Sending the old Bill round! I'll not have it!"

'Then he thumps on Mrs D's window like he wanted to smash it, and she looked right feared, so I goes up to him and I says, "Now then, Jake, what's up mate?" 'cos I used to know him a bit when I was a kid, and he looks at me and blast I thought he was going to smack me one, his eyes were that glazed over and his breath smelt strong, I could tell he was pissed.'

'Oh Ronnie, love, he didn't hit you, did he?' said Beryl.

'No, he didn't, but only 'cos I got the trolley between me and him.

'"What's it to you?" he says, all belligerent, trying to push his face at me; I swear he would have nutted me one if he could, he were that fired up, but at that moment Stan Godley appears.

'"Well, if it isn't Jake Buckland," he says, all quiet like, but firm. "I remember when you were a laddy in the first year, my, you've grown," and Jake he just looks at him for a moment then shakes his head and says, quieter like, "Ah, Mr Godley, sir, you still here?" and Stan says, "What's all this about, Jake?" and he ushers him into his office.

'Well I didn't hang around, but later I asks Stan what happened and he said it was about that Jimmy Buckland not coming to school and the welfare officer took a copper with him 'cos he daren't go on the site without protection. And Jake Buckland, what's Jimmy's uncle and guardian or suchlike 'cos he's not got no parents, poor lad, he's been served with a Section something-or-other notice about attendance. He'll get fined if the nipper don't attend school and if he don't pay, well he'll probably get locked up-like his brother Isaac. It's a family hobby!'

'What is the world coming to?' commented Beryl, taking the jam tarts out of the oven.

I heard a sequel to this story from Dwayne in registration a few days later.

'Saw Jimmy at the weekend,' he said to Peter Slingsby.

'Oh yeah? What's he doing with himself, the lucky bugger?'

'He's working with his Uncle Jake, on the scrap. He gave me two packets of Dunhills.'

'Who did? Jake Buckland?'

'No, you daft bugger, Jimmy. He says they've got loads of fags, they got 'em off a lorry what stopped at some layby or other.'

'Cor! Give us one,' begged Peter.

'I left 'em at home,' said Dwayne. 'Old Crumpet's always on the rampage, it's not worth it and I hate that fucking dancing. I'll get you some if you like. Hey, Big Ears, mind your business!' He interrupted himself to address me, cuffing me round the left ear at the same time. 'And he says his Uncle Jake's going to do old Crumpet's Jag for sending the welfare round.'

Two days later Mr Crumb's Jaguar had the tyres ripped and the paintwork badly scratched while he was attending an evening governors' meeting.

'You should have seen him, spitting fire he was!' said Ronnie, telling me about it when he arrived back that evening. It was only just getting dark and he had asked me to feed the wildfowl and shut up the chickens for him as he would be late home. 'Mind you, I can see he might have been pissed off, it's a beautiful beast that Jag and it'll need a whole new paint job, let alone four new tyres. It'll cost him a packet,' he pronounced gleefully.

'Did you see anyone prowling around?' I knew it was part of Ronnie's job to open and lock up when there was an evening governors' meeting and also to meet Mrs Westley-Lewis's taxi and escort her to and from the meeting. He would have been about in the car park, I reckoned.

Ronnie looked furtive.

'No, I fucking didn't. I've got better things to do than hang around in the carpark all night. I'm not a security guard. I took the opportunity to clear out the library cupboard, which needed doing mind you, but also gave me a chance to earwig on the meeting. You never know when you might pick up something useful.'

'Did you, Ronnie?'

'No, I bloody didn't. Just had to listen to Old Crumpet droning on and on. I tell you, all them governor twats looked glass-eyed after half an hour, and as for that old bird, Mrs Westley-bloody-Lewis, I swear to you she was fast asleep with her head slumped sideways on Old Crumpet's shoulder. Woke up with a gasp and a splutter, she did, when he heaved her off sideways, with a, "That is my report, Madam Chairman." Anyway, when I took her out to her taxi I saw the Jag. I wonder if Old Badger saw anything. I bet it was pikeys!'

'It was! It was Jake Buckland!' I stated, proud of my insider knowledge.

Ronnie turned on me. 'And how do you know that, boy? You haven't been hobnobbing with them pikeys, have you?'

'No, I heard it at school,' I replied airily.

'Well, whoever did it, there'll be trouble,' said Ronnie. 'I got away as soon as I could when I saw Old Crumpet's face.'

He was right. There was trouble.

Nobody had ever seen Mr Crumb angry before. In fact, no-one had ever seen Mr Crumb express any strong emotion. I had seen him show satisfaction over the entrapment of some unfortunate smoker; I had seen him wrinkle his nose in distaste when Mr Godley made his regular speech in assembly about the urine on the urinal walls, but passion had seemed foreign to him. He was the original cold fish. But now that his pride and joy, his classic XJ12, had been mutilated, and deliberately, he was beside himself with fury.

We were summoned to a special assembly the next morning, which was a Friday, and we didn't usually have assembly on Fridays.

Mr Godley tried to warn us.

'Now, school,' he said, 'we have called you all together this morning for a very special reason. Something quite dreadful has occurred, and I want you to be especially quiet and listen very respectfully to what Mr Crumb will say to you.' He paused, jerked his head and looked meaningfully in the direction of certain pupils. 'And I strongly suggest that those of you who feel it would be entertaining to do anything other than sit completely still and quiet while he is talking should think again, for this matter is of the utmost seriousness.'

Everyone was very quiet. I thought that at the very least someone had been murdered.

'Now stand!' Mr Godley commanded, and we leapt to our feet, as Mr Crumb strode onto the stage.

I was shocked; I had never seen Mr Crumb stride. Normally he shambled around gazing at the floor with his hands clasped behind his back under his academic gown as if he was wearing a bustle. But this entry was athletic and determined, back straight, arms swinging, gown swirling, and his face, normally so indeterminate like an out-of-focus photograph, was firm and set like granite. His voice too had been transformed.

'Now listen here, school,' he began and then paused (which in itself was a shock, because it was a contrast to the customary monotone), 'and woe betide any of you who so much as move a little finger while I am addressing you.'

We sat like statues with mouths open in amazement.

'Yesterday evening, between the hours of 6.30 p.m. and 9.30 p.m., an act of sacrilege occurred at this school.' His voice quivered and rose to what was almost a squeak. 'A classic XJ12 Jaguar, a coupe, one of only ten models produced in its year and therefore rare and valuable as well as beautiful, was damaged by an act of deliberate and totally unbelievable evil, that I… that I…' He stopped, and his face contorted as he struggled to control his feelings. Because I thought he was about to cry, I felt embarrassed and wanted to look down but didn't dare move. '…that I find it almost impossible to believe if I hadn't seen it with my own eyes.'

He took a deep breath, and I took one too.

'I do not need to tell you that the person who committed this unspeakable act will be immediately expelled from this school.' The word 'expelled' was uttered with a spray of saliva, some of which, I am sure, reached the front row of Year 7.

'Now, I want you to help me, school. If any of you know the perpetrator of this… of this… act of cruelty, or if you know anything at all about how it might have happened, you are to give this information to Mr Godley immediately after this assembly.' He looked at us all and then said something that was totally unexpected. 'Please,' he begged, and then hurried from the hall.

There was a collected exhalation and fidgeting and people looked at each other uncomfortably.

'OK school,' said Mr Godley, who also looked uncomfortable. 'I will be in my office after this assembly if there is anyone who wants to tell me anything. Would members of staff allow pupils who wish to see me permission to be late for their lesson.' There was a pause as he seemed to search for words and his head jerked violently. 'I think you all understand how much Mr Crumb's motorcar means to him and how priceless it is because of its particular history. So I hope that you will search for some… for some compassion in your response to his plea. That is all. Dismissed!'

As we left the assembly hall everyone looked round at everyone else to see if anyone was headed in the direction of God's office. We all knew who was guilty – the rumour of Jake Buckland's threat had spread round the school – but I suppose we were looking to see if anyone would snitch. I don't know if anyone did. Why would we? I'm not sure if adolescent pupils like us knew what compassion was, and we certainly didn't connect it with someone like Mr Crumb, who was not only a teacher but a *head* teacher.

*

When I got home from school that day, I sought out Ronnie to see if he knew anything more about what everyone in the school was talking about. I found him attacking the back hedge, which was always the sign that he was in a bad mood. I should have left well alone.

'You know Old Crumpet's car, Ronnie?' I started.

'Mr Crumb to you, Stephen,' was his reply as he removed a particularly thick and prickly branch with a vicious swipe of the shears.

I should have read the signs and left him, but I was full of the story and all Mum had said was 'Really dear?' when I tried to tell her.

'You should have heard what he said in assembly,' I said, and I began to mimic. 'If anyone saw anything…' but I was interrupted quite viciously.

'What is this? A fucking witch-hunt? I've already had a grilling from Stan Godley and Old Crumpet more or less accused me to my face of damaging his bloody car. I can do without it, boy, so be about your business before I tell your mother it was you with your catapult and not me with the lawnmower what cracked the front room window.'

'But I didn't, Ronnie!'

'Exactly! Now bugger off!'

I found out later that Mr Crumb held Ronnie responsible for the damage because he was on site during that evening and should have provided better security. I suspect that Ronnie was so upset over this accusation because he felt guilty that he was in the cupboard listening rather than looking after the school's security. However, from that day on Mr Crumb could not be persuaded that Ronnie was not responsible for the damage to his precious car and his attitude to him changed from polite disinterest to a targeted vendetta. As for Ronnie, his former contempt for Mr Crumb because he was 'one of them big-headed bossy teachers' was transformed into vitriolic and implacable hatred.

'I'll swing for that bastard Crumb, I tell you,' blurted Ronnie, as he burst into his shed just a few days later. I was painting a chicken coop with some left-over timber preservative and he had slammed the door so hard I splattered it onto my trousers.

'Oh shit!' I exclaimed, noticing that they were my school trousers and thinking of Mum.

Ronnie was so worked up he didn't correct me for swearing. He picked up a bit of wood he was working into a walking stick and began to whittle it frenetically with his penknife.

'I don't know why he's suddenly got it in for me! What have I ever done to him? Who is it who does all this unpaid overtime for him, trying to keep his bloody school in one piece, even decorating his office over that weekend. And this is the way he rewards loyalty. Bastard!'

I was worried that he'd do himself a mischief with the knife, so I tried to divert him.

'What's happened, Ronnie?'

He stopped whittling and looked up at me. His face was twisted as if he was in pain.

'He's given me a bloody written warning, Stevie! Me? What's always worked my fingers to the bone for that school. There's no-one can say that school isn't looked after properly, even old Mrs

Westley-Lewis always compliments me on how nice the front flower beds look. And he's gone and given me a written warning for bloody misconduct, as if I'm some idle layabout getting a telling-off from my boss.'

'But why, Ronnie?'

'He says I should have stopped them pikeys trashing his car, as if I haven't got better things to do of an evening than stand guard over his precious Jag.'

'But what is a written warning, Ronnie?' I asked. 'Warning about what?'

His answer was a sob. 'It's a warning that he wants to sack me, Stevie.'

I was shocked. I couldn't imagine Sir Willyum's without Ronnie. But as I didn't know what to say I dipped my brush into the preservative and went back to my chicken coop.

Ronnie had stopped whittling and was staring at the shed wall as if he was watching his own future humiliating dismissal. A few minutes passed in silence and when he spoke again his voice was so quiet it was almost a whisper.

'But I'll get my own back, you wait and see. I'll make him pay, if I have to swing for it.'

I went on with my painting. Then, after a few minutes, I think he remembered I was there.

'You won't tell Beryl, Stevie, will you! I don't want her worried, bless her. Keep it just between us, eh boy?'

'Yes, Ronnie.'

I felt very flattered that he had asked me to keep his secret. It made me feel very grown-up.

Chapter Ten

'What's the matter with you? You're wriggling like an eel. Got ants in your pants?'

We were on the way back home after a visit to Welney Washes for some fishing.

'I need to piss real bad,' I said.

'Why didn't you go behind those bushes when we packed up?' said Ronnie in exasperation.

'Didn't want to go then.'

He went on driving at his steady pace. We were on the Wisbech bypass, a long sweeping stretch of single carriageway lined by orchards.

'But I'm desperate, Ronnie,' I pleaded.

'What am I supposed to bloody do about it?'

But at that moment, with a deep sigh, he suddenly swerved into a layby and slammed on the brakes.

'Get a move on!'

I got out of the van and looked for a gap in the bushes. The grass at the edge of the layby was muddy and I had to scramble down a steep slope to reach a suitably hidden spot to relieve myself. I was surrounded by rubbish and piles of dog shit. It smelt horrible.

It was as I turned back, zipping myself up and looking for somewhere on the bank to get a purchase for my trainers that I noticed I was not alone. In front of me, looking down at me from the top of the bank, was Mr Crumb. He didn't look much like the Mr Crumb I knew because he was dressed in a grey windcheater and open-necked shirt, but it was definitely him. It was a big shock because he was the last person I expected to see, and I immediately felt very guilty. What do you say when you're doing up your flies in a ditch and you meet your headmaster? But as I was wondering how to deal with this situation, Mr Crumb turned and walked away, and I realised that he had not recognised me, or even noticed that anyone was there.

I climbed up the bank and trotted back to Ronnie's van.

'Guess who I saw in the…?' I began, but Ronnie interrupted me.

'Shh!' He pointed ahead of us and put his finger to his lips.

I looked where he was pointing. The layby was a long one and about twenty yards ahead of us Mr Crumb was struggling to lift a rolled carpet out of the boot of his car.

'Should have bought an estate version,' I said, trying to be clever.

'Shh!' Ronnie said again.

'What?' I said.

'Who is it?'

'Old Crumpet! I was just about to tell you, I saw…'

Ronnie was not listening to me.

'Old Crumpet it bloody well is, and what's he doing, Stevie?'

'He's getting a carpet out of the back of a car. Oh, and now he's dragging it to the bushes and, wait for it, yes, he's hurling it into the bushes. So what?'

'But what is he actually *doing*?'

'I dunno. He's just dumping an old carpet.'

'No Stevie, he's not "just dumping an old carpet" as you put it; he's fly-tipping, that's what he's doing. And, Stevie, fly-tipping is against the law, punishable by a hefty fine, I expect.'

I still didn't get it.

'But only if someone reports him.'

I broke off. I had finally got it.

'You wouldn't, Ronnie!'

'Wouldn't I now?' There was a malicious gleam in his eyes.

He slumped down in his seat and peered over the dashboard, gesturing for me to do the same. Mr Crumb came back from the bushes, wiping his hands on his trousers and looking around furtively. I held my breath.

'Looks like he's just dumped a dead body, don't he?' Ronnie hissed.

'Perhaps it's Mrs Crumb wrapped up in the carpet,' I said, giggling. 'He's murdered her 'cos she found out about his porn magazines. Is there a Mrs Crumb?'

'Hallo! What next?' said Ronnie, for Mr Crumb hadn't finished. As we watched, he dragged a pile of black rubber material out of the boot and hurled it in the direction of the dyke where the carpet lay.

'What's that?' I asked.

'Carpet underlay. Our Crumpet has been doing a spot of decorating.'

'Mrs Crumb nagging him!' I contributed.

By the time he had finished, Mr Crumb had deposited two bulging bin bags, a few empty paint pots and a rusty spade to join the carpet and underlay.

'Looks like she got him to clear out the garden shed too!' said Ronnie.

He grinned and rubbed his hands together.

'I think we'd better get out of here, Stevie!' and he put the van in gear and his indicator on to drive out of the layby. I looked out of the passenger window and saw Mr Crumb about to get in to the car. At that moment he looked in our direction and I saw a look of recognition on his face. He might not have recognised his pupil but he knew his caretaker's van.

On the way home Ronnie was very cheerful.

'Are you really going to report Mr Crumb?' I asked.

'Yes, I really am. Why?'

'Because I think he recognised the van.'

'So what? All I am is a concerned citizen doing my duty. So what if he does know it was me that reported him? What can he do to me?'

Ronnie did report Mr Crumb to the council. He did it as soon as we got home that day.

'Yes, I'd like to speak to someone about fly-tipping,' he said into the telephone in his front hallway. 'Yes, I'll hold, thank you.' He winked at me. 'Yes, I want to report an incident of fly-tipping… Er, why do you need my name? I didn't do it… Oh, I see, well yes, my name's Rawlinson, Ronald Rawlinson, Number 2, Spark's Cottages, Wrong Drove… Yes, that's right, it happened in the layby on the A47 just after the Shell Service Station, do you know the one I mean? Yes, he just dumped a carpet, some underlay and an old spade, threw 'em in the ditch… No, I didn't get the registration number, no need to, I know him… Gerald Crumb, C R U M B, don't know exactly where he lives, somewhere in Wisbech, but he's the headmaster at Sir William Smith High School… Yes, that's right Easton St. Matthew… Oh, isn't it? Well it's bloody disgusting whatever it is and there should be a law… What? Oh, littering, well same thing… Yes, thank you, good day to you too.'

He put the phone down and rubbed his hands together. 'That'll cook his goose, Stevie my boy.'

'But what will happen, Ronnie?'

'They'll fine him, that's what'll happen. Apparently, it's not fly-tipping, it's littering, but all the same thing, it's against the law, and I hope they screw him good and proper. Now let's get the gear unloaded.'

*

Mr Crumb did find out who reported him because one morning a couple of weeks later I saw round one of the retaliations.

I was, as usual, standing outside the staffroom waiting for teachers to collect their registers. I was a bit early and so I saw Mr Crumb drive into the school and park in his parking slot outside the front entrance. Then, instead of coming straight into school, he opened the boot of the car and took out a can of what looked like engine oil. I assumed that he was going to top up his oil and, sure enough, he opened the bonnet, but instead of pouring oil into his engine, he looked around, as if to make sure no-one was watching, and then, slowly and deliberately, poured the oil into the middle of the next parking slot, all over the 'VISITORS' which Ronnie, helped by me in the last summer holidays, had carefully painted in white. What on earth did he do that for? I thought, but then forgot about the incident.

But later, when Ronnie arrived home in a foul mood, I learnt why Mr Crumb had done it.

'I don't know where Ronnie's got to,' said Beryl. We were visiting next door, Mum for a cup of tea and me for a plateful of scones. 'He said he wouldn't be late tonight, there's no after-school stuff and all he has to do is lock up. Ah, that sounds like him.' We heard him push open the back door and stamp his feet on the doormat. 'Had a good day, dear? The tea's just made.'

'No, I bloody haven't had a good day,' said Ronnie, still stamping his feet. 'Had to spend half the day trying to clean an oil-stain right in the middle of the visitor's parking space. Pints of the stuff, there was, and it had soaked right into the concrete. I had to get down on my hands and knees to scrub it with oven cleaner in the end. WD40 just wouldn't shift it. And then tonight I had to re-paint the bloody visitor's sign.'

'Oh, dear,' said Beryl, pouring him a cup of tea. 'I don't know why you bother, love, it's only a carpark.'

'But it's right in front of the entrance, and it's where visitors park. I don't want people to think I don't keep the place clean. It was probably some parent with an old jalopy.'

'No, it was Mr Crumb,' I interrupted.

'What?' Everyone looked at me.

'It was Mr Crumb. I saw him this morning. He poured oil from a can all over the parking space.'

'Did he now?' said Ronnie. 'Well, that's very interesting.' He looked thoughtful. 'Perhaps that's why Stan Godley told me to clean the stain because Mr Crumb had noticed it and wanted it shifted before Mrs WL arrived this afternoon.'

'But surely a headmaster wouldn't do that sort of thing, not on purpose,' said Mum.

'This sort of headmaster would,' said Ronnie. 'But two can play at that game. He'd better watch out.'

'Now Ronnie,' said Beryl. 'Don't you go and wind Mr Crumb up or you'll regret it. He is your boss, after all.'

But Ronnie wasn't listening to her. He was planning the next act.

And so began the feud between Ronnie and Mr Crumb. Looking back now, I can see it was very childish of both of them, and it had quite serious consequences eventually, of course, but at the time it seemed to be great fun and I enjoyed hearing about each latest instalment.

A couple of days later, when I arrived at the school office to collect the registers, all I could see of Mrs Duckworth was her backside, as her head was inside the bottom drawer of a filing cabinet which stood in the corner of the school office. Mr Godley was standing next to her and they were whispering fiercely at each other.

'But I don't know where they are, Stan!' she said. 'I put them back in their case and in this bottom drawer of this filing cabinet, where I always keep them. I'm sure I did.'

Mr Godley's tick was very bad. I thought his head was going to come off sideways.

'Are you absolutely sure, Maureen?' (Jerk!) 'It's easy to mislay something when you're very busy.'

Mrs Duckworth bristled.

'I am absolutely sure, Stan. I never mislay anything.'

'Of course, Maureen.' (Jerk, jerk!) 'But what could have happened?'

'Perhaps someone has stolen them?'

'But why? Why would anyone want to pinch Mr Crumb's binoculars. It's not as if they are particularly valuable, but don't tell him I said that.' He looked nervously towards the door into Mr

Crumb's office and jerked his head four times.

'Perhaps it was a pupil, some sort of prank, I wouldn't put it past any of these kids,' said Mrs Duckworth.

'But how could they have got in to the filing cabinet?' (Jerk!) 'Don't you keep it locked?'

Mrs Duckworth looked affronted.

'Of course I do! The only other person who has a key is Ronnie.'

My ears pricked up.

'Where is he now?' whispered Mr Godley, and he jerked his head towards Mr Crumb's office.

'He's ranting and raving in there! Oh, what shall we do?'

I don't know if they ever found Mr Crumb's binoculars, but I certainly knew who had taken them, and it wasn't any kid.

Later that week, there was another crisis in the school office. I was passing through reception at break time to avoid the playground, when I saw that Ms McCarthy was in the school office, so I decided to hang around and think of something to say to her about photography. She was standing behind Mrs Duckworth who was on the phone; it looked as if she was waiting to ask her something. Mr Godley was fussing over the photocopier. Suddenly Mr Crumb's door burst open.

'Mrs Duckworth, I do not expect you to go into my drawers, I thought you understood that.' Mr Crumb looked very cross; his hair was stuck up on top and his face was very sweaty.

Mrs Duckworth dropped the phone.

'But I haven't, Mr Crumb!' Mrs Duckworth's face was also very red. 'I would never do such a thing!'

I could hear a squawking from the phone, but she ignored it.

'But the bottom drawer in my desk is always locked, Mrs

Duckworth. Please explain what has been going on – my desk drawer has been unlocked and some of my er… private papers have been removed. Are you the perpetrator?'

'Oh, Mr Crumb, sir! As if I would! How can you think it?'

I thought Mrs Duckworth was going to cry; her face had collapsed into crinkles. Mr Crumb looked at her as if she was a nasty taste in his mouth.

'Oh, I am sure Mrs Duckworth wouldn't…' said Mr Godley, his tick going nineteen to the dozen.

'Then who has, Mr Godley? And where are my country-dancing magazines? They are not where I left them.'

'Er… I'll see if I can find them, headmaster.'

Mr Godley looked desperately round the office, as if they might suddenly materialise. He began to pick up and put down various piles of paper on Mrs Duckworth's desk, riffling through them. Then he lurched to the reception counter and began to scrabble about in the lost property box.

The phone was still squawking, its receiver hanging on its cord from the desk. Ms McCarthy quietly replaced it.

Mr Godley fished out a muddy plimsoll and a football sock and suddenly swooped.

'Ah!' he said, waving a magazine. 'Is this what you've lost, sir? It seems to be…'

He broke off and gasped.

Ms McCarthy took the magazine from him and thumbed through it. She frowned and handed it to Mr Crumb.

'I hope this isn't yours, Mr Crumb. I'm all for being open-minded but this trash is so sexist.'

Mr Crumb blushed purple and snatched the magazine from her.

'How did this happen? I want to know what has been going on, Mr Godley.'

Mr Godley jerked a lot.

'Well, er… I am sure it couldn't have been Mrs Duckworth, Sir, and, er… the only other person who has a full set of school keys is Mr Rawlinson, and he wouldn't…'

'Rawlinson?' spat Mr Crumb. 'I might have known!' And he marched back into his office.

Mr Godley and Mrs Duckworth looked at each other.

'What was all that about?' asked Mr Godley.

'I don't know, Stan, I really don't,' said Mrs Duckworth.

But I did.

Later, in the shed, I told Ronnie what had happened.

'He went purple when Mr Godley got out one of the magazines,' I told Ronnie.

He chuckled.

'I can just imagine it!'

The next day, a very windy one, someone upset all the playground rubbish bins in the middle of Period 3, just after Ronnie had finished his litter-pick.

'But it might just have been the wind,' I argued, when he told me about it.

'Yeah, and pigs might fly,' was his retort.

The following day Ronnie used an electric drill in the corridor outside Mr Crumb's office.

'He was livid! "What exactly do you think you are doing, Rawlinson? Haven't you got better things to do?" he goes in that snotty voice. "I'm putting picture hooks in, sir," I says, "so as we can hang some nice pictures in this corridor, where the visitors come."'

Then there was the visit of the health and safety officer, not due for another five months, because 'there has been a complaint,' and the twenty-page form Ronnie had to fill in before the visit. That was followed by the 'accident' to Mr Crumb's assembly book when it fell into the cleaning bucket and had to be dried on a radiator, causing the pages to stick together. For two days Ronnie couldn't find his trolley, always kept in reception, and had to carry deliveries by hand all over the school. He found it in the skip, just before it was due to be emptied. And then, finally, there was the furniture spray on the stage.

It happened in final assembly. As the end of the summer term drew near I had begun to count off the days until that glorious last day of term, when, traditionally, we did not do any work but played hangman while the teachers said they had to clean out their cupboards. And we always went home early.

'Bloody stupid idea!' Ronnie used to say. 'Just so the teachers can get away to bloody Majorca or wherever they go on their posh holidays. And who is it that has to tidy up their bloody classrooms, eh? Yours truly! There's books all haywire and litter all over the floors 'cos the kids have been messing about all morning!'

By the time final assembly arrived, when Mr Crumb would give us a sermon about 'one more year of spiritual growth' and Mr Godley would give us a lecture about not getting into trouble with the police during the holidays, we were as high as the proverbial kites, and Mr Godley had trouble getting the assembly hall quiet enough for Mr Crumb's entrance. But eventually he seized a moment of relative quiet and said, with a very big jerk, 'School Stand! Quietly!' and we all stood up for Mr Crumb to come into the hall and up the stairs onto the stage.

It was as he walked in his academic gown towards the lectern that he slipped on something and, flailing his arms to try to re-gain his balance, he looked like a young cormorant attempting a first flight. At last, after what seemed an age of flapping, his legs slid from under him and he landed with a thump on his backside.

There was a collective gasp and then the assembly hall roared with laughter. Even the teachers laughed, and Mr Godley, hurrying across the stage to the rescue, was smirking along with his tic. Mr Crumb was eventually helped to his feet and propped up against the lectern, where he looked out on a sea of hilarity. All the pupils were laughing, even though the teachers had controlled themselves and were trying to quieten everyone down with lots of shushes. It took Mr Godley some minutes to restore order and even then, for the rest of the assembly, which Mr Crumb conducted doggedly, there were occasional titters and little groups of pupils would break into giggles.

'Take the names of those pupils not showing respect, Mr Godley,' Mr Crumb interjected into his monologue, but that was an impossibility, as sometimes a whole line would just collapse in helpless laughter.

However, the assembly did end eventually, and, as I was in one of the last lines to leave the hall, I saw Mr Godley on his hands and knees on the stage feeling the floor.

'It's furniture polish or some such thing, sir,' he said, smelling the floor.

'Send Rawlinson to me at once, Mr Godley.' Mr Crumb gathered his dignity in the arms of his academic gown and swept off.

'Had me in his office, he did,' said Ronnie, later. 'He didn't beat about the bush, either. Just told me he was sacking all the cleaners for gross misconduct, something about being negligent, and endangering people's safety. I says to him, "You can't do that sir, it's not fair, it wasn't them, it was me what forgot to clean up the stuff when I spilt it," and he looks at me sort of glowering with his eyes and he says, "You haven't heard the last of this Rawlinson! Go away!" So I went.'

It was then, I think, that Mr Crumb decided to get rid of Ronnie, come what may.

Chapter Eleven

The summer holiday had arrived.

As I travelled home that day, the world I could see from the bus seemed to glow with colour under the dazzling fen sky and, cycling back down the drove, I could smell the winter wheat ripe for the harvest. In front of me stretched countless days of freedom. I am sure those summers were not always hot and sunny, although that is how I remember them, and the days when I set off to explore with a jam sandwich, a bottle of squash and binoculars, seemed endless, although I always had to be home by six o'clock for tea. After tea there were still the evenings, with long windless dusks when the bats flitted around the trees by the cottages and Ronnie and me sat outside his shed and he talked of his childhood and told me stories about shooting characters. Most of all I looked forward to the summer holidays because they gave me six weeks of freedom from the attentions of Dwayne & Co.

But that year it didn't turn out quite like that.

We rarely went away for a summer holiday. I now realise that was because my mother could not afford it. In fact, I wonder now how she managed to bring me up the way she did on the part-time job at the Shell garage. I don't remember feeling that I wanted for anything, I was always well-fed and respectably clothed, with birthday and Christmas presents that I had asked for always provided. But there was little left over for treats. Seaside holidays were not part of the childhood I can remember, although Mum had photos of me as a toddler on the beach at Cromer on the last holiday before my dad died.

But that year we went away for a caravan holiday at the seaside. Ronnie and Beryl always had a week away in the summer in Beryl's sister's caravan on a site at Hunstanton, and as this year Sandra had 'upsized' to a much posher van with two bedrooms and a separate shower, they invited us to join them.

'That's so kind of you, but we couldn't,' said Mum, to my annoyance, when they first suggested it. 'It's your holiday and we wouldn't want to presume. You need some time on your own, you must get fed up with Stephen always under your feet.'

I scowled at her.

'Rubbish!' said Ronnie. 'He's no trouble, most of the time.' He winked at me. 'Besides it will be company for Beryl, a woman to natter to when I'm fishing.' Ronnie enjoyed beach fishing when he was on holiday.

'Oh please, Mum,' I begged. 'Can we go?'

Mum looked worried. 'But things are a bit tight at the moment,' she said, 'and I couldn't see myself not making a contribution to the costs.'

'Now look here, Myra love, we don't pay anything for the van. Sandra lets us use it buckshee 'cos we're family, and the only expenses are food and stuff that we'd be buying if we was at home. And if you like, you could give us a few bob for your keep.'

'We could go shopping together,' said Beryl, 'and then you could pay half, just as if you were shopping for yourself. Come on Myra, it'll be lovely. You need a break and Stevie will have a wonderful time, a real seaside holiday, bless him.'

So we had our caravan holiday and, by luck, the sun shone for five out of the seven days. I remember days spent in a haze of sea and sand and ice cream whenever I wanted it, as Beryl spoilt me shamelessly. I remember beating Ronnie at crazy golf (although on reflection I am sure he fiddled the scorecard), and learning how to cast out over the waves with his huge sea rod, although I never caught anything. I remember hours spent at low tide searching the rockpools for crabs and the cliff bottoms for fossils. I remember a wonderful afternoon's boat trip along the coast to see seals. I remember going on the waltzers with Ronnie and how green he looked afterwards. I remember playing cards at the little caravan table in the evenings, when my mother revealed herself, to my surprise, as a competitive card player. I remember sitting on the front eating fish and chips and watching people walk by – which is when we saw Dwayne, a memory I would rather forget.

'Just look at that woman, Beryl!' said Mum. 'How can she flaunt herself like that?'

'Deary me, she must be at least size 20,' said Beryl, who was herself overweight.

They were looking at a very fat woman, dressed in a pair of tight pink shorts and vivid green halter top, who was swaying along the promenade towards us, buttocks wobbling in time with her enormous breasts. A few yards behind her shambled an equally fat boy, who was stuffing a hot dog into his mouth and dripping tomato ketchup down his T-shirt.

Ronnie looked up from his chips.

'Why, it's Mrs Tubbs!' he remarked. 'You know, love, the school cook. There's certainly plenty of flesh to flaunt, eh Stevie?' He gave me a huge nudge in the ribs.

'Ronnie!' said Beryl, 'not in front of the lad.'

At that point Mrs Tubbs saw us.

'Well bugger me, fancy seeing you here!' she said, and she stopped in front of us.

Dwayne sauntered to a halt. He hadn't noticed me. I gave my newspaper of chips a lot of attention, head down.

'Down for the day, Daphne?' said Ronnie.

'Yes. I looked out of the window this morning and I said to Dwayne, I said, "I fancy a day at the seaside today," so we came on the bus. A lovely ride it was, wasn't it Dwayne love?'

Dwayne looked as if he hadn't enjoyed it much.

'Can I have an ice cream, Mum?'

'In a minute. Don't be so rude, can't you see I'm talking to Mr Rawlinson and his wife and,' noticing Mum and me, 'why, it's Mrs Stringer and Stephen. Look Dwayne, it's your little friend.'

Dwayne noticed me and smirked. I stared at him, trying to look daggers.

'My feet are killing me, up and down this front. I think I'll join you, if you don't mind,' she said and she plonked herself down next to Mum and mopped her forehead with a handkerchief. 'Wow! That's a hot ol' day!'

'It's a lovely afternoon,' said Mum.

Mrs Tubbs scrabbled in her large canvas handbag and withdrew a fat leather purse.

'Here Dwayne, take this fiver and run along with Stephen and get yourself both an ice cream from that kiosk. And bring me a cuppa, two sugars. Can I get your good selves anything?'

'No thank you very much, we've just finished our lunch,' said Beryl.

Dwayne took the banknote eagerly. I sat where I was, trying to be invisible.

'Go on Stephen,' said Mum. 'Mrs Tubbs has offered you an ice cream. Go along with Dwayne, and what do you say?'

Reluctantly I slid off the wall.

'Thank you, Mrs Tubbs.'

'That's all right, dear. Now you go along and keep my Dwayne out of trouble, he needs a nice friend like you.'

Dwayne joined in, putting on a very polite voice. 'Come on, Stephen. What flavour would you like?'

We set off towards the kiosk, me keeping a good distance between us. My mouth felt dry but I knew I'd be all right if we kept in sight of the adults. I glanced back. The women were talking but Ronnie had stood up with chip papers and was making for the waste bin by the kiosk. Dwayne looked sideways and must have noticed this too for he put his arm across my shoulders. I squirmed away, but he was too strong for me and held me to him in a firm grip on my right shoulder.

'Not very friendly, are you, Sydney?'

When we got to the kiosk he released me, and I winced and rubbed my shoulder. Ronnie had finished at the bin and joined us.

'I'll get these, lad,' he said, 'you put that fiver in your pocket for later eh?' He winked at Dwayne. 'You and Stevie could have a go on the slot machines, eh?'

'Oh, thanks Mr Rawlinson,' said Dwayne, all smarmy. 'We'll have a lovely time, won't we Syd… Stephen?'

'Stevie's been nagging me all week about those bloody machines, haven't you, lad?'

I nodded and tried to smile. 'Yeah, but I don't think I feel like it this afternoon. I don't feel very well.'

Ronnie looked hard at me.

'Can I help you?' said the lady in the kiosk.

'A cup of tea, two sugars, and two ice creams, please. What flavours, boys?' said Ronnie.

'Chocolate!' said Dwayne, in a flash. 'With two flakes!'

'Stevie?'

'Vanilla please,' I said.

'That's three pounds seventy-five. Sugar's on the counter.'

Ronnie paid and carried the cup back for Mrs Tubbs. We were given our ice creams. Dwayne began to saunter along the prom, one arm firmly round my right shoulder, the other holding his ice cream while he slurped it.

'Come on, Sydney. Enjoy your nice ice cream.' He pinched the skin on my upper arm.

'Ouch! That hurt! Get off!'

'Eat your ice cream!' he hissed.

Obediently, I licked. It tasted like runny cardboard.

'D'you wanna go on the machines?' asked Dwayne, slurping.

'No, thanks.'

'What about the dodgems? We'd get two goes for a fiver,' he said with his mouth full of ice cream.

'No thanks!' The idea of being chased by Dwayne in a dodgem car made me shiver.

'Why don't we just go on the beach and paddle then, like good little boys?'

'No thanks.'

'You're not much fun, are you, Sydney?'

Dwayne finished his ice cream and flung the end of the cone on the ground.

We had reached the public toilets.

'I need a piss! Come on!' said Dwayne.

'I think I'll just go back,' and I turned to go back.

'Oh no you don't!' and his arm grabbed my shoulder again.

'Ouch!'

'What a cry-baby! I'm only being friendly!'

In spite of my protests and wriggles he guided me into the men's toilets. Once there he had me up against the wall.

'Get off!' I shouted, hoping that someone else on that promenade would also need the toilet.

He grinned. 'Are you enjoying your ice cream, Sydney?'

He got hold of my right hand, which held the ice cream cone, and slammed it against the wall. The cone fell to the floor.

'Ow!' I shouted. My knuckles really hurt.

'Oh dear, you've dropped it! Look, it's got piss on it!' He kicked it towards a nasty-looking puddle in the corner by the urinal.

I heard the toilet flush in one of the cubicles and prayed that someone would emerge to save me.

'You'd better pick it up, mustn't drop litter, must we?' He pushed me towards the corner. I landed painfully, giving my face a good whack on the wall, which was why I didn't see what happened next. I heard it though.

'Ow!' Dwayne screamed.

I turned to look. Ronnie was holding Dwayne pinned against the wall by his shoulders. He was struggling and flailing his arms, but although Ronnie wasn't a tall man he was very strong and he held him fast. He leaned his head forward until his face was less than an inch from Dwayne's spluttering.

'Get off me!' shouted Dwayne. 'You're hurting me!'

Ronnie spoke quietly and calmly. 'I'm not hurting you, you great big wimp, but I sure as houses will if I ever again see you lay a hand on Stevie.'

'Leave me alone, you bully!'

'You're the bully, you scumbag. If you want to pick a fight with someone, choose someone your own size. Now run along back to Mummy.' He let him go.

Dwayne sniffled. 'You're not supposed to hit a child,' he whined.

'I didn't hit you. I gave you a friendly word. Now bugger off!'

Dwayne summoned up the dirtiest look he could muster, and then slunk away.

'You just wait!' he hissed.

I thought he had addressed that final comment at me. But I was wrong. He had aimed the venom at Ronnie, as we were to find out when we returned from our holiday.

'Are you OK, boy?' asked Ronnie, and he pulled me to him in a short fierce embrace.

'Yeah, I'm all right. I just tripped over when he pushed me.'

He held me away from him and examined my face.

'No serious damage done as far as I can see,' he said. 'A bit of a graze on your forehead there,' he lifted my fringe, 'but I don't expect your mum'll notice if you're careful. Now, tell me, Stevie, and I want the truth, mind, how long has this been going on?'

'How long has what been going on?'

'Don't mess with me boy, you don't need to. How long has that scumbag been bullying you.'

I looked into his eyes and saw so much love and concern it embarrassed me.

I looked down and mumbled, 'For quite a long time.'

'That's not an answer. How long? A couple of weeks? A term?'

I thought back to when it all started, to how much I had looked forward to secondary school, to all my excitement on that first morning, to how Ronnie had taken a photo of me in my new uniform before I left for the bus, how proud Mum had looked; and then I remembered the whispering, 'Sydney! Sydney!' I wanted so much to tell someone, to ask for help, to lose the burden of fear, and I looked up at the man I trusted so much, who had always protected me and been there for me.

'Since my first day at Sir Willyum's,' I sobbed, and I threw myself against Ronnie and held on to him as tightly as I could, squashing my glasses against his chest.

He held me as I cried and there we stood until I had cried myself out. We broke away as a man came in and headed for the urinal.

'Just splash your face in that wash basin,' said Ronnie, to cover my red face and obvious distress. I did as he said, and we left the toilets.

'You just leave this to me,' he said. 'Heads will roll.'

'No Ronnie, please don't say anything at school. It'll only make things worse. It always does.'

'But he can't be allowed to get away with it.'

I remembered that final threat. 'But he'll say I'm a grass and then everyone else will join in and it'll be even worse. Please! Don't say anything.'

'But you can't go through your school life being bullied all the time.'

'It's OK, honest it is. Most of the time I avoid him, different classes and that,' which wasn't strictly true. 'Everyone does it, it's just normal, pushing people around,' which also was a lie.

'He needs someone to give him a right seeing to, that's what I think,' he grumbled.

'Someone did. When he had a fight with Connor Soames in Year 10 he came off worse. He only picks on me because I'm smaller and he can get away with it,' and because no-one likes me enough to stick up for me, I wanted to say, but didn't because that would be revealing even more of my misery.

'I think I'll have a word with Stan Godley all the same,' said Ronnie.

'Please don't. It'll only makes things worse.'

'We'll see.'

I spent the rest of that holiday worrying about what would happen if Ronnie talked to Mr Godley. I knew what would happen if he did; Mr Godley would have what he called 'a quiet word' with me at the beginning of term about how I was getting on and did I have friends and did I know what to do if I was ever unhappy at school and all that sort of thing. But what could I say? Teachers often had 'quiet little talks' like that and felt that by doing so they had solved the problem. If only they knew what was really going on.

Of course, I was worrying about the wrong thing, wasn't I?

*

It was the same two grey-haired women from the Child Protection Team that interviewed us, but this time the interview took place at Ronnie's. They arrived while we were unpacking.

'Now what?' said Mum when she saw the police car draw up as she was putting the suitcases back on top of the wardrobe.

'You haven't been getting into any trouble, have you Stephen?' She looked suspicious.

'No!' I felt aggrieved that she didn't trust me.

She didn't look any less worried when the two women, still in saggy cardigans, knocked next door. I was worried too. Had Mrs Darbyshire been making up another set of lies about Ronnie?

But it had been Dwayne who had carried out his threat. He hadn't told his mother about the confrontation at Hunstanton, but he had phoned *Childline* and reported Ronnie's behaviour as a physical assault in a public toilet. I learnt this three quarters of an hour later, when they knocked on our door and, much to my mother's shock, said they wanted to interview me in the presence of my parent.

'So we meet again, Stephen,' said the fat one.

'What has he done?' demanded my mum.

'Stephen hasn't done anything wrong, Mrs Stringer,' said the thin one. 'But he is a witness to an incident that has been reported to us by a child victim of an assault by an adult male in a public place.'

My mother looked confused. 'But when? Where?'

The fat one consulted her notes. 'On 27th July in a public toilet on the promenade at Hunstanton, Norfolk,' she read.

'But that was…' said Mum.

The thin one ignored her. 'Now Stephen, this is about Mr Rawlinson…'

'Again!' said the fat one.

For the second time I found myself defending Ronnie against an allegation. I listened to Dwayne's version of events and trod carefully over whether I had been 'pushed over by accident when he tried to stop my ice cream being dropped on the floor'. But I did defend Ronnie vehemently: no, he had not hit Dwayne; yes, he had spoken sternly to him and he did hold him by the shoulders but that was because he thought he had pushed me deliberately.

'And are you sure it was an accident when you fell, Stephen? You are telling the truth, I hope.'

I opened my mouth to tell another lie, but fortunately I was saved by my mum.

'He doesn't tell lies, officer,' she said firmly.

As soon as they had gone, leaving us with the information that it was an 'on-going investigation' and that they might need to interview me again, I rushed next door. Ronnie was sitting at the kitchen table. His mouth was set tight and he was very pale. Beryl was in floods of tears.

'Oh Ronnie! Just when I thought all that nastiness was over! What will people say?'

'They can say what they bloody like,' said Ronnie. 'I was defending our Stevie from a right nasty piece of work and I'm not ashamed of it.'

I suddenly felt very emotional and went to stand next to him. I put my hand out to put it on his shoulder, but then stopped. He looked quite fierce.

'But what about your job, Ronnie. How will you hold your head up?'

'Stop your wailing woman! I've done nothing wrong, I tell you.'

'But…'

The telephone rang.

'Oh dear, who can that be?' said Beryl, moving to the hall. 'What a time to ring, just when…' She stopped herself and turned back to

Ronnie. 'You don't think that Susan Chichester has heard, do you?'

'Rubbish, woman. Answer the bloody phone, will you?'

Beryl disappeared into the hall and, together, we listened.

'Hallo? Wisbech 489761. Who is it?' she demanded.

There was a pause and her voice softened. 'Oh, hallo Mr Godley, I didn't realise it was you, sorry if I was a bit sharp, we've just had a bit of a shock… Oh, you know about it… Well yes, they've just left, and very unpleasant they were too, accusing my Ronnie of… Yes, of course, sir, of course you can… Yes, we'll be in… No, it's not inconvenient… We look forward to seeing you then… Thank you, sir, bye.'

She came to the doorway and we both turned to face her.

'That was Mr Godley, Ronnie. He's coming round to see you.'

'Well, at least I'll get some sense out of him,' said Ronnie.

'Yes, he'll sort it out. He knows what's what.' She sat down and took a deep breath of satisfaction. Then suddenly she stood up again. 'Oh deary me, and the house in such a state too, with us just getting back from the caravan and everything all over the place. Now have I got enough milk, because Mr Godley'll want a nice cuppa, bless him.'

'I could do with one too,' said Ronnie.

I wasn't there when Mr Godley arrived, as Mum had hauled me back next door to sort out my bedroom, but I looked through the window and noticed that he had a very serious look on his face when he got out of his car and trudged up the path to Ronnie's front door.

Afterwards I couldn't get Ronnie to tell me what they had talked about. All he would say was, 'Stan Godley will sort it out, boy, don't you worry.'

'But, Ronnie, what about Mr Crumb and your warning thingy? He might sack you!'

He laughed, but not very convincingly. 'Don't you bother about that. Old Crumpet's all wind and piss I tell you.'

I don't know exactly what Mr Godley did, but I expect he had a nice talk with Mrs Tubbs and a not so nice talk with Dwayne. What he said to the two grey ladies I don't know, but all that happened was that Ronnie got a letter telling him he was on some sort of child protection list because there had been more than one allegation against him. I didn't think that was fair.

'But they're false allegations,' I argued. 'It's Ashley and Dwayne who ought to be on a police list, not you!'

'Don't you fret, boy,' said Ronnie. 'If being on a list is the worst thing that ever happens to me, I don't mind.' Ronnie was wrong about that, of course. 'Mind you, I intend to keep well away from that toe-rag young Tubbs, and I suggest you do too, Stevie.'

'I'll try,' I promised him.

I wish I could, I thought.

Chapter Twelve

But that wasn't the only thing that happened in that eventful last summer holiday. Although Jimmy Buckland had left school he did not leave my life.

It was a wet Saturday afternoon in August, one of those occasional summer days when it starts fine and sunny and then the rain just descends in straight lines and you get soaked within a few moments. I was cycling back from the Marsh, where I had been searching for any unusual visitors on early migration. I had just reached the first sea bank and settled onto the long straight King John's Mile (which was actually three miles), head down and dreaming of dry clothes and doughnuts for tea if Mum had been shopping, when my front tyre went flat. I slithered to a halt, got off, wiped the rain off my glasses and examined it. Sure enough, there was a sharp bit of shingle still attached.

'Fuck!' I said to the bike, as there was no-one else within miles.

I got off and began to walk, feeling, if it was possible, even wetter than before.

I had made it as far as the turn-off for Walsh's Dyke, when I heard the sound of a vehicle behind me. I stopped and dragged my bike onto the verge, as the road is not wide. When I looked back I could see a dirty grey pick-up truck approaching. I waited, but instead of driving past me, it stopped next to me, and the driver's door opened.

'Want a lift, laddie?'

It was Jake Buckland, and next to him, in the passenger seat, was Jimmy.

'No thank you very much,' I said. 'I'm fine.'

'Got a puncture? It's a long way to civilisation. 'Why…' as he peered at me through the rain, '…it's that lad was in your class, Jim, what's 'is name, Myra Coatley's boy?'

'Stephen Stringer,' said Jimmy, and I looked up at him, rather startled, as he had used my real name. 'Hi, Steve! How're you doing?' He sounded as if we were best mates.

Jake got out of the pick-up, and without asking me, took the bike from my grasp and slung it into the back of the pick-up.

'There, lad, that's your bike picked up anyway, and if you want to see it again, you'd better get in too, or these nasty pikeys'll nick it, like what they always do, eh?' He nudged me hard in the ribs and bellowed a huge deep laugh.

'Come on, Steve, there's room,' said Jimmy, patting the seat, so I stepped up and slid across the driver seat to join him, not seeing what else I could do.

'What yer been doing?' he asked, as we drove off.

'Nothing much.' I was still wary of him.

'Come on, mate, don't be like that!' He put his arm round my shoulder and squeezed.

I flinched. I had been on the receiving end of other such physical approaches of mateyness, particularly from Dwayne Tubbs, and they were usually very painful.

'It's OK, mate, honest!' he said softly, and he withdrew his arm, with a pat on my back. 'We're good mates, Steve and me,' he said to Jake, who was negotiating the narrow bridge over Walsh's Dyke.

'We've got a good understanding, haven't we?' He grinned at me.

I searched his face, but it was bland and without any obvious guile. The malice I remembered from our encounter in the changing rooms was absent from the clear blue eyes, one of which winked at me.

'You been bird-watching, eh?' he said and he slapped the back of his hand against my binoculars, which I wore round my neck. 'Steve's a bird-watcher, Uncle,' he said.

'Is he now?' said Jake. 'I quite fancy the birds too, especially on Saturday nights when they're all dolled up with legs up to their fannies, eh Jim?' The huge bellowing laugh again roared out of him.

'No, Uncle. Proper birds, with wings 'n that. Steve here's quite an expert. He gave a talk once in English, didn't you Steve. Knows all their names 'n that.'

'Good lad,' said Jake. 'I like to see young-uns what take things seriously. And good to hear you remembered something from that bloody school, Jim.'

By now we were on the main road.

'Could you drop me at the top of Wrong Drove, please, and I'll walk from there,' I ventured.

'What, in this fucking rain. With a puncture to mend when you get home? No way. We'll get that puncture fixed first, eh, Jim?' he said and he accelerated towards Wisbech.

'Yeah, course,' said Jimmy, and he winked at me again.

'And then we'll drop you home. I'd like to say hello to Myra again after all these years. My, was she a stunner when she was fourteen! Not that she had eyes for anyone except John Stringer. We called him Sydney, you know, family name I think.'

'Really?' said Jimmy, winking at me.

'Yeah. Pity what happened to him. My sincerest condolences, lad, about your dad.'

'Thank you, sir,' I said.

After that I kept quiet. I wasn't sure what to make of what was happening to me. I hoped they'd drop me home well before Mum got back. I didn't think she'd be so keen to meet Jake Buckland again after all these years.

By the time we reached the traveller site on the main road, it had stopped raining and the sun was just emerging from the bank of grey cloud disappearing towards the Wash. I had never been on a traveller site before, although I had passed this one lots of times.

The first thing I noticed was the dogs. As we turned in from the main road we were surrounded by a pack of them barking and jumping up at the pickup truck. I was used to dogs; Ronnie's Gyp had been in my life for as long as I could remember, and I was used to the occasional scrap over territory between a couple of the retrievers on a shoot. But this leaping baying pack was quite frightening. However, Jake and Jim opened the pickup doors without concern and dropped down among them.

'Quiet you buggers!' commanded Jake, aiming a boot at the nearest, and they circled away, fawning close to the ground, tongues hanging out. 'Come on lad, they'll not harm you. It's only coppers they eat!' He held out a hand to help me jump down, grinning.

I didn't see how I could refuse, and so I slithered across the seat and accepted his help. Once I was on the ground, he lifted my bike out and wheeled it one-handed towards a large mobile home which was parked in the corner of the site. The dogs dispersed, except for two that followed closely in his heels. Jimmy and I followed too. He leant the bike against the steps of the mobile and leapt up the three steps, pushing open the door.

'Esme, my love, can you find some pop and chocolate biscuits. I've got a couple of starving young-uns here! You take your mate inside, Jim, and introduce him, and I'll get to grips with this puncture.' So saying, he swung the bike upside down one-handed, propping it on its handlebars, and swung the back wheel.

'Now then, where's the damage?'

'No, it's all right, I can do it, if you've got a puncture kit,' I said.

He smiled at me. 'No, lad, you're soaking wet, get inside and stoke up. I'll have done this in a jiffy.' He began to root around in the back of the pick-up.

'Come on, Steve!' said Jimmy, and the use of my real name once again beguiled me.

I followed him into the van.

It was not at all what I had expected. My only experience of gypsy vans had been the ones that used to be parked on the field behind our cottages when I was very young and when the gypsies still came to our area fruit-picking. Those vans had been small and shabby, with rounded roofs and little chimneys, and, although I had never been inside one, I had imagined them to be pokey, dark and crammed with shelves full of china. The inside of Jake's van was a revelation. It was huge, even bigger than the caravan at Hunstanton, and I couldn't believe how spacious it felt.

'This is a mate I had at school,' said Jimmy. 'Steve, this is my auntie Esme.'

The woman was not at all like the gypsy women I remembered seeing fruit-picking. They had had long black tangled hair and earrings, wore brightly coloured skirts and didn't look too clean; this woman was very different. For a start she was blonde and wore her hair short and shaped to her head. She wore jeans and a plain black T-shirt, and she looked squeaky-clean. She was the sort of woman my mum would have described as 'nice-looking'.

'Hi. Make yourself at home,' she said. 'Jim, you know where the coke is. Get your friend a drink.' Then, noticing my bedraggled state, she added, 'Wow, you're soaked! You'll catch your death. Jim, take him into your room and he can take those wet clothes off. He looks your size, give him some jeans and a T-shirt.'

Jimmy's room, leading off the little corridor that led from the main room towards the back of the van, wasn't much smaller than my own bedroom at home, with a bunk bed and fitted wardrobe and chest of drawers in matching pine. On the top tier of the bunk bed a little boy, about five years old, was sitting watching a cartoon on a small TV that was fixed to the top of the wall.

'This is my cousin Abraham,' said Jim. 'Say hallo to Stephen, Abe!'

He turned and looked at me. I expected him to make some comment about me being a Gorgio, but all he did was stare at me with huge brown eyes and put his thumb in his mouth.

Jimmy opened one of the drawers and rummaged around, emerging with a pair of jeans and a white T-shirt.

'These should fit you. You're not such a little squirt anymore are you?'

I looked closely at him, wondering if he was taking the Mickey, but he just smiled in a nice sort of way and said, 'The bathroom's just on the right there, if you want to get changed.'

Even my mother couldn't have objected to the clothes, which were clean, ironed and smelt of the kind of softener that Beryl used and Mum thought was a waste of money. The bathroom was another shock; it had a proper shower in a glass cubicle as well as a bath and a toilet with a fluffy mauve toilet seat cover. There was a vase of artificial flowers on the cistern. Living in a cottage with a bathroom converted from the coalhouse, with a solid old iron bath and an old-fashioned toilet which you flushed with a chain hanging from a cistern above you, I was very impressed with this luxury.

'Here, let me put these wet clothes in a bag for you, or shall I pop them in the washer, it's no trouble,' said Esme.

'No, it's all right,' I said quickly, thinking of how my mother would react to the idea of having to pick up her son's laundry from a traveller site, and I grasped the bag firmly. 'My mum'll do them.'

Jimmy threw me a can of coke, cold from the fridge. 'Here, man!' he said.

I felt very grown-up; the only kind of coke I ever had was warm and flat from a bottle that Beryl kept for me.

'Come on,' he said, and headed out through the door. 'Do you want a go on the bike?'

I followed him across the centre of the site. The dogs were lying around in a huddle outside one of the vans. They lifted their heads but seemed to have accepted me. A few children were jumping up and down on a trampoline. It could have been a scene in any suburban garden.

Behind one of the vans was a motocross bike. From our cottages, if the wind was in the right direction on a Sunday afternoon, we could sometimes hear the bikes being ridden at the stadium outside Wisbech, and I knew that some of the older boys from our village messed about on bikes like this at the gravel pits outside Kings Lynn. I thought they looked tremendous fun. As soon as I saw this one I wanted one.

Jimmy got onto it and started it up. 'Come on!' he said.

'Really?' I said. 'I mean, are you allowed?'

'Yeah, of course I am, it's mine,' he said. 'Are you coming or not?' He revved it hard.

I perched on the back of the seat while he stood on the pedals in front of me, and he set off, down the field, through a gap in the hedge and into an apple orchard, where he showed off by riding, slalom-like, in and out of the rows of trees. Eventually he came to a halt.

'Do you want a go? The throttle's a bit fierce, so watch it,' he said, climbing off the seat.

Did I want a go? I don't think Jimmy could have done anything more effective to gain my trust than offering to let me ride his motorbike that afternoon. I did not think about where it might have come from, whether it was actually his or not, whether we were trespassing or not; all I was bothered about was riding that motorbike. I think that was the first time for several years that I had 'played' naturally with another boy and I relaxed and thoroughly enjoyed myself. By the end of half an hour I was whooping as loudly as he was as we swept around a corner or dipped down and out of a dry ditch.

Later, back at the van, I shared chocolate digestives with Jimmy. While we were playfighting over the last one in the packet, Jake reappeared with my bike.

'There you are, lad. All done and dusted.'

'Thank you so much,' I said.

'No trouble, son. Has Jimmy been entertaining you?'

'Yes, thanks, I've had a wonderful time,' I said, and I looked at Jimmy and grinned. 'His motorbike's fantastic!'

'Told you it was his, did he, the lying toad?' said Jake, taking a playful swipe at Jimmy, who ducked but continued to grin.

Suddenly aware of the time, I got hold of my bike.

'I'd better be off,' I said. 'Thanks for the coke and biscuits and the ride on the motorbike, and, oh, the clothes and… everything.'

Esme appeared in the doorway with the bag of my wet clothes.

'Here you are, love. It was a pleasure to have you. Come again.'

'Yeah, any time, lad,' said Jake, 'that old motorbike's always hanging around.'

I looked at Jimmy; I felt I needed his endorsement of this invitation.

'Yeah! See yer around, Steve!' he said, and he offered his right hand in a high-five. It was a sign of acceptance.

Chapter Thirteen

And so began my friendship with Jimmy Buckland. The temptation of the motorbike was powerful, and desperate to be accepted by my peers, I wanted to believe that Jimmy was being honest when he sought my company. I spent many days of that summer holiday at the traveller site, pedalling there each morning when Mum thought I was out bird-watching or spending time with Margaret, as I did not dare tell her who I was keeping company with.

It must have been hard on Margaret, as she had no other friend, but I couldn't help it; letting rip all over the countryside on the motorbike or accompanying Jimmy when he joined Jake and his cousin Georgie in the pick-up on their forays for scrap-iron was much more fun than spending time with Margaret, and anyway, I had become embarrassed at the way she clung to our friendship. After all, she was a girl, we had different interests and she was certainly not the kind of girl a thirteen-going-on-fourteen-year-old might be interested in because she was a girl. She didn't have legs like Josie.

The only time I saw her during those six weeks was when I came across her on my way home from the site late one afternoon. She was walking back from the bus stop, shoulders hunched. She looked sad and lonely. I couldn't avoid pedalling past her and I couldn't bring myself to be rude, so I stopped as I came up to her and got off my bike.

'Hi!' I said.

She looked round at me and her face lit up.

'Stephen!'

She looked so happy to see me that I felt guilty.

'Are you all right?' she said. 'I thought you might be ill or something as you hadn't come round. I thought you said that when the holiday came we were going to do photography.'

I remembered how, showing off, I had promised to teach her how to compose a photograph, like Ms McCarthy had shown me. I had forgotten all about it.

'Yeah, I'm fine,' I said. 'I've just been quite busy.' That sounded lame, and as she didn't say anything I felt that I had to go on. 'I've been building something in the garden with Ronnie, er… an extension to the chicken shed.' She was silent as we walked a few paces. 'Er…' I continued, 'and I've been helping Mum decorate my bedroom.' I couldn't think of any more lies.

'Wow, you have been busy,' she said. 'What colour is it?'

'What?' I said.

'Your bedroom. What colour is the paint and all that? And did you get new curtains? I want some in pale lavender, but Rene says they're too dear.'

'Er…' I wasn't good at fabricating interior design details, so kept with what I knew. 'Blue… er… it's just the walls… er… but it looks nice.' I tried to think of something to change the subject.

'Do you think I could come round to see it some time? I've never seen your room and you've told me so much about it. You could show me your fossils and things. I wouldn't be any trouble, your mum wouldn't have to invite me to tea or anything, I'd just like to see it,' she finished rather sadly.

I felt even more guilty. We had been friends for nearly two years and I had never invited her home. In fact, she had only ever met my mum once, when we were waiting at the bus station on the way home after my dentist's appointment and she and Irene got on the same bus. I had kept her a secret because I was ashamed of being friends with her, and, walking along the road with her that afternoon, I felt more ashamed of her than of myself, God forgive me.

'I'll ask my mum and let you know,' I said rather too quickly, and I looked at my watch in an ostentatious way. 'Oh, bloody hell, it's getting late, Mum'll slaughter me. Must go, see yer!'

I got on my bike and rode away from her.

But Margaret wasn't the only person I neglected that summer. I stopped spending so much time with Ronnie. In earlier summer holidays I had been his constant companion. Sometimes he had taken me fishing, sometimes I went with him to school, where he spent some days doing minor maintenance and decorating, the kinds of things he couldn't do in term time, and I would be his assistant. Or else there was a DIY project at home, and this year he had said he wanted to extend the chicken shed and could I help him. We would work together happily for hours, then sit outside the shed while he talked shooting.

I could never hear enough of the stories he told of the old days, when his grandad and their mates went wildfowling. According to Ronnie, the weather was always, 'Fucking near to freeze your balls,' the birds always flew straight over the guns and the wildfowlers never missed, except when some wonder-dog fetched a winged bird and swam back with it against the tide, or some such story.

'Mind you,' he would add, 'there weren't near as many pinkfeet as there are today. My old grandad would think it was Christmas every day to see them all on Westley's beet tops.'

In the past I had never tired of these accounts, repetitive as they were, and I had followed Ronnie's lead in idolising the great names of the sport of wildfowling, especially the famous Kenzie Thorpe, who had been one of Ronnie's grandad's mates.

But now I had other interests and other heroes. I was infatuated with riding the motorbike and spending time with Jimmy, a proper friend at last. I hadn't realised how much my soul had yearned for acceptance, and I found myself accepted, not only by Jimmy, but also by his family and the other travellers. These were not the 'thieving pikeys' I had been brought up to shun, who either stole from you or tricked you and who fought in the Wisbech pubs every Saturday night. These people were friendly and open and generous. In particular I began to admire Jake Buckland, who made a bit of a favourite of me. He was such a larger-than-life character, whose sense of humour was as huge as his voice. His traveller lore, recounted as we sat on the steps of the van or drove back to the site with some scrap, began to sound as interesting as the world of shooting.

'We're true Romany,' he would say, 'not like those dirty Irish tinkers. My old man, Jim's grandad that was, he was the last in our family to live on the road with the 'orses when he was a nipper. Travelled all over eastern England he did when he was a kid, and used to tell me stories about it, about the big 'orse fairs they used to hold. And they'd travel down to Epsom every year for the Derby and meet all the rest of the family. There'd be hundreds of Romany there, he used to tell me. We're all settled now, there's no future on the road no more. And the 'orses – old Tipsy there and Tiger,' and he would jerk his thumb to where two stocky little ponies grazed on a patch of grass adjacent to the main road, 'they're just for the little old lasses to pet and for old time's sake, I suppose. But we still meet up sometimes, all the family. Last year we went to Great Uncle Joshua's funeral in East Yorkshire. All the Bucklands were there, weren't they Jim? Hundreds of the buggers. Breed like rabbits we do, eh love?' He swiped at Esme's bottom as she came down the steps with a basket of washing and roared with laughter.

I am sure Ronnie noticed my absence, although he never made any direct comment about it. Once or twice he would ask me if I fancied a day fishing.

'Oh, I can't today, Ronnie,' I would bleat. 'I promised Margaret I would show her…' something or other, or 'I need to change my library books…' I would think of some excuse. He never reminded me of my promise to help him with the chicken shed, although the extension never got built.

Once, when I'd just arrived home and was parking my bike, I overheard him talking to my mum in our kitchen, where he was fixing a broken hinge on a kitchen cabinet door.

'Where's that lad of yours got to, Myra? I never seem to see him nowadays?'

'Really?' said Mum. 'I thought he was your shadow.'

'Not now he isn't. Off on his bike as soon as you're out of the house to catch your bus, love. Can't catch up with him. I don't know what he's doing with himself out on his own all day.'

'Oh, I think he spends a lot of time with that Margaret Thompson, her that lives at the reservation with her sister. Nice girl I think, met her once at the bus station; quiet, polite, not sluttish. I'd rather he spent time with a girl like that than… well, Ronnie, you know better than me what these girls are like nowadays.'

'Mm,' said Ronnie. 'Perhaps he does like spending time with her, but it doesn't seem natural for a boy of his age, you know, spending so much time with a girl like her. I wonder…'

At that moment I thought I'd better make an appearance.

'Hi Mum! Ronnie! What's for tea?' I began to talk about what I fancied to eat and what was on TV that night and anything to stop her from continuing to wonder where I had got to all day.

Ronnie went back to his DIY without another word. I didn't notice if he looked sad, but I expect he did.

*

I wasn't able to keep my secret forever. As Ronnie would have put it, 'the shit hit the fan' on August Bank Holiday Monday.

It had been very hot and very dry for several weeks that August. The TV news talked of a drought and Ronnie had spent hours watering his vegetables with the garden hose. That morning Jimmy and I were in our den. We had built it out of some broken pallets we had come across in the corner of the orchard next to the dyke. We had kitted it out pretty well. I had contributed a mug, which I retrieved from the dustbin when Mum threw it out because it was chipped and, she said, carried germs. But all the rest of the furnishings were provided by Jimmy, whose family's trade was picking up other people's throw-outs. We had two old car seats, a moth-eaten travel rug, an orange box for a table, topped by a white china ashtray (Jimmy had introduced me to smoking), and an old milk crate in which we kept the coke which Jimmy filched when he could.

As it was a bank holiday we had planned to have a feast, and

I had that morning smuggled out of our freezer one of the three packets of sausages that Mum had bought when there was an offer. Jimmy had said he would bring some matches and we would build a fire, 'Like my grandad used to do when they went on the road.' The twigs and branches we found on the floor of the orchard were tinder dry, which was a good thing, as we had no idea how to make a fire, and we had very few matches left in the box by the time our fire obliged us by not going out. Then we encountered another problem; how were we to cook the sausages? We had not thought of this before and had no frying pan or forks, only Jimmy's penknife, but eventually we managed to spear two sausages onto twigs and hold them over the flames.

By then we were more thirsty than hungry, as it was very hot, and so, propping the sausages against the burnt ashes of the fire to continue cooking, I said: 'I'm fucking parched. Chuck me a coke!'

'Never mind fucking coke,' said Jimmy. 'I've got something better than that.' He opened his rucksack. 'Have one of these if you're thirsty,' he said, revealing a six-pack of lager. 'It's a bit warm, but I don't have a cooler, man.'

'Fucking hell!' I said. 'Where did you get this from?'

'Uncle Jake got it cheap, duty free, from some mate of his. I went to fetch it with him, loads of it there was and as I was helping him unload it I hid a couple of packs. Here, catch!' He slid a can out of its plastic ring and threw it at me. 'Cheers!' he said, opening a can. He lifted his head back and poured the overflowing beer into his mouth. He wiped his mouth with the back of his hand. 'That's better! Aren't you going to drink yours?'

The only alcohol I had ever drunk was a small glass of sweet sherry at Aunty Sandra's twenty-fifth wedding anniversary when I was nine and I hadn't thought much of it. But this was beer and I was with my mate and it was a cool thing to do, so I opened the can and there was a frothy surge of warm hoppy liquid which I spilt all over my jeans. I sipped it. It didn't taste particularly nice, I remember, but it was easy to drink, and I was soon on my third can.

It was then that I began to find everything that happened so irresistibly funny that I couldn't stop giggling. I giggled at the sausages being burnt, at Jimmy singeing his trainers by sitting with his feet too close to the fire, at the sudden collapse of the springs in one of the car seats, at having to pee in a bush and falling over when I was zipping myself up, at being chased by Jimmy and falling over in a tangle with him wrestling. It was even funny when, having picked ourselves up, we found that the fire had begun to spread through the dry grass along the dyke edge. It was very funny trying to stamp it out, and not managing to stamp where I had intended and falling over again. And it was hysterical wrestling with Jimmy and rolling over and over in the grass.

It was as we lay alternately panting and bursting into giggles, that Jimmy suddenly shouted, 'First goes on the bike!' leaping to his feet. He was faster than me but as he started it up I jumped onto the back, and away we went.

The alcohol had certainly affected Jimmy. We swerved violently from side to side as we rode through the orchard. We just missed getting caught up in the orchard gate and sped off across the adjacent field. Jimmy seemed to be possessed, and I was just as excited, hanging on for my life and thumping him on the back.

'Faster! Faster!' I shouted.

Neither of us saw the combine harvester until we were upon it. Jimmy suddenly swerved, so violently that the motorbike tipped sideways and landed on its side. I was flung off and it was pure luck that I was thrown out of the path of the huge machine. I rolled over and over and then lay still. I felt as if I had been punched very hard all over.

'Hey you!'

I heard the shout as the combine engine suddenly stopped and, looking up, saw Jimmy running away across the stubble. I got to my feet and started after him, but I was so queasy that I didn't get very far.

'Oh no you don't!' shouted the driver as he came after me.

I glanced round, and as I did so, I tripped and fell. I didn't try to get up and was suddenly very sick. I lay with my face on the hot stubble and felt all the strength drain out of me. I couldn't have run away if I'd tried; I couldn't even get up on my own. The driver hauled me to my feet.

'What the fucking hell do you think you were doing, eh? You stupid little bugger! You could have been killed. Them wheels don't take prisoners!'

He was a well-built man with a very sunburnt forehead and he was wearing a cotton face-mask. He dragged me roughly over to the combine harvester and propped me up against the side of it and wrenched the face-mask down.

'I've a good mind to give you a fucking hiding right here, but I tell you, that'll be nothing to what your dad does to you when I tells him. Hey, son, are you all right?' I had begun to crumple downwards. I felt so ill that all I wanted to do was to lie on the ground. He knelt beside me.

'Just you stay here, right? I'll radio for some help. You don't look too well to me. Now don't you go and run off when my back's turned, do you hear?'

At that moment I couldn't have run if I was about to be eaten by a lion, which fate I felt preferable to my present condition. I moaned. I was vaguely aware of him climbing back into the combine's cab. I lay with my eyes closed and even then the world was turning in circles at an alarming rate.

It was as I was being carried on a stretcher across the field some time later that I heard the sirens, but I wasn't at all interested. I felt so ill that if the world had been ending I would have just lain there with my eyes closed hoping it would end soon so the turning would stop.

'That's the fire brigade!' said someone next to my head.

'Yeah, looks like the stubble's on fire. See the smoke? Tinder dry it must be. We haven't had rain for weeks. It only takes some fool throwing away a lighted fag, or some bloody kids lighting a fire.'

I didn't want to hear any more. I just wanted the voices to stop. My head was hurting.

*

Much later I was sitting with a basin on my lap, into which I had been sick several times, in a curtained cubicle at the hospital, next to a worried-looking mother. Ronnie hovered behind her, cap in hand and looking uncomfortable. A policeman pushed his way through the curtains.

'Right then,' he began, taking out a notebook. 'I take it you're Stephen Stringer?'

I nodded.

'I'm PC Travister, and my colleague, PC Davies, is interviewing a…' he consulted his notebook, '…a Mr Ryan Forbes, who I believe was a witness to an incident involving a motorbike and two lads. What's all this about, son? I hear you've had an argument with a combine harvester. Not very sensible, you're bound to come off second best.'

'What did you say?' gasped Mum.

'It's all right, Mum, it wasn't very serious…' I began.

'Not very serious! When I've gone on and on at you to be careful on your bike with these roads nowadays. You know what happened to Duncan! Sorry Ronnie, but I can't help saying it. What were you thinking of? Where were you? How did it happen?' Her voice cracked.

'Exactly, madam. That's what we all want to know,' said the policeman. 'Especially as this young man was apprehended by the said Mr Ryan Forbes in a field trying to run away from the crashed motorbike and, what is more…'

I heard a gasp from Mum. 'Motorbike?'

'…what is more,' he continued, 'the fire service is at this moment damping down a stubble fire in the said field. According to the fire officer, upon investigation it appears that the said fire was caused by the spread of a small cooking fire which had been started outside some kind of shelter constructed out of pallets taken from the pallet store in the corner of the said field. Now lad, does this sound familiar to you?'

I looked up at him. He had a knowing look in his eyes. I turned my head, which still hurt, and looked at Mum. She looked horrified. I looked over at Ronnie.

'Bloody hell, Stevie!' he said.

Later, having been discharged from the hospital with nothing worse than a large bruise on the back of my head where it had hit the ground when we crashed, I attended the police station in Wisbech with my mum and Ronnie.

I was told I was lucky not to be badly injured, or even dead, but at the time it didn't feel like luck, because I had to answer a lot of questions which I would rather my mother had not heard. She sat stony-faced next to me throughout the ordeal. Ronnie sat on the other side of me and PC Travister sat behind a table. I felt surrounded by adults.

'So you were at your "den" with your friend, you say? Can we have his name please?'

I paused a moment, not because I didn't want to tell on Jimmy as I was far beyond such niceties by then and I still had a terrible headache, but because I didn't want Mum to hear who it was.

'Stephen!' she said, in a warning voice, when I didn't answer.

'Jimmy Buckland,' I said.

The policeman looked sharply at me.

'Buckland, you say? Do you have an address for this Jimmy Buckland?'

'I don't know exactly,' I said miserably, 'but he lives at the traveller site on the Wisbech bypass.'

I heard Mum's in-drawn breath.

'Fucking hell, Stevie!' whispered Ronnie.

I couldn't look at him.

'And this motorbike you were both riding, where did that come from?'

'It's Jimmy's. We often ride it around the site and on the fields and the orchards and that.' I ended lamely.

'Ah!' muttered Ronnie.

'So this is where you've been disappearing to every day,' said Mum, 'when you've been telling me you're with that nice girl Margaret or out bird-watching.' Her voice began to rise. 'You've been lying to me, Stephen, when I trusted you. And associating with those dirty didicoys. How could you? Well, don't think you're going to be gadding about the countryside after this!'

'Mrs Stringer, please,' said PC Travister. 'I understand how you feel. I'll let you deal with him later. But now, if you don't mind, there's something more serious I need to ask him.' He turned to me. 'Now, Stephen, I want you to tell me the truth. You're in enough trouble already and look at the worry you're causing your mother? So, if I were you, lad, I'd forget about any tall stories about that there motorbike, and just tell me as it is, do you understand?'

'Yes, sir.'

'It was Jimmy's motorbike, you say?'

'Yes, sir, that's what he told me.'

'This lad's not a liar, officer,' said Ronnie.

'No, I don't think he is, sir. In fact, I think he's basically a good lad, but he's taken up with the wrong company. Now, Stephen, what if I were to tell you that a motocross bike answering the description of the one you over-turned in that field, which is now in our pound, has exactly the same chassis number as one which was stolen from… er…' he consulted his notes again, 'the yard of a farm near Swaffham at the end of May? What would you say to that, eh?'

I stared at him, open-mouthed.

'What did you say?' croaked Mum, and she covered her face with her hands.

'Oh, bloody hell!' said Ronnie.

No-one moved for a moment. I went on staring at him, speechless.

Then the police officer broke the spell.

'Ah, I have my answer, don't I lad? It's not as bad as you're thinking, Mrs Stringer. It's obvious to me that your lad had nothing to do with that, although I'm pretty certain his friend young Jimmy Buckland and his uncle Jacob know a thing or two about it. Now I tell you what I'm going to do. I reckon your lad is guilty of nothing more serious than choosing the wrong friends, which is not a hanging offence. And he's had a nasty fright too. I'm not even going to issue him with a caution, and I am going to release him into your custody, which I am sure will be pretty uncomfortable for him, which is as it should be. You've given your mother a nasty fright, Stephen, and you should be ashamed of yourself. And I'm taking a risk with not taking this further, so don't let me down, son, eh? Do you understand?'

I didn't answer for a moment. Everything was moving too fast for me.

'Stephen!' said Mum, warning again.

'Yes, sir. Thank you, sir.'

I was grounded for the rest of the holiday, not even allowed to visit Ronnie in his shed, and no matter how many times I told Mum how sorry I was it didn't shift the pained look on her face or encourage her to hold any conversation with me except in monosyllables.

An immediate problem was the retrieval of my bike, which was still at the traveller site. The following evening Ronnie drove me to the traveller site, with Mum sitting next to me like a prison warder.

'I'm not going in there, Myra. Sorry, but I don't want no trouble with that Jake Buckland,' said Ronnie, when we got there.

'No, Ronnie, I don't expect you to. Stephen got himself into this mess, and Stephen can get himself out of it. Now, Stephen, you get out and go and ask – politely mind – if you can fetch your bike. And while you're there you can tell that Jimmy Buckland that you're not allowed to play with him anymore.'

I did as I was told. It was quiet on the site. I walked over to the van. It felt as if there weren't as many people around and there were no children except Abe, who was sitting on the van steps eating a chocolate bar, with chocolate all over his face.

'Hi, Abe,' I said.

He just stared at me and said nothing. My bike was no longer leaning up against the end wall where I had left it. I knocked on the van door. Esme opened it.

'Hallo Steve, love,' she said. 'I'm afraid Jim's not here at the moment. He's gone away for a few days with Jake. They're visiting family up north.'

'They've scarpered,' said Abe, through a mouthful of chocolate.

'Abe!' said Esme sharply. 'Just go inside for a minute!'

'Oh, that's all right,' I said, relieved not to have to face Jimmy. 'I've just come for my bike. I left it here yesterday.'

'Oh, did you? I haven't seen it.' She looked around. 'Where did you leave it?'

'Up against the van.'

'Oh dear. Now where can it be?' She looked vaguely around the site. At that moment a tall man with a lot of ginger curly hair came around the corner of the next-door van.

'Jonny!' she called. 'Have you seen Steve's bike? He said he left it up against the van yesterday?'

The man stopped.

'Was it a Raleigh racer, blue paint?' he asked.

'Yes,' I said. 'I wasn't able to fetch it yesterday…' I began.

'You're lucky,' he said. 'It's in the back of the pick-up and we're just loading up. I thought it was one Jake had picked up somewhere. You come along with me, lad.'

Sure enough, my bike was in the back of a pick-up at the other end of the site. Jonny hoisted it out.

'Thank you very much,' I said, meaning it. What would Mum have said if I had lost my bike too?

It was much later that evening that I remembered the binoculars that I thought I had left hanging from the handlebars; but at that stage I didn't dare mention them.

I was glad to get back to school for the autumn term. Being confined to the house during that very hot final week of the summer holidays had been miserable and it wasn't only the temperature that was stifling. I tiptoed through each day, wondering if my mum was ever going to smile at me again.

11.30 a.m. Lesson 4

Chapter Fourteen

The last lesson of the morning on that day was drama, which I had always hated, and which was even worse now that I had to spend it working with Margaret. I remember being very grumpy in that particular lesson and telling her I had a headache and didn't want to make up a radio broadcast on stranded seal pups because it was 'a naff idea!' How sad to think it was my last conversation with her and my last ever lesson with Ms McCarthy.

My regular Sunday photography expeditions with Ms McCarthy had resumed in the Autumn Term. My mother thought that these were official school trips and so I would be properly supervised and unable to associate with boys she considered 'undesirable'. I didn't disillusion her, and she had no idea about the Harley-Davidson or the visits to the flat in Wisbech.

One Sunday afternoon in late September, as we were packing up the equipment after a trip, Ms McCarthy told me about the exhibition.

'I've used one or two of your photos, Steve, in an exhibition I've been setting up in Kings Lynn. Would you like to see them?'

'Really? What, in a real art gallery?'

She laughed. 'Well, not exactly, it's just an exhibition some friends and I have put together. It's at the museum. We're starting a branch of S.A.B.'

'What's that?'

'*Save all Birds*. It's an organisation that campaigns to protect wild birds. I could take you into Lynn after school on Thursday if your mum wouldn't mind.'

'Oh, yes please.'

I was thrilled at the prospect of seeing my own photos on display.

'Mum! Guess what?' I burst out when I got home that afternoon. 'Ms McCarthy has said she'll take me to see my photos that are in an exhibition at the museum in Kings Lynn on Thursday, she'll take me after school, it's all right it won't be late.'

'Exhibition? What sort of exhibition?' Mum sounded suspicious as she carefully ironed the collar of one of my school shirts.

I was impatient, as usual, with my mother's slow solicitude.

'A photo exhibition, Mum, I've just told you. It's about wild birds and things.'

'And where is it being held, this exhibition?'

'At the museum, Mum, I've just told you. Can I go?'

'Mm, we'll see,' which usually meant, I knew, yes.

Ronnie also happened to be in the kitchen. He was on a step ladder replacing the tube in the kitchen light, which had blown the previous evening. When Mum left the kitchen to take the ironed clothes upstairs, he said: 'I'd be careful about getting too chummy with that Miss McCarthy, Stevie, if I were you.'

I looked up at him. 'Why?'

'Just something about her, Stevie. She's not *one of us*.'

'What do you mean, "not one of us"? She's really nice.' I felt irritated by his attitude and rather defensive.

'You'll see,' he said. 'Just be careful. Keep your distance, is my advice. Hand me that tube will you.'

Afterwards I puzzled over this conversation. What did Ronnie mean? No, Ms McCarthy was not at all like Ronnie or Mum or even like any of the other teachers. She had bright red dyed hair, which I knew Mum would have disapproved of, and she rode a motorbike, which would have appalled Mum (had she known) and she didn't have a telly, which would have just bemused everyone. Yes, she was different from us in some ways but I didn't understand why that meant I should avoid her. Eventually, I remember, I concluded that Ronnie was jealous because I had chosen to go out with Ms McCarthy rather than go fishing with him and I realised that he had stopped going fishing on Sundays. It made me feel a bit smug to think he cared that much.

I think he must have said something to my mum, because next day she said: 'About this exhibition, with your photos…'

'Yes, Mum. I can go, can't I?'

She was cutting my sandwiches and took her time over the reply.

'It's like this, Stephen. I think I would like to see these photos of yours. It's not every day that your son has something on display in a museum. So what I think we'll do is…'

She moved to the drawer under the sink and looked inside for polythene sandwich bags. I waited, hoping.

'…we'll go together, you and me, this Saturday. Ronnie says he'll take us.'

'Oh Mum!' I gave her a hug. 'That would be great!' I loved the idea of showing off my photos to my mother.

She looked pleased.

'Now, you need to say to that Miss McCourtney…'

'Ms McCarthy, Mum.'

'...yes, well you tell her – politely, mind – you tell her that you're going to the display with your mum on Saturday and therefore her kind offer of a lift will not be necessary, thank you very much.'

We all went together, the following Saturday, Mum and Beryl squeezed into the passenger seat of Ronnie's van, and me in the back with the fishing gear and some sacks of mixed corn. It was quite an occasion, as we went to MacDonald's first, ''Cos we're all very proud of you, Stephen, so we thought it'd be a treat for you, and we've got to eat dinner somewhere, so it might as well be here,' said Mum. It *was* a treat for me, as the only time I had ever been to MacDonald's was when we went to visit Auntie Deirdre and Uncle Richard in Milton Keynes.

Everyone else seemed to enjoy the meal too. Beryl asked quite loudly, 'Where are the knives and forks?' but Mum said it was like having a picnic.

'Use your fingers, love,' said Ronnie. 'When in Rome do as the Romans do.' He stuffed about six fries into his mouth and grinned.

The S.A.B. display was in a corner on the first floor of the museum. It was set out on a long trestle table, with a green display board balanced on the back of the table. In the middle was a large poster which read 'Do you care about birds?' with the 'you' in big red italics, and underneath a picture of a man in a deerstalker hat aiming a shot gun at a flying pheasant. There were piles of leaflets on the table, with the poster picture on the front, and next to them an exercise book and a pencil attached to it by string. 'If you would like to join S.A.B., please give your details below' was written at the top of the page, and four people had written their names and addresses.

But I was mostly interested in the photos. There were four photos, which had been enlarged to 18 x10 size. Two of them were mine, one of waders low over mudflats and another close-up of a black-headed gull. I hadn't felt as proud of myself since my picture of the three kings had been posted on the classroom wall when I was six.

'Well, which ones are yours, then?' asked Mum.

I pointed them out.

'Mm,' she said. 'I see.' I could tell that she was pleased.

'Oh Stevie,' said Beryl. 'You are a clever boy! Isn't he Ronnie?'

I looked expectantly at Ronnie. What would he say? I wondered. He had picked up a leaflet and was reading it, a slight frown on his face. He looked up.

'What?'

'I said Stevie's very clever. His photos are lovely, aren't they?' said Beryl.

'Oh, the photos? Yes, very good, boy. They're very good.' But he didn't look as I had expected him to look; he looked worried.

Just then Ms McCarthy came up the stairs with a man with long hair tied in a pony tail who was wearing a fringed suede jacket. They were carrying plastic cups of tea.

'Steve! You've come!' She hurried towards us. 'And this must be your mum. How do you do, Mrs Stringer.' She held out her hand. 'I'm Sidney McCarthy, Steve's teacher. You've got a very talented son here!'

Mum shook her hand and smiled awkwardly. I blushed even more.

Ms McCarthy turned her attention to Ronnie and Beryl. 'Hallo, Mr Rawlinson, nice to see you without your broom for once.'

I felt my mum stiffen; I think she thought that was rude. Ronnie just grunted, like he did sometimes when he didn't know what to say.

'And is this Mrs Rawlinson? How do you do? What's it like being married to the fastest litter picker in the West, eh?'

Beryl didn't understand what she was talking about and looked overwhelmed.

'This is Jed. He runs S.A.B. with me.'

'Hi,' said Jed.

'Are you interested in joining us?' asked Ms McCarthy. 'No membership fees, it's completely free. We are a voluntary organisation and just give our time when we can.'

'Not at the moment thank you,' said Mum, still a bit stiff.

'What about you, Mr Rawlinson?'

Ronnie didn't answer. He was still reading the leaflet. He was a slow reader.

Beryl nudged him in the ribs, but when he didn't say anything, she said, 'I don't think I will today thank you. I'm already in the WI and do the church flowers every other week.'

'I'll take some leaflets,' said Ronnie suddenly.

'Of course, take as many as you want.' She gave him a handful. 'I've already handed them out in the staffroom but perhaps you have some friends.'

There was a silence. It was as if no-one knew what to say next.

'Well, we'd better be getting back,' said Mum. 'Thank you, Miss… er…'

'Call me Sidney, please.'

'Thank you for allowing Stephen to use your camera and taking him on these trips. We're very grateful.'

'It's a pleasure, Mrs Stringer. Hope to do it again soon, eh, Steve?'

'Oh yes, please, Ms McCarthy,' I said.

'Well, that's as maybe,' said Mum.

I remember feeling a bit worried at that; it usually meant no.

As we left I saw Ronnie pick up the rest of the leaflets from the table.

'What do you want all those leaflets for, Ronnie?' I asked, when we were outside the museum.

'That's what I want them for, boy,' he said, throwing them all into the litter bin outside a newsagent's shop we were passing.

'Oh Ronnie, what a waste,' said Beryl. 'Someone else might have been glad of one of them leaflets, even if you didn't want them.'

'They're better off where they are,' said Ronnie. 'We put rubbish in the rubbish bin, don't we?'

*

Ronnie continued to worry about the S.A.B and Ms McCarthy. A few days later I found him in his shed. He had Felicity, one of the ferrets, on his lap and was stroking her and just staring into the distance. I got Myrtle out of the hutch and she ran up my arm and sat on my shoulder. I laughed and wagged one finger at her: 'Don't you dare nibble my ear, miss!'

Ronnie took no notice, which was unusual; we often played together with the ferrets. He seemed preoccupied.

'Did you have that drama today, boy?' he asked.

'Yes, why?'

'With that Miss McCarthy, her with the motorbike?'

'Yes, and it's Ms not Miss.'

'Whatever. I can't get my tongue round that "ms-ing"; sounds like someone's false teeth have slipped.'

He said nothing more for a bit.

'And what do you do in those drama lessons, eh?'

It was obvious something was niggling him.

'I dunno. We do drama, plays and things.'

'But what exactly are the plays about, Stevie? What does she tell you?'

'I dunno. We make them up. She gives us subjects and we sort of make them up. Why?'

'But what sort of subjects does she give you?'

'I can't remember. Oh yes, yesterday we had to do something about family rows. Why do you want to know? If you're so interested why don't you come and listen?'

I said it for a joke, but Ronnie wasn't in a jokey mood.

'I might just do that, Stevie. I might just do that.' He suddenly stood up. 'Here, put her back for me.' He handed me Felicity.

Ronnie did begin to visit my lessons with Ms McCarthy, making up excuses that to me sounded lame. As the weeks passed it felt more and more like spying.

'Just need to check the lights,' he would announce, as he set up a ladder and climbed up to fiddle with the strip lighting. Or, 'Just need to find out if you've got the right number of chairs, Miss McCarthy,' and he would hover for a few minutes, making a big show of counting chairs.

As the weeks passed he became more and more obsessed with Ms McCarthy, always asking me whether she had talked to me, what did she talk about on those 'fucking photography trips', had I been in the art room store cupboard (which she had by then converted into a dark room) and 'what was the fucking point of a dark room when Boots can develop 'em?' He always led up to had she given me any more stuff about 'that fucking S.A.D. or

S.A.B. or whatever the fuck it is.'

I began to think that he was jealous because I liked her instead of him. This made me cross. Why shouldn't I like her? Why should I only be friends with people Ronnie approved of? He wasn't even my real dad, I argued to myself. (God forgive me, what better dad could I have had?) But I was thirteen, no longer a child, I thought, and needed to flex my independence muscles.

I hid my developing friendship with Ms McCarthy from him, and from my mother too, from whom it was essential, of course, to hide the motorbike, but who I felt would also somehow disapprove of Ms McCarthy, although I couldn't put my finger on exactly why. I certainly didn't tell them about the S.A.B. meeting I attended one Saturday in Wisbech when I was supposed to be changing my library books.

I wish I hadn't gone to that S.A.B. meeting.

Ms McCarthy had told me about it at the end of an art lesson. These little tête-à-têtes at the end of lessons were becoming a problem for me because, although I was privately proud of the attention she was giving me, I didn't want to appear to be a 'teacher's pet'. Therefore, on this occasion, rather than lingering behind when the rest of the class had left, as I usually did, I began to hurry away. But it didn't work.

'Stephen! Just a minute!' she called as I was half-way out of the door.

Oh no, I thought.

I turned. Unfortunately, Dwayne was behind me.

'Sydney!' he said. 'Miss wants you!'

Ms McCarthy had turned away and was carrying something into the cupboard.

'Don't keep her waiting, she probably wants to give you a blow job,' he said.

I began to walk towards the cupboard, but he held out his arms to prevent me passing him.

'Naughty! Naughty! Fancy wanting to have sex with a teacher in her cupboard!'

I turned away from him, but Keydon Bartley was behind me, and, catching on, he was holding out his arms too. They advanced on me. I tried to dodge away but wasn't fast enough – I never was – and Dwayne caught my arm and swung me round so that he was holding me with my back up against his chest and his arm round my neck. He was very strong and although I struggled, I was held firmly. He put his mouth to my ear and I could feel his hot breath.

'Do you know what we do to teachers' pets, Sydney?' he whispered hoarsely, right into my ear. It almost hurt.

Then, as Ms McCarthy emerged from the cupboard, he released me quick as lightning.

'Just fetched Stringer for you, Miss, I don't think he heard you. Here he is.'

'Thank you, Dwayne,' said Ms McCarthy, looking suspicious.

When Dwayne and Keydon had gone, Ms McCarthy said, 'Are you all right, Steve? I thought I saw Dwayne assaulting you. You would tell me if you were being bullied, wouldn't you?'

'It's nothing, Ms McCarthy, we were just messing about,' I said. She might have treated me like a friend, but I couldn't trust her with that kind of truth. Teachers just didn't understand about bullying.

'Well, I wondered if you would like to come to our next meeting of the S.A.B. It's on Saturday afternoon at 2.30. I thought It might interest you because we've got Jason Duffy, the wildlife photographer, coming to show us some of his work. We meet in the back room of the White Bull, it's a pub in Wisbech market place. I could pick you up.'

I thought quickly. In a way I didn't want to go, as I somehow felt Ronnie wouldn't like it. I remembered how he had thrown away the S.A.B. leaflets. On the other hand, it was very tempting; I would like to see the work of a professional photographer and I also felt, as usual, proud that Ms McCarthy should invite me. Then I thought of a way to go without anyone at home knowing.

'I'm getting the bus into Wisbech on Saturday afternoon anyway, to change my library books. I could come afterwards, if I have enough time.'

'OK,' she said. 'I'll see you there.'

'Yeah,' I said, 'I'll try to come,' which, I felt, left me some wriggle-room in case Mum decided she wanted to take me shopping on Saturday for new school shoes. I turned to leave.

'Oh, I've just remembered,' she said. 'As you're under eighteen, you'd better come in by the side door of the pub, the one that opens into the alley by W.H. Smith, do you know where I mean?'

I didn't, but I said I did. I knew where W.H Smith was.

I had never been in any of the pubs in Wisbech; none of them were the kind of pub that did family lunches and my mum would never have had lunch in a pub anyway. I knew there were a lot of them.

'More pubs per head of population than anywhere else in England, according to my old dad,' Ronnie had told me.

I saw a lot of their patrons on my Saturday trips to the library. Saturday was market day, when they served all day, and by late afternoon there would be groups of men with glass tankards spilling out of pub doors or spread-eagled snoring on the benches in the public gardens. There would be a thick smell of smoke and beer as I wound my way through the market stalls and I would sometimes be accompanied home on the five o'clock bus by a swaying, muttering drunkard who had to be reminded by the bus driver where to get off.

The White Bull was right in the middle of the town centre and, sure enough, there was an alley between it and W. H. Smith. I found a heavy door with a leaded window at the top of it and I turned the big brass handle. It led into a dark corridor which was very quiet. I stood for a moment, blinded by the darkness after the bright street, and then a door on my left opened and a fat woman carrying dirty plates pushed through, bringing with her a surge of noise and a smell of food. She propped the door open with her enormous backside and called back, 'Was that two sausage 'n mash, you said?'

Then she saw me. She let the door swing shut.

'Well, hello there, laddy. What can we do for you?' She had a red face and a wide smile.

'I'm looking for the S.A.B. meeting,' I ventured.

'And what's that when it's at home?'

'Save all Birds. It's an organisation. They've got a meeting here, I think.'

'Just a minute, darling,' and she swung her hips at the door again.

'Is there some meeting here today, Bert?' she screeched.

A man's voice answered. 'Back room, Sadie! It's three sausage 'n mash and a ploughman's.'

'Through there, darling, past the ladies, and up the stairs. You'll find it,' she said and she bustled away to the kitchen.

When I arrived in the upstairs back room, there were lots of seats set out for an audience although there were only a few people there. Ms McCarthy was helping to erect a screen at one end of the room and didn't see me, but Jed was by the door offering the exercise book and pencil and said 'Hi!' I said 'Hi' too, signed my name, and went to sit at the back on the end of a row.

An elderly lady in check trousers and a green quilted body-warmer was sitting in the row in front of me. She turned and peered at me over half-glasses, then returned to her perusal of one of the S.A.B. leaflets. A woman came in carrying a supermarket carrier bag full of shopping and put it under her seat. There were one or two other Jed-like men wearing jeans, and one had a beard.

Altogether about twenty people were at the meeting, and Jason Duffy was very good. His photos were amazing, and he was good at explaining where he'd been and how he'd got the shot and I was impressed with his knowledge of birds.

After his talk, Ms McCarthy, addressed the audience.

'On behalf of everyone here, Jason, I'd like to thank you very much for that fascinating talk. Shall we show our appreciation in the usual way?' We all clapped.

While we were doing that Ms McCarthy took a photo of us – I didn't realise until I felt the flash – and then she took one of Jason in front of one of his photos on the screen. Then she addressed everyone, a bit like a school assembly.

'Now, I'd also like to thank you all for coming this afternoon. I know we all could have been watching Man U thrash Barcelona,' (there was a ripple of laughter), 'but you chose to join us instead. For those of you who are new to us, we are an organisation devoted to the protection of our wild birds. We hope that you will want to become full members; details are in the leaflets by the door.'

On cue, Jed held up some leaflets and everyone looked at him.

'But before we all go can I interest you in our first direct action campaign. We all know that the birds we love face many threats in this modern world. Their habitat is disappearing, and they are affected by the chemicals we use in modern agriculture. But in addition, some are still being cruelly and wantonly killed for sport, even though we are approaching the twenty-first century. S.A.B. wants to make a stand about that, so if you are interested in standing with us, please stay behind for a few minutes at the end of this meeting, when we will be planning our anti-shooting campaign.'

I froze. Anti-shooting? What was all this about? I wasn't against shooting, I was for shooting, if I ever thought about it, which I didn't because I had grown up with shooting. I had a shotgun, I shot pigeons with Ronnie, I went wildfowling with Ronnie, I was a junior member of the local wild-fowling club and took part in their clay-shooting competition for under-eighteens, which I had won last year. I was also one of the beaters on the club's game syndicate and I helped Ronnie rear the pheasants. Why was Ms McCarthy talking about anti-shooting? She hadn't ever said anything about this to me, even when I had talked to her about pheasant shooting.

Suddenly I felt a deep unease, as I remembered a conversation on a recent photography expedition. I had been showing off, telling her about how to rear young pheasants, and she said, 'How do you know all that, Steve?' So I told her about the rearing pens Ronnie had constructed next to the copse by Big Field, and how we would keep the feeders and drinkers topped up through the summer and how in September we would put the birds in crates and drive around the syndicate's fields and release them ready for the start of the shooting season.

'And when is that?' she had asked.

So I told her. God forgive me, I even told her when our next shoot was.

Now I remembered Ronnie's comment, 'She's not one of us,' and I understood what he had meant. I shouldn't be here, I thought. I got up quickly and made for the door. Unfortunately, Ms McCarthy saw me.

'Steve! Are you going already?'

'I'm sorry, Ms McCarthy, but I don't want to miss my bus,' I called back, and I escaped.

I almost ran back to the bus station, wanting to put as much distance as possible between myself and S.A.B. and when the bus driver asked me, 'Had a nice afternoon, sonny?' I felt guilty, as if he might know about my betrayal.

When I got home, Ronnie was at the kitchen table eating doughnuts.

'Here he is mother! Stevie, you're just in time, I was about to eat the last one!'

He grinned at me, jam around his mouth, and in that instant I felt a sharp pang of love so intense that it made me gasp. Oh Ronnie, I said (in my head), I'm sorry!

'You look peaky,' Mum commented. She always knew if something was wrong, even if she didn't know what it was. 'Are you sickening for something? Mrs Shenfield's eldest's got chicken pox, and you've never had that.'

'I've got a bit of a headache.'

'Early night for you, young man,' she said. 'Do you want the last doughnut?'

'No thanks. I'm not hungry. You can have it Ronnie.'

At that moment I would have given Ronnie anything in the world. Instead, I felt I had given him perfidy.

The next day we were most of the way through the art lesson and I was beginning to hope that perhaps Ronnie wouldn't interrupt the lesson that day, when he opened the door and stuck his head in.

'Stephen Stringer needed in the office!' he announced.

I went bright red as everyone looked at me. My heart began to beat fast. What had happened? Why was Ronnie bringing the message? Had something happened to Mum?

'What have you been up to, you naughty boy?' said Josie, and everyone sniggered.

'There's no need for that, Josie,' said Ms McCarthy. 'You'd better go and see what it's about, Stephen.'

As soon as we were outside the door I turned on Ronnie, who was looking very upset.

'What is it? What's happened? Is it Mum?'

'Your mum? No, it's nothing to do with your mum. It's about you, and what I've just found out.' He glanced towards the classroom windows. 'Come with me a minute, Stephen.' He ushered me down the mobile steps and around the back where the skip was parked. I was really worried; he never called me 'Stephen'.

'What's all this about?' he demanded, waving a newspaper in front of me.

'What's all what about, Ronnie?'

'This here photograph in the local paper, that's what. What do you think your mother's going to say when she knows who you've been associating with?'

He thrust the paper at me. He had drawn a big ring in felt tip round a photo half way down a page. My heart missed a beat. It was the photo taken at the S.A.B. meeting the previous Saturday, and there was my face in the back row. Ms McCarthy must have sent it to the local paper to get publicity.

'There I was, just having my normal cuppa and catching up on the news, when I sees this. Our Stevie in a picture with them!' He pronounced the word as if he was spitting at them. 'And I warned you! You've got to keep away from that bloody woman, that one in there, Stevie!'

'Ms McCarthy? But why, Ronnie? What are you talking about?'

'Because she's evil, that's why. She's an anti. They're all evil. They want to destroy our way of life, Stevie, and you must keep away from them. I mean it boy!'

He was red in the face and trembling all over; he looked as if he was about to burst into tears. It was most un-Ronnie-like. I had never seen him in such a state.

'Ronnie, don't be daft.'

'I mean it, Stevie!' He grabbed me in a tight hug. I was excruciatingly embarrassed. When I was a little kid, Ronnie and I often hugged each other, of course, but that hadn't happened for some years. I usually gave him and Beryl a brief hug when they gave me a Christmas present, but that was just politeness. And to do it at school, where other pupils might see. It made me angry with him. What was he doing behaving so strangely, being so vulnerable? This wasn't what I expected from the man I had always admired. I pushed him away.

'I must get back to the lesson. It's embarrassing to be called out like that. We'll talk later, right?' I said, my words sounding strangely adult and detached, even to myself, and I moved back towards the mobile classroom.

'Just be careful, Stevie! She's got her mind set on ruining us.'

I told myself I didn't have the first idea what he was talking about. I was furious with him, but the incident worried me badly, not just because I had been found out in a lie but because I *did* know what he was talking about, and I felt very guilty again about the meeting I had attended and the book I had signed my name in.

In the days that followed Ronnie criticised Ms McCarthy whenever he talked to me although he didn't mention S.A.B.

'She shouldn't be allowed to bring that motorbike to school, I say, it's not appropriate for a lady teacher. Gives the lads ideas seeing her in them leathers she wears.'

'I dunno what you see in them drama lessons, Stevie, all that dancing around pretending you're a tree. I went in there yesterday to see to the radiator that's leaking, and everyone was lying on the floor with their eyes shut listening to some weird art-farty music. They all looked asleep except for two boys who were kicking each other. Waste of time I say. Kids go to school to learn things not lie around going to sleep.'

'That Miss McCarthy's got me going in two nights a week to lock up after some bloody rehearsal. And you should see the mess that's left behind, crisp packets and everything all over the back of the stage.'

'There was clay trodden into the art room floor again today. That bloody art teacher needs to get the bloody kids to clear up properly. Why does she have to get them to use clay anyway? Haven't they got pencils? When I was at school art was drawing things.'

I had been dreading the next lesson with Ms McCarthy. I was sure she would ask me about the meeting or, heaven forbid, ask me to join the anti-shooting campaign. But I had my excuse ready;

I would invent a shopping expedition with my mum as I really did need new school shoes. But Ms McCarthy was not in school for our next lesson, so we had extra Maths with Mr Godley instead. But I couldn't dismiss the most serious worry of all. Why had I told her about the syndicate shoot? Had she remembered? What was 'direct action'?

I was to know the answer the next Saturday.

Chapter Fifteen

It was October, and the beginning of the game shooting season. The wildfowling club ran a small pheasant-shooting syndicate for members, leasing the shooting rights on farm land near the Marsh from Mr Westley-Lewis, the biggest farmer in the area. It was an amateur affair, but great fun. Ronnie was its part-time gamekeeper, and I was his assistant. We reared a few dozen pheasants each year to add to those that sneaked over from the inland part of the farm, where Mr Westley-Lewis held regular shoots for what Ronnie called 'the toffs'.

Ronnie was in charge of organising our shooting days and seemed to thoroughly enjoy this authority, running about with his whistle and shouting things to us beaters like, 'Keep the line bloody straight in the middle there – you'll let 'em through!' and, 'Keep your spacing, damn you, I could drive a bus through that gap!' while we trudged across the vast muddy fields driving the birds before us towards the guns who were lined up along a hedge in the far distance.

On the Saturday of the first shoot Ronnie and I set off early.

'I've put your little old 20 bore in as well, Stevie. We're a bit short of guns today, and you can walk a couple of drives and see to the ones that fly back, O.K?'

Normally I would have been thrilled. Ronnie kept my specially-adapted 20 bore shotgun in his gun cabinet with his own guns and

I was allowed to use it only rarely and under his direct supervision. Being a walking gun on the shoot for the first time showed he trusted me, which made me feel sick because I knew how I had let him down.

'You don't look very pleased. You've been on at me long enough about it,' he said when I didn't reply.

'Oh, sorry, Ronnie. Of course I'm pleased. Thanks!' I tried to look pleased.

In spite of my apprehension, the morning went well. We didn't see a lot of birds on the first few drives, but the few there were flew in the right direction, helped by us beaters swishing our sticks against the vegetation and shouting at them. There was a lot of shooting, but not many birds fell from the air, which was usual for our syndicate.

'Waste of bloody time sending 'em over if the guns miss 'em every time,' moaned Ronnie, as usual.

There was a lot of shouting and whistling at dogs, most of whom took no notice of their masters' directions but still managed to retrieve the birds that were shot. I shot one cock bird that tried to fly out sideways over a dyke, and Gyp went after it, brought it back sopping wet and shook himself all over me. Normally I would have been really chuffed to have shot my first pheasant at a shoot, but I was still anxious. I had a premonition that something was going to go wrong. And I was right.

They arrived during our lunch break. You can see a vehicle miles away in that landscape and any strange car is conspicuous. We had just settled down with our sandwiches in the yard at the top of Big South, sitting on last year's dusty straw bales under the Dutch barn or perched on the edges of various bits of dilapidated farm machinery, when Ronnie, who always noticed things first, said, 'Now who's that bugger?'

A white Bedford van with something painted on its side was making its way along the concrete road from King John Bank and, as we watched, it stopped at the farm gate half a mile away. This had a padlock on it and a sign that said 'Private'; only farm workers and people like Ronnie had a key. This, Ronnie had told me, was to ensure that members of the public used only the official marsh entrances and didn't spend their time driving along the concrete farm roads trying to find the beach.

'They think 'cos it's a coastline on the map there must be sand and donkeys and deckchairs and whatever, the hignorant buggers!'

Two men got out of the minibus and seemed to be studying the gate.

'Private! This means you,' muttered Ronnie.

But the men turned and went to the back of the van, opened the door and took out something, although it was too far away to see exactly what it was. They began to do something to the gate. Ronnie's eyes were sharp.

'What the fuck? They're bolt-cutters. The buggers are cutting the padlock!'

Sure enough, after a few minutes the gate swung open, the men got back in the van and it drove through the gate and began to make its way towards us. As it approached, the writing on the side of the minibus became clearer: 'Save all Birds!' I tried to disappear behind the straw bale.

'What the hell are that fucking crowd doing here?' said Ronnie.

I knew exactly what they were doing here. They were on their anti-shooting campaign and whatever was going to happen next was what Ms McCarthy had called 'direct action'.

What kind of action? I wondered.

The van drove onto the yard and parked about twenty yards away from us. The doors opened and six people got out and, once again, the back of the van was opened and several long poles were taken out and handed round. These turned out to be the poles for three banners which were unfurled and held up facing us. The banners read 'STOP SHOOTING FOR SPORT', 'KILLING IS NEVER IN SEASON' and 'THINK BEFORE YOU FIRE'. On the end of one banner was a figure I recognised because of the red hair that was bursting out of a brown woolly hat – Ms McCarthy! I crouched lower behind the bale.

The syndicate members looked a bit lost. This was not usually what happened in the lunch break. Someone laughed nervously. Someone else grunted and spat ostentatiously. One of the dogs, who had been lying around waiting for the next instalment of fun, began to bark, and was told, 'Jess! Shush!'

'What's all this about?' asked Tom Spedding, who was a special constable.

'Leave this to me!' said Ronnie.

He had been standing in front of the rest of us staring at the newcomers as they drove from the gate, arrived at the yard and set out their banners. I could not see his face, but his shoulders had tightened. He carried his open empty gun across his left arm, just as he had taught me, and now, without turning, he called, 'Stevie! Come here!' in a voice I could not ignore. I slunk from my hiding place towards him and, without looking at me, he took his hands out of his pockets and held out the gun for me to take.

'Check this properly and put it in the van!' he said, then he set off in a steadfast march towards the banners.

He stopped about ten yards from them. The banners had sagged a bit as he approached but when he stopped they were once again swung up into position. No-one spoke and no-one moved. I was mesmerised; it reminded me of those scenes in cowboy films where the hero confronts a line of baddies. Then, as if rehearsed, a cock pheasant flapped out of the blackthorn hedge, cackling, and fled into the sugar beet.

'This is private property, and you're trespassing, so you need to get back in that van and bugger off sharpish!' shouted Ronnie.

One banner sagged again, but the others held firm. I recognised the voice that shouted back.

'We reserve the right to protest against inhumane slaughter of defenceless creatures in the name of sport. You should be ashamed of yourself, Mr Rawlinson!' called Ms McCarthy.

'We have the lawful right to lawfully pursue game with a lawfully-held firearm with lawful permission of landowner in lawful season,' spluttered Ronnie, 'so you can mind your own fucking business, Miss Mc-whoever-you-are and fuck off before I shoot a fucking hole in your fucking banner!'

The protesters did not move but I heard Ms McCarthy laugh.

'You really shouldn't threaten us with a firearm, Mr Rawlinson,' she said and she began to chant something. At first I couldn't catch what it was, but then as her collaborators began to join in I realised what they were chanting.

'Save all Birds! Save all Birds! Save all Birds!'

It went on and on. Ronnie just stood there for a minute, while it washed around us.

'Save all Birds! Save all Birds!'

Then he suddenly shouted, 'Fuck you all, fucking townies!' He turned and marched back towards us.

'Save all Birds! Save all Birds!'

It grew louder and louder and the banners swayed in time.

'I'll call the coppers, Ronnie,' said Tom. 'That'll shift em!' He made for his car, which had a car phone, as his day job was some kind of regional sales distribution, of agricultural machinery, if I remember rightly.

'Don't need you to tell me how to run the shoot, Tom Spedding!' snapped Ronnie. Then he saw me, still standing where he had left me, his gun in my hands: 'What did I tell you to do, boy? Why can't you do as you're fucking told for once!'

I turned towards the van with tears smarting my eyes.

Ten minutes later, with the syndicate members still standing around unsure what to do and Ronnie pacing around the yard, and with the chanting somewhat diminished in volume but still steady in rhythm, a police siren could be heard in the distance. The chanting faltered. A police car was approaching, and as it negotiated the corner by Prentice's Cottages the chanting died away. Banners were rolled up and packed into the van, along with their handlers, and the van reversed, spun a bit on the mud then made its get-away. We stood and watched as it was intercepted just before the gate.

'That's cooked *their* bloody goose, no doubt!' said Ronnie, but he did not look pleased, just angry. We all suffered; nothing we did was right for Ronnie and it was a thoroughly miserable afternoon.

I was glad when it was over and we had distributed the pheasants, loaded the van and were on our way home. Ronnie did not say a word to me during the whole journey, and I felt too laden with guilt to say anything. Once I stole a look sideways at him; his face was set hard in a way I had never seen before.

When we arrived back home, Ronnie stopped the van outside our front gate, which was not like him; usually he drove round the back of the cottages and I helped him unload and stow the stuff in his shed and hang the birds in the porch.

'Out you get!' he said.

I opened the van door, feeling utterly miserable.

'Do you want me to clean my gun?' I asked.

'No. I'll do it.' His face was still set rigid.

I got out and went to the back door of the van to retrieve my bag and then trudged, head down, towards home. But as I unlatched the gate, I heard Ronnie's voice calling.

'Stevie!'

He was leaning across towards the passenger door and spoke through the open window. I turned.

'Come here, son.'

I walked up to the window. He was leaning back in his driver seat, staring into the distance.

'It'll be OK, boy, don't you worry. I just need some time to think things through, that's all, work out how they knew where we were,' (I suddenly felt very sick), 'and suchlike, and then I'll sort it.'

He looked at me and tried to smile, not very convincingly. I nodded at him, not knowing what to say. He turned back to stare into the space beyond the windscreen.

'It's just that there's two sorts of people in this world, Stevie. There's us, and there's them.' He paused, as if searching for words. 'There's us that live like we've always lived in these parts, and there's them that live in towns and don't know what's what. There's us that are part of what's natural, like old Charlie Fox trying to get his supper in my chicken run, and there's them that are anti-nature and like their chicken wrapped in polythene from the Co-op. There's us, that mind our own business and let live, and there's them that poke their noses into other people's lives and tell them what to do. Do you understand, boy?'

'Yes, Ronnie.' I thought I did understand, but I didn't realise how profound his words were.

He looked at me closely.

'Good! And, Stevie, what you've got to understand too is that *she,*' he pronounced the pronoun with a sharp hiss, '*she's* one of *them!*'

I opened my mouth to answer him, to confess my guilt to him, to promise undying loyalty to him, but he cut me off before I could say a word.

'Now off you go, boy, your mother'll be wondering where you are and my tea'll be baking solid in the oven, if I know my Beryl.' He put the van in gear and drove around the back. I often wonder if he knew what I had done.

I spent that evening on an emotional roller coaster. One minute I was vowing to myself to have it out with Ms McCarthy and tell her how wrong she was. Then I was wallowing in the dread of how I was going to extricate myself from what I saw as my friendship with her. Then I was following Ronnie into battle to save our shooting culture. Then a sharp pang of guilt would consume me at the thought of Ronnie finding out that I had given Ms McCarthy the date of the shoot. Then I was being disappointed that I would lose the opportunity to use Ms McCarthy's camera.

'What's up with you? Are you sickening for something?' asked Mum, when I had refused a second helping of treacle tart, which was not like me.

'No, Mum, I'm just a bit tired after the shoot.'

'Mm,' she snorted. 'Over-tired more like. Early night for you, my lad.' This was her trusted cure for anything that ailed me, physically or psychologically.

'OK, Mum.' I would be glad to be on my own in my room to sort out my tumultuous brain.

Mum stirred her cup of tea, peering sideways at me.

'I knew there was something the matter with you when you didn't come in gabbling nineteen to the dozen about how many birds had been shot and suchlike. What's the matter, Stephen, love? Didn't the shoot go well? Come on, spit it out!'

I was bursting to tell someone what was racing around in my head but could not tell my mother. I felt it was too emotionally complicated and that she would not understand. Looking back, I realise that I was probably very wrong and that behind her off-hand manner she was very perceptive, particularly with regard to me. Anyway, I fell back on the drama.

'It's just that there were some antis at the shoot, Mum, and we had to call the police.'

'Antis?'

'Yeah, with banners and that, protesting, you know.'

'Well, good job Ronnie was there. I'm sure he knew what to do. Now, off you go, there's plenty of hot water, get yourself a bath, you'll be filthy dirty from all that mud and it'll calm you down. You're just over-excited.'

I did have a bath, but it didn't calm me down and I spent the rest of that evening and the whole of Sunday worrying about my next lesson with Ms McCarthy, which was on the Monday morning. By then Ronnie had 'thought things through and got it sorted' (or so he thought), as I was to see.

Chapter Sixteen

By Monday morning I had plucked up courage and determined to tell Ms McCarthy that I didn't want to go on any more photography expeditions. At the end of the drama lesson I hung around a bit, sorting through my bag as if I was looking for something. I was soon the only person left and could approach Ms McCarthy, who was wheeling the TV stand back into the store cupboard.

'Can you hold the door, Steve.'

I held the door for her while she stowed the trolley. Then she closed the door and locked it. She turned to me, and I took a deep breath ready to blurt out the little speech I had prepared. But she stole my thunder.

'Did you enjoy your day out at the shoot, Steve?'

I am sure my mouth dropped open. I know I went very red. I was speechless for a moment. She smiled at me.

'It looked like fun. It's just such a pity that you kill the birds, isn't it? Can't you just fire blank bullets or something?'

I didn't know what to make of this. Was she being serious or was she joking? I decided to pretend I hadn't heard and I launched into my well-rehearsed spiel.

'Er, Ms McCarthy, my mum says she doesn't want me going on any more trips with you. It's the motorbike, you see. She worries a lot, 'cos my dad had an accident.'

This was, I had convinced myself, not a total lie; my mother knew nothing of the motorbike, although she would have stopped me riding on it if she had known, and she certainly did worry a lot.

Ms McCarthy leaned against the table and folded her arms. She looked at me thoughtfully but said nothing. I felt I had to fill the silence.

'She's very grateful for what you've done for me, letting me use your camera and everything, but she just thinks…' I ground to a halt. Ms McCarthy was still regarding me, that smile on her face.

'Well, that's a pity, Steve, because I was looking forward to the next trip. I had planned to take you to the Ouse Washes, because I know how much you love the birds…'

I winced. It was a trip I had suggested.

'I'm very sorry…' I began.

'…but never mind. You can still do some photography with me. I've asked Mr Godley if I can start an after-school photography club, and you can be my first member. How about that?'

'Er… that will be very nice Ms McCarthy, but… er… (I thought desperately of an excuse) I have to get the bus home after school and… er… Mum worries if I'm out late.'

I knew she was looking at me in that nice way she had, but I couldn't look her in the face. The moment stretched uncomfortably.

'Steve? Look at me!'

I could not disobey a teacher. I looked up.

'Has anyone been putting pressure on you about this? This isn't anything to do with the other kids is it? I know how difficult it is if you're seen as a teacher's pet. Has Dwayne been saying anything?'

'Oh no, Ms McCarthy. It's nothing like that.' It was such a relief to tell the truth. I think she believed me.

'Well, promise me one thing, Steve. Don't give up the photography. You're very good at it.'

'Yes, Ms McCarthy.'

I kept that promise.

As I left the drama mobile I bumped into Ronnie, on his way in. He was carrying a bucket and mop, so he could have just been about to clear up some mess, but I suspected that this visit to Ms McCarthy was for a different reason, particularly because he didn't even notice me and looked as if he was about to go into battle. I decided to hover and listen, worried for him.

'Yes, Mr Rawlinson?' Ms McCarthy's voice had lost its warmth, I noticed. 'Can I help you?'

'Yes, Miss McCarthy, as a matter of fact you can. You can do two things for me. Firstly, you and your mates can stop poking your nose into things you don't understand, and you can keep away from our shoot. Is that OK with you?' He sounded quite calm and reasonable.

'Well, no, Mr Rawlinson, as a matter of fact it is not OK. We have a right to protest peacefully, because this is a democratic country, although you and *your* mates might not have noticed that, with your noses stuck firmly in the nineteenth century. Nowadays it's the twentieth century and in the twentieth century it's not OK to butcher innocent creatures for fun.'

'Is that so?' said Ronnie. I could tell he was getting stressed as his voice was tighter.

'And the second thing?' said Ms McCarthy.

'What?'

'You said there were two things I could do for you. You have told me what the first is, now what is the second?'

'Right, yes, I'll tell you what it is. It's about the lad, Stevie. You can keep away from him and stop putting ideas in his head what are not appropriate.'

'I beg your pardon, Mr Rawlinson.' I could tell Ms McCarthy was getting angry too. 'Are you accusing me of inappropriate behaviour with a pupil, because if you are…'

'What I mean,' interrupted Ronnie, 'is that Stevie doesn't rightly know what's what about things. He's been brought up in a certain way. And he doesn't need any of this anti shit pushed down his throat by a teacher what he feels he can't say no to.'

'Mr Rawlinson, what is your relationship to Stephen Stringer?'

'Relationship? We're not related, if that's what you mean. I live next door.'

'I see.'

There was a pause.

'Is that all?' Ms McCarthy's voice was like steel. I had never heard her talk like this.

'What?'

'Do you have anything else to say to me, because if you haven't I would be grateful if you would leave my classroom.'

'Yes, I have got something else to say to you, young lady, you can do something about the way you park that bloody motorbike of yours. You're taking up the whole of a parking space. It's not happropriate, if you must know, to come to school on a motorbike, you being a woman and all!'

I could hear Ms McCarthy laughing as I scooted down the mobile steps. I didn't want Ronnie to come out and catch me eavesdropping.

After this incident I felt angry and confused. I was angry with Ronnie, for not being clever, like Ms McCarthy was, and for letting her get the better of him in that conversation; and I felt angry with Ms McCarthy for taking advantage of him. I also felt angry about what he had said about me. I was old enough to make my own decisions about what I did and what I believed, and who I was friendly with, or so I thought. How dare he treat me like a child? I remembered the excitement of my times with Ms McCarthy, how grown-up she made me feel, and how much I wanted to live like her, to live in a flat with a friend (not with my mum in a horrid little cottage in the middle of nowhere), to have hundreds of books on my shelves and to have conversations about art and philosophy in the evenings instead of watching the telly with Mum. For the first time in my life, I realised that there was a way of living that was different, and I yearned for it. Why had I just told Ms McCarthy that I didn't want to spend any more time with her? What a fool! What would I rather do on a Sunday – speed through the countryside on a Harley-Davidson and then lounge on a sofa listening to heavy rock music and eating doughnuts, or sit on the bank of the Middle Level watching a float in the hope of a catch and listening to Ronnie going on about the geese, *again*? At that moment there was no question which I would choose. I also felt angry with myself for ditching the opportunity to change my life, and I burnt with disappointment all day.

After school, as I made my way across the car park towards the school buses, I saw Ms McCarthy at her motorbike. She was loading papers into the saddlebag. I stopped and watched. She began to put her helmet on; she was obviously about to leave, and I felt that if she drove away I would somehow lose the chance to change what had happened. Without thinking what I was doing I ran across the car park.

'Ms McCarthy?'

Suddenly I had no idea what I was going to say. How could I explain to her the tumult I was feeling?

'Why hallo, Steve? What can I do for you?' She smiled as if we were still friends, as if nothing had changed, and she bent again to pack her saddlebag.

'Er… I… er…' I did not know how to say it and looked down at where my right foot was scraping the tarmac as I searched for the right words.

'What is it?' she asked softly. 'You can tell me, you know.'

I blurted it out suddenly. 'I think I would like to go on some more trips with you and I think I can persuade my mum. The Ouse Washes sounds fun and if you have already arranged it, I don't want to let you down; and my mum wouldn't like that either,' (which was true).

I went on studying my foot. She didn't answer immediately, but she sighed, lifted my chin and smiled at me. It was such a tender smile. The moment stretched. I was oblivious of where we were, in the staff carpark, either side of a motorbike, surrounded by the bustle of noisy pupils and the sound of buses' engines revving. It was one of those perfect never-to-be-forgotten moments. Then she sighed a second time and shrugged her shoulders.

'Oh Steve! I am so sorry to have put you in this position. I didn't realise what pressure I was putting on you. Poor you!'

It was as if she understood perfectly everything I had been thinking and feeling all day.

'Oh, but you haven't put me under any pressure, it's not your fault, it's just that…' I gabbled.

'Steve! Listen! I have really enjoyed your friendship and I will never forget how you have trusted me and returned that friendship. I hope you will still come to my photography club and, remember, you did volunteer to help backstage with the school play, but I really don't think it is a good idea to continue our meetings out of school.'

'No, Ms McCarthy! Please don't say that!'

'Yes, Steve, I must say it, for your sake. You are a pupil and I am a teacher and… look, Steve, don't misunderstand this, but I have become very fond of you. I don't expect ever to have children, but if I did have a son, I would want him to be like you.'

I didn't know what to say.

'And then, of course,' she went on, 'there's the difference in our ideas, isn't there? Don't think I haven't understood the importance of shooting in your life.'

'But it doesn't matter…'

'Yes, it does Steve. It is your upbringing, and it's been a very fine upbringing. I have the greatest respect for the history and traditions of the fens, and in a way I admire people like Mr Rawlinson, although he wouldn't believe it, would he?' She laughed. 'I also understand that he is very important in your life and, how can I put this? I think you should love him and support him.'

'But…' I didn't know what to say. Suddenly there seemed to be far more than a motorbike between us.

'And I also think that you should forget about me. She took a deep breath, put her helmet on and swung her leg over the Harley. 'Now, out of the way, or you'll get run over. I'm in a hurry tonight as it's Kath's birthday and I've got to buy some champagne.' She started the engine.

The Harley-Davidson burst into life and began chugging.

'Forget me, Steve!' she said and began to ride away.

'I couldn't ever forget you,' I said, but she didn't hear me. She was already out of the gate and accelerating away.

A loud hooting interrupted my musing. I looked up. My school bus was parked right outside the carpark entrance, blocking everyone. Dick was gesturing at me to hurry and then he leant on the horn again. I rushed to the bus.

'Come on boy, get a wiggle on,' he said as I climbed up. 'What's got into you? We don't usually have to wait for you. Chatting up your girlfriend, were you?'

He was just joking, of course, but I felt a piercing stab of humiliation, aware of the listening ears behind me, which belonged to watching eyes which had noticed me in a way they didn't normally.

Sure enough, next day I paid for it. Dwayne waylaid me between lessons, pushed me into the cloakroom and grabbed me in a headlock.

'Now then Sydney, what's this I hear about you grassing to a teacher in the carpark, eh, you tittle-telling little nark?' he hissed, and he squeezed my throat as I fought for breath.

But we weren't alone in the cloakroom.

'Leave him alone, you bully!' said Connor Soames, emerging from a corner with Josie Davenport in tow, hastily doing up the buttons on her shirt. Connor was in Year Ten and thought himself very cool and vastly superior to us Year Nines. Josie was always hanging round him.

Dwayne tried to save face.

'Who says?' he sneered, but he let me go.

'Me!' replied Connor, and he walked right up to Dwayne and stared in his face. 'Do you want to do something about it?'

Josie giggled. I disappeared.

After that, although she was always very nice to me, greeting me if we came across each other round the school and asking me if I was all right when I arrived for a lesson, Ms McCarthy didn't try to continue our friendship. I did join the after-school photography club, and I relished every minute of being with her, but she treated me just like the other pupils.

The last time I had any kind of special conversation with her was the time when she gave me the photos. She did it in quite an off-hand kind of way, as we were all leaving the art lesson.

'Oh, Stephen,' she called, 'don't forget this. You've left it behind.'

I stopped and turned around. She was holding out a roll of thick paper, about a foot long, secured with an elastic band. I didn't know what it was, but I didn't know what else to do except to take it from her. I tried to stuff it into my school bag.

'Thanks,' I said, and made my escape.

Looking back now, I can see how ungracious my behaviour must have looked to her, but I was aware how curiously some of my fellow-pupils were looking at me, although, fortunately, Dwayne was away that day.

Later, in the school library, I had a chance to see what she had given me. I slipped the elastic band off and unrolled the stiff paper. The two photographs I had taken which had been used in the S.A.B. display at the museum lay before me, curled up at the ends. Each one had a white cardboard frame, and at the bottom a printed title in italics *Foraging on the Shore Line* and *Flying Free*, which I thought were rather good, and underneath *Stephen Stringer, Snettisham*, 1992. On the back of each one she had written, 'From Sidney McCarthy.'

'Oh, Stephen, they're lovely! Are they yours?' asked Margaret, who had helped me undo the packaging.

I didn't answer. I just sat and looked at them and felt like crying. I still feel the tears smarting behind my eyelids when I think of that moment.

*

However, the row between Ronnie and Ms McCarthy was not over.

One day, about a week after that first shoot I noticed that throughout the school there was a scattering of posters on the boards, and they were S.A.B. posters, rather like the ones I had seen at the exhibition. When I first saw them, I studied each one and thought about the message they were portraying. There was one which showed a retriever carrying a dead mallard and it reminded me of Gyp fetching a duck out of a creek and bringing it to us, wagging his tail. 'Stop this Slaughter!' read the rubric. I just couldn't marry up the idea of 'slaughter' with the happy hours I spent wildfowling with Ronnie and Gyp on the Marsh. How was it wrong to shoot a bird if you were going to eat it for dinner? I wondered. How was that different from eating a pork chop?

Ronnie would have said it was less cruel: 'Them poor ol' pigs, they know what's going to happen to them, you know, you can hear 'em start that squealing when they get to the slaughter house even though they're still in the trailer; they can smell the blood I reckon. That wigeon I just shot, Stevie, he didn't feel no fear, one minute he was flying free, the next he was dead, bang. That's the way I'd like to go.'

However, the S.A.B. posters went the way of all Sir Willyum's's display material, and two days later they had all been torn away from the wall. Ms McCarthy didn't give up, though. I knew it was her (because who else would it have been?) and anyway I saw her one morning at the end of a corridor, replacing them. But the new posters also got ripped away, and it happened that same day. This went on for four days.

When I thought about this, I decided that someone was deliberately tearing them down, because, on examination, I noticed that they had all been pulled away from the four drawing pins holding them, which were still in place, and I had a good idea who it was, too. My suspicions were borne out when, on my usual morning visit to Ronnie's office one morning, while I was listening to him going on about some delivery or other, I noticed the screwed-up posters in his waste bin.

The battle of the posters came to a head a few days later. I came in on the end of it when I turned the corner towards the music room with Mr Took's register. I took a step back again, around the corner.

'I've got every right to put up these posters, Mr Rawlinson. I have checked with Mr Crumb and he has given his permission.' Ms McCarthy sounded well in control of the situation.

'Is that so?' spluttered Ronnie. 'Well, in my opinion Old Crumpet doesn't know his arse from his elbow, let alone knowing what's healthy for youngsters to see on their walls. It's bloody propaganda, that's what it is. That's how Hitler started, with that there propaganda!'

'Don't be ridiculous, Mr Rawlinson! This has got nothing to do with fascism. Save all Birds is a perfectly legitimate organisation with legal charitable status and it's extremely healthy for young people to think about issues such as blood sports.'

'Bloody rubbish, that's what it is. Putting ideas in their heads, turning them against their heritage. What you call in your fancy way 'field sports' is what their dads have done and their dads before them in these parts. Shooting's in their blood, woman, and you can't change that.'

'Perhaps. And now, if you excuse me, I am going to go to Mr Crumb and complain about your behaviour, as I am pretty certain you have been tearing these posters down.'

Ms McCarthy did complain, but not to Mr Crumb in person, of course, because he delegated her complaint to Mr Godley. I heard about it because when I got home that day Beryl was having a cup of tea and some cake with Mum in our kitchen.

'He's in a terrible mood today,' she was saying. 'I've sent 'im outside to trim the 'edge, I reckoned using shears would help him get it off his chest. This bit of lemon drizzle is lovely, Myra.'

'Thank you dear. What's eating Ronnie?'

'Something to do with posters. I didn't really understand what he was going on about.'

'Stephen!' said Mum, noticing me, 'take your uniform off before you do anything else, I don't want it messed up.'

'Can I have some cake?'

'No, you'll never eat your tea. You can have some afterwards.'

I went upstairs and changed my clothes and then sought out Ronnie, who was still going at the hedge as if it was a line of anti-shooting banners, with Gyp sitting at a safe distance wondering what was happening.

'Hi, Ronnie,' I said.

He didn't stop his frantic clipping.

'Afternoon!' he said.

I stood and watched him for a bit, wondering whether I should say anything about the posters.

'If you've got nothing better to do than stand around doing bugger all you can tidy up that log pile for your mum, boy!'

He was certainly in a bad mood, so I did as he suggested and left him to vent his anger on the hedge. Judging how the land lay, Gyp joined me. Ronnie kept cutting.

Chapter Seventeen

During that autumn the feud between Ronnie and Ms McCarthy continued to simmer. At first, we thought the involvement of the police had put a stop to S.A.B. campaigns at our shoot.

'They've been told, good and proper, that it's trespass unless they've got the permission of the landowner, and Westley-Lewis ain't going to give his permission to a load of antis, I can tell you that,' declared Ronnie. 'And anyway, there's a new padlock on that gate, so they're fucked.'

Sure enough, the next shoot was free from trouble, so we thought the problem was over. The following fortnight, however, when we were on the last drive, which was always on Wide Acre Field, driving the birds towards the sea wall, I noticed, way to the left in the distance, a small huddle of people walking along the top of the sea wall towards us. It was a wet and windy day, not the kind of weather when you expect to see people hiking or birdwatching, and suddenly I had a sinking feeling. I was sure that Ronnie had noticed them too – his eyes were sharp – and I looked over towards where he was advancing in the middle of our beaters' line, but was too far away to see his face. He was behaving as if everything was normal, striding out across the beet ridges, whacking the leaves with his stick and singing out that strange cry, half yelp, half hiss, that's used to move the birds forward.

When the group of people got nearer, I could see that they were carrying poles; it was the S.A.B. group, and I realised what they had done to circumvent the gate. The sea wall is a public right of way and they had just parked at one of the marsh entrances and walked the four miles, carrying their banners with them. When they saw us, they increased their pace, and were in time to set themselves up in a row on top of the wall above the line of guns, who were standing in the lee below them. It was blowing a gale, so I couldn't hear if they were chanting anything this time, but I could see that the guns were unsettled, looking over their shoulders uneasily.

It took us about another ten minutes to walk the birds, as Wide Acre is one of the biggest fields on the farm. Just at the point when the pheasants, having been driven over the ground away from our advance, find that there is nowhere to go but up, and when the guns should have had a good chance of shooting one or two as they flew low into the wind and away over the sea wall, the protesters started to wave their banners and I could hear spurts of their shouting in between the wind gusts. The pheasants certainly flew, but, startled, flew straight up before they reached the wall, turned and flew back over our heads.

Ronnie swore loudly and screamed at Benny Rugdale, who was our walking gun.

'Over, damn it! Over!' (This was the signal to shoot 'returning birds'.)

Benny raised his gun and aimed but they were all far too high, or perhaps he was as startled as the pheasants, as he let them all fly back without taking even one shot.

'What the fuck, Benny!' yelled Ronnie, but it was too late. The birds had found a safe haven in the vegetation of the field behind us. The line of guns in front of us were frozen in the act of taking aim but had nothing to aim at; they looked a bit like a painting of a shoot that Ronnie had on his sitting room wall. The drive, normally our best, was a total disaster, and not one bird was shot. The protesters' cheers did not help matters.

When we caught up with the guns, and Ronnie had blown his whistle, Tom Spedding said, 'You want to call the coppers again, Ronnie!'

'No point, Tom. The slimy bastards are on the public footpath. We can't do nothing. Let's just hope it's a long, wet walk home!' he spat emphatically.

They did get very wet, because they stayed on top of the wall in the wind for another half hour, while we packed up and eventually drove off. Ronnie and I were the last to leave. I was very disappointed, as Ronnie had promised to take me on the Marsh for flight that evening after the shoot. The geese were in and I was desperate to bag my first goose.

'There's no point, Stevie. All that gallivanting and noise on the wall has frightened off any duck for miles around, and the geese'll sense it and come out down the coast. I'll take you soon, lad, don't you fret. You'll get your goose.'

On the way back along the concrete farm road to the gate, we came upon Benny Rugdale on his bike, gun slung across his shoulder, pedalling into the wind and rain. We stopped to give him a lift, putting his bike in the back of the van.

'What are you going to do about them prustaters, Ronnie?' Benny asked. 'They're spoiling our sport.'

'I dunno, yet, Benny. I know what I'd like to do.'

'What's that, Ronnie?' I asked. I couldn't see that we could do anything.

'I'd like to poke one of their poles up where the sun don't shine, for starters.'

Benny laughed and I joined in. I loved it when Ronnie treated me like a bloke.

'But seriously, I'd better get my thinking cap on. Messing up a day's pheasant shoot is one thing, but when the bastards start waving and shouting near the Marsh, screwing up my fowling, that's serious. I'm not going to let a gang of lefties stop me doing what my dad did and his dad before him. We've always shot the Marsh, it's our right as long as we're over the wall and on the foreshore. Why, wildfowling on this Marsh is famous, it's in books and such.'

'Well, that's not going to help me, Ronnie,' said Benny. 'I've never been much shakes at that reading, but I'll tell you what, I can give 'em a good right and left!'

'Pity you didn't do that today, Benny. We might have had a bag for our pains. Here you are, mate.' He drew up in front of Benny's cottage. 'Help Benny with his bike, Stevie, there's a good lad.'

Ronnie was quiet for the rest of the journey.

'Is there anything we can do, Ronnie?' I asked eventually.

'I'm thinking on it, Stevie, I'm thinking on it.'

*

He didn't just do a lot of thinking in the next week or so, he also took some action.

One evening after tea, when I went to visit Ronnie in his shed, I couldn't find him. I went to his back door and poked my head into the kitchen. Beryl was sitting at the kitchen table with a cup of tea reading *Woman's Weekly*.

'Beryl, where's Ronnie?'

'He's in there.' She jerked her head towards their living room, 'but I wouldn't disturb him if I were you. He's taken over the dining table and turned off the telly, just as *Coronation Street* was starting. Said he couldn't concentrate with all that noise. So I'm sitting out here, I know my place, I'm just his wife of twenty-four years.' She huffed and put on her martyr look.

'What's he doing?'

'Writing letters.'

'What?!'

I had never even seen Ronnie with a pen in his hand. Curious, I moved towards the living room door.

'I wouldn't disturb him if I were you, Stevie, he's got a bee in his bonnet about that S.A.D. thingy, and he's writing a letter to the Duke of Edinburgh, and he's in a right ol' mood. Well, I'm not clearing up after him, I'll tell you that, the floor's covered with screwed-up paper and as for his language,' she huffed again, 'good job the Duke of Edinburgh can't hear 'im!'

He had heard my voice.

'Stevie,' he yelled. 'Come in here and help me with this bloody writing lark. I'm buggered if I can get the lines to keep straight, they keeps wandering like a dog's hind leg.'

And so I became his scribe. He was, indeed, surrounded by screwed-up sheets of writing paper, and the latest attempt, I could see, was covered with crossings-out. I did my best, as although my handwriting wasn't over-neat, it was certainly more legible than his, and I found, when I read through what he had written, that I could spell better too. I can't remember exactly what the letter said, but this is the gist of it:

Dear Prince Philip,

I am writing to you because I expect you to stand up for the shooting man, what with you being a good shot when you have them shoots at Sandringham, so Reg Prentice, your keeper what retired in '86, tells me. Our shooting syndicate is being pestered by antis and they're frightening the birds and spoiling our sport. Please have a word with Her Majesty (God save her) to get the government to make a law about waving flags and shouting when a God-fearing Englishman is out with his gun and not on a Sunday, because we know the law, which is more than them antis do, with their trespassing and breach of the peace and what-have-you. And while they're about it, the government can ban the S.A.B.

Yours truly,
Ronnie Rawlinson

At first, being in the top set for English, I tried to re-arrange this into what Miss Ferguson would describe as standard English, but when I read it out to him, he objected.

'No, Stevie, that's not what I said. I want him to know exactly how I feel. He's a shooting man and he'll understand. You write it out just like what I said.'

So I did as he asked, and then, to his direction, wrote, in capital letters on the envelope 'DUKE OF EDINBURGH, BUCKINGHAM PALACE, LONDON'. I was about to put the letter in the envelope and seal it, when he stopped me.

'No Stevie, we've got to do some more writing, lad. I'm going to screw that S.A. bloody B. if it's the last thing I do. We've got plenty more work, son.' This was not exactly accurate, as, during the rest of the evening it was me that did the work, copying out the letter four more times, with slight changes, and inscribing five more envelopes to 'THE MAYOR OF WISBECH', 'RICHARD WAINWRIGHT, MP', 'BRITISH ASSOCIATION FOR SHOOTING', and 'MR WESTLEY-LEWIS, LANDOWNER'. When I had finished, Ronnie put each one in its respective envelope, licked the seal and thumped it closed with his fist.

'Where's the stamps, woman?' he asked Beryl, who was passing through in her dressing gown and curlers.

'Where they always are, in the sideboard drawer, and you needn't think I'm going to get them for you.' She was still in a huff.

Three weeks later Ronnie received a very posh cream envelope, with 'Buckingham Palace' in silver print on the flap. He was very excited.

'I told you he'd listen to me. That's a man what knows what's what about shooting,' he said with satisfaction.

But all the letter said was, 'Dear Mr Rawlinson, His Royal Highness thanks you for your letter but regrets that he is not in a position to help you. Yours sincerely, D. Potter, Assistant Equerry.'

*

I wasn't enjoying the fortnightly Saturday shoots anymore. Ronnie would be tight-lipped and frowning, not at all like himself, and did a lot of shouting and swearing at people and dogs because he was so stressed. The guns were grumpy because they kept on missing birds and it was always us beaters that got the blame.

And then there were the protestors. They were well-organised and operated in a sort of pincer movement. Every Saturday when we arrived at the gate onto the private farm road two or three were there, with their banners. They didn't say anything, they didn't try to stop us unlocking the gate and driving through, but it was very inconvenient because, rather than unlocking the padlock and leaving it open for the next syndicate member to lock it again, as we usually did, we had to lock the gate again each time after we had driven through, in case they sneaked through after us. I found this particularly embarrassing, as I was always the person who did the gate, and I hated having their eyes boring into my back as I fumbled with the padlock key, especially if it was Ms McCarthy or Jed.

The other half of them came trekking along the sea wall and camped by the Marsh entrance. To a casual observer they were just bird-watching, because they spent a lot of time looking through binoculars and taking photographs. But those binoculars were often trained on us, and it made me feel very uncomfortable to be under surveillance. We no longer shot the field directly underneath the sea wall, but we could still see them from several of our afternoon drives and whenever they heard the guns they picked up their banners and started waving them.

However, although Prince Philip hadn't been interested, one of the letters I had copied out so painstakingly did have consequences. It must have been about a month later that we had a visitor during our lunch break. A Land Rover drove onto the concrete pad and out got a fat man in a brown waxed jacket and green wellington boots.

'That's Westley-Lewis,' muttered Ronnie. 'To what do we owe

this honour, I wonder. Mm, perhaps he's seen my letter.'

The man walked straight up to Ronnie.

'Ah, Rawlinson,' he said.

'Afternoon, sir. Come to join us? They're flying nice and low in this fog, and you're very welcome to show us how it's done.'

'I need to have a word with you,' said Mr Westley-Lewis, ignoring Ronnie's attempt at flattery. 'We've got a problem with this shoot.'

'Have we, sir? In what way?'

Everyone had drawn close to listen.

'I've had the press nosing round. Some little pip-squeak from the Wisbech Times had the audacity to knock on my door a couple of evenings ago. Wanted to ask questions about some animal welfare organisation protesting at your shoot. I didn't give him the time of day, of course, sent him off with a flea in his ear, almost forgot about it. But then my foreman Joe Tate gave me a call earlier today and told me he'd been out checking on the yield in East Angle and he'd seen some people waving banners at the gate.'

'Ah,' said Ronnie.

'So I came out myself to see what the hell was going on and came upon this group of wasters hanging around the gate. They had the audacity to wave a banner at me – at me, on my own land, mind you! I soon told them to go back where they had come from, that they were trespassing and I'd call the police...'

'Did you, sir?'

'…and they started telling me that they were on a public road and had the right to protest or some such rubbish. Well, I told them where to get off, I can tell you, and I've come to tell you, Rawlinson, that I'm not having it, do you hear, I don't want no loonies on my land and I certainly don't want the press involved, do you hear?'

He had worked himself up and his face was red and sweating.

'Well yes, sir, that's exactly why I sent you that letter, a copy of the one what I sent to His Royal Highness. You did get it sir?'

'Letter? What letter? I'm talking about people trespassing on my land, man!'

'So what do you think we should do about it, sir, if you don't mind me asking, you being a Justice of the Peace and with you knowing so many important people?'

This question seemed to floor Mr Westley-Lewis. He stopped in mid-bluster and I could almost see the thoughts flitting across his brain until one took hold and grew.

'Mm. Well, I could give old Des Stibley a ring, I think he's still Chief Constable, ask him if he fancies a round of golf, get him to twist someone's arm, something like that.'

'That sounds like an excellent idea, sir,' said Ronnie.

'Well someone needs to do something round here,' contributed Tom Spedding. 'I'm not paying my syndicate fee for next season if my shooting's going to be fucked up again.'

Mr Westley-Lewis turned and looked at Tom as if he was some reptile that had just crawled out of the undergrowth.

'You'll not have any shooting, my man, if this doesn't get sorted out; I didn't offer you lot the lease to get all this trouble. When is it due for renewal, Rawlinson?'

'That'll do, Tom,' said Ronnie, and he began to usher Mr Westley-Lewis back towards his Land Rover. 'I'll see what I can do too, sir; I'm sure we can get this thing sorted out. No need to take drastic action.'

When he had opened the Land Rover door for Mr Westley-Lewis and waved him away, Ronnie returned to where we were all standing.

'You need to keep your bloody big mouth shut, Tom Spedding!' he said.

*

At the end of the afternoon, when we reached the gate on the way home, the protesters had been joined by a woman in a long red coat and black fashion boots and a man with a baseball cap on back-to-front who was taking a photograph of the banners.

The woman approached the driver side of the van while I was fiddling with the padlock, but I saw that Ronnie had wound up the window and was staring fixedly ahead. Seeing me stop and look up at him he gestured with impatience. As I pushed the gate open, he revved hard and drove the van at speed through the gate and up the road about twenty yards and I had to run after him as I was frightened he wouldn't wait for me. Panting, I climbed up into my seat as he accelerated.

'You need to get a move on, Stevie. We don't want our pictures in the paper, do we?'

'Why not, Ronnie? It might help,' I said.

'We don't trust the press, Stevie, that's why not. They'll twist things any which way they want to sell their bloody newspaper.'

However, he wasn't successful at evading the press. When we turned down our drove he looked in his rear-view mirror and muttered, 'The bastards have followed us!'

'But I thought you wanted to tell the local paper – that's why you sent them the letter.'

'Don't argue, boy! You don't know what you're talking about! Shut that bloody door!'

Sure enough, when we arrived outside our cottages a Ford Escort was close behind us. It stopped outside our front gates as we drove around the back and as we began to unload the van as usual we were approached by the reporter and her cameraman.

'Do you think we could have a statement?' she called. 'It's Mr Rawlinson, isn't it?'

Ronnie looked at her.

'And who are you?'

'We're from the *Wisbech Times*,' she said, taking a notebook and pen out of her pocket. 'I believe that you were in charge of the pheasant shooting taking place on Coast Farm this afternoon. I wonder if we could have an interview, Mr Rawlinson.'

'*Wisbech Times*, eh?' he spat. 'Well, I'll tell you what you can do, young lady, along with that there friend of yours, you can go straight back to the *Wisbech Times* and have your tea, 'cos it's teatime and that's what I'm going to do now. So goodbye. Come on Stevie, we'll unload later.'

Unfortunately, we didn't escape that easily. Before we could turn away, there was a flash, and the moment had been recorded in black and white.

'This is private property, so you can take your bloody camera and your girlfriend and you can bugger off before I set my dog on you, do you hear?' shouted Ronnie.

The thought of old Gyp, currently curled up in the back of the van, attacking anyone except with hot doggy breath and a sloppy tongue made me giggle.

'It's not bloody funny, Stevie. This is a serious matter.' He said, marching up his garden path.

The story appeared in the *Wisbech Times* on the following

Friday. Many years later, when I was visiting Wisbech as part of my preparation for this book, I decided to see if could find it in the newspaper's archives; but the *Wisbech Times* had gone the way of most small local newspapers, and its old office in the market place was now a nail parlour.

I went to the public library where I had spent so many hours as a child. It looked very different, with automatic doors and scanning machines and a huge area devoted to computers.

I went to the desk and asked to look at the *Wisbech Times* archive.

'What year? 1993?' asked the librarian.

'No, I'm interested in 1992 please. I don't mind waiting if you have to find it. I'll have a look round.'

'Oh, I assumed you'd want 1993, because of the… you know, the… what happened on that day,' she said. 'We're always being asked for that day so we keep it quite handy. Are you researching for a book? We had someone last year who was doing that. There are a couple of books about that day in our local studies section. Do you want me to fetch them as well?'

Her perkiness seemed out of place.

'No thank you, just the archive for 1992.' I didn't need to read about what happened on that day in 1993. I had been there.

She bustled away, and I amused myself by browsing the shelves, noting that those well-loved natural history classics that I had devoured as a boy had been replaced by large glossy coffee-table books linked to television wildlife series. When she returned with a pile of large navy-blue lever arch files I settled at a table in the reference section and soon found both the photo taken at the S.A.B. meeting and the shoot story, dated November 25th 1992.

'ANTI-GUN PROTESTERS STORM WILDFOWL SHOOT.' The

headline makes me feel angry even now, because of its inaccuracy and bias; S.A.B. was not an anti-gun organisation, it wasn't a wildfowl shoot and there had been no storming.

'What do you fucking expect?' Ronnie would have said. 'Liars, the lot of them. If they can see a story they don't give a fuck whether it's right as long as it sells papers!'

The story beneath that headline was more accurate. There was a lot of quotation from 'Sidney, call me Sid, McCarthy, a local secondary school teacher and chair of the local branch of the "Save all Birds" organisation', along the lines of, 'We protest about the wanton slaughter of defenceless creatures,' and, 'We would like to see the law changed so that shooting a bird with a gun becomes illegal.' There was a description of our shoot as a 'game-shooting syndicate operating regularly on land owned by local landowner Roger Westley-Lewis, J.P., well-known as the president of the local branch of the Conservative Party, who refused to make any comment'. Ronnie featured briefly in the text as 'Gamekeeper Ronald Rawlinson refused to make any comment'.

The photo taken at the back of the cottages, in which a skinny boy wearing glasses with an armful of dead pheasants was looking at a nondescript-looking man in a large shapeless smock and a flat cap with an open shotgun slung over his arm, was one of several scattered about page 4, where the story, such as it was, unfolded. The front-page picture was of the line of protesters with their banners, posed in front of the sign 'Coast Farm'. I can see why Mr Westley-Lewis was so angry.

That was, surprisingly, the only newspaper story about the protests at the shoot. I looked for any press follow-up in the following weeks but found nothing, perhaps because a scandal involving the wife of the Chairman of Wisbech Borough Council and the Council Treasurer, who suddenly re-located together to the Cote d'Azur with much of the council's money, took over as a more newsworthy.

I don't remember Ronnie's reaction to that newspaper story, although I do remember Beryl rushing in one teatime waving a copy of the *Wisbech Times*.

'Look at this Myra, here's my Ronnie and your Stevie in the paper! Fancy that, and on page 4 too, not in the back pages with the classifieds. There's the van in it too, covered with mud, I'm always going on at him about giving it a clean, and it says Mr Ronald Rawlinson though no-one's ever called him Ronald since our wedding when I had to nudge him hard 'cos he didn't recognise the vicar was talking about him. It's just not like Ronnie is it to be called Ronald, sounds too much like that ventriloquist's puppet on the telly, Ronald something or other what rhymes, what's-his-name?'

We had looked up from our sausages.

'Ronald McDonald,' I said.

'Sit down, Beryl,' said Mum. 'Stevie, get Beryl a chair, and slow down a bit love, you're all of a flummox.'

Beryl sat and spread the newspaper out on the table and Mum moved the tomato ketchup to make room. We gathered round Beryl and looked at the paper.

'You look such a scruff,' said Mum.

'But at least he's face-on, Myra. My Ronnie's not looking at the camera properly. Typical, he never has liked his photo being taken.'

'We didn't know it was going to be taken,' I said.

'Don't contradict Auntie Beryl, Stephen. It's not polite from a child.' She began to read the story.

'But I wasn't…'

'Shush, Stephen, I'm reading. Sit down and finish your tea.'

Never one to let a sausage go uneaten, I did as I was told and that is perhaps why I did not remember the details of the newspaper story, because at that moment we heard the toot of Ronnie's van as he turned into our back area.

'Oh, there he is, back from locking up. I must show him this!' Beryl gathered up the newspaper and rushed out of our back door.

'I wouldn't be in any rush, Beryl love,' Mum called after her. 'I don't think he'll be very happy to read it.' But Beryl had already gone.

*

The last few shoots of the year passed uneventfully. We had become used to our 'friends' with the banners.

'Christ, it's bloody cold today,' said Tom Spedding at the end of one particularly bitter December day, stamping his feet. 'Them buggers are likely frozen solid, banners and all.' He jerked his head towards the sea wall, where the protesters, bundled up in scarves and woolly hats, struggled to hold their banners in the wind.

'Serves 'em right,' said Bennie. 'Hope they all gets that pewmonia!'

'Well, I hope they buggers off right fucking smart when we pack up. If they mess up our fowling tonight I might get really pissed off,' said Ronnie.

'After the geese, Ronnie?' said Bernie. 'They're on the beet on Steward's these last few days, 'bout twelve thousand, I reckons, and it's full moon; they'll be flitting about all night.'

Because of the protesters on the sea wall, we had stopped our habit of staying for evening flight after the shoot, but earlier in the week Ronnie, having consulted his tide tables, had planned to go out that evening to have a go at the geese, which would be flighting late under the full moon. I had begged to be allowed to go too, as my greatest ambition at that point in my life was to shoot a goose; I saw it as a kind of initiation. Mum had said yes because it was a Saturday and there was no school the following day.

I must have looked worried as he went on, 'Don't you worry, Stevie, they'll not hang around freezing their arses tonight, mark my words. I'll get you under a goose, boy. But you'll have to use my 12 bore, don't think your little old gun is man enough for a big ol' pinkfoot. Do you think you can heft it OK?'

'Yes, of course I can Ronnie,' I said.

I knew his gun was still a bit too long in the barrel for me and heavy too, but I'd rather have died than admit it.

That night under the moon was all I had ever imagined, and I will always remember it; not just because I did shoot my first goose but because it was the last time I can remember when the two of us were really happy together.

It was a very cold night and very dark. A stiff north-easterly breeze was stinging my face as I carefully plodded after Ronnie's wader-prints across the Marsh out from the sea wall and towards the sea, while Gyp ranged around us, nose busy and tail wagging. He loved the marsh smells. After half a mile of squelching and slithering and scrambling across muddy pools and creeks, we settled in a particularly deep creek where we could crouch, our waders in a foot of sea water, our backs against the muddy creek edge. Gyp sat in front of us, ears erect.

'Are you OK, boy?'

'Yes, Ronnie.'

I was shivering uncontrollably, partly with cold, even though Mum had insisted I wore several extra layers, but mostly with excitement.

'Good lad! Now we wait for 'em. That tide's still ebbing. They'll come, you wait and see. Now, what you want to do is to stick your hands inside your pockets, and, see here,' he handed me a little pouch, 'you put this in your right-hand pocket to keep your trigger finger warm. We don't want you missing at the crucial moment, do we?'

The pouch was warm, a hand-warmer fuelled by lighter fuel, and I clutched it tightly, as if my life depended on it, continually flexing my right forefinger, as if pulling a trigger, while my left hand, my nose and both my feet gradually lost all feeling, frozen solid.

We waited for two hours. Gyp curled up on the mud and went to sleep. We were two round balaclavas stuck out above a landscape of black mud and black tufts, with a vast dome of blackness above us, patterned by a scattering of stars. Every so often Ronnie would shift his position and mutter, 'They'll come, they'll come!' Once he lit a cigarette and puffed at it impatiently, a tiny red glow in the starlight. I didn't dare to move, and I ached with cold.

It was nearly half past eleven when a faint rim of light could be seen over the sea horizon. Gradually, inch by inch, minute by minute, a huge full moon rose into the scudding clouds. The landscape around us was transformed. In the moonlight, the Marsh had been colour-washed with a palette of greys and the water in the pools and creeks was gently glimmering.

And then we heard them! Faintly, far in the distance, the unmistakeable cry of the pink-footed geese, calling to each other that they had eaten their fill and needed to fly to their roost on the mudflats. Ronnie tensed.

'There they are! You beauties!'

Gyp woke up. Gradually, the sound grew louder, more insistent.

'They're coming!' Ronnie whispered, and he slipped two cartridges into the barrel of his open gun.

Gyp began to quiver. I turned my head towards the seawall behind me, straining to catch a first glimpse. Ronnie closed the gun with a firm click and handed it to me.

'Here you are, Stevie. Remember, they've got to be low enough for a clean kill; we don't want no winged birds, Gyp's past chasing across the Marsh. Just hold your horses until I give you the word.'

I raised the gun to my shoulder and pointed it upwards. I didn't notice its weight or how unwieldy it was for me. I was focused on the approaching geese.

The first skein was high, far above us and to the left, their calls carried on the wind, and pitching out towards Bulldog Sand. Then more from the same direction but swerving towards us.

'No, too high, boy!' warned Ronnie.

Like etched silhouettes, they flew straight across the disc of the moon and disappeared into the darkness.

But more were coming. From all directions behind the sea wall they came, skein after skein, thousand after thousand. Amid the loneliness of the wide marsh we were suddenly overwhelmed with the clamorous sound and insistent movement of a multitude of living things. It was as if we were in the midst of them, part of their community, listening, as they did, to the cries of their leaders and following the urge of the soaring wings in front of them. They were all too far and too high for a shot, not that I was aware of the gun in my hand. And then there was a pause. Their sound was now less insistent, a comfortable settling far out on the sands of the Wash, a mile or more beyond us. I imagined them paddling around in their groups and eventually tucking their heads under their wings to sleep, bellies full.

'Is that it?' I whispered.

'Just you wait, boy. There'll be stragglers.'

Sure enough, a few minutes after the main groups had disappeared and the Marsh was again quiet, we heard the cries, louder, nearer, but fewer. We turned to watch for their arrival, and then, so low that it seemed that we could even hear the swish of their wings, a party of six geese flew straight towards us.

'Here he is, boy. Your goose! Aim for the one at the front; you've got two barrels in case you miss. Remember, follow the flight with your arm.'

I missed the first, but got the fifth in the line, and it dropped out of the sky about fifty yards away. I was sure I could hear the soft thud of it hitting the mud.

'Fetch!' commanded Ronnie, and Gyp bounded towards it, returning a few moments later with my goose, a big wet bundle of grey feathers, which he deposited into Ronnie's hand before shaking himself wetly.

It was my first and my last goose. We were never under the geese again that season, and although I did not know it at the time, it was also my last shooting season. After what happened on that day I gave up shooting.

When we arrived back home, in the early hours, Ronnie said, 'Now, you slip in quietly, Stevie, you don't want to wake your mum up, and you need to get your head down and get some sleep.'

'But Ronnie…'

'I'll hang up your goose for you, and it'll still be there for you tomorrow, don't you fret.'

But the advice wasn't needed, for Mum was still awake and as we drove around the back the kitchen light went on and there she was, in dressing gown, making sure I had been returned in one piece.

'Look Mum! I got a goose!' I held it by its feet and tried to hold it aloft in triumph, although I couldn't manage that very well, it was so heavy.

'Very nice, dear. Now you say thank you very much and help your Uncle Ronnie with the birds and that and then you get in here and get off to bed. It's nearly two o'clock.'

To me, 'Thank you very much' was hardly enough.

'I did it, Ronnie!' I grinned.

He grinned back.

'Yes, Stevie, you did it. You got your first goose and I tell you, boy, you'll never forget this night. You are now a fully paid up member of the wildfowling community and you've paid your dues, as it were. You now have a special link with them geese, Stevie. You're a hunter and they're your prey; you're part of the natural order, is how I sees it. You've brought home a nice fat bird for the table and when you eat it, and your mum's good at goose pie I know, you'll be giving it the respect it deserves.'

He was right. I have never forgotten that night.

'Yes Ronnie. Thank you, Ronnie.' I hugged him impulsively, goose and all, burying my face in his muddy salty-smelling coat, which is a smell, too, that I have never forgotten.

Chapter Eighteen

I witnessed the big bust-up between Ronnie and Ms McCarthy. This was because it happened after school. I was on the bus and our bus was waiting in the long line of buses to turn out of the Dog and Duck carpark.

I was gazing vacantly out of the window when I saw Ronnie's van turn in at the school gate, hooting loudly and narrowly avoiding Mrs Pritchard who was driving her little Ford out of the same gate. He screeched to a halt in the staff carpark. What's up now? I worried. I knew that there were no after-school clubs because it was a Friday, so Ronnie shouldn't have been back at school to lock up until after 6 p.m.

He leapt out of the van door, left it open and ran across the car park waving what looked like a white envelope. Then I saw where he was heading.

Ms McCarthy was packing her saddle bag and putting on her helmet. As he reached her she swung her leg over the Harley-Davidson, started the engine and kicked the stand away. But she couldn't ride away because Ronnie was standing right in front of her. He was red in the face and shouting, although I couldn't hear what he was saying. He kept pointing with his right forefinger at the envelope which he held in his left hand and then he thrust the envelope into Ms McCarthy's face. She didn't move except to take off her helmet, placing it on the petrol tank and folding her arms. There she waited, perched on the motorbike seat, listening to Ronnie's tirade.

Other teachers, on the way to their cars, had noticed what was going on and went up to Ronnie and began to talk to him. Mr Dawson got hold of Ronnie's arm and tried to lead him away, but Ronnie swung his arm at him, knocking his glasses sideways and pushed him so that he staggered backwards and nearly lost his balance. I gasped.

'What the fuck are you doing, Ronnie?' I whispered.

Then Ms McCarthy must have decided that enough was enough and she put her helmet on, put the bike in gear and went to ride forward, but instead of moving out of the way, Ronnie rushed at her and pushed her violently. She fell backwards and sideways and the bike fell on top of her. I didn't see what happened next, as the teachers rushed forward and at the same moment my bus started to move and we drove away from the school.

Desperately worried about what could have made Ronnie so angry, and whether Ms McCarthy had been hurt, I could not settle when I got home. I went outside and fussed about in the wildfowl pen, throwing the ducks some grain, watching them, but not really seeing them, just filling the time until I heard Ronnie's van. Eventually, Mum called me in for tea and while we were eating I heard the van arrive.

I looked up and started to get up.

'Sit your bottom down, boy, and finish your tea,' said Mum. 'You've been like a cat on hot bricks ever since you got home. I don't know what's up but whatever it is it can wait until you've eaten your tea and done your homework.'

'It's Friday, Mum, I can do it later in the weekend.'

'Don't argue, Stephen. Just eat your tea.'

When I did get to escape next door, Ronnie was not to be seen.

'He's in his shed,' said Beryl, when I put my head in at their kitchen door. 'And he's in a right ol' mood. Got some letter from that Mr Westley-Lewis, something to do with shooting and a lease or some such thing. I don't understand half of it.'

He was sitting in his shed, which wasn't unusual because he spent a lot of time in there. He'd made it very cosy, with an electric fire, a saggy old armchair and a battered table where he used to load cartridges and tie flies. There were hooks on one wall for his waders and shooting clothes. His metal gun cabinet was attached to the brick wall of the house and his fishing rods stood in one corner. And the whole place was stuffed full with things: piles of old Shooting Times, a rat trap, an old cracked aquarium, some pewter pots, a scythe with a broken handle, a red tool box, open and overflowing, a fish crate picked up on the tideline because it 'might come in useful…'

In the corner was the ferret hutch, and on this evening the ferrets were 'having their evening constitutional', as Ronnie would put it. Myrtle always the more curious, was, true to her name, ferreting in the corner under the fishing gear, but Felicity, Ronnie's favourite, always affectionate, was curled up on his lap. He was stroking her absent-mindedly, gazing out of the un-curtained window at the darkness. This was not like him; he was usually doing something when in his shed.

I shut the door carefully. He looked up briefly, but then returned his gaze to the window.

'Make sure that door's shut. Myrtle's loose and investigating.'

'Hi Ronnie.' I didn't know what else to say.

It was very quiet in the shed, except for a scrabbling in the corner. I approached him and put out a hand to stroke Felicity. She was sound asleep.

'You'd best get your homework done, boy. I'm not in the mood for company right now.'

I could feel my eyes smarting. I blinked.

'Why? What's the matter, Ronnie?'

He looked at me. I tried to look directly back but was struggling not to cry.

'You might as well know, boy, as it affects you as well as me. She's taken our shooting, Stevie.' He finished the sentence with a sob and bit his lip, turning his head away so I would not see.

I swallowed.

'Who has? Who's taken our shooting, Ronnie?'

'That witch, that McCarthy woman, her and her fucking cronies.'

'But how, Ronnie? What's happened?'

'What's happened is that I've just got a letter from Mr high-and-mighty Westley-Lewis who's pissing his pants about publicity and he's gone and taken away our lease for next season, that's what's happened, boy. And what that means is that we can't shoot on his land anymore and, what's worse, we can't get through his bloody gate and along his bloody road to the Marsh entrance like we've done for years and years and I'll tell you what, Stevie, I'd like to… I'd like to…' He broke off.

I said nothing because I didn't know what to say. I swallowed again.

'I tell you one thing, Stevie, I wish that woman had never come anywhere near Sir Willyum's.'

And so did I. At that moment the enormity of what I had done was revealed to me.

'So do I, Ronnie, and I wish I had never…'

But he didn't let me confess, stopping me with, 'But I've had a few words with her, I can tell you that. I showed her the letter, told her what she'd done, and do you know what she said? She just smiled and said, "I'm glad, Mr Rawlinson." Yes, that's all she fucking said, she's fucking glad, fucking glad that she's taken my shooting away, I tell you I'd like to…'

'Yes, Ronnie, me too,' I whispered.

'But it didn't turn out well, Stevie, when I told her. I got sort of carried away, and she sort of fell, I must have given her a bit of a push, I was that mad I can tell you. Anyway, Stan Godley sorted it out. He's a good chap, that Stan Godley, he took me inside and made me a cup of tea and calmed me down a bit, and he called the ambulance too.'

I looked at him, startled.

'The ambulance, Ronnie?'

'Well, a Harley-Davidson's mighty heavy, boy, and it fell on top of her. Serve her right! It's not natural her riding that motorbike, being a woman and all, now is it? Mind you, I didn't mean to hurt her.'

It must have been very heavy for it certainly did some damage to Ms McCarthy. When she returned to school two weeks later she arrived by taxi and was on crutches with her left leg in a long cast. But by then the consequences of Ronnie's 'bit of a push' had already caught up with him.

We were having Sunday dinner with Ronnie and Beryl when the police came.

'That's a police car, Ronnie,' said Beryl, as a car pulled up outside.

'Probably lost their way looking for some pikey what's gone thieving or got into a fight last night. I'll see if I can help them,' said Ronnie, and he got up from the table and went into the hall just as the doorbell rang.

'Mr Rawlinson?' we heard.

'Yes, that's me, officer. Can I help you?'

'Can we come in, sir?'

'Yes, of course, come in. We're just having out tea.' Ronnie ushered two policemen, caps under their arms, into the entrance of the dining room. One of them was Tom Spedding.

Beryl got up and began fussing.

'Oh, do come in, officers. Why it's Mr Spedding. How's Dorothy? Can I get you a cup of tea?'

Tom smiled at her uncomfortably.

'No thank you, madam. We don't want to interrupt your meal,' said the other policeman.

'Is there somewhere we can talk, Ronnie. In private, like?' said Tom.

'Er… yes, of course.' Ronnie sounded unsure of himself.

Mum took charge.

'We're were just going to clear up, weren't we, Beryl?' she said, picking up her plate and mine and stacking them, with my half-eaten roast pork squashed underneath.

'But Mum, I haven't finished…' I began.

'Come on, Stephen, we'll help Auntie Beryl wash up,' she said, pushing me in front of her into the kitchen. 'Are you going to bring the rest of the plates, Beryl. And put the kettle on, dear, I'd love a cuppa.'

Ronnie was left in the living room with the policemen, while we sat around the kitchen table.

'There you are, Stephen, finish your dinner,' said Mum, excavating my plate. 'Do you want yours, Beryl, love?'

'No, thank you Myra. I'm not sure if I could eat anything now, not with the coppers being in the house, even if it is only Tom Spedding.'

So we sat, wondering what on earth the police were doing talking to Ronnie. We could hear voices, but nothing was distinguishable, except an occasional exclamation from Ronnie: 'But I didn't mean nothing...' and 'I'm telling you, it was her that caused it all…' I began to think I knew what it was about.

After about fifteen minutes, the dining room door opened, and we could hear more clearly.

'Well, it's just a caution on this occasion, Mr Rawlinson, but I suggest that you are very careful about your behaviour in future. You should get the paperwork through in a few days, it comes from Cambridge. No, it's all right, sir, don't get up. We'll see ourselves out.'

Beryl and Mum looked at each other. The front door opened and shut, and we heard the police car start up and drive away.

When we went into the living room Ronnie was sitting with his elbows on the table and his head in his hands.

'Ronnie?' said Beryl. She went up to him and put her arm round him. 'Are you alright? What did they want?'

He looked up at us, as if seeing us for the first time, and shrugged off Beryl's arm.

'Don't fuss woman. I need to get me thoughts together.'

'But Ronnie, what was that about your behaviour and that. You're not in any trouble are you, love?' She began to cry.

'We'll be off now,' said Mum. 'Thanks for a lovely dinner, Beryl, do pop round later if you want a chat, love.'

'But Mum, we haven't had pudding yet,' I said.

'Come on, Stephen,' said Mum firmly, walking through the kitchen to the back door. 'You've got homework to do, no doubt.'

I followed her, and we left Ronnie to tell his wife what had happened. He told me later, when I ventured out to look for him in his shed.

'She reported me to the coppers, Stevie, that stupid cow!'

'What? Ms McCarthy?'

'No, not her. That fat cow what was waiting at the school gate for her daft lad. Said I'd deliberately pushed that motorbike over onto your teacher. It broke her leg, apparently. "We've had information from a Mrs Dulcie Darbyshire," they said, all hoity-toity. "What she witnessed constitutes common assault, bla bla bla." I tell you, boy, I never meant to hurt the lass, did I? If she must career about the countryside on that machine, it serves her right I say. But it wasn't deliberate. I've never raised my hand against a woman, that's not the way I was brought up.'

I was shocked and rather frightened.

'What will happen to you, Ronnie? You won't have to go to court, will you?'

My mind was full of ideas gleaned from TV detective series. I couldn't voice my greatest fear, that Ronnie would have to go to prison.

'No, of course not, boy. They've given me a caution. And I'm sure that bastard Tom Spedding was enjoying it, grinning all over his face he was. The other one wrote it down on some form or other and asked me to sign. They'll send me a copy, he said. Don't you worry, that'll be the end of it now, just you wait and see.' He made an attempt at a grin.

But, unfortunately, it wasn't the end of it for Ronnie.

It was the beginning of it.

*

It was a fortnight later when the bombs fell. Looking back, I think Ronnie might have been able to cope with one of them, or even with both, if they had not happened on the same day.

It was Beryl who brought the news.

'Oh no,' muttered Mum, 'what now?' as she heard Beryl's wailing in our kitchen. We were upstairs, sorting through my clothes, as I was beginning to grow and several pairs of trousers no longer fitted properly.

'Myra! Oh Myra, what shall I do? Myra, where are you?'

'I'd best see what's happened,' said Mum, sighing. 'You go on trying on those trousers and keep the piles separate, right?'

She hurried down the stairs. I ignored the trousers and stayed at the top of the stairs, where I could hear what was being said in the kitchen.

'Now what is it, dear?' began Mum.

'Oh Myra, he's lost his job! That Mr Crumb he's sacked him.'

'What? Ronnie? What for?'

'I don't rightly know, but it's something about that time he pushed that teacher, the one with the motorbike and the police coming. Oh, what shall we do?' Beryl began to wail again.

'Now sit down dear and get yourself calm. I'll get you a cup of tea, and you can tell me properly what's happened.'

I wanted to hear what had happened too, but not from Beryl.

I came downstairs and walked through the kitchen with a breezy, 'Hi, Beryl!'

'Where are you off to? Have you sorted those trousers?'

'Yes, Mum. I'm just going to check my bike light.'

Ronnie was where I thought he would be. He was at the bottom of the garden; I could see the cigarette burning.

'Hi Ronnie!' I tried.

There was no answer.

I tried again. 'Are you all right? Beryl said…'

'Go away, Stevie!' His voice was gruff and kind of broken.

'But, Ronnie…'

'I said, go away! Do as you're told, boy, for Chrissake. I don't want you at the moment.'

I felt the tears smarting. I wanted desperately to comfort him, to make it all right for him. I felt that I had never loved him so much, and his rejection hurt deeply. I waited for a few minutes, but, frightened of making him angry, eventually I crept away and left him. I tried the shed door, thinking I'd wait for him there, play with the ferrets perhaps, but it was locked. So I went inside, where Beryl was blowing her nose hard.

'The worst thing is, Myra, he won't talk to me about it. He just gave me this letter, said, "He's given me a month's notice, the bastard!" and stomped off down the garden.'

'What did the letter say?'

'Oh, something about "gross conduct" and "bringing the school into disreputation", or some such term. I don't rightly understand it all.'

'But they can't do that. There should be a disciplinary hearing, dear, with the governors, I expect. That's what happens in these sort of cases. Then he can explain his side of it, and I'm sure Mr Godley would speak up for him.'

'But Mr Crumb hates him, Myra. Oh, what shall we do?'

At that moment we heard the van start up.

'That's him, off out, listen to him taking it out on that poor van.' The engine was revving wildly.

Without thinking, I rushed out and ran after the van as it turned out of our back alley and started down the drove.

'Ronnie! Ronnie!' I shouted, waving frantically. 'Wait for me! Take me with you!'

But he didn't stop. He probably couldn't even see me. I stood and watched as the van's back lights grew smaller and smaller until they eventually disappeared altogether.

12.20 p.m. Lunchtime

Chapter Nineteen

It was lunchtime. Normally I would eat my packed lunch in the canteen and then make my way to the library. But today my sandwiches were in the form room bin and I had no appetite anyway. I was worried sick about what I had to do that lunchtime with the airgun I had smuggled into school. It had all started on a cross country run in PE, exactly one week earlier.

That February was a very cold one, and the wind stung my cheeks as I battled against it round the first bend. But I was soon out in front of the rest of the class because I was good at cross country running. It was on the second circuit, as I passed the corner of the playing field flanked by bushes and long grass, when a hand reached out and grabbed my ankle. I fell heavily.

'Gotcha!'

I recognised Dwayne's voice. Before I could gather my breath to yell, I was dragged into the bushes and a hand was put over my mouth. It belonged to Keydon Bartley.

'Don't even squeak,' he told me, 'or it'll be worse for you!'

I couldn't have made a sound if I had tried because I was gasping for breath, but I began to struggle to get up.

'Don't even think about it!' warned Dwayne as he kicked me in the ribs.

I could not help a muffled yelp.

'Shut your mouth, Sydney, or there'll be more where that came from,' said Keydon.

'Shh!' hissed Dwayne.

All three of us froze. I don't know why I didn't make a noise, but I didn't. A group of boys shuffled past, panting. Then Dwayne peered out at the field from behind the bush.

'All clear! Those were at the back.'

'Now listen Sydney,' hissed Keydon, obviously enjoying his borrowed power. 'Have you met my dad?'

I shook my head.

'Well, you don't want to, 'cos he don't like anyone upsetting me, right?'

'Shut up, Keydon!' said Dwayne. 'Your dad's a fucking wimp!'

'No he is not!' shouted Keydon, and he let go of me to face up to Dwayne.

I decided to use this opportunity to make my escape. I knew I could run faster than either of them. But I wasn't quick enough; Dwayne moved amazingly fast for a fat boy. He caught hold of me by my T-shirt and wound me in.

'Not so fast Sydney. We need to have a little chat with you, 'cos there's something you ought to know.' He was grinning. 'Tell him, Bartley.'

I looked from one to the other, wondering what this was all about.

'I saw you with your girlfriend on Saturday afternoon,' said Keydon. 'I saw you having it off with that fat cow Margaret Jackson what lives on the reservation, right?'

'Yeah,' said Dwayne. 'Bartley told me all about it and we had a right laugh. Fancy fucking an ugly bitch like that. I'd have to put a bag over her head and even then I'd need to hold my breath.'

'So would I,' said Keydon.

I thought desperately about when Keydon might have seen me and Margaret together recently, as I no longer spent a lot of time with her, and then I remembered when, the previous Saturday, cycling home down the drove I had seen her taking a puppy for a walk. I had stopped because I didn't know about the puppy and she had told me she was walking it for Mrs Beacon. Thinking about it, I had a vague recollection that a car had passed us.

'What if we told everyone about your girlfriend, eh? Would that be nice?' said Dwayne, still grinning.

No, it wouldn't be nice. I imagined the humiliation; the whispers, the laughter, the crude comments. I would have done anything at that moment to prevent other people knowing about my friendship with Margaret. I wished with all my heart that I had never got to know her. In that moment I hated her.

'Well, would you like that, Sydney?' said Keydon.

'Well?' prompted Dwayne, with a kick.

I shook my head.

'Thought so!' said Dwayne. 'Now listen carefully, Sydney. We've got a friend what wants to have a little word with you, 'cos he thinks you've got something he wants, right?'

'Oh yeah? What?' I had no idea what he was talking about and guessed it was bravado.

'Never you mind. You know the war memorial in Marwell?'

Marwell St John's was our nearest village. The war memorial wasn't in the centre, like most fenland villages, but on the edge where the disused railway line crossed the road at an old level crossing. I knew it well; I had often explored along the overgrown railway lines.

'Well, do you?' he said, and kicked my shins.

I nodded before Dwayne could prompt me again.

'We'll see you there Saturday morning at eleven o'clock. Right?'

I nodded.

'Don't be late!' warned Dwayne, with a final kick, 'or everyone will know about you and Fat Mags.'

'What happened, Stringer?' asked Mr Parkin, as I pulled up at the end of the run. 'It's not like you to be last home.'

I affected to limp a bit.

'My ham string pulled, sir.'

He didn't even notice that Dwayne and Keydon had not returned from the run.

*

I was there by nine thirty on Saturday. I biked around for a bit, but I had an hour and a half to kill, so I sat for a bit by the railway line to see if I could see anything interesting. Although there was some scrabbling in the silence, not even a rat materialised, and I soon gave up being a naturalist. My heart wasn't in it; I was too nervous. Eventually, I got up and biked up and down the main (and only) street in Marwell St. Johns.

What was this meeting about? What would Dwayne and Keydon do to me at the war memorial? I spent some time wondering why I was so keen to keep to the arrangement? How soft was I, to deliberately put myself in their power rather than avoiding them at all costs? Perhaps I should just cycle home and forget about the whole thing. Perhaps it was just a prank, to frighten me, and they would have already forgotten about it. Perhaps when I got back to the war memorial at eleven o'clock they wouldn't be there. I actually set out to go home, feeling rather brave. After all, I was thinking, what can they do to me that's any worse than what they usually do?

Then I saw Margaret. As I turned the corner at the top of King John's Bank, I came upon her and Doreen waiting at the bus stop. All my resolution disappeared. There she was, in her old mac (it was drizzling), feet planted firmly apart, in that sturdy stance that was, perhaps, so reassuring in a friend but so unsexy in a girl. Why was she so fat? And why was she carrying a plastic carrier bag? At that moment I felt a surge of distaste, even fear of contamination. What if Dwayne & Co did what they said they'd do? What if I had to endure the taunts that would follow if they started a rumour that I was Margaret's boyfriend?

She saw me and waved.

'Hi Stephen!' she called. 'We're off to the car boot, d'you want to come?'

I wanted to cycle away, but it was too late to pretend that I hadn't seen them. I had been brought up to be polite and just couldn't ignore a direct question.

'Oh, no thanks. I'm… er… going to try to see if… look for a pair of kestrels… see if they're still around… and Mum wants me back early for lunch,' I finished lamely.

'Stephen's a bird-watcher, remember Rene?' said Margaret, proudly.

'Is he now?' said Doreen, as if birdwatching was a sin.

'Do you want to some round for tea? We're having pancakes. Is that all right, Rene?'

'I suppose so,' said Doreen.

'Er… I'm afraid I can't, er… we're… er… my aunty's coming to tea today.'

I had never lied to Margaret before.

'Oh, never mind. Come round tomorrow if you like.'

'OK.' Tomorrow was so far in the future that I couldn't even remember what day of the week it was.

'Tomorrow's church,' said Doreen.

'Yeah, I know, Rene, but not in the afternoon. Stephen can come round then, can't he? After I've done Bible study.'

'I suppose so,' said Doreen, and she looked at me sternly, 'but he needs to get saved.'

I felt terribly guilty that I wasn't saved, that I was a liar, that I was a coward, and that I was betraying Margaret. Thankfully at that moment the bus rounded the corner.

'It's late,' said Doreen. 'As usual.'

When I arrived back at the war memorial it was five minutes to eleven. I slid to a halt and looked round, my legs astride my bike, clutching my handlebars with sweaty hands. It was very quiet. All I could hear was the distant murmur of traffic on the main road. Then a crow started its call, startling me.

Then I heard another more sibilant cry from the other side of the railway track: 'Pss! Sydney! Here!'

I saw an arm emerge from behind the old signal box and beckon me urgently. I obeyed it, dismounting and wheeling my bike across the grassy level crossing and around the brick building. It grabbed me and hauled me off my bike, pulling me through a doorway.

It was dark inside the signal box. The equipment had been long dismantled, and all that was left was a narrow but very tall brick room, with the roof caved in at one side, allowing some light to filter down to the filthy concrete floor. There were some sacks and broken bottles in one corner and a pile of broken wooden roof joists in another. It was full of the biggest spiders' webs I had ever seen. It smelt of damp rotten wood.

There were three boys inside: Dwayne, who still had hold of me, Keydon, who was smoking, and Jimmy Buckland. That was what surprised me. I had not seen him or his uncle for some months. I thought he had moved away forever, along with my binoculars.

'Welcome to our humble abode, Sydney! So glad you could make it,' said Jimmy.

'Seen your girlfriend recently?' said Keydon.

'She's not my girl… ow!' My reply was cut off by a punch to the belly from Dwayne. I doubled up in pain. Keydon giggled.

'No need for that, Tubbs,' said Jimmy. 'We just want you to do a little job for us, right?'

'Right?' echoed Dwayne.

'What job?' I said quickly, before Dwayne could punch me again.

'You go shooting don't you? I remember you told me all about it,' continued Jimmy.

'Bang! Bang!' said Keydon, pretending to shoot me.

I nodded cautiously. 'So what?'

'And you live next door to Rawlplug, who's got loads of guns, right?' said Jimmy.

'Bang Bang! Bang Bang!' Keydon pretended to shoot several people who were lurking in the corners of the signal box.

'For Chrissake grow up, Bartley!' said Jimmy.

Keydon sat down on a box, looking cowed.

'Well, has he?' continued Jimmy.

'Has he what?'

'Has he got guns?'

'Yeah, why?'

'Well, we want you to get us a gun,' said Jimmy.

'What? You must be crazy!'

'Are you calling me crazy?' Dwayne pushed me up against the wall.

'Give it a break, Tubbs!' said Jimmy.

'What do you mean, a gun? I can't get you a gun. What do you want with a gun?'

'We're gonna murder Mr Crumb!' said Keydon, and he giggled again.

'I wish you'd shut up, you stupid twat,' said Jimmy.

I must have looked as shocked as I felt.

'We're not going to really shoot anyone, Sydney, honest we're not,' said Jimmy.

'Worse luck!' said Dwayne.

'But what do you want to do with it?' I asked.

'We want to put the wind up old Crumpet, that's what. Just for a laugh. Make him think it's the I.R.A. Set off the fire alarm, everybody out, police arrive, school closed down, stuff like that.'

'Yeah, it'll be great,' said Dwayne, grinning. 'I can just imagine the look on Old Crumpet's face.'

'Yeah! No more school!' said Keydon.

'But how would you… where would you… when?' I stammered.

'Don't you worry your little head about all that, leave the "when" and "how" to me. Your job is to get me a gun. No need for ammunition, just a gun. It's just for frighteners.'

'But I can't,' I said.

'Oh yes you can,' said Dwayne, and he pushed me up against the wall.

'I don't care what you do to me, I can't just give you a gun. It's against the law. You can't use a gun unless you've got a shotgun certificate and anyway we're all too young. I only use one when I'm with Ronnie 'cos he's an adult with a certificate.'

'Fuck the law!' said Dwayne.

Jimmy laughed. 'Don't be such a little wimp, Sydney!'

It was that last comment which really hurt. This was the person who had, I thought, been my friend. And he'd still got my binoculars.

'But I can't just get a gun, they're locked away.'

'That's your problem. Your job is to get us a gun.'

'But…'

'Or we tell everyone how you fucked Fat Mags, right?' said Dwayne.

'But I haven't got any guns. Ronnie keeps them.'

'Yeah, we know all about you and Rawlplug, 'said Dwayne. 'That pervert!'

'Surely he'd do his little lover-boy a favour,' said Keydon.

'But I can't…'

'Can't you?' said Dwayne. 'Do you want me to persuade him, Jim?' He held me up against the wall.

Keydon guffawed, nervously. I swallowed.

'Leave him be, Tubbs. That's not the way,' said Jimmy. 'Now, Steve, my friend, what if I told you that I'd still got something of yours that you left behind by mistake when you were visiting, eh? What if I said you could have this something back, being as they were your dad's, or so you told me, eh?' He paused, looking at me. I stared back. 'Do you understand me?'

I nodded.

'So it's a fair exchange, right? You get me some kind of gun, you get your binoculars, right?'

'Binoculars? What, like Old Crumpet's? What's he want them for?' said Keydon.

'I bet he uses 'em so he can spy on Fat Mags and see her undressing, eh? Has she got nice big titties, eh? And what about that arse?' said Dwayne.

'Yuk!' said Keydon.

Jimmy ignored them. 'Well?' he asked me.

'OK,' I said.

What else could I have said? I missed my binoculars terribly as I could no longer watch birds properly. They were the most valuable thing I had ever owned. They had been my father's and were the only thing I had of his. I had never dared to admit to Mum that I had lost them and had taken to carrying their case around pretending that they were inside.

'When do you want it?' I asked.

'Next Saturday, same time, same place.'

'What?' I gasped. Having so little time somehow made it worse, as if it wasn't going to be difficult enough anyway to smuggle a gun out of a locked gun cabinet.

I spent the next few days in a mental frenzy. How could I get hold of a gun? At first my brain refused to work at all and all I could think about was what it would be like if everyone at school knew about Margaret and me. I went alternately hot and cold just thinking about it. But then I pulled myself together. If I was to get out of this I needed to do 'my job' for Jimmy, so I put all my efforts into trying to think how to smuggle a gun out of Ronnie's gun cabinet. I lived my ordinary life in a daze; all I could think of was what I came to regard as 'that bloody gun'. At night I lay awake for what seemed like hours. I could no longer think straight about anything, let alone guns. Eventually I would fall asleep, and wake the next morning after dreams in which I ran after Ronnie along the sea wall to the sound of gunfire, or I shot Mr Crumb who was standing on the war memorial looking at me through his binoculars. I got up each morning with my stomach in knots.

Now, when I think about it, I wonder why I didn't just tell an adult – my mum, Ronnie, Ms McCarthy, Mr Godley – about my predicament. Somehow that solution never occurred to me, for the same reason that I had never revealed to anyone the extent of the pain and humiliation I suffered at the hands, and mouths, of my fellow pupils. It was as if I existed in a separate world, with its own morality and rule of law, which I had no choice but to obey; a parallel world to the 'real' world of adults, a world where power was wielded by those who could instil the most fear, where there was no sense of fairness and where to be a 'grass' was a worse crime than to be a torturer.

*

I was so overwhelmed with my own problems that Ronnie's situation didn't really register properly. But looking back now, I can see that it was the visit from the firearms officer that was the final straw that finally broke Ronnie.

On Thursday evening I was wiping up after tea and the draining board was piled high, when Mum said: 'Come on, buck up Stephen! If you're not careful, you'll wipe the pattern off that plate. Always day-dreaming you are at the moment, that's when you're not up in that room of yours. Ronnie must wonder what he's done wrong. When he was putting a new fuse in the washing machine this afternoon he asked me if you were all right as he hadn't seen you for a few days. Poor chap, he's that screwed up with losing his job and all that, and he still worries about you, bless him. And you look pale.'

She put a soapy hand under my chin and raised my head to look at her.

'What's up, son?'

'Nothing. Ow, Mum, that was wet!' I scrubbed my face with the tea towel, embarrassed, as always nowadays, by my mother's affection. Keen to avoid any further discussion I made an extra effort, wiping the rest of the dishes at breakneck speed, hoping to be able to disappear upstairs where I could worry alone. But it was not to be.

'No you don't, my boy!' said Mum as I made for the stairs. 'You get out there and talk to Ronnie. He's in his shed probably. Beryl says he's always in there nowadays, she can't get a word out of him. At her wits end she is. But he always talked to you. You just spend a moment thinking of all the things he's done for you; it won't hurt you to give him half-an-hour, will it?'

She was right, of course. I felt at the time that the last thing I wanted to do was to listen to anyone else's troubles. I had become obsessed with my own. But I did feel sorry for him, so I did as she said. I was glad that I did, because by visiting Ronnie in his shed that night, the solution to my problem dropped, ready-made, from heaven.

Ronnie's shed was in as much turmoil as he was. In the past, although it had been stuffed with 'things', it was all in order, everything in its place with Ronnie knowing exactly where to lay his hand on what he wanted. But during the last few weeks the shed had become as chaotic as him. When I look back, I don't really understand how I missed seeing Ronnie's disintegration. His once sunny disposition had disappeared, and he looked constantly miserable. His moods were unpredictable; I would often come upon Beryl crying in our kitchen because, 'I don't know what to say anymore, Myra, everything I say is wrong,' and my reluctance to spend time with him was partly because of the recent occasions when he had bawled me out – unfairly, in my opinion. As I gazed at him in his shed on that evening I saw someone I hardly recognised. For a start he seemed to have shrunk. He had never been a tall man but he seemed somehow diminished, sitting there in his chair, and, most surprising, he wasn't doing anything: he wasn't whittling a piece of wood, or making an old crate into a place to store his wellie socks, or plucking a pheasant, or petting a ferret. He was just sitting hunched up staring at the wall. He had his shotguns lined up on the table in front of him, and there was a tin of gun oil and his cleaning kit on the table.

Around him everything seemed to be a mess and the things usually lined up in order on the shelves – tools, tins, little boxes, bits and pieces – were all in a muddle on the floor. It looked as if he had started a spring-clean, like Mum did, by moving everything away from its place, but, unlike her, he had put nothing back. There were heaps of stuff everywhere and the metal gun cabinet was open with the keys hanging from the lock, which was most unusual because Ronnie was obsessive about never leaving it unlocked, let alone open.

When I went in he looked up. But he did not grin at me, as he usually did, or even scowl at me, which he used to do when I had done something wrong. He didn't say, 'Now then, Stevie, how's things?' or 'Now don't you be disturbing me, young fellow, I'm busy and haven't you got any of that ol' homework.' He didn't push his cap back off his forehead or jingle his keys in his right-hand pocket like he usually did. He just looked blank. The most disturbing thing of all was that his eyes were not only expressionless but had lost their vivid blue colour and were dull grey. It was frightening.

'Hi, Ronnie,' I said.

He didn't answer. He was staring at the wall again. I sat down on a box and wondered what to say.

'Are you all right?' was what I eventually came up with.

It didn't work. He went on staring. A few very uncomfortable minutes passed; it was like trying to communicate with someone you didn't know.

'What are you doing?' I tried.

'What does it look like, lad?'

Well, at least he recognises me, I thought. I felt a bit more encouraged.

'Do you want me to help?'

'With what?'

'Shall I put the guns back in the cabinet?' I asked.

'No, leave them be. I want to keep them in sight, while I can.'

'What do you mean?'

'They're taking my guns, Stevie, the bastards are taking my guns!'

'Who are? What do you mean?'

'It's the bloody coppers, that's who it is. I've just had a visit from old Brian Forbridge, what's done the firearms sustificates for Cambridgeshire for as long as I can remember. Thought it was just the normal check, like, to see the gun cabinet and my shotgun papers and suchlike. But oh no, it was to take my guns from me, and to think that I always pass the time of day when I sees him.'

'But why, Ronnie?'

He looked up at me. 'Why? It all goes back to that group of fucking antis and that teacher you're so fond of. I got a bloody caution, didn't I? And on top of all that palaver from the mother of that daft lad! Well, now look what's happened! "We need to revoke your certificate, Mr Rawlinson," he says, all hoity-toity like, not at all like he usually talks to me, "the police computer shows a caution against your name and our policy is… blah, blah, blah!" I tell you, boy, I'll swing for them two women, that fat cow with the big mouth and that anti witch. I've said it before and I'll say it again! I'll swing for 'em'

'But what will happen to your guns, Ronnie, and the shooting, and…'

The enormity of what had happened dawned on me. Ronnie was losing his guns and so he wouldn't be able to shoot, he wouldn't be able to go pigeon shooting, he wouldn't be able to bring back the occasional pheasant from the Marsh edge; and, oh God, he wouldn't be able to go wildfowling, there would be no more 'going after the geese'.

'Well, he says, does Brian bloody Forbridge, that I will have to re-apply for a sustificate, "Sometime in the future," whatever that means, and he will confiscate my guns and, "Take them into safe keeping," that means throw them in a pile at the nick no doubt, unless I can get someone with a sustificate to look after them for me, so I've gone and seen old Benny Rugdale and he said he'd take 'em, so I'm just getting them cleaned and ready like.'

I didn't know what to say. I felt desperately sorry for him and as I looked at his hunched back I really wanted to help him. I put a hand on his shoulder in a tentative way.

'Do you want me to help you tidy up in here?'

He looked surprised. 'Why?'

'Well… er… it looks a bit untidy.'

'If you want.'

I looked round at the mess, not sure where to start. I got up and began to pick up screws and put them back in their little cardboard box. It was then that I saw my airgun, leaning up against the wall, not in the gun cabinet where it was usually kept. Given to me by Ronnie on my tenth birthday, I had rarely had a chance to use it because although it wasn't legally necessary to keep an airgun in a secure gun cabinet, Ronnie was a stickler for gun security.

'I'm not locking it up 'cos it's a gun, Stevie,' he had told me. 'There's nothing dangerous about a gun in itself. It's them what use 'em that's sometimes dangerous and even an airgun can cause a nasty accident in the hands of a nutter and I don't trust them pikeys not to poke around our property when we're out. So I'll keep it locked up when you're not using it, right? If you need it for a good reason, we'll get it out.'

Unfortunately, 'good reasons' for a boy to use an airgun without direct supervision hadn't often occurred over the years, and it had lived propped up in the dark in the gun cabinet. I had almost forgotten it belonged to me. My mind raced as I tried to think of a 'good reason' for removing it.

'Er… you know my airgun?' I began.

He looked at me but didn't seem to have registered what I said.

'What?'

'My airgun. Could I… er… could I… er… use it to… er…' Suddenly it came to me, and the words rushed out. 'Could I take it to school so I can give a talk in English, on Monday that is, this coming Monday, I'd look after it ever so carefully and give it in at the office as soon as I got to school to be locked away until I needed it. It would help me get a better mark if I could talk about something I know like shooting, and Miss Ferguson said she was interested and could I bring it in?' My anxious gabbling died away, as Ronnie didn't seem to be hearing me. 'Ronnie?'

'What?'

'Can I take my airgun into school for a talk in English?'

'Yeah, if you like.'

I was shocked. I had expected him to object and had been gearing myself up for an argument. I picked up the airgun and made my escape before he could change his mind.

'What's that you've got?' said Mum as I passed through the kitchen.

'Just my airgun,' I said airily.

'Does Ronnie know you've taken it out of the shed?'

'Yes Mum. I'm just going to take it apart to clean it. It's all right. Ronnie said it's all right, he's cleaning all his guns.' It felt such a relief to be able to tell a partial truth.

Mum looked at me closely.

'Your hair needs a cut. I'll take you this Saturday, I can't trust you on your own, last time you came back with that mucky gel stuff all over it. We'll get the nine-thirty bus.'

I thought of the war memorial and Dwayne and Jimmy waiting for me. I thought of what they might do, if I didn't turn up…

'But Mum…'

'No, Stephen, don't argue with me. We're going and that's that. You can change your library books while we're there.'

'But…'

'Stephen!'

I knew that warning in her voice. I slunk away to my bedroom.

Once there I pondered my new problem. How was I to get the gun to Jimmy? Once again I spent a restless night worrying, and I still hadn't solved the problem when Dwayne offered me the solution on a plate the next morning in registration.

'Ah Sydney,' he shouted as I slid into my seat and Mrs Pritchard opened the register. 'You all right, mate?' He put his arm around my shoulders and gave me a painful man-hug.

Mrs Pritchard looked up. 'It's nice to see you two getting on so well,' she said. 'But can we have some quiet, Dwayne, while I call the register.'

'Yes, Miss.' He turned around in his seat and bawled at the class. 'Quiet! Shut yer noise! Miss is doing the register!'

Afterwards, when Mrs Pritchard had disappeared into her storeroom, he turned to me again. The bonhomie had gone, and his eyes glinted in malice.

'Well, Sydney?'

'What do you want?' I whispered, trying to wriggle out of his grasp.

'Just being friendly, Sydney. Wanted to remind you about our little meet-up on Saturday morning? You still coming?'

I gulped. 'I can't.'

'Of course you can,' he hissed, leaning over me.

'I've got to go out with my mum. I can't get out of it.'

'Poor little mummy's boy, eh? Never mind your fucking mum, remember what we said if you didn't come up with the goods, yeah?' He turned round to Peter Slingsby. 'Hey, guess who we saw Sydney with? He's got a new girlfriend. It's…'

I broke in, frantically, tugging at his arm. 'No, I've got the… I've got it all right. Honest I have. It's in my bedroom. It's just that I can't do it Saturday. I can do it Sunday, or Monday. Yes, on a school day I can do it. Please believe me, I've got it, it's just that I can't do it Saturday.'

He looked at me and I could see his little brain working. He wasn't sure what to do. This wasn't in the script.

'We'll have to see,' he said. 'I'll talk to Jim.'

On Friday morning Jim's message came back. It was hissed into my face along with a strong whiff of cheese and onion crisps and plenty of saliva, when I was waylaid by Dwayne under the stairs between Period 1 history and Period 2 design tech.

'Monday lunchtime. Corner of the field. Edge of the dyke opposite the allotments. Or else!'

My relief was tempered by a further problem. How was I to take the gun to school on Monday? Even when it was dismantled it wouldn't fit into my school bag and I knew Mum would never allow me to cycle off for the bus with a gun on my handlebars.

That evening I rooted around in my room and eventually found, on top of the wardrobe, Uncle Doug's old cricket bag which he had given me some years before. Now, having wiped off the dust with a dirty sock, I found that the dismantled airgun, wrapped in a sweater, and with my PE kit stuffed at one end, fitted in quite neatly.

I had therefore set out on this Monday morning with the bag balanced on my handlebars.

'What on earth is that you're taking to school?' Mum had asked, when I said goodbye to her.

'My cricket bag, Mum. You remember, what Uncle gave me. We're doing cricket in PE this morning.'

'What? In this weather?'

'Yeah, we do nets in the gym if it's raining.'

She looked puzzled. 'But you told me you were doing cross country in PE at the moment. I washed and ironed your green T-shirt not your whites.'

'Yeah, I know. Mr Parkin is always changing his mind. Bye, Mum!'

Dick had chuckled as I lugged the bag onto the bus.

'Running away from home, lad?'

I smiled weakly. 'I'm just taking something into school to show the teacher.'

That lunchtime I didn't go to the library as I usually did. Instead I collected the cricket bag from Mrs Duckworth and set out to walk as unobtrusively as possible out of the school building. I strolled across the playground, avoiding the lunch queue and the games of football, and around the edge of the field, trying to appear as if it was perfectly normal to carry a cricket bag to some imaginary cricket pitch on a cold wet day in February.

I reached the corner of the playing field which abutted onto the allotments. The fence was broken down at one spot next to the dyke. I clambered through, crouched in the nettles and settled down to wait for Jimmy.

I waited a long time, but he didn't show up. The only living creatures that did were a couple of ducks, hoping for a hand-out. It was very cold, and the rain was light but steady. I was soon wet through and had to keep wiping the rain from my glasses. What if he didn't come? What if I had gone to all this trouble for nothing? What if they were just having me on? What if they started rumours about me and Margaret anyway? I shivered.

Eventually, I heard the bell for the end of lunchtime. What was

I to do now? I hesitated, but eventually decided that being late for afternoon lessons would lead to awkward questions and compound the problem. So I put the bag in the nettles and hurried back. I would check at the end of school, and if it was still there I would take it home again.

I didn't need to do that because Jimmy launched his escapade that afternoon.

1.20 p.m. Lesson 5

Chapter Twenty

On Mondays Year 9 had country dancing Period 5, and I arrived for the lesson feeling very worried. What had happened to my airgun? Was it still in the nettles, or had Jimmy found it? Where was he? I glanced over at Dwayne as we lined up outside the assembly hall. I had noticed that he wasn't in afternoon registration but he had reappeared on the way to the hall for country dancing and he was larking about with Keydon. I hoped he'd forgotten all about what was supposed to happen, and I began to work out how to lie about the permanent loss of my airgun as well as my binoculars.

Mr Took bustled up and pushed open the hall doors.

'In you go, Year 9,' he said.

He trotted over to the grand piano, and began to open it up, as we followed him, finding seats on the low gym benches which were placed around the walls. By the time both Year 9 classes had assembled there were nearly sixty of us, waiting miserably for our weekly dance.

As soon as Dwayne got into the hall he went straight to the fire doors and pushed the bar to open them, letting in a draft.

'Shut that bloody door, Tubbs,' shouted Stacey O'Rourke. 'It's fucking freezing in here.'

'Oh sorry!' said Dwayne. 'I thought it'd be nice to have some fresh air. It smells in here; someone must have farted. Wasn't you was it, Stace?' He pulled the door shut, or so I thought.

'Tosspot!' said Stacey.

Mr Crumb arrived, his country dancing music book under his arm.

'Stand, Year 9,' said Mr Took, and we shambled to our feet.

'Take your places for Apple Tree Square!' Mr Crumb rubbed his hands together. He obviously enjoyed these lessons and his voice was a bit more animated than usual.

We shuffled around, trying to remember whether we started in two lines or in squares.

'Come on now squares of eight, how many times do I have to remind you? Would the boys in that far corner do some simple arithmetic, then they might notice that there are ten people in their square, you need to lose two now get yourself organised. That square over there will have to manage with seven, just pretend there's someone there Bristow. As usual now, from the beginning, thank you Mr Took. One two three!'

We began to dance. It was faltering, it was confused, it wasn't synchronised, and it wasn't in time with the music, which Mr Took thumped out, trying desperately to slow down when we were obviously miles behind and then speeding up frantically when Mr Crumb called out, 'Let's have some energy, some verve!' But somehow we got through the first square.

'All change!' called Mr Crumb, as this was supposed to be where we moved to our left and joined the adjacent square. We had been practising this move for weeks but still quite a few people didn't know their left from their right, or chose not to know, because it always turned out to be a mess, with lots of people squashed into one square and one or two squares disappearing altogether.

At this point I found myself opposite Dwayne. His piggy eyes gleamed when he noticed this and, sure enough, when we got to the first 'two steps forward and clap' move, he used the opportunity to slap me round the head rather than clapping his hands.

'Ouch!' I couldn't help shouting.

'Quiet there concentrate on your moves that boy,' called Mr Crumb.

I tried to obey him, but with half an eye on Dwayne's next moves. Sure enough, at the twirly bit in the middle of the square, Dwayne trod firmly on my foot, and I limped through the next three moves.

'No no that's all wrong, stop everyone! We will need to go through it all again, will you never get the sequence right, how are you going to be ready for the Easter fete? Stop everyone!'

Mr Took stopped playing mid-bar. We stopped dancing. I had stopped next to Dwayne in the middle of the 'up to the top' move.

'What's happened to the gun, Sydney!' he hissed. I ducked and missed the slap intended for my head.

'Those two boys stand still,' said Mr Crumb.

At that moment the fire doors crashed open and a figure in jeans and bomber jacket, with a green knitted balaclava over his face rushed in. It was obviously Jimmy and he was carrying my airgun.

'Hands up or I'll shoot!' he shouted in an awful mock-Irish accent.

Josie Davenport screamed. Keydon Bartley giggled. Stacey O'Rourke, who was Irish, gasped, 'Mary, Mother of Jesus!'

Then for a long moment it was completely silent in the hall. All I could hear was Joanne Bevington's constant sniff.

'I said, hands up!' said Jimmy. It was as if he didn't know what to do next.

Dwayne came to the rescue. 'It's the I.R.A! Help! Sound the alarm!' He rushed towards the door, straight at Mr Crumb, who put out an arm to catch him. Dwayne stopped. Josie screamed again, and some of the girls joined in, but in a half-hearted sort of way. Everyone looked confused.

'Back in your place, Tubbs,' said Mr Crumb, pushing him away with a moue of distaste. Keydon laughed and then stifled it.

Mr Crumb turned towards Jimmy, who was still standing in the same place, but whose weapon had begun to wilt.

'I don't know who you are but I suspect that you are a pupil at this school and that this is what is called a "prank". I need to see you outside my office at the end of this lesson what are you waiting for boy now go. Get back into position Tubbs and you can see me at the end of the lesson too for disruptive behaviour. Where were we Mr Took?'

Dwayne slunk back to the square. Everyone else shuffled around back into some sort of shape, and Mr Took played a chord. Jimmy was left with the gun slumped at his side.

'Well what are you waiting for boy I said my office toute suite,' said Mr Crumb, and he clicked his fingers.

'Fuck you! 'said Jimmy. 'And fuck your fucking gun, Sydney!' He threw my airgun towards me. Then he disappeared through the fire doors.

'Mr Took please retrieve that firearm and at the end of the lesson take it to the office and ask Mr Godley to call the police for its confiscation now everyone begin the second square.'

The lesson proceeded. As a lesson it didn't seem any different from hundreds of others I had endured at Sir Willyum's, but I was still very anxious. I knew I would have to go to Mr Godley at the end of the lesson to try to explain why it was my airgun and to get it back somehow. I remember longing for the end of this awful day and getting home to tell Ronnie about the geese I had seen that morning from the school bus, and asking if I could go wildfowling with him.

'That was a shambles,' said Mr Crumb. 'I don't want to dwell on such ridiculous behaviour but I warn you,' he peered around until his eyes settled on Dwayne with venom, 'that I will not stand for any further disruption to our work on Apple Tree Square, take your places and I expect it to be perfect or we will be practising after school, I hope I make myself clear, thank you Mr Took.'

Somehow, we found ourselves in some sort of approximately correct formation while Mr Took waited, hands poised above the piano keyboard, a painful look of despairing encouragement on his face.

We began to dance. The next fifteen minutes of the lesson were uneventful. We completed three changes of Apple Tree Square twice, and although none of us ended up where we were supposed to be, we did manage to keep the formation. Even Mr Crumb seemed satisfied.

'That will do, thank you Mr Took. It still needs plenty of rehearsal but we will leave it for now, I want to practise some steps, there are still some boys who are out of beat in the skipping sequence, now listen year nine I want you standing in a space facing me and quietly, Dumbridge you are clumping remember that this dance is an expression of joy at springtime and I want to see you light on your feet like a spring lamb not a carthorse.'

Brian Dumbridge, all six feet and ten stone of him, went red and began an exaggerated tiptoe towards a space. Someone giggled, I couldn't see who because I was in the front.

It was at that moment that the nightmare began.

'Headmaster! Headmaster!' gasped Mrs Duckworth, bursting through the hall doors.

'What is it, Mrs Duckworth? Can't you see I am teaching?'

'But I think this is very urgent, headmaster, you see it was when I went to the ladies that I saw him and I couldn't believe my eyes at first headmaster because, well, I thought I must be seeing things but no I was sure it was…'

'What is very urgent Mrs Duckworth, stop gabbling woman you are making no sense.'

Someone giggled.

'There's a man with a gun, headmaster!'

'Yes Mrs Duckworth there was someone with a gun but it was I am afraid a very stupid prank and the perpetrator should be outside my office.'

'Yes headmaster, but…'

'I am not having my country dancing lessons continually interrupted by foolishness Mrs Duckworth, now go and find Mr Godley and tell him to deal with that stupid boy.'

'But it isn't a boy, headmaster, it's…'

'I really don't care who it is or isn't Mrs Duckworth I am not having it disrupt this lesson do you understand now go away, Mr Took would you be so kind as to play bars… er…' he consulted his book, 'bars 45 and 46 on page 13 thank you.'

'But headmaster…'

A loud bang was heard, coming from the front of the school. Mrs Duckworth stopped, with her mouth open. A girl screamed.

Mr Crumb gulped.

'It's a bomb!' someone shouted.

But I knew that sound and I knew that it was no bomb. It was the sound of a shot gun.

Ms McCarthy burst into the assembly hall. Her eyes were scared, just like a rabbit in the headlights when Ronnie and I went rabbiting at night on Westley's farm.

'He's shot her!' she shouted in a sort of gasp.

Mrs Duckworth screamed, a loud piercing scream. But no-one else made a sound. It was as if we were frozen.

'What?' whispered Mr Crumb. 'In my school?'

Still no-one moved. No-one shouted, no-one else screamed, no-one ran for the door, ran for cover, ran anywhere. Mrs Duckworth was shivering fiercely but did not reach for the fire alarm, which was by the door. She did not seem capable of movement.

'Quick!' cried Ms McCarthy. 'Get the children out. He's got a gun, I tell you!'

But it was too late. Behind her, the hall door was pushed open again and a figure took a step inside. He was pointing his shotgun at Ms McCarthy's back and in the very instant that I realised it was Ronnie (but that new Ronnie, that different Ronnie, that Ronnie I did not recognise, with face set rigid and dead eyes), he pulled the trigger.

I did not hear the boom, although it must have been deafening as I was only a few feet away. All I saw was the look of surprise on Ms McCarthy's face and then, slowly, she crumpled forwards and landed in a heap at the side of Mr Crumb. Ronnie just stood in front of the door and calmly broke the gun, spilling two empty cartridges onto the floor. He felt in his pocket, took out two more cartridges

(I noticed from the red colour of the cases that they were BBs for goose shooting), slipped them into the barrel and closed the breech with a loud click.

Mr Crumb, released at last from his frozen stance, turned around just as Ronnie completed re-loading. He caught the next shot straight in the chest and fell backwards. I heard his head crack on the polished wooden floor.

Then there were screams, lots of screams, and, as if a spring had been released, everyone began to move, running in different directions.

'Quick! Under the piano!' I heard Mr Took call from behind me.

'Oh my God!' shouted Mrs Duckworth and I saw her collapse in a faint.

I still could not believe what I was seeing. This was Ronnie and he had just murdered two people in front of my eyes. He began to advance slowly towards the screaming, rushing pandemonium. He passed very close to me but did not seem to see me. I turned and watched as he pointed the gun and slowly spun it across, as if searching for a target that wasn't moving. It settled on Margaret, who was, like me standing stock still. She was looking at me and she looked quite beautiful for an instant, like a Madonna, and that is how I remember her, not as the crumpled heap lying on the hall floor.

Ronnie re-loaded again and began to stalk round the hall, picking off pupils as they tried to escape. I saw Peter Timms shot as he huddled on a bench against the wall wailing. I saw Mr Took shot as he crouched behind the piano, sheltering two girls under his arms. I saw Josie shot in the back, that beautiful back, as she tried to get through the fire door, which was crammed with panicking pupils. I saw Dwayne on his knees, tears streaming down his fat face, begging for his life.

'Don't shoot me please!'

Ronnie turned towards him, aimed and shot.

Somehow that sight galvanised me.

'Ronnie! No!' I shouted. 'No!'

He turned towards my voice, the barrel pointing straight at my chest and I thought he was going to shoot me. I felt my bowels loosen. I stared at his strange face; it was as if he was in the most terrible pain. He looked at me for what seemed like a long time, although probably it was less than a second. Then I saw his lips move, and, although I could not hear him in the noise and I am no lip-reader, I knew exactly what he said.

'Stevie?' For an instant, his face softened. Then he turned and left the hall, head bowed.

At that moment the fire alarm sounded.

Afterwards

Chapter Twenty-One

I have no recollection of the next few hours.

I am told that the fire alarm triggered a mass evacuation of the school and that excited happy-go-lucky pupils from the rest of the school were met by panicking Year 9s running for their lives and screaming about a gunman on the loose. The panic spread so that any semblance of evacuation drill was impossible and, rather than assembling in lines on the playground, pupils ran away, screaming, across the playing field, out of the front of the school and across the car park, spilling on to the road outside and into the arms of parents, who had arrived in their cars as usual ready for the end of school, some of whom were huddled around Mrs Darbyshire, who was slumped in a heap by the gate. She had been waiting as usual for Ashley when Ronnie got out of his van and shot her. It had been that first shot which we heard in the assembly hall, and which had alerted Ms McCarthy, who, on her way from the art mobile to the staffroom had seen a man with a gun walking into school in front of her.

I found out afterwards that Mr Took, badly wounded by a shot to the shoulder, had shepherded many shocked pupils from the assembly hall and into the adjacent classroom, where he ordered them to hide under the desks, and then, by a superhuman effort and losing blood copiously, dragged the teacher's desk against the door before collapsing. I am told that Stacey O'Rourke tried to staunch his bleeding with her hands, praying to 'Mary, Mother of Jesus' all the time, and that she was covered in blood from head to toe when the paramedics finally lifted her away.

I am told that Mr Godley heard the shooting when trying to understand what Old Badger was trying to tell him. It had been the second time that day that the tramp had come into reception and attempted to communicate his concerns about why Ronnie had hidden a gun in the mini-bus garage two nights before and had retrieved it that morning. Sensing that something was wrong, the old man had clung onto Mr Godley's jacket and, struggling to utter the words which were blocking up his voice, managed to whisper the word, 'Shotgun,' which came out slurred as 'Shogn' and which Mr Godley did not understand.

The sound of the gunshots, though, led him to race in the direction they seemed to come from in time to see a man with a gun running away from the hall, and at that point he smashed a fire glass with his fist, setting off the alarm, and arrived in the hall as pupils ran screaming past him. He found me standing alone among the bodies and I am told he took me in his arms and hugged me, as if to enclose me from further harm, and that he did not let go until the first policeman arrived and said, 'It's all right now, sir, you can let him go. He's safe.'

I am told that the news of the shooting spread fast, as pupils living in Easton ran to their homes crying about a gunman on the loose, and that, even in the days before social media communications, parents soon knew and, during the next thirty minutes, arrived in cars from all over the district, desperate to find their child alive. The taxi driver who was waiting to pick up Aaron Browne, who had special needs, called the police with a 999 call on his car phone and they arrived within fifteen minutes. Soon the surrounding area rang with the sirens of police cars and ambulances and eventually even the fire crew turned up to find a real emergency at Sir Willyum's at last.

I was disentangled from Mr Godley's embrace and taken by a policewoman into Room 2 to join my classmates, who had emerged from beneath the desks but were crying and shivering with shock. From there Mr Took was carried out by paramedics and taken to the hospital at Kings Lynn. They didn't manage to save him. I am told that I sat where I was put but said nothing, even when I was asked how to contact my mother, and that I appeared not to hear anyone. Gradually, over the next hour, parents arrived to take the other pupils home and I still sat there until eventually they did contact my mum, I don't know how, and I don't know how she got to the school – I expect Mr Simpson from the garage brought her – but she did come to collect me and I was taken home.

I am told I continued to sit and say nothing in Mr Simpson's car and later in the kitchen, where my mum had wrapped me in a blanket and made me a cup of cocoa. She tells me she was at her wit's end, not knowing how to deal with a child who had, as it were, come back from the dead, but wouldn't say anything.

'He's in shock!' Beryl told my mother. 'He'll come round.'

My first memory when I did 'come round' was the smell of cold cocoa. I was sitting at the kitchen table with a blanket round my shoulders and my mother was stroking my hand.

'Geroff, Mum!' I said, and snatched my hand away, embarrassed by this excess of solicitude from a parent whose normal response to any catastrophe involving me was, 'You'll live!'

My mother burst into tears, which was even more embarrassing, and I shrugged off the blanket.

'Oh Myra, love, it's going to be all right,' said Beryl, who was occupying the third seat at the table, and she passed Mum the box of tissues. Of course it wasn't going to be all right. It would never again be all right, not only for me, but also for her, poor woman, although she did not know that at the time.

'Is there anything we can get you, dear?' she asked.

I was suddenly very thirsty.

'Can I have some lemonade?' Lemonade was strictly for special occasions in our household as orange squash was cheaper, but I felt I warranted some special treatment.

'Of course you can, Stevie love,' said Beryl. 'Where does your mum keep it?' Mum was still blowing her nose and wiping her eyes.

'I'll get it,' I said, glad to escape all this emotion, and I went to the pantry.

Then there was a sharp knock at our front door.

'Whoever's that?' asked Mum, looking startled.

'I'll go,' I said, as I was already on my feet and it would get me out of the kitchen.

I had to unbolt the front door because normally we never used it. That necessitated fetching a chair from the front room because I couldn't reach the top bolt, but eventually I pulled it open. On the doorstep stood a policewoman in uniform and a man in a raincoat with a crew cut.

'Good evening, sonny,' he said. 'Is your mum in?'

'Can I help you?' asked my mum, who was behind me.

'We wondered if you could tell us how to contact…' he consulted a small black notebook which he took out of his pocket, 'Mrs Beryl Rawlinson? I believe she lives next door, but we couldn't make anyone hear.'

'Oh, she's here, officer. We've had a bit of a shock, you see. Beryl?' she called.

Beryl came to the door, looking flustered.

'Yes? What is it?' Her hand flew to her mouth. 'It isn't Ronnie is it? There hasn't been an accident? He went out this morning and he isn't back yet. Oh, please tell me he's OK.'

'I think it might be better if we had a word in private, madam,' said the detective.

'Come in, come in!' said Mum. 'Use the front room, Beryl,' she said, and led the way, turning on the light and drawing the curtains. 'Come on Stephen,' she said to me when Beryl and the two police officers were seated, and we left them.

It was very quiet for a few minutes. I drank my lemonade and Mum put the kettle on and put a teabag into a mug. Then, from the front room, we heard a loud wailing. It sounded as if someone was being led in to hell.

'Oh my God,' said Mum. 'What's happened now? Has someone shot Ronnie?'

'No Mum,' I said. 'Ronnie did the shooting.'

*

There was a nationwide search for Ronnie, and his face filled the television screen that night. I think it was a photo pasted from the Fenland News, some group photo taken at a shooting club dinner and blown up so that his face was just a blur. I didn't recognise him; this wasn't the face that I knew so well, with its squashed nose and smiley eyes, and neither was it that tortured mask that had confronted me a few hours before in the assembly hall. Where had he gone? I was desperately worried for him.

In the meantime, Easton St Mathew and Sir Willyum's had become suddenly famous. That evening, while Mum sat next door with Beryl until her sister arrived from Swaffham, I came downstairs from my bedroom, where Mum thought I was 'forgetting things' by 'having an early night'. I sat and watched the six o'clock News and then the seven o'clock News on the other channel. It showed policemen standing in front of the school gates, through which the staff carpark, empty, could be glimpsed. There was an interview with a man from the Education Authority in Cambridge and Mr Khan from the village shop, who said that everyone was shocked and no-one could believe what had happened. There was also a shot of our road, cordoned off by yellow tape with police cars parked at an angle, and a reporter was shown talking outside our cottages. Mum had drawn the curtains earlier 'out of respect', but if I lifted the corner of the curtain at the front room window I could see the TV cameras. And from the kitchen I could see forensic people in white overalls in Ronnie's garden. In the distance I could hear police sirens, and overhead a helicopter hovered over the fen fields, searching.

Far into that night I lay awake, as my mind re-played the dreadful memories over and over again, and every time the re-play reached the point where Ronnie stared into my face and then turned and ran from the assembly hall, I reached the same conclusion. I had to find him.

When midnight found me still sleepless, I knew where he was likely to be, and I knew what he would have done to ensure that he wouldn't be found. I got out of bed and began to pull on some clothes over my pyjamas, straining my ears for the sound of Mum's steady breathing from her bedroom next to mine. I crept down the stairs, remembering to avoid the creaky bit, and quietly turned the key of the back door. I could feel a cold wind on my face when I looked out and I went back inside and carefully reached down my shooting coat from the peg and wound a scarf round my neck. Then I pulled on my wellington boots, because it would be wet underfoot.

It took me half an hour to walk up the drove to where I had left my bike that morning. Out of habit I looked both ways before wheeling it across the main road, but only empty tarmac stretched either side of me in the darkness. As I pedalled doggedly along the endless concrete farm roads towards the marsh, the weather worsened, and a fine cold sleet began to blow off the North Sea right into my face. The journey seemed to take forever, although in happier days I had cycled this route a thousand times with a cheese sandwich in my pocket and my binoculars across my shoulders. But today I carried nothing but despair.

Earlier that day I had been buttressed by shock, which had enabled me to sit impassively in the classroom where we had been gathered to wait for our parents. It had helped me to describe calmly and objectively what I had seen to the quietly-spoken lady detective who called at our house that evening. It had also helped me to reassure my mother that I was all right and would go to bed early and swallow a few mouthfuls of the cocoa she had again prepared for me 'for the shock'. Bless her, she had no idea how to deal with this horror, so resorted to the soothing administrations that had made me all right again when, as a small child, I had grazed my knee or lost my favourite marble down a drain. But during the long hours of that night, as the events I had witnessed played repeatedly in slow motion across the screen inside my head, the shock had dissolved and I was left with a solid lump of pain in my chest. What was this life about, if someone like Ronnie, who I not only loved but revered, could do what he had done? Where was the sense in it? I felt the certainties of my existence shifting. I felt very alone in that cold dark landscape.

Eventually, after about an hour of hard physical effort and tortuous soul-searching, I reached my destination. There was, on the sea side of the sea wall about a mile from the Marsh entrance, a wrecked houseboat, the only one left of the line of houseboats just like the one in which Ronnie had been brought up. It had been used by wildfowlers in generations gone by as a home from home when the geese were in. Next to it was a particularly deep creek, which hardly ever dried out even at neap tide and over which a plank bridge had been constructed by the wildfowling club. This constantly-flooded piece of salting was favoured by the duck, and by Ronnie, who would often settle himself there with his gun, half-hidden by the houseboat, to wait for a flight when the tide was high under the moon. Nearby, on the other side of the sea wall, was a ramshackle barn with a half-collapsed corrugated roof, and I guessed that he would have hidden the van in there, unseen by the police helicopters and probably one of the last places to be reached by the search parties.

Sure enough, there he was. I was shivering uncontrollably when I found him, partly from cold, but also from the fear of what I would find. He was lying on his back right under the bridge, with his boots half-submerged, and the gun was lying across his body where it had fallen. I can't tell you about the look on his face because his face and most of his head weren't there anymore. I was glad about that because all the way down to the Marsh along that never-ending road I had wondered what he would look like. What would the face of a murderer look like, and how would it be different from the familiar face of Ronnie?

I knew what I had to do. It was as if all Ronnie's teaching, all the years of watching him and helping him and learning from him, had coalesced and prepared me for this moment, for this ultimate act of homage.

'OK Ronnie,' I said, 'We'll just wait for the tide to turn.'

I settled down to wait beside him.

Several hours passed. Sometimes I heard a helicopter in the distance and I held my breath, crouching. But apart from that I was alone. Never had a salt marsh felt so empty, and I could not help remembering the hours I had sat like this, waiting for the evening flight, but with Ronnie. Later the rain stopped and the wind died down as a muddy moon rose slowly, bringing into relief the grey details around me. In the moonlight a few wigeon, unsettled from their roost, got up, flapping, but then saw me, and wheeled away to settle again, their heads under their wings. As the moon rose higher behind the heavy purple clouds I heard the geese, returning late from the feeding fields, and as the sky above me suddenly cleared I saw them, skein after skein, fly past in tribute. Then I felt it was the right time and I took him on his last journey.

Taking hold of his boots I dragged him out from under the bridge and along the creek towards the sea. It was very hard work. I had never thought before how heavy a corpse was; the expression 'dead weight' is exactly right. But I pulled him, slowly and arduously, inch by inch through the wet mud, stopping for breath with almost every tug as I was by then exhausted physically as well as emotionally.

By now the moon, full and perfect, was overhead and I could clearly see the ripples as the tide began to flow. Ronnie had taught me well, and I knew the full moon indicated a spring tide and that the marsh where I was standing would be under water in an hour or so. So I left him in the creek, where he settled with a squelch in a few inches of water and mud and I went to sit on top of the sea wall to watch over him. All I could see of him from my vantage point were his boots sticking out stiffly, legs spread, and this made my vigil easier, because I did not want to dwell on what the rest of him looked like. I knew that in a few hours he would be submerged and that when the tide eventually turned and began to ebb, he would float out into the cold grey Wash.

Sitting there, I remembered how he had planned his funeral.

'When I get my final come-uppance,' he would pronounce to Beryl, 'I don't want none of that religious squit. Just get me cremated. No fuss, short and sweet – there's enough insurance money for that – and then sprinkle the ash on the Marsh. And don't you grieve for me then, girl, the Wash'll take me where I want to go.'

At least I could do that for him. I waited until the boots were covered with water and had begun to float just under the surface, tossed about by the advancing waves, and then I turned and left him.

I did not forget the gun. Ronnie's lessons had sunk deep: you never leave a firearm unattended. I retrieved it from the bridge and, balancing it somehow across my handlebars, I began to pedal back, stopping off at the pair of abandoned farm houses at the corner of Big Jim's Acre, because I remembered that in one of the gardens Ronnie had shown me an old well partly covered with a concrete slab. I dropped the gun into the black hole and, with a heave that almost made my heart burst, I pushed the slab in place to conceal it. Then, having recovered my breath but feeling totally drained of sensation as well as strength, I mounted my bicycle and slowly rode home, turning one leg after another, like an automaton.

Three weeks later, Ronnie's body, by then, I expect, badly decomposed, turned up on the beach at Snettisham. I was disappointed as I had hoped that it would somehow disappear forever into the oceans of the earth. I did not want a post-mortem. I still don't.

If you were to ask me, after all these years, what I thought about the events of that day, I would not be able to answer you. And if you asked me, knowing that I was perhaps the person who had been closest in the world to Ronnie Rawlinson, why he did it, I would say, 'I have no idea.' Others have tried to answer that question. I could refer you to Why did he do it? A study of the Easton St Mathew Shooting by R.S. Steele or to the chapter in David Hearse's The Psychology of School Shootings. The published extracts from the Dayning Report into the shooting might also interest you; it would certainly fill in some gaps, as, of course, I did not know until later some of the things that had been happening inside Ronnie's head which I knew nothing about at the time. In writing this book I have merely tried to tell my story of what happened on that day.

*

There was something else I had to do. The following Saturday I biked to the traveller site to ask Jimmy for my binoculars.

'Is Jimmy there?' I asked when I had negotiated the dogs and saw Jimmy's auntie Esme hanging out the washing.

'No love, he's not and I don't know where he is. Hang on, I'll ask Jake.' She shrieked towards the van. 'Jake! D'you know where Jim-boy is?'

After a long minute, the van door opened and Jake stuck his head out yawning.

'Wha' yer say, petal?'

'Here's young Steve, Jimmy's friend. D'yer know where he is?'

He rubbed his tousled hair with both hands and yawned again.

'Hi, Steve, my man. How'yer doing?' Then, as he seemed to wake up, 'What a terrible to-do at the school, eh? Can't get it out of my head!' He yawned. 'Old Ronnie Rawlinson, eh? Who would have thought it?'

I interrupted him. 'Do you know where Jimmy is?'

'Can't say as I do. Haven't seen him for a day or two. He might have gone off with my cousin Georgie to Doncaster. When did they leave, Esme? Yesterday, wasn't it?' But she had returned to her laundry. 'D'you want him for anything in particular, or were you just passing the time of day?'

'I came for my binoculars. He… er… he borrowed them in the summer and… er… said I could have them if I called round. They're a Zeiss pair with a black leather strap.'

Jake's features quickened and I saw a glimpse of the Jimmy eyes.

'Binoculars you say? Well, let me see.' I could see his brain working. 'I seem to remember a pair of binoculars what Jimmy was playing around with in the summer. Would they have been yours?'

'Yes, that's right. I left them here on the day of the f… on the day I was last here. I haven't been back since because er… er… I've been busy, but I saw Jimmy last Saturday and he said I could have them if I came round.'

'Oh dear, that's a bit of a problem,' said Jake, his face beaming with innocence. 'I remember them binoculars quite clearly now. Nice piece of gear. Must have cost a tidy sum. Well, I'm afraid I've got bad news for you, Steve, my lad, and I'm truly sorry and I'll flay the hide off that Jim-boy when I next see him, but he told me he'd found them. I even gave him a few quid for them and then they went as part of a deal I had with an associate of mine in Newmarket. What a shame! If only I'd known they were yours.'

'Oh,' I said. I didn't know what else to say. I felt overwhelmed by disappointment.

'Here lad,' he said. 'Do you want to come in the van and have a coke or something?'

'No thanks,' I managed to say. 'I'd better be going.' I couldn't wait to get away.

I never saw Jimmy again. By the time he got back from Doncaster, if he ever did, we had moved, and things were never going to be the same again. Losing my binoculars was just subsidiary damage.

February 13th 2018

Chapter Twenty-Two

'Stop it! Listen! You've got to stop dancing!' I shout at the whirling figures around me.

I am a child again and I am at school. I am in the school hall at Sir Willyum's. I am surrounded by people who are dancing Apple Tree Square and the music is being played faster and faster on a piano. I am trying to stop them dancing as there is something vitally important I must tell them. I rush around, reaching out to them, but as soon as I touch them they fall down at my feet. When I look down at them I see their faces looking up at me and I know that I once knew them but I cannot remember their names. I am suddenly out on the Marsh beyond the sea wall and their faces are becoming submerged, so I grasp hold of their wellington boots and try to pull them out of the advancing sea. But their faces begin to sink beneath the waves and I have to let go or I will drown, and they float away from me out to sea, and I run up the bank and along the wall, suddenly afraid for my life. And as I run I hear the gun shots and I count them as I run and when I get to thirteen I turn and scream, 'Ronnie! No!' into the barrel of a shot gun.

*

I hadn't wanted to go to the twenty-fifth anniversary

memorial ceremony.

I thought I had put it all behind me, that I had got on with my life, that I had, if not forgotten, at least not been affected by what happened on that day. I made every effort to forget.

In the first days and weeks afterwards I had refused, point-blank, to talk to anyone about it. I would not even let myself think about it. Some counselling lady came to see us, sent by the police I think, but I said I didn't want to talk about it, that I was all right.

'But thank you for coming,' I added, thinking I had better be polite because Mum was looking at me hard, like she did when she thought I was hiding something.

I was left in the kitchen while Mum showed the lady out, but I heard what she said in the hall.

'I think he's probably in shock, poor lamb. I'll leave my card, so you can contact me if he wants to talk. I'm sure he will eventually. In the meantime, just try to make life as normal as possible for him. He'll survive; children are amazingly resilient, you know.'

Mum put the card on the shelf above the kettle, but afterwards I threw it away. Why should I need help, I argued to myself. I had survived, not like Margaret, and Dwayne, and Josie. And Ronnie. I forced my mind away from thinking about them.

In fact, I survived well. I completed my secondary education, more successfully, probably, and certainly more happily, than I would have done if it hadn't happened, as Mum wouldn't stay in the cottage and we moved to Milton Keynes to be near my aunt and uncle. There I attended a big comprehensive school where I did very well and then went on to Leeds University. I have worked as a research biologist for *Natural England* for nearly ten years, for I have never lost my love of natural history although the rugged upland pasture in the Peak District is a world away from the wide spaces of the Wash. I am currently settled with a long-term girlfriend, and marriage and children are probably on the horizon.

It was Suzie who persuaded me to go back for the memorial. We were visiting my mother for the New Year weekend and it was Sunday lunchtime.

'You'll never guess what I found the other day, Stephen,' she said, doling out the roast potatoes.

'Go on, surprise me, Mum.' I wasn't really listening, being more interested in my dinner.

'It was in Mr Simpson's Christmas card…'

'Mr who?'

'You know, at the garage, where I used to work. He always sends a card every Christmas and he always puts the village newsletter in as well, so I can keep up-to-date, I suppose, although I've no wish to really. But it's a kind thought.

'Get to the point, Mum,' I said with my mouth full.

'Well, in the newsletter there was all about some memorial because it's twenty-five years since it happened. Doesn't time fly?'

'Twenty-five years since what happened, Mrs Stringer?' asked Suzie.

'You know, Stephen. That day when it happened, when…' She stopped in mid-sentence. 'Perhaps it's best not to talk about it.' She picked up her knife and fork.

My Suzie is not renowned for tact. 'The shooting, Mrs Stringer?' she persisted. 'Is that what the memorial's about?'

'Well, yes dear. I take it Stephen's told you about it. It was all very unfortunate, you know, and to think that he lived next door.'

'Let's change the subject, shall we?' I said.

Later, on the drive home, Suzie was equally persistent.

'You can't avoid it forever, you know, darling.'

'Avoid what?'

'The fact that the man next door was a mass murderer and that you witnessed it.'

'It's over and done with, Suze. It happened on that day, and I was lucky, and I survived. I've put it behind me.'

'But you haven't, have you?'

'What do you mean?'

'What about your nightmare? The fact that I'm woken up at least once a fortnight by your screaming?'

'Oh, *that*.'

'Yes, that. It's obvious to me,' she said. 'You say you've forgotten all about it, but your subconscious hasn't, has it? You need help, Steve, so that you can forget it properly. You've just sublimated it, or whatever it's called.'

'Since when were you a psychiatrist?' (Suzie is a graphic designer.) 'And before you suggest it, I'm not going to any head doctor.'

'No, I wasn't going to suggest you did. But I do think we ought to go to the Memorial. I think it would help if you allowed yourself to mourn properly. Anyway, I'm curious about what you've told me about your childhood and the fens.' She scrabbled about in her bag. 'Here it is!'

'Here's what?'

'Your mum gave me that newsletter about the Memorial. I said we'd take her with us, but she didn't want to, said her arthritis was too bad to sit that long in a car. But she thought it would do *you* good to go. She said you'd never faced up to what happened, that you'd never allowed yourself to mourn for him.'

'Did she now?' I said, wondering why it was that my mother, who had always seemed somewhat distant to me, and certainly not over-affectionate, understood me so well. Suzie understood me too, which is why I did go back to Easton St Mathew for the Memorial.

*

'But it's so flat!' said Suzie as we set out along the A47 from Peterborough towards the east.

We had made good time on the motorways, but it was late afternoon as we started to trundle along at 40 m.p.h. behind a beet lorry. The sky had that mauve greyness that I remembered so well, when the clouds pile up either side of the straight road like mountains. A vivid orange sun was dipping in my rear-view mirror, its light reflected in pink streaks on the underside of the clouds. Lines of pylons stretched in receding diagonals towards the horizon, where a group of wind turbines did not turn in the dank still air.

'That's what everyone says!' I replied. 'But I don't remember it like that. I suppose I thought the whole world was flat. Anyway, what I remember most is the sky, how huge it is. Just look at this space!'

'It makes the houses look so tiny. Look over there, past that line of trees. They look like dolls' houses.'

'Mm. I used to live in a cottage like that, and Ronnie and Beryl lived in the one next door. Our nearest neighbours were three quarters of a mile down the drove.'

'You must have felt so isolated.'

'It didn't feel like that. It was just what I was used to.'

It was almost dark by the time we reached Wisbech. We had

arranged to stay in the Rose and Crown hotel and after unpacking we set off to explore. The centre of town was much quieter than I remembered. The market place had been pedestrianised and where market stalls had once stood, and I had threaded my way through the crowds on a Saturday afternoon on my way to the public library, there were now seats and bollards and big stone containers of drab-looking mini-shrubs surrounded by used cigarette-ends. The signs prohibiting 'troublesome van-dwellers' from frequenting the pubs had gone, and so had most of the pubs. There was just one branch of a national pub chain with smokers spilling out onto the pavement outside and the sound of cheering from inside where the mid-week Sky broadcast of a premier league football game was being shown, according to the advert in the window. Most of the shops had changed too; the pork butchers, where I had queued with Ronnie for the Christmas pork pies, had closed, and there was a 'Business To Let' sign in the window. The fishmongers had become a charity shop, one of several along one side of the square and, next to the bus station, the Queen's Theatre, where Beryl had played bingo every Friday evening, had been demolished to make way for a small shopping mall, where only two of the sites had been opened by national clothing chains, the rest standing empty.

'Let's see if the bus station is still there,' I said, and it was. As we arrived a blue bus turned in and disgorged its two passengers. The bus driver stood up and stretched, then began to wind his destination board from 'Wisbech Bus Station' to 'King's Lynn via Duck's Drove'.

'That's our bus!' I cried. 'That goes past the top of our road.' I looked at my watch. 'That'll be the last bus, the six forty-five, it'll leave in about five minutes.'

We stood and watched as an old lady with a wheeled shopping basket clambered on board, followed by two young men in dark hoodies. Then the engine started up and the driver backed the bus, its warning bleeper sounding, prior to the big sweep as it drove out on to the roundabout. And as it went, my memories followed, and I was again journeying home after an afternoon in the library, my nose pressed to the steamed-up window to see the statue of Thomas Clarkson and the Town Bridge, surrounded by the noise of chattering women and the throbbing diesel engine as it inched its way through the traffic. I stared after that bus and felt a lump in my throat.

'Come on, let's get a meal,' said Suzie, squeezing my hand. 'You can show me all your old haunts tomorrow. We'll have time; the memorial service isn't until two o'clock.'

*

It was strange to drive myself along that familiar road, through the edge of town, past the football ground and the big haulage depot and out into the fen countryside. The little bungalow at the corner just before the double bend, which had been half-hidden by an old Bramley apple orchard and outside which a faded sign had read 'Honey for Sale', had been extended with a huge conservatory, and the orchard cleared for a wide sweep of lawn and a swimming pool. But at the 'reservation', the row of council houses at the end of Duck's Drove looked just the same, with several old cars at the side of the end house, which I am sure had been there for over twenty-five years.

We turned on to the dual carriageway and crossed it.

'That's where Duncan was killed,' I said.

'Who was Duncan?' Suzie asked.

'Ronnie's son.'

'You never told me that before.'

'I'd forgotten; but seeing where Mum had trained me to get off my bike and walk across the road reminded me, and look, that's where I used to wait for the school bus. I used to leave my bike behind the tatey grave on that concrete there.'

'Tatey what?'

'It's what we called a potato clamp, where they're stored.'

Now in front of us stretched Wrong Drove and there, in the distance, was a cyclist, battling against the wind. I was transported back in time and was again a thirteen-year-old boy on the way back from school, to the two isolated cottages which were my home, to Mum and changing my uniform and bread and jam at the kitchen table under the clothes drier, and into the garden before it got dark where the chickens needed to be fed and where Ronnie would stop his digging, push his cap back on his head and greet me with a wide grin and, 'Now then, lad!'

But the memory was to be broken. When we reached the end of the drove I stopped in confusion.

'What the hell?'

'What is it, darling?'

'They're not there!'

'What aren't there?'

'The cottages! Our cottages. They've gone!'

'Are you sure? Perhaps you've turned down the wrong road. It's been a long time.'

'Are you saying I don't know where my home is?'

She didn't say anything else. We sat in the car and looked out of the windscreen. Where the cottages had once stood now there was nothing. Not a brick remained; the buildings had been razed to the ground and all that was left was the foundations. I could see where the dividing wall had been and where the outhouses had stood. Only the old iron stove, which had stood in Ronnie's shed, was still there, isolated among the tall grass and nettles. Around the edge of what had been the two cottages and their gardens and the roadway that led round the back was a tall wire fence, and there was a metal sign at the front: 'Plot of land for sale. For development. Deadman and Stanes, Estate Agents, Wisbech 735671'.

'Aren't you going to get out and have a look?' ventured Suzie.

I did not answer immediately. Instead I took a deep breath, then reversed the car, changing the gears viciously.

'There's nothing to see, is there?' I said, driving away.

After a while Suzie said, 'Perhaps they demolished the cottages because no-one would live there, you know, because of what happened on that day.'

I thought about that all the way to Easton St. Matthew. Was it that simple? I had tried to demolish what had happened on that day too. Had I succeeded?

*

There were a lot of cars in Easton St. Matthew, parked all the way along all four roads leading to the village centre. We found a parking space in a cul-de-sac, part of a new housing estate half way along Church Lane, and walked back towards Sir Willyum's.

Perhaps it was because I had been searching for parking, perhaps it was because I was surprised by all the traffic, but I hadn't really looked at the school on the way in; and now, when I did, I couldn't believe what I was seeing. The school was no longer there. The car park was still there, on this afternoon filled with cars in reserved slots, and supervised by pupils in blazers, but the rest of the school had disappeared. All that remained was the old frontage, with its two entrances for 'BOYS' and 'IRLS', but that had been re-built and turned in to a double arch. On a bronze plaque high up on the wall between was written: 'This memorial garden is on the site of Sir William Smith High School, where thirteen people died on 13th February 1993. May they rest in peace'.

We followed a stream of people through the left-hand archway into the garden, which was laid out in a large circle, covering most of what had once been the main block. Beds planted with small evergreen shrubs lined the outside perimeter, next to a gravel pathway which encircled a lawn. In the middle of the lawn was a bronze statue of a girl and a boy, hand in hand, knees raised, as if skipping together. On the plinth beneath the statue were engraved these words: 'They dance in heaven', which made me snort with derision.

Suzie looked at me. 'I think it's very touching.'

'But they're dead and there isn't a heaven.'

'I know, but perhaps it helps people to think of it like that. You're just a cynic.'

'Perhaps. But the idea of Old Crumpet dancing the Apple Tree Square through all eternity just makes me feel rather sick, that's all.'

I looked beyond the garden. In the distance, where the playground, the science and technology block, the gym and the playing field had once been there were now rows of houses. The only building still standing was the mobile classroom that had been the art room, where Ms McCarthy, bless her memory, had taught us and where I had learnt how to develop photographs in the back cupboard she had adapted as a dark room. Next to it on a stand was the large label: 'Memorial Visitor Centre. Open 10 a.m. – 4 p.m. Tuesdays, Thursdays and Saturdays. Entrance Free. Donations welcome'. It was a Sunday, but it was open, and people were passing in and out.

'Do you want to take a look?' asked Suzie.

'I'm not sure. I think I'd like to remember it as it was.'

'But if you don't, you might wish you had later. Come on! This trip is all about laying ghosts.' She took hold of my hand and drew me to the steps and up to the door.

Inside it had been transformed into a small museum. The walls were covered with displays. On one side was the history of the school and of the villages it served, with photographs and printed information. Beneath the displays, items were set out on tables: exercise books; textbooks; football boots; a trumpet ('Oh, I had forgotten about the Boys' Band!' I exclaimed); and in pride of place a class register, just like the ones I used to carry around the school every morning. I looked more closely. It was open at the week beginning 13th February 1993, but had just one entry, for Monday.

'Oh, it's our class!' I said, and I pointed to an entry. 'Look, here's me! And Dwayne Tubbs, after me. He was always after me!'

A few people turned and looked at me curiously.

'Why are some names highlighted?' asked Suzie, bending over the register. 'Look, there's Josephine Davenport, Margaret Jackson, Oh,' she suddenly raised her hand to her mouth, 'are they the ones that were…?'

I did not answer. I was seeing them as they had been. I was re-living those nightmare moments in the school hall all those years before.

'Come on!' I said at last. 'Let's see the rest of it.'

Another display mapped the events of that day as seen by officialdom, with extracts and photographs from local and national newspapers, and then a series of displays which told the story of the demolition of the school and the establishment of the memorial garden.

And then we came to Ronnie. At the back of the room, in a corner, was a small display about the school caretaker. Under a headline which read 'Caretaker turns mass murderer in school horror' there was a short resume of his life and one small photograph, a headshot of the sort taken in a photo booth for a passport, which had probably been attached to his application form when he had first started the job all those years ago. It didn't look like Ronnie. Not only was he much younger than I remembered him, but he was staring at the camera as if it would bite him.

'Is that Ronnie?' asked Suzie, peering closely at it.

'No,' I said. 'That's not the Ronnie I knew. He wasn't like that. He was…' But I couldn't explain.

'Look at him!' said a woman behind us. 'Evil personified. You can tell just by looking at him!'

'They say he was mentally ill,' said her companion. 'But they ought to have vetted him when he joined the school. You can't be too careful where there's children.'

I felt a surge of anger. 'Come on, let's go! I've had enough of this!'

I strode out of the mobile and across the garden, Suzie struggling to keep up with me in her high heels. I had meant to go straight to my car and drive away, to have nothing more to do with it. I meant it when I said I had had enough. It was all too painful. But as I tried to get through the garden entrance I came face to face with an old man, and, angry as I was, I didn't look closely at him. Like one does, we performed the 'after you' dance, both stepping to the same side when trying to avoid each other.

I smiled politely. 'Sorry!'

'Stephen Stringer! I do believe it's you! After all these years, boy,' said the man, and he put out his hand.

I was startled out of my thoughts and looked closely at him as he shook my hand. He looked familiar but for a moment I could not place him.

'You're the spitting image of your father, Stephen, do you know that? He was a good lad too. Now, what on earth happened to you?' His head gave a huge sideways jerk, helping me to realise who he was.

'Mr Godley!' I said. 'How are you, sir?'

'Twenty-five years older, my boy, and feeling it more every day.'

He was unmistakeably Mr Godley, although he had very little hair left on his head, and he was much shorter than I remembered, with bowed shoulders.

'I often wondered what happened to you, Stephen. You had so much talent. And then, it must have been such a shock for you. Well, it was for us all. Who would have thought that Ronnie… and he was like a father to you, I know.'

I did not know what to say to that. He patted my shoulder.

'And look at all this!' he gestured to the memorial garden. 'The school gone as well. I never understood that. There had been a school on this site for so long. I don't see why it couldn't have continued. After all, there was a lot of good in Sir Willyum's as well, wasn't there?'

'When did it happen, sir? Closing the school, and all that? I moved away with my mum and we haven't kept up with it, I'm afraid.'

'Very wise your mother was, Stephen. She gave you a new life. As for me, I stayed on, of course, didn't know what else to do, but then they decided to demolish the school and bus all the kids into Wisbech so I retired. My wife had been nagging me to give up for some time, and somehow I never got back my energy, after… you know… after what happened on that day. Funny, isn't it, but the only thing I can remember about that day is holding you, Stephen, just after… it happened. I'll never forget that.'

'Neither will I, sir,' I said.

He wiped an eye.

'Well, Stephen, are you coming to the service? We'd better be getting into the church, or there'll not be any seats. There's a big crowd due to attend, big wigs and everyone. But it's good that you're with us, Stephen, to help us to remember that some survived.'

After that I couldn't walk away and leave him, and so we went into the church with him.

*

Attending the memorial service in St Mathew's made me feel as if I was a boy again. It was like walking in file over the road with Mrs Pritchard and my form to attend the annual carol service on the last day of term before Christmas. But this time the hymn singing was far heartier, and the vicar was a woman and not old Reverend

Chadwick with the fat belly under his cassock that had made him look pregnant. And, of course, it wasn't Mr Took playing the organ.

I thought the service would be just like all church services, and because I wasn't religious I expected to go through the motions of standing and sitting and bowing my head as a way of being polite. I remembered what it was like to sit in those hard pews and what could happen under the cover of the high wooden backs. But as the service proceeded I began to find meaning in what was happening, in spite of myself. It was the opening address by the vicar that caught my attention first.

'We are gathered here to remember the thirteen whose lives were cruelly cut down on this day twenty-five years ago and to mourn their loss. This was not a natural disaster but an act of evil that we can scarcely comprehend…'

I began to think about that. An act of evil? Was Ronnie evil? I wrestled with this notion while we sang 'Fight the good fight!' and 'The day thou gavest, Lord, is ending'. The mayor of Wisbech then read that bit from Ecclesiastes that begins 'For everything there is a season, and a time for every matter under heaven…' The words began to speak to me: 'a time to be born, and a time to die… a time to kill and a time to heal… a time to weep and a time to laugh… a time to mourn and a time to dance… a time to keep, and a time to cast away… a time to keep silence, and a time to speak…' And in my mind I went on with the quotation: a time to forget, and a time to remember. I had spent twenty-five years forcing myself to forget; it was now time for me to remember.

At the end of the service we stood in silence as thirteen children, specially chosen as being in Year 9 and living in the village of Easton (so the order of service informed us), read out a name of someone who had died on that day, lit a candle and placed it on the altar.

'It's fourteen, not thirteen,' I muttered.

'Shh!' hissed Suzie.

'But there's no candle for Ronnie,' I whispered.

I still feel the same way. In bed at night I still cry behind my eyes, not for what he did but that he is gone. Of course, like everyone else, I mourn the loss of those who were killed that day: poor Margaret, and Ms McCarthy, and Mr Crumb and Josie, and the others… even Dwayne Tubbs didn't deserve such an end. I have found, over the years, that I feel more than most people for a beetle squashed under a casual foot or a hedgehog under a speeding car. You see, I grieve for all those who find themselves cut off in the midst of life when a normal day suddenly disintegrates into death.

And for those who are squashed, but survive, like me, remembering is a continuing horror. I will never forget, but I have written this book and tried to lay my ghosts. Pity me, if you will, but spare a thought, too, for the man I loved, whose ghost, if it exists, is sitting in a creek on the Marsh and waiting for the geese.

Printed in Great Britain
by Amazon

76413239R00208